# Hers³

# Hers[3]

**BRILLIANT NEW FICTION BY LESBIAN WRITERS**

**edited by Terry Wolverton with Robert Drake**

ff

**Faber and Faber, Inc.**
**An affiliate of Farrar, Straus and Giroux**
**New York**

Faber and Faber, Inc.
An affiliate of Farrar, Straus and Giroux
19 Union Square West, New York 10003

Library of Congress Cataloging-in-Publication Data
Hers[3] : brilliant new fiction by lesbian writers / edited by Terry Wolverton with
Robert Drake.
   p.   cm.
  ISBN 0-571-19962-3 (alk. paper)
   1. Lesbians—United States—Social life and customs—Fiction.  2. American
fiction—Women authors.  3. American fiction—20th century.  4. Lesbians'
writings, American.  I. Wolverton, Terry.  II. Drake, Robert.
III. Title: Hers three.
PS648.L47H482   1999
813'.540809206643—dc21                                          98-33106

*For Ana*

# Contents

# Contents

# Introduction

"So what do you want to hear about the state of lesbian fiction today?"

I'm struggling with the introduction to this anthology. The manuscript is late, the publisher is anxious. I can't seem to generate the precise insights and witty commentary needed to encompass the twenty-one stories that appear between these covers. What theory will definitely fix them in their categories, contextualize them in their time? What argument will justify their collection here, their jostling for position in the literary marketplace?

I'm at my cluttered desk, staring through mini-blinds at the angled sunlight that signifies a California October, the phone receiver lodged between my ear and cramped right shoulder. I'm talking to the woman who should be my girlfriend, should be because we're both crazy about each other, that deep, stubborn kind of love that can withstand all sorts of torture and not evaporate. But she stopped sleeping with me four months ago because she claimed she couldn't see a future for us.

"I can break your heart now or I can break it later," she told me at the time but, ventricles bloody and dangling, we still go out to dinner or the movies most weekends, still can't stop ourselves from buying spontaneous presents—scented soaps or CDs or thrift store sweaters we know the other will like. Hers is still the name on the card in my wallet that reads: In Case of Emergency, Contact . . . Neither of us has been willing to cut the cord, to extinguish the undercurrent of desire that sparks our interactions. We talk on the phone almost every day.

My friends have had to listen to every detail of the saga. "Last night she called to say how much she loves me." "Today she told me she thought we should stop having contact." Concerned and infinitely patient, they tell me this will someday be a story I'll write. A lesbian story. To me it seems like a story that's been written far too often, but I don't tell them that; they're only trying to console me.

The suffering has not done wonders for my productivity. I've got fifteen other projects just as urgent and unfinished as this one. They're piled on my desk, scattered on the floor beneath it; they taunt, reproach. I ignore them. I write her long E-mails that I usually don't send, or play computer solitaire until two in the morning, hand after hand of Forty Thieves while I mentally revisit every twisted aspect of my love conundrum.

The woman who should be my girlfriend is at work. She hates her job with the phone company—the mindless detail, the repetitive routine of it—so she welcomes my call, the chance to engage her brain in something different.

She's been helpful in the past. She is, in fact, the woman whose smart suggestion led to the titles of this series of anthologies, years ago now, before I ever knew that I would love her. "So what do you want to hear about the state of lesbian fiction today?" I beseech her.

"Just that people are still writing it," she answers. This matter-of-factness is only one of the things I adore about her.

Yes, my dear, they are.

Two hundred and four stories just for this volume of *Hers*. I read them all throughout June and July—endless, hot, weepy days when I tried desperately to reconcile her decision to stop being my lover with my unquenchable feelings for her. Each day I'd work my way through another stack—so many lesbian stories, yet none could seem to provide a happier resolution for mine.

I have in the past—and publicly—complained about the preoccupation with relationships in the writing of lesbians. *Write about your work, write about the larger world in which you live,* I've exhorted. *We are about more than who we sleep with,* I insisted, and I believe it still, but I haven't embodied it these past months. True, I've shown up to teach my classes, completed projects for clients, etched words onto pages, met (eventually) my deadlines. I signed a book contract, traveled to Chicago to pick up a Lambda Literary Award, led a writing retreat in France, but I moved through these activities like someone in a dream, one only half remembered. When fall arrived, signaled by the shift of light, the slanted shadows, I could not begin to think where summer had gone. The only things palpable to me this whole long season have been the throaty purr of her voice, her luminous gaze like dark moonlight, my skin shrieking with the absence of her touch.

Is this why so many of the stories collected in this volume have to do with romantic love? The promise of love, the search for love, lost love, love regained, the sad aftermath of failed love, the things one is driven to do in the absence of love—a full three-quarters of the stories here dwell in this terrain. Of course, they do so with wit, with bravado, with tenderness, with insight, with skill. Whatever the experiences—lived or imagined—that inspired them, the authors of these stories have transformed them into art.

Some shimmer with sexuality, the ripe beginnings of desire and possibility. Some sting like the kiss of a whip—the power of withholding, the poignancy of opportunities wasted, connections missed. A few present stern lessons about the lengths to which we'll go in order to find and preserve intimacy. A number record in brutal detail the devolution of affections that leaves us setting mattresses aflame, skirmishing over the division of household items, talking fervently to wrong numbers, or sifting through photographs that now seem to tell a different story from the one we once thought we knew so well.

The selections here that are not about romantic love are largely about childhood, and still about the fragile hope of finding connection, or the devastation of losing it. Lesbian or not, these are the most human of themes; perhaps this longing for attachment is the very impulse from which the urge to tell stories springs.

*What do you want to know about the state of lesbian fiction today?*
*Just that people are still writing it.*

We're still writing these lesbian stories because we're still living them. Trying to erect a delicate architecture with whatever materials we have on hand: our treacherous histories; the collected wisdom of therapists, recovery programs, self-help books; a trove of allusions from pop songs and movies; the hunger that rises without regard for caution; whatever scrap of trust we're still able to muster. The woman who should be my girlfriend and I tried to construct a meaningful bond, but the foundation cracked beneath us, the roof caved in. Now we sit in the rubble, staring at each other with bemused expressions, still reluctant to seek other shelter.

That will change, eventually. My friends tell me this will someday be a story I will write. Then I will wield the powers of invention, of skill, of meaning. I will craft a plot that makes sense, create characters whose motivations I understand, inject just enough irony to keep it from collapsing under the weight of sentiment. It will be a lesbian story. A work of fiction.

Almost as if it happened to someone else.

TERRY WOLVERTON, 1998

# Hers³

# Tokyo Trains

**PAT SCHMATZ**

Sabrina went to Tokyo to ride the trains. Most particularly, she went to ride the Yamanote Line between eight and nine on weekday mornings.

The Yamanote Line is a loop around Tokyo. It stops at all of the Tokyo stations, including Tokyo Eki. There, connections can be made to the bullet train to travel throughout Japan at over one hundred miles per hour, always on time, everywhere. It stops at Ikebukuro and Shibuya, which are major hubs for other local train lines. All day long, the Yamanote runs around and around the huge snarling, belching, filthy beast that is Tokyo, moving throngs of salarymen and office ladies and schoolchildren and foreigners and teachers and sightseers and shoppers. Everyone rides the Yamanote sometime, and many people ride it every day. Especially, many people ride it every day between eight and nine in the morning.

Sabrina spent three years planning her trip to Japan. She wanted to ride the trains. She wanted to ride bullet trains and commuter trains, subway trains and local trains and express trains. She wanted to go long distances and short distances, she wanted to ride the same car every day for a while and then she wanted to try different lines at different times. But more than anything else, she wanted to ride the Yamanote during rush hour.

She decided this when she saw a special on television about Tokyo and overcrowding. They showed a packed platform with a mass of people waiting to board. The train pulled up, and faces were literally smashed against the windows. Some people got off the train—barely enough so that the people on the train could breathe. Then the mass on the platform began to power its way into the car. They turned around and backed in. Somehow, they all managed to get on the train, but the doors could not close. At that point, the conductor on the platform put on his white gloves. With his gloved hands, he pushed the people in so that the doors could close. When Sabrina saw this, she made up her mind to go to Tokyo.

Sabrina was "Miss Murphy" to a classroom of second graders back in California. Her life consisted of the children at school, her dog, a literature discussion group, and occasional university extension courses. At thirty-five she was single and not particularly interested in an intimate relationship. After years of therapy, she considered herself fortunate to have survived her childhood with her wits and personality intact, and had been told by more than one professional that it was a miracle that she was not a sociopath. She considered it a fabulous success that she was able to relate to second graders, and to their parents when she needed to. She had a dog which she did not beat or kick; they had a warm and mutually respectful relationship. Sabrina also considered this a success. She had several casual friendships, centered on activities such as hiking and reading books.

This is not to say that Sabrina was asexual. She was simply not interested in one-to-one, intimate relationships. She liked human contact. She liked physical contact. She did not like it to be acknowledged.

Sabrina arrived in Tokyo in October. After three years of planning and saving and fantasizing, she had taken a semester's leave of absence to travel throughout Asia. She had spent three weeks hiking in Nepal with a women's adventure group, and now she was on her own for two months in Japan. She planned to study the Japanese language and culture, and to travel throughout the country by train. She was staying for a month in a foreigner house in Tokyo, and she had to ride the Yamanote Line every single day, to sightsee and go to the library.

Sabrina rode the trains out of necessity from the moment she arrived in Japan. But for the first week, she took great care not to ride at rush hour. She learned about the ticket wickets and the maps and the ways of the trains and their passengers. She studied maps, she studied money, she studied language. She learned the kanji characters for the different stations around Tokyo. Finally, on her second

Monday in Japan, she felt secure enough and confident enough to attempt the train ride that she had been anticipating for three years.

It was all that Sabrina could do not to run to the station in the morning. She was awake at five o'clock. She went downstairs and put a hundred-yen coin into the slot which turned the shower on. She carried an extra coin with her, and slid it in when the shower stopped, allowing herself an extra five minutes of hot shower on this morning. Then she went back upstairs and dressed carefully. Levi's and a casual cotton sweater and tennis shoes. As a foreigner, she was going to stand out no matter how she dressed, so she might as well go for comfort and confidence.

It was a crisp, clear morning and she walked down the street to the bakery. She treated herself to several pastries and an orange juice. By six-thirty, she was dressed and fed and ready and there was nothing to do but wait. She tried to read and couldn't concentrate. She was already so completely turned on with anticipation that it was all she could do to keep herself from masturbating. But she wanted to wait, to make this first time everything that she had dreamed of. Finally, she left for the train station.

She walked through a labyrinth of winding narrow streets. There were shops and houses close on either side of her, pedestrians and bicycles passing almost close enough to touch her, and the streak of narrow bright blue sky overhead, between the rooftops and balconies that were draped with drying laundry and bedding left out to air.

When she came out on a main street, the one that led to Ikebukuro station, her pulse increased with the increasing pace around her. There were cars and buses and taxis, bicycles and people hurrying hurrying hurrying toward the train station. The noise of Tokyo was rising to its daytime pitch, as trains rattled overhead and horns honked and music played from the shops which were opening and the city stretched and yawned noisily as it woke and snorted its way into a day.

When Sabrina arrived at the train station, it was a thrilling throng of humanity, moving politely in all directions at once. She followed the green "J.R." signs which funneled her toward the boarding platforms for the Yamanote Line.

It was exactly eight o'clock when Sabrina bought her ticket and climbed the stairs to the platform. She stood in line with men in suits. It was very crowded. Sabrina's face was flushed and her heart pounded. She carefully maintained her distance from the man in front of her so that her body was not quite touching his. Still, her skin was tingling with the excitement of the near-contact and the warmth of the bodies all around her. When the train pulled up, there were faces smashed against the window just like on the television program, and her stomach quivered.

The doors opened and many people poured out. Sabrina's line moved her onto the train car, touching her now, pressing up close all around her. She was pushed farther into the car and could see that the seats were all folded up against the sides, transforming a perfectly civilized train into a human cattle car. She couldn't see the conductor on the platform. She didn't know if he was pushing people in. She had seen him earlier, but he hadn't had gloves on. She wanted to see the conductor, but her view was blocked by ears, shoulders, chins, and tops of heads.

This sight, along with the tightening press of bodies around her, intensified her excitement. Her chin almost rested on the head of an old woman in front of her, and the pressure was particularly strong on her right arm and shoulder from a man with wide shoulders and graying hair. She could smell aftershave, stale coffee, and tobacco. Her body was very warm now, and her heart was pounding so rapidly that she wondered if the man who had his chest against her back could feel it. Her legs were weak, but she was packed in so tightly that she could not possibly fall.

Sabrina had heard about the train perverts who grabbed and fondled women on the trains. She could certainly see how it would happen, and hoped that it wouldn't. The sudden presence of an unwelcome hand would ruin everything. It would instantly put her into intimate contact with that person, whether or not she could trace the hand to its shoulder and face. No, it was the anonymous close contact that she craved, the press of bodies all together by chance and circumstance, rather than by intent.

The train lurched into motion, and they all rocked and swayed as one large body. Nobody looked at anyone else. Sabrina's hands were pinned to her sides, and the warmth and the pressure and swaying motion pulsed around her entire body. She closed her eyes, to better feel the sensations. She carefully kept her mouth closed and her face masked, but her pulse raced and she was soaking wet, more turned on than she had ever been. The movement of the train soared up through the soles of her feet like one giant whole-body vibrator. As she inhaled, she imagined the molecules of air that she breathed moving into her nose and down inside her body, then back out, into the bodies pressed around her, and then back into her own again. She felt it, felt the presence of carbon dioxide that had just come from the source of warm pressure against her back, her right shoulder, her hip. She felt her body melting into the same breath, the same heartbeat as all of the bodies touching her and the other bodies touching them. She knew that beneath those masks, the blank and staring faces, they must be feeling what she was feeling.

Sabrina held her breath. She was riding on that moment, that glorious moment just before orgasm, the moment of the best feeling in the entire world, a moment that she wanted to stretch into hours. She concentrated on keeping her face still and relaxed, resisted rubbing her pelvis into the hip in front of her. The train stopped, and the jerking motion followed by the sudden increase of pressure as the doors opened and bodies surged for the door pushed her over the edge and she couldn't help breathing heavily, but resisted making the sound that longed to swell from deep inside of her.

The bodies pushed her off the train and she didn't resist, although she had not planned to get off yet. She let them push her and spin her and send her along the platform until finally the crowd opened enough so that the constant pressure was gone and there was only occasional bumping as people rushed by her on their way to the stairs. Sabrina was panting now, and she looked for a place to sit down. There was none. She leaned against a post and watched the conductor. There was no expression on his face, none at all. He put on his white gloves.

People packed themselves into the train as tightly as they could go. Sabrina didn't take her eyes off the conductor's face. It was a good face to look at, with high cheekbones coming down to a narrow chin, a small mouth, and very wide-set eyes. A young and handsome face that betrayed nothing. The hands went carefully to backs and shoulders and pressed them further into the train.

As the doors closed and the conductor turned around, Sabrina glanced down, but his jacket came over his pants in such a way that she couldn't tell if he had an erection. She thought his face looked flushed, and hers certainly was, as she moved toward a second orgasm, this time touching herself with her hand in the pocket of her Levi's reaching for her clit, not even caring if the people on the train noticed, watching the young conductor and imagining those gloved hands pushing her into the waiting breathing crowd, wanting for the first time in her life to feel the touch of one individual on her body, and knowing that she was going to enjoy the next three weeks in Tokyo very much indeed.

# While
# Pilar Tobillo
# Sleeps

**AMELIA MARIA DE LA LUZ MONTES**

My lover lives July during just about any month of the year. That's
what she tells me. I want to believe her. We're in the middle of December and we just met, so there are no Julys between us. July in Tacuba is
warm and rainy. But today is not July, not rainy. It is December when
the city is under smog cover, under coat cover—when everyone hud-
dles into the Iglesia San Gabriel because the vaulted ceilings and
stained plaster covering the walls look wet. Only in December do we
begin to imagine a main street, Calle Remojo, a slab of shimmering
concrete—an urban mirage. December brings the limosneros down
the Tacuba metro steps because there the roof reaches over their
heads like nowhere else and the temperature seems warmer. But in
her apartment, December suddenly is a wet July. She is lava, raining in
buckets brimming of sauza, crackling barrels full of Nayarit tomatoes,
squeezing each one above my head making my hair red, crimson, vermilion. She sizzles like the moment a plump drop of sweat falls from
her scuffed piano-playing fingers onto hot oil. I believe she lives July
because the weather in here burns and reminds me I'm at tropical lat-
itude, where the lightning bolts strip the skin in zigzags.

Some people can be hesitant at first. They want the lights off or
shades drawn. Some have to begin with small talk or lay out ground
rules. Others come with prepared instructions or introductions. Not
July. Everything begins *in media res* or, in this apartment, *in media
insula,* an island without introduction or ending: only action, the
body engaged, potent, kinetic. My coat and shirt had been discarded
long ago and not by me. Had she always been naked? I know she had

clothes on before we entered and yet somehow I missed the transition, the shedding. I watch her walk toward the windows, watch her hands touch veiled drapes. The delicate material gathers in her palm. I revel in that moment of gauze gathering, watching each fold multiply in her hand like memories accumulating in gorgeous pleats. Perhaps I am a collector of memories. Perhaps. A moment such as this one brings every sense alive but for a purpose. So I can play it over and over, adjusting here a glance, there a touch, a smell or sound. Memories are reliable, pliable. The actual moments, sadly, are as delicate as gauze, fleeting in their movement—the way I see her now. She unhooks the latches and pushes open the panes of glass, a glass that plays with my eyes, that begs me to check again what I have seen. It is early afternoon and people must be looking up to the balcony, to this glistening woman whose arms are outstretched, opening French doors. I imagine a dark watercolor figure on the pavement, looking up, a smudge of sienna for an open mouth on a surprised face.

She laughs, "You know that song 'Bésame.'"

I close my eyes and I can hear her bare feet coming closer, her breath on my face. She is whispering "Bésame" lightly on my neck. I can feel the timbre of her voice against my skin—"Bésame" on the round curve of my shoulder, my belly, my thigh. I join her in a soft chorus exchanging delicate vibrations from lips to skin—

Some people pick up the pace, change positions, lead the action. My lover stays and stays, drinking in every nuance of touch, kiss, caress. And when it is almost too much, she comes in a cascade of words about fruit of all things—wanting to devour each morsel.

"Casaba, guayaba, granada."

"What are you saying?" I whisper.

"My ancestors' ashes," she says in winded phrases.

Her voice—musical, enticing. I follow her out of my body up to the city's foothills and she's laid out the ashes—gray fragile offerings on the edge of hills full of fruit trees and bushes: mango, tamarindo, tejocote. I keep thinking any slight breeze will scatter them. Her voice brings me back to her. She touches a mango tree, a tejocote. Its leaves appear abundant in her hands and before I know it, her body is laced with its greens and browns. She beckons me closer. The fragile gray lines around us become vines abundant with tamarindo pods, tamarindo filaments. I can hear her laughing and we both watch the mango grow tall above us, twisting up and around. We're wrapped up, fitting snug within the midst of all this foliage. And we feel each inside of each—the rain we pour, steamy and sweltering. I can't see her because I'm coming too, but I can feel her move my arms away from her and above my head, letting me swing from the bough of her ancestral vine tree—my mouth open, filling full with the juice of casaba.

"I'm famished." She watches herself in front of the mirror near the bedroom door. "I know exactly what I want to eat."

I smile. "Casaba?"

She looks at me strangely. Hadn't she remembered anything? She looks at me as if I had appeared from nowhere and doesn't ask any more of me. No hugs, no whispers. Some people demand sentimentality after sex—you know, enveloping hugs, indecipherable whispers, what we call promises, promises. Maybe it isn't such a bad idea—to linger and pretend. I feel my hand smooth the lemon-colored sheet still slightly damp and quite warm. All five feet of her glistens in front of the bed and mirror like an illusion—like the mirage on Calle Remojo. I want her all over again, but she's gone like the rain. December. Not a cloud in the sky. Just cold. I can hear her bare feet downstairs on the wooden floor of the kitchen.

"Are you hungry?" she calls.

I lie there listening to the refrigerator open. I imagine her eyes skimming over tiny black seeds on cut papaya, the bit of rust on the jar of *pico de gallo*, or a bowl of marinating red onions. Maybe she would have these. The refrigerator door closes. Pots clatter. She hums a strange tune which is interrupted by successive chopping on wood. I listen and watch the gauze curtain unfurl gently in the breeze of the afternoon. More clatter. She moves in my mind from one kitchen activity to the next: mortar in one hand, pestle in the other—a desire for the smell and taste of cumin, cinnamon, pepper. The smells move my feet first. They plant themselves on partly cool wood floor and rumpled cotton bedsheet. I decide to forego covering myself and half wonder which is more vulnerable in this place: being naked or clothed? And will it be someone else I meet downstairs—someone who remembers nothing—or will she still be naked and glistening, smelling of food and sex, her body giving everything away all over again? I quietly step my way down a rusty wrought-iron staircase—a narrowly circular one. I can't remember climbing it. Halfway down I see her. The yellow and blue tiles in the kitchen make her brown skin darker—her black hair richer. July smiles at me, beckoning.

Ten crushed garlic cloves she throws in the pot and doesn't wait for the onion, but snaps the green beans clean, smooths the yellow and orange peppers with oiled hands larger than mine.

"How can you cook so efficiently right after what we just did?"

"It cools me down . . ." She pauses as if she really meant to say something else. She looks at the pepper. "No," she says. "No, actually, it just prepares me for mi segunda lluvia."

My second rain. She doesn't even look at me because I know what she means. Her *segunda lluvia* may or may not include me. She takes the avocados, peeling them two at a time.

"This caldo is my favorite." She smiles. "You're lucky today. I don't make it often."

"What is it called?" I ask.

Her eyes scan the red and orange colors of the liquid. "I didn't know for a long time what to call this. I had to eat it enough times to let the name come to me." She takes her finger, dips it in the soup, lets it linger inside her mouth. "I call it caldo ahuehuete," she says, her finger tracing the lines of her mouth.

The soup I taste is quite different from the one I order at the restaurant down the street from here—the one across from the church of San Esteban Popotla. The ingredients may be the same, but maybe the distinctive smells make the difference, or the colors. Perhaps it is July from whose prodigious hands this soup appears. Yet, maybe the difference lies simply in the name. After all, the ahuehuete is the tree every one of us knows—the gnarled and sorry tree across from Popotla under which Cortés is said to have bowed low, weeping over the death of five hundred Spaniards at the hands of Aztecas. I can taste anger in this soup—inflamed malevolent spices.

*It's only soup,* I whisper, as if to remind myself.

She dips the ladle into the pot. "Some people tell me it's only soup. Others say it's something else."

"Really?" I say, watching her pour the reddish liquid into the bowl. *Did she hear me?* "What do others say?"

"Oh—some want to call it an aromatic." She takes another bowl but does not fill it. "Others say medicine—herbal elixir."

She doesn't move when I take her hand from the bowl and bring it to my lips. She watches me, as if intrigued. I kiss her warm hand again and my lips find her upper arm, the nape of her neck, my eyes covered by the blackness of her hair. She smells of the ahuehuete tree after a rain.

"You eat," she says, brushing away the last of my kisses. "I need to play before I eat."

She was the one saying she was famished—yet she cooks, serves me soup, and immediately heads for the piano in the next room. The aroma of food may not always be the trigger for hunger. Maybe coupling the scent of a savory broth with musical notes is all she needs for heightened pleasure. I take a few spoonfuls of liquid, feel it burn down my throat. I close my eyes and see her fingers moving furiously from one end of the keyboard to the other. She's playing a song I've never heard. It sounds strangely indigenous as if she transposed an ancient song and instrument into her own odd melody for the piano.

*Who are you?* I want to ask. *Tell me everything about you.*

She abruptly stops and changes octaves to warmer, deeper tones. I come near and sit with my July, who I know full well is not really mine—whom I hardly know.

"Would you like more?" She slows the tempo.

"More soup?"

She laughs. "I only cooked one thing today. But if you like, I'll cook something else next week."

"I'd love to," I say, watching her fingers glide over the edges of ebony keys.

"Love to what?" She looks up, her green eyes sear into me as if she already knows everything she'd like to know about me.

"Love to see you again—see you next week."

I don't know which is better—hearing her play or watching her abruptly stop, head for the table, and sip the spicy liquid from my spoon. She doesn't just put the spoon in her mouth. She sips the liquid first and then takes each vegetable one at a time, her thick lips enveloping the orange pepper gently, then the yellow one.

"I know what this is missing."

I have no idea what she means. I have everything in front of me I would need.

"Jalapeños."

"Really?" I say. "I didn't think of that."

"How could I have forgotten? It's just not spicy enough."

"I thought it was just right." I take the spoon and taste it once more, picturing her lips, full and spicy, around mine.

"Do you like jalapeños?" she calls from the kitchen.

"Not as much as my sister did," I answer. "She ate them like a snack—right out of the jar."

"My mother used to tell us kids that while she breast-fed us, she would have lots of jalapeños with every meal. She said it gave us strength."

I want her to keep talking, to let me know every detail about her life. I want to know who she looks most like—her father or mother. Does her mother have the same arched nose, the same straight hair cut softly around a perfectly round face? Or is it her father or some distant relative who has such big hands and feet? What mix of peoples has gifted her with such smooth chocolate skin? Does her bold stature come from the jalapeños her mother ate?

"So you agree with your mother about the jalapeños?" I ask, dipping my spoon in the bowl.

She reappears next to me with an open jar of the green plump chiles. She takes one and squeezes it over my bowl, then onto my spoon. Her lips barely touch when she breathes in the juice. Her eyes close shut and she is off somewhere else.

"Mierda mama, pura mierda!" she cries. "Oh, that's good. It's sweet, you know, like the lemon on papaya."

"I believe you," I answer.

She takes the spoon full of soup and fills my mouth. It burns sweetly.

"There," she says. "Now you are full of mierda. Full of shit," and she laughs before taking the bowl into both her hands and suddenly drinking the liquid down as if it were a shot of tequila.

She gasps loudly when my watch suddenly beeps the hour. "What time is it?"

"Five o'clock," I say, hating myself for owning that watch.

"I've got to go," she says, getting up. "You need to go too."

"Can I see you again, can we make plans?"

"In a week," she calls from the kitchen. "Thursday."

"Where?" I move to the kitchen, closer to her, wanting to breathe in her pepper smell so I can remember for a week.

"Where we met."

---

*Where we met.* She wants to meet me at the cemetery again. I had been at the cemetery this morning because my American cousin, Ricura, asked me to visit the grave of Pilar Tobillo—Ricura's grand obsession. There's this legend about Pilar Tobillo. Her soul, they say, is lost—a traitor to her Spanish blood. She was once the toast of Mexico City, performing repeatedly at the Palacio de Bellas Artes. In the 1950s, Tobillo was at her peak. She was also married to Spanish royalty and mistress to a Mexican official. Some people say it was her dancing that ruined her. Others say it was the stage curtain of the Palacio that bewitched her—the glass theater curtain designed by the famous artist Dr. Atl—the one made of countless opalescent crystals depicting volcanoes in the Valley of Mexico. It was there one afternoon, reported various newspapers, that she was caught with "un limosnero—Indio—who had a long black braid and was of a slight build." Someone reported seeing Dr. Atl's crystal volcanoes reflected on their bodies. Another saw light streaming from their feet. Most, however, reported them fleeing the building naked. For years afterward, people would report having seen Tobillo dancing Aztec dances on the top of Popocatépetl or the Pyramid of the Moon. Dolls and statues were made of Tobillo clad in feathers and crystals. Some say she is still alive. Others believe her grave does not really contain her body. Ricura has always loved the intrigue. I wonder if Tobillo and her indigenous alliance is simply a tale—a ploy to make us sympathize with Cortés under the ahuehuete tree.

When we were growing up and Ricura came to visit, she pretended to be the famous Tacuban dancer who, as Ricura explained, "was my Aztec hero." Ricura dressed herself with feathers on her head, a long serape over her torso, and tiny jingles around her wrists. "I am Tobillo," she would proclaim to us in the living room, stamping her bare feet on the floor.

"Eres pocha!" my father would tell her disdainfully—"una gringa!"

My other cousins from Mexico City would laugh at her. "If you want to be Tobillo, you need to learn Nahuatl. She knew."

"Don't encourage her," my mother would say. "You'll make her into an Indita."

I hated it when my parents would start on this subject. "Aren't we all Indios?" I would tell everyone.

My mother and father would frown. "You can say that here in this house, but don't say it if you want a high-profile job."

"My job," Ricura was emphatic, "is to be Pilar Tobillo in Los Angeles."

Everyone would laugh.

But Ricura never forgot Tobillo. I would have forgotten her had it not been for Ricura's stubborn fidelity to her Spanish-turned-Aztec dancer. Ricura loved Tobillo, loved how she refused to dance the same dance. One August, Ricura asked me to go with her to watch old movie clips—all that is left of Tobillo's image—old and damaged. Ricura begged me to see Pilar beat out the rhythm of *La Jota Aragonesa.*

"This is a piece from her early career. Watch the movement," she'd tell me. "Watch her rhythm."

I was confused. "Why do you want to see her dancing flamenco?"

Ricura always became impatient with me. "Because you can still see the Aztec influence. Haven't you read about her performances—how her movements have also been interpreted as indigenous?"

"No. I can't say I've read about that."

"I read it in Los Angeles. A Mexican art and dance historian wrote it! Haven't you heard about it?" Ricura threw up her arms in frustration.

I said nothing, more out of embarrassment than disregard for Ricura. I simply shrugged my shoulders. She responded to my silence by twirling her long chestnut hair around her right index finger. I knew she was angry. When Ricura is angry, her thick eyebrows become tightly knit so that her long face casts a dark look my way. There is a certain loveliness to Ricura's anger—a somewhat furious energy that electrifies her body. Her anger motivates me out of a kind of slumber. Her body folds like her eyebrows: long, lean legs cross tightly, hands grip at folds of clothing. I can see the white of her knuckles. If I wait long enough, she makes another attempt at me—unknitting, uncrossing herself—gesticulating once again and entreating me to see her side, her perspective.

"You see, they never filmed her doing other dances—especially Aztec ones." Ricura's hazel eyes brightened. She smiled slowly. "But she found a way even in these. Watch the film and then maybe you will see."

———

A cracked, filmy Pilar raises the castanets above her head, her spine arched like an arrogant peacock in a severe unfurling of overexposed ruffles, lifting her heels, toes pointed, while the film jumps, skips off its sprocket, and there's a moan from the audience and the projection room. There's another moan and Pilar's image trembles and doubles, then finally settles into focus while her partner enters from the left, joining her in the rhythmic clicking, in the sudden accelerated sound track. Two of them now—only Pilar and her partner—the music fast and swift bringing them into a circle of arms rattling castanets, rattling a "ha!"—their lips a tenth of an inch apart, large and sultry. Then the camera spins straight into Pilar's face. For a moment she seems suspended in air—her eyes dark and almond-sized, tainted with spidery film smudges. I close my eyes. The high speed of the music makes me dizzy—makes me imagine Pilar skipping the sprocket, suddenly twirling round and hitting the heels of her shoes hard onto wood. But the shoes disappear. The film cuts to bare feet bedecked in strange jewels. Silver-ringed toes on wood change the tempo. I hear a high-pitched singing from her open mouth, an unknown refrain—language strangely familiar. Her partner has disappeared and Pilar Tobillo's presence consumes all of the stage like a whirling memory of something I once knew. I can hear Ricura's breathing beside me, or is it mine that has accelerated? The image on the screen is surrounded by feathers, long and glorious. Tobillo takes them, glides them across her body, across the stage. She twirls again and again. Suddenly the film abruptly turns a sepia, a burnt sepia. Flame begins from the left corner, then up the middle, and the audience directs loud whistling and hissing at the projection room. "Estúpido!" "Pendejo!" they yell. The music gets louder and louder while its notes become long-drawn-out and out of tune. More hissing and yelling. The theater goes dark.

I feel Ricura's hand on mine, her breath close to my ear. "I want her soul," she says.

But how can we have anybody's soul, let alone Pilar's soul? Ask Ricura, because even though she's never seen someone die she will tell you she knows. She says the soul is like a white grayish cloud, a puff of smoke, an aspiration hardly pronounced. She says some people have seen it float out of the newly deceased's mouth and into their own. Those who want their loved one's soul only need open their body for it. She says others who have felt the soul say it simply brushed past them, or they felt a breeze but the soul never stayed. Still others say it interrupted the electricity in their house and they were using candles for the week the soul was there.

"It seems to me," I remember telling Ricura, "that it's all up to the soul and not up to us. So you may want it, but you may not receive it."

"You don't know." Ricura shot an angry look my way. I could see her hand muscles tightening. "You don't know."

Ricura called a month ago and asked me to go see Pilar Tobillo's grave. She was doing research on famous Tacuban dancers and would I just see what was written on the gravestone. I was reluctant at first. It seemed such a trivial request. And as for her studies on famous dancers or anybody famous—I believe when you die, that's it. Finished. You did what you could, you had one chance, and being remembered or putting something memorable on your grave or leaving something behind is all just mortal desperation. Who remembers? I certainly don't. In fact, I almost forgot to fulfill Ricura's wish until early today when I had gone to the outskirts of the city for business. The cross of Calvario Cementerio was right in front of my view and then Ricura's words hit me: "I'm telling you to go now, because I know it'll take you a month to get there."

"You know me too well."

"I do." She laughed. "My paper's not due till the end of the term. Call me as soon as you get it." There had been a slight pause. "Make sure you write it down."

"You know me too well."

"Oh and just one more thing. Please remember not to step in front of the gravestone where the remains lie."

"What?"

"You know, the old belief about waking up the dead and how if you step where they've been lying—it's bad luck—you interrupt their sleep."

"Okay. Yes, Ricura. I got that."

Ricura knew I never liked lingering on the phone, so she ended the conversation quickly. "Say hello to everyone—tell them I called—if you remember! Adiós."

"Left area—on the hill." The bearded attendant pointed from the cemetery office door. "Follow the marked numbers—Tobillo is in the 900 plot area."

I decided to walk from the office lot. This morning was an unusually sunny day for December. Very warm. The smog was nonexistent, so I could see the miles of large ashen gravestones. In December, the climate is so dry and cold that the stone begins to take on a hard pumice look, so the view looks eerie—like an empty lava field. The only inhabitants are grotesque-looking angels, their wings chipped, faces wind-blown or washed away from summer rains, or columned monuments cracked in half from earthquakes. Ricura tells me that on the Day of the Dead, spirits are visible. She says one can see souls encircling the sky above the cemetery. Ricura believes all of this because she's not here all the time. She only visits Tacuba in the summers when cemetery stones are brilliantly shiny from constant tropical rains. The legends remain new to her. She doesn't see the city year-round. I suppose I could compare her view of Tacuba to one's image of a new lover in one's life. You can easily idealize a new lover, enamored of the mystery, of your own fictions you make of her. After you know the truth, Tacuba just becomes like el centro Distrito Federal—all smog. Just the smog, Ricura, just the smog. I know she doesn't like hearing this, so I don't try to convince her.

By the time I arrived at plot number 941, I could see that a funeral ritual had just ended. Various people clad in black were exiting the east gates. A few looked back to gesture at the one person who had stayed behind. They were making the sign of the cross to her. She did not respond but simply stood watching them leave. The young-looking woman was not dressed in black but in flowing reds and greens. She was barefoot. My eyes caught the luminous beadwork on her bodice and then I saw her perfectly round pensive face. She walked around the hole as if inspecting its contents. Suddenly, she was on her hands and knees. I could see her reaching down into the hole and drumming furiously on the coffin with what seemed like long reed-like canes. She wasn't crying, wasn't saying anything. The drumming was rhythmic, the beats contagious. I hadn't noticed I was stamping to the rhythm when she happened to look at me. She looked apprehensive.

"Not on the remains!" she yelled, pointing a cane at my feet.

I looked down. My feet were moving rhythmically right on Pilar Tobillo's grave. I panicked and jumped but only to land my right foot on another grave, stepping back to land upon a third. Finally, my feet found themselves once again at the edge of Tobillo's grave. *Ricura need not know,* I whispered to myself. I stood there listening, rubbing

my hands together—feeling a desire to clap to the sounds a few feet
away.

The drumming became louder. After a while, I wondered if it was
coming from below or above me. The woman kept staring, her eyes
large and dark. I left Pilar for the moment and went to the source of
rhythm on impulse. Something pulled me, beckoned me to sit next to
the drumming woman, to feel her body move to the rhythm, until she
abruptly stopped.

"Did you wake the dead?" She looked down at the box below.

"I don't know," I said. "I wasn't watching."

She turned to look at me. "What were you watching?"

*I was watching how beautiful and strange you are, how I want to touch
those lips,* I thought. "I was watching your drumming," I said.

She leaned over and whispered, "That's not what you were watching."

I brushed my finger over her lips. She didn't move away but opened
her mouth slightly. In fact she was quite bold. Her full lips met mine—
wet and warm. She dropped the canes and I let her take my arms
around her perspiring back. She touched my skin with her dirt-
stained hand, rubbing grit softly against my temple. The next thing I
knew, we were on our way to her apartment.

"Was that a song you were playing?" I whispered to her in bed.

"In a way," she said. "I wanted to make sure she was dead."

I thought of Ricura, who reminded me that we always need to know
if a person is dead. Too many people have been buried alive not only
in Tacuba but throughout Mexico—people buried in less than twelve
hours. Some people swear they knew their loved one was dead. They'll
tell you they saw the soul leave the body. But who's to say the soul
doesn't choose to return? My own mother swears she heard her
father scratching and clawing the box as she left the graveside with
the family.

"They buried him only five hours after they say he died," my mother
would always tell me, shaking her head. "I knew he was alive even
though Tia Chala said he was dead. Tia Chala kept pulling me away
from the burial site as I kept telling her to listen to the box."

Ricura told me last summer that the burial practice was a curse on
all of Mexico.

"I wouldn't go that far," I told her. "Wasn't it simply because people
did not embalm?"

"Hundreds of Aztecas were buried alive by Cortés' men." Ricura's eyes searched my face. "How could they not curse Mexico before they died?"

I guess I should have agreed. Instead I said nothing. Now I find myself with a woman who makes sure people are dead.

"Are you sure drumming on the coffin works?" I asked July, kissing her scuffed knuckles.

"It's the only way. The song wakes anybody up. It made you dance on Tobillo's grave—and the two next to hers."

I thought about that and wondered if Pilar had heard me. "Oh shit!" I yelled.

"What? What's the matter?"

"I forgot to write down . . ."

"Write what?"

"Oh, you'll think it's silly—I was going to write down the epitaph from Pilar Tobillo's grave."

"That's not silly," she said. "I've seen lots of people do that. You know how famous she is."

"Well, do you know what it says?"

"No, but then I don't really look at epitaphs. I like to notice the grass over the remains, the cracks in the ground—that tells me more."

I kissed her. She circled her body around mine. I realized then it was July, not December. The rains had come and Pilar Tobillo was probably somewhere above us, while in Los Angeles, I imagined Ricura speaking in Nahuatl and stepping to strangely familiar rhythms. I can't say if this is true. I don't know. I can only tell you I am with July in December while Pilar Tobillo sleeps.

# What We Forgot to Tell Tina About Boys

**ELLEN HAWLEY**

My niece has been old enough to hold a conversation for something like twelve years now, and what I've learned in this time is that the more I care about the topic, the less likely I am to say the right thing to her. This has been true for a long time, but I'm painfully aware of it right now because I've spent the past two hours waiting for a doctor to stitch up the cut under her eye, and I still haven't figured out what to say about how she got hurt.

I drive her home and shut off my old Honda in front of my sister's house. Neither of us makes a move to get out. In the bleak orange of the streetlight, Tina looks like she's spent the last two days riding the hound. The bruised side of her face is away from me, by the window.

"I don't want to go in," she says. "I don't want to hear it from her."

*Her* is my sister, Katy, and there've been times that I haven't wanted to hear it from her either. I don't say this to Tina. I say, "She's worried about you. She loves you."

Tina rolls her eyes and I shrug, maintaining my traditional sympathy with both sides. I can remember still what it was like to be fifteen and hemmed in by my parents' love when that wasn't what I wanted anymore—or what I thought I wanted. I wouldn't mind burdening Tina with a bit of my own love, but it won't help just now. I look away from her, at the windshield, which is beaded with tiny drops of rain, only a fraction heavier than mist. Each bead holds a glint of orange from the streetlight. With the heater off, I'm starting to feel how damp my clothes are.

"C'mon," I say. "Let's get it over with."

She doesn't argue. Outside of the car, it's cold. I'd put a hand on her shoulder if she were either younger or older. I hug my raincoat closed instead. Tina wears a light windbreaker and she leaves it open, as if cold and rain don't touch her. Her hair hangs over her shoulders, looking damp and defeated.

I've been close to Tina since she was tiny. Her father left before she was born, and I never expected to have kids of my own. Until I saw Tina's bunched, newborn face, I had no idea that I even wanted kids. So we both had a gap in our lives. I told myself I could protect her from Katy's fierceness. Infants inspire all kinds of delusion. I thought I could protect her from everything. I used to worry that sooner or later I'd embarrass her—the way I dress, the fact that I go out with women—but that doesn't seem to bother her. She's at that age is all, and I'm on the other side of the dividing line. It would be the same if I were straight.

Katy opens the door for us as we come up the walk and she hops backward to let us through. She's been on crutches for less than a week and is awkward with them.

"So how're you doing?" she asks Tina.

"Fat lot you care," Tina says, marching past her and up the stairs, wet jacket and all. I hang my raincoat on a peg while Katy swings to the base of the stairs and plants herself there.

"Hey," she yells upward. "When did I get to be the enemy? Hunh?"

Tina doesn't answer. The door to her room slams. Katy holds her position long enough to accent Tina's silence, then adjusts her crutches, stumps in a circle, and swings back to her chair in the living room. She heaves the leg with the cast onto the hassock and leans her crutches against the wall.

A part of me would like to be upstairs, waiting with Tina in case she wants to talk, but it's not a big enough part. We're dividing up by age, and I follow Katy meekly into the living room.

"What did *I* do to her?" Katy asks when I'm settled on the couch. "Can you tell me that?"

I shake my head, no, I can't.

"She's fifteen," I say as if this explained everything.

"I should've taken her to the hospital myself, shouldn't I?"

I nod at the cast. "She can see how it is."

"I should've taken her. I should've called a cab."

She lets her breath out in a sigh as solid as the weight of her leg dropping onto the hassock. Our mother used to sigh like that, as if breathing out were a luxury she couldn't afford very often.

"So *you* tell me," she says. "How is she?"

It takes me a few seconds to realize I can actually answer this—that I don't have to account for Tina's whole person.

"They don't think it'll leave a scar," I say. "It looks worse than it is."

"I wish it would leave a scar." She juts her chin out, daring me to argue. "I don't want her to think things like this happen and you just walk away from them."

"He ever hit her before?"

Her chin drops back to its normal position.

"If he has, he didn't leave marks."

We nod like the middle-aged women we are, remembering how little an adult really knows about a child's life and how little our parents knew about ours.

"I know this much," she says. "He likes to control her. Who she talks to, who she sees, what she wears." She laughs sourly. "He's a perfect little wife beater in training."

My mother's sigh comes from me this time. It releases a weight in my chest, but a second later the weight's back again, as heavy as before.

"You want some coffee?" I ask.

"Sure, make us some coffee. Throw caution to the winds. We should get drunk, only I don't feel like it."

I heave myself off the couch.

"Tinaleh," I yell up the stairs. "I'm making coffee. You want some?"

I'm standing the way Katy stood to yell up at Tina, head tipped back, time suspended, breathing suspended, waiting for normal life to rush in and fill the vacuum. My voice is cheerful and witless and I wonder if there's some way I can divorce its owner.

Tina yells no as if I'd offered her a raffle ticket on a three-month jail term; as if this were the third time I'd offered it to her. My mother sighs through my lungs again and this time I expect her and I'm glad to hear from her. I want to know if she has advice for us. I want her to tell us it will all work out—that sooner or later Tina will grow up, and when that happens she'll develop some sense. I want her to tell us who the enemy really is, because that seemed a lot clearer when she was alive. All through the McCarthy years, when my father was expelled from the union he'd helped organize and moved from one underpaid job to the next, getting fired whenever the FBI took it into their heads to visit him at work, she kept our anger focused away from individuals. She told us people were misled, or naive, or ignorant; at her angriest she said they were crass, or narrow-minded. She never let us see them as the enemy. The enemy was the ruling class, the bosses, the government. No one you met on the street. No one you knew at school. No one you went out with.

In the kitchen, I put the kettle on and dump out old coffee grounds. While I wait for the water to boil, I squirt soap around the top layer of dishes, wash them, squirt more soap, and wash the next layer. I haven't done Katy's dishes like this since she was too pregnant to get to the sink. Our father had just died, and his absence stunned us into the closeness he'd always wanted for us. An offering to his memory, maybe, or a rush to make ourselves back into family for Tina's sake, although we didn't know her name yet, or her sex. It's hard to say what drove us then.

I miss those days.

"Knock it off in there, will you?" Katy yells.

The kettle screams before I decide whether to knock it off or not, before I decide whether to yell back that she damn well waited until I'd done a lot of dishes before she objected. I pour water into the coffee filter, watch the level drop, pour more water, and wait for the last drips to squeeze through. From the other room, I hear the whump of Katy rearranging her leg on the hassock and I'm coldly furious, all of a sudden, that she can make this much noise just sitting still. I don't want to go back in and sit with her. I don't want to excuse her temper on account of her leg or her daughter or the phases of the moon. I don't want to figure out what she did wrong or what she can do now that would make it right. I don't know what will make it right. I'm an outsider here—an aunt, not a mother. I've never known this so sharply before. I don't make the decisions; I'm not the one who got us to this point.

I set Katy's coffee on the arm of her chair and she curls a hand around it, which is as close as she'll come to saying thanks. I'm cold to the bone and wrap both hands around my own cup. I want to go home, put on a load of wash, and make a lunch for tomorrow. I want to do anything other than settle in for a piss-and-moan session with Katy. I'd work an extra shift right now if I could arrange for someone

to call me. I blow on my coffee, forcing a storm across the surface. I
run out of air and steam rises in front of my face.

"Did she talk to you at all?" Katy says.

"A little."

I blow into my coffee again and sip it, scalding my tongue. I'm
aware of Tina upstairs, out of sight, either listening to us or else not listening—I don't know which. She didn't tell me anything particular
when we were at the hospital, but even so I feel wrong turning around
and talking to Katy about it. Or maybe I only feel wrong talking to
Katy because Tina may be listening. Whatever the reason, it's not powerful enough. Katy's the one sitting across from me, her leg pinned to
the hassock by her cast, and I never could hold out against her for
long. I look at the cat, who's asleep in front of the heat vent, and I
watch his ribs rise, then fall, then rise again before I answer her.

"She wants to help him—" I say.

Katy snorts.

"And I want to nail his hide to the garage door."

I snort back, half amused, half angry that she cut me off.

"I expect I'm part of what she wants to save him from."

"Not the part she mentioned. She talked about his family, mostly.
His stepfather. School."

"Yeah, she's told me about the family."

We stare at the center of the room, somewhere between her white
plaster foot and the dirty plates on the coffee table.

What Tina told me about the boy's family is that a couple of months
ago the father took the door off Darren's bedroom and won't tell Darren where he put it. He says Darren shouldn't do anything in private
that he can't do in public. Sometimes he prays over Darren and sometimes he tells him to get out and never come back, he's seen as much
of him as he ever wants to. "I mean, he hits him and all that," Tina told
me, "and I know my mom thinks that's the worst thing you can do, but
it's the other stuff that really gets to him. You know, like the door and
all."

I didn't argue about what Katy thinks. I listened and I nodded and I
let her talk. She was passionate about how badly Darren's treated, and
she reminded me a lot of the way Katy used to sound. Katy runs an
emergency child care center, and when she was first setting it up I
used to hear the same protectiveness from her, and almost the same

voice. She still sounds like that from time to time, but less often now, and less powerfully.

"She told me he gets blamed for everything at school, even when it's not his fault." I look up. "I'm quoting."

The doorbell rings, sending the cat streaking for the basement. The cat door flaps closed behind him.

Katy swings her leg down and reaches for her crutches.

"I was afraid of this," she says.

I flip the outside light on and wait for her at the door. Standing politely on the porch steps is a teenage boy—thin, nice-looking, maybe half a foot taller than either of us, his curly hair glistening with drizzle and soft in the yellow porch light. Katy comes up behind me and mutters, "Shit."

"You want me to open the door?"

She nods and hops backward to give me room. I follow her onto the porch, standing behind her.

The boy is separated from us by nothing more than a screen door and his own good manners. If he wanted to, he could open the door and slam a fist into either of us as easily as he did into Tina, but he doesn't take his hands out of his pockets. He has coffee-and-cream eyes with lashes a model would die for. It's hard to see any danger in him.

We stand there for several long moments, trying to sort out our roles. He kicks lightly at the top step and looks down like a bashful suitor.

"Tina in?" he asks.

Katy shakes her head.

"I don't want you seeing her anymore. And I don't want you in this house."

"Could I just talk to her for a minute?"

Katy shakes her head again, but we don't leave, we stand there looking at him, inviting an argument.

"Look, I just want to tell her I'm sorry. I won't move off the step here."

He holds his shoulders hunched. Behind me, through the door I left open because it seemed safer to have an open door at our backs, heat flies out of the house and disappears into the damp air without warming anybody. The street's shiny with rain.

Katy stumps sideways, ready to go back in, and I move aside to give her room. The boy has one hand on the doorframe and is saying, again, that he just wants to talk to Tina. From above the porch, Tina yells, "Darren?"

He backs up until he can see her.

"Hey, I was just asking your mom if you were in. Come on down here."

"I don't want to see you again. Ever." She yells this at full dramatic pitch but without slamming the window. Katy and I stop where we're standing. I feel like I'm watching the balcony scene from some insane rewrite of *Romeo and Juliet*.

"I didn't mean to hurt you. I was out of my head, okay? I went crazy."

"You did hurt me."

"Tina, I'm sorry. I'm sorry. Okay? I'm sorry."

"You didn't even ask if I'm okay."

"Are you okay?"

"No, I'm not okay. I'll probably have a scar for the rest of my life."

"Listen, I'm sorry. I'll do anything. Really, I'm sorry."

"Don't talk to me."

The window slams shut. Across the street, the lights go off so the neighbors can see what's happening without having to watch through their own reflections in the glass. The drizzle seeps down. Even under the porch roof, damp air slides through the weave of my sweater and flattens itself against my skin.

"Ti-naa," Darren calls, the last syllable stretching out long and desperate. "I love you, Tina!" He's crying. His jacket's open and he has no hat. He's wet, he's cold, he's younger, I swear, than any human being should have to be, and he may or may not have a roof over his head tonight. He's braying his love under the eyes of a block full of strangers. He breaks my heart. Katy completes her interrupted turn and I follow her into the house, shutting the door and turning off the porch and hall lights so that we too can watch him without seeing our faces.

"I'll call you," he yells up to Tina's closed window. He walks a couple of steps toward the sidewalk and yells, "I love you." He waits there, hands stuffed back into his pockets, then he turns toward Lake Street and walks off, head low, rain drizzling down the inside of his collar. At the edge of Katy's yard, he turns back and yells, "I love you," his voice breaking on the word "love." A piece of broken glass glitters at his feet.

The fan on the furnace hums, cranking out heat to replace what streamed past us into the dark. Tina's quiet upstairs, not climbing out the window after him, not agreeing to meet him in a graveyard, or wherever it was that Juliet met Romeo, but even so, I'm not ready to believe it's over. It's more than his pain that draws her. It's that he can stand on a wet sidewalk and bellow that he loves her. It's that she can yell back that she never wants to see him again and know that she will. He's the roller-coaster ride of a lifetime, and the one thing guaranteed to give her mother fits.

"You think she'll talk to me?" Katy asks, looking out into the empty street.

"I'm not betting on this one."

"Thanks a bunch."

I shrug. Katy doesn't move.

"You think she really believes I don't care how she is?"

"I think she's just mad. Or embarrassed. Or something. Hell, I don't know. She knows you care about her."

She nods toward the dark.

"I should've called a cab. I should've been there."

I shrug. The lights go on across the street.

"You know she went with me when I broke this damn thing?" She moves her leg a couple of inches to show me what she's talking about. "She was sweet."

"I don't think that's the problem."

She shakes her head and draws a deep breath, straightening herself. She says, "Well, shit."

She swings to the base of the stairs and hands me one crutch, using the other one and the banister to lever herself up. I follow two steps behind, braced to catch her if she falls, convinced that if she does I'll go down with her.

At the top, I hand her the crutch and turn to go back, but she calls my name and I stop.

"Come with me?" She nods sideways toward Tina's room. She says it the way thirty-odd years ago I might have asked her to come with me into a dark basement, or past a group of older kids who'd threatened me. I squeeze her arm for a second, too close to tears to say anything, and I nod. She nods back, sets her jaw, and knocks on Tina's door. When Tina doesn't answer, she knocks again.

"What?" Tina yells as if she'd been knocking all night.

"I want to talk to you."

"So?"

Katy takes this as shorthand for "So what are you doing in the hall?" instead of "So what do I care?" Maybe you have to be a mother to hear it this way. Maybe you have to have Katy's fierceness. I'd have gone back downstairs. Katy opens the door and swings over to the bed. I hesitate on the far side of the doorway until Katy motions me in.

"Don't go away. Maybe you can keep us from saying anything stupid to each other."

"She's not God," Tina says.

From the furthest reaches of Katy's lungs, our mother sighs.

I slide down to the floor and lean my back against the wall. The weight on my chest has eased. Katy thinks she needs me and that makes me as happy as if it could fix everything.

Tina's sprawled in an old armchair, arms folded across her chest, her jacket a wet pile on the floor beside her. The bruise around her eye has darkened and her shoulders have pulled the India-print spread off the chair's back and arm so that I'm staring at white cotton padding where the fabric's worn through.

"Well, what?" she says.

Katy pulls herself back on the bed so she can lean against the wall.

"Let's start over, okay? How's your face?"

"It hurts."

"You want some aspirin?"

"I took some."

The phone rings. All three of us freeze. I say I'll get it.

"If that's Darren, I don't want to talk to him," Tina calls down the hall after me.

"Tell him I'll call the cops if I so much as see his shadow," Katy yells.

A boy asks for Tina. Maybe it's Darren; maybe it's not. How am I supposed to know? I hear traffic in the background. I can't think what to say and he asks for Tina again. I tell him primly that she can't come to the phone right now. I stop myself before I ask if I can take a message. As I lower the receiver to the cradle, I hear his voice, tiny and angry, pleading, "Just let me talk to her. Just let me *talk* to her." I break the connection.

A few seconds later, the phone rings again. I hang up. I wait for it to ring a third time, but he must be out of quarters. I lean against Tina's doorframe.

"I don't want you to see him anymore," Katy says.

"I already told him." Tina's voice rises, aggrieved. "You always make it sound like everything's up to you."

"I heard you *tell* him. What I worry about is whether you mean it."

"You're going to make it so I have to go back to him just so's I can make my own decisions."

Katy closes her eyes, leans her head against the wall, and groans.

The phone rings.

"I want to talk to him," Tina yells after me, making no move to get to the phone.

I pick up the phone and set it down. It rings again. I hang it up. I expect two more calls—change for a dollar—but nothing happens.

I stand in Tina's doorway. The silence is as thick as blood, which is thicker than water and one hell of a lot more complicated.

"Let's start over," I say.

We're quiet for a minute, none of us making eye contact. I'm trying to find a way we really can start over, but I can't think of one. Tina's slumped sideways in the armchair, her face turned toward the window, toward Darren's absence. She looks teenaged and misunderstood and sulky. Katy's eyes are still closed. After a while she opens them and without looking at Tina begins to talk. Her voice has lost its edge and is quiet, as if she's thinking out loud. This is Katy at her most calculated, but she's no less effective just because I know the game.

"The first time I ever saw an adult hit a child, I was downtown with Mom," she says.

She has Tina's attention now, although Tina's as cagey about showing that as Katy is about claiming it. Her face is still turned to the dark window, but her body's come into focus differently.

"We were at Eighth and Nicollet. I remember a scaffolding over part of the sidewalk for some kind of construction. The boy was a year or two older than me, so he would have been seven, maybe. Eight. I'm guessing."

She looks at me, says, "I don't know where you were," and lets her eyes go out of focus again.

"The man was hitting him with a belt. I don't remember the boy crying, or anybody saying anything. I don't even remember the belt landing. It's like a snapshot—the man, the boy, the scaffolding, the belt, a crowd of people standing around them on the sidewalk. Until right then, I didn't know things like that happened. I knew kids got hit, but I didn't really understand that they got hurt. I hadn't put that part of it together."

A pause. The rain's gotten heavier and taps at the glass.

"I watched them until Mom pulled me away. Later on I asked her why she didn't do anything about it and she said, 'I couldn't.'"

She pulls at the skin around the base of her thumbnail.

"I thought about that for a long time, why she couldn't step in there and stop the man." She looks directly at Tina. "I don't know how clearly you remember her, but she was one powerful woman. Not physically, but emotionally." She lets her attention drift away from Tina again. "Morally. She always told us that things had to be changed if they weren't right, and here she was saying she couldn't do anything. It still bothers me."

Tina turns a little further to the window.

"That and knowing I wanted to stay and watch. Like I was some kind of tragedy vulture."

A car goes by outside, dragging its muffler for blocks before it fades away. I'm not sure what the point of Katy's story is. Maybe there is no point. Maybe she only told it because it crossed her mind, and because she doesn't know what to do now any more than our mother did all those years ago.

The phone rings. I hang it up without answering and wonder if it might have been somebody other than Darren. I go back to Tina's bedroom and sit on the floor. It's like stepping onto a raft: chair, bed, braided rug, silence, the blue-and-white spread crushed behind Tina's shoulders, the dark panes of the window, the three of us, all adrift in the damp night.

"You don't understand," Tina says quietly, as if she were answering something one of us had just said. "It's not like that. He didn't mean to hurt me."

Katy groans. Tina turns on her angrily.

"He didn't. He's like the boy you saw getting beaten. You should understand that if anybody does."

"I understand that children who get hit learn to hit," Katy snaps back. "What I don't understand is why you want to put yourself at ground zero."

"He doesn't *want* to be that way. You don't know him." She's leaning forward, intense, concentrated, pure. A single drop of this child should be enough to save a world, although it isn't, somehow.

"You can't save him," I tell her. "If he wants to change, maybe he will, but until then you can't save him."

"You don't think anything can change. You think every kid who gets hit is going to be an abuser unless you do something personally. Don't you? Don't you?"

I'm torn between yes and no and shake my head without saying anything. It's Katy, for whom this is meant anyway, who commits us by saying, "I'll tell you what I believe. I believe you're not doing either him or yourself any good by letting him hit you. Think about what it does to him if you don't care about yourself."

Tina leans back into her chair and says, in her best sullen teenager voice, "So what if I don't think about myself. *You* don't think about me."

Katy rises to the bait as surely as I would and says of course she thinks about Tina, it's just this damn cast on her leg. It's hard to get around . . .

"You won't let me meet my father," Tina says. "Because *you* don't want to see him. You don't care what I want."

She crosses her arms, grimly triumphant.

"I'm not going to get started on that."

"See?"

This is where I should have stopped them from saying anything stupid to each other, but as Tina more or less predicted, I have no idea how I could have done that, and it all happened too fast anyway. I sympathize with both of them. Kids should know their parents. I'd want to if I were Tina. On the other hand, I've met Tina's father. He's a charming man, or at least he was when he became her father. He had a story for every occasion, and not many of them turned out to be true. By the time Katy left him, the only thing she knew for a fact was that he drank too much.

She never told him she was pregnant.

Once, years ago, I threatened to tell Tina about him myself if Katy wouldn't, but I never found the right moment. And I wasn't sure enough that Katy was wrong. She was trying not to say anything bad to Tina about her father. When Tina was eighteen, if she still wanted to find him, Katy said she'd do what she could, but until then the best thing to do was to leave it alone.

Tina and Katy leave a moment's pause, as if even Tina's afraid to push this too far. Out back I hear the sound of breaking glass and I follow it through Katy's dark bedroom. I rest my forehead on her window. Nothing's moving in the alley, but my stomach won't unclench. *To understand all is to forgive all,* someone once said. I can't think who, but the quote comes to me in French. Voltaire, then? Baudelaire? I doubt Voltaire ever forgave anybody, and I don't know a thing about Baudelaire. Whoever it was, though, he had the luxury of distance. Even my mother never quite talked about forgiveness. "In a decent world," she would have said about Tina and Darren, "things like this wouldn't happen." It's what she always said when she didn't have a solution.

In the indecent world we have, Darren lopes around the corner of the garage carrying the plastic bucket Katy uses to set out the recycling. The picture's oddly domestic. Cold rises from the windowpane and into my skull. Tina comes up behind me. We watch Darren like he's a movie. It's not until he throws a bottle at the house that I'm jarred into motion. More glass breaks while I pick up the hall phone and dial 911. The woman who answers wants my name. Her computer must tell her where I'm calling from, because she reads me the address, asking if it's correct. She asks Darren's race. *Race,* I think blankly. Black, white, Indian, Hispanic, Asian; choose one. I have no idea what race he is, or whether he fits any of the categories.

"I don't know," I say.

Outside, Darren's yelling Tina's name again. More glass breaks.

"Is he black?" she asks. "White?"

"I don't know," I tell her before she can read me the rest of the menu. "For Chrissake, I don't know."

What I do know is that I sound like an idiot. The two things an American can be expected to notice about a person are their race and their sex, and I've managed not to register one of these.

Tina comes out of Katy's bedroom and asks what I'm doing. I turn my back without answering. The woman at 911 is still trying to sort out Darren's race.

"I don't *know,*" I tell her again. "He's throwing goddamn bottles at the house. I don't *care* what race he is."

"It's strictly for identification," she says. "I have to ask."

"They'll hurt him," Tina wails to my back. She's frantic, almost howling, and hanging on my arm. I pull away from her and she grabs the phone cord and yanks it out of the wall. I yell at her and she backs away, looking surprised and holding the end of the cord in her hand like an astronaut floating away from the ship on a line. I've still got the receiver in my hand and the vague feeling that it's supposed to be useful. We've both come unmoored. The gravitational force of our lives has let us slip. More glass breaks. Katy swings into Tina's open doorway and stops there, watching us. The thought comes to me that I should have checked with her before I called 911, and I dismiss it. Katy doesn't know what to do either. And she said she'd call the cops. The phone rings downstairs. Tina drops the cord and dashes for the stairs. I hang the receiver up neatly, just as if this mattered, before I follow, calling her name, not the way Darren's calling her in the alley but sharp, commanding, the way I used to call her when she was little and I could bark her name to stop her from running out between parked cars. Behind us, Katy also barks her name.

Tina grabs the downstairs phone, yells that there's no problem, and yanks the cord loose. Not far away, a siren screams, and then another. She whirls toward me in tears.

"They'll hurt him."

"He'll hurt us."

"He won't."

"You want a mirror?"

"It's not the same." She's crying full out now. "You called the *cops*. You're the one who taught *me* about cops."

I did teach her about cops. I told her stories from before she was born, about demonstrations I'd been part of that were peaceful until the cops waded in. When she was twelve, I took her to a rally against police brutality—a sad little gathering, maybe twenty or thirty people in front of the courthouse after a black kid got his head cracked open somewhere between the time he was put in the car and the time they delivered him to jail. What was I supposed to do? Tell her the world is one big Disneyland and then wait for her to turn on me later because I lied to her?

"They're all we've got right now," I say.

The sirens scream to a halt. A red light's flashing through the front window like a strobe.

"I'm going outside," she says.

I nod. I'm not sure going outside is a good idea—it probably isn't—but the agreement's pulled out of me by her tone, which has dropped

back into the rational zone. Katy launches her crutches down the
stairs and is working her way down step by step on her hind end. I follow Tina out the front door and stop above her on the porch steps.
Below us, Darren's backed against the wall of the house, holding the
hollow pole from Katy's bird feeder across his chest like a kung-fu
fighter on television, only with none of the grace. He's trapped in the
dark corner formed by the house and the neighbor's fence, trying to
hold off two cops, who've sprouted in the rain on Katy's front lawn,
large and blue and frightening, and he's yelling at them to kill him, to
go ahead and shoot him. *Hysteria,* my mind tells me, but even as the
word forms, I see that one of the cops has a hand riding on his gun.
*That's ridiculous,* my mind announces in a clear running commentary.
*This is a child. No one's going to shoot him.* Some less articulate part of my
mind disagrees. It tells me childhood's no protection. It says Darren
may understand the world better than I do. I put a hand on Tina's
shoulder and hold tight.

The cop with the gun is talking to Darren quietly, in a steady drone
under Darren's yelling. The other cop has his club out and is swinging
it hungrily, wordlessly, as he moves in.

"Come on," Darren yells. "Shoot me. I don't care." He swings the
pole awkwardly.

The drone of the cop's words bores its way through the yelling. He's
also saying, "Come on." Come on what? My ears tell me he doesn't
want to hurt anyone. My eyes register the gun under his hand.

The front door opens and I hear Katy swing across the porch to
stand behind me. The cops have closed the space between themselves
and Darren, and the one who's talking puts his left hand on the pole.
It's an odd, low-key gesture, his hand wrapping around the pole, the
two of them measuring each other for the space of a breath before
Darren yanks the pole violently and throws it over the fence behind
him, into the neighbor's yard. He spreads his arms wide.

"Shoot me. I want you to do it. Shoot me."

His voice is raw and I believe he means it. I also believe that even
now he knows whom it's safe to hit and whom it isn't. He's not going
to get himself shot if he can help it. He sobs and yells and lets himself
be spun around so they can pull his hands behind his back and handcuff him.

Halfway down the walk, he wrenches against the hands on his arms
to turn and bellow, "I love you." They yank him forward and Tina

sobs, lurching onto the walk to follow him. Katy yells at her to stop. I still have hold of her shoulder and she pulls me down a step, into the rain, but she hesitates there. I drop my voice to what I hope is a whisper, telling her for God's sake to stay out of it or they'll take it out on Darren. She shakes her head no but stands still. He bellows her name. She screams that she loves him. The cops fold him, bellowing, into the back seat and slam the door, cutting off Tina's name. I tighten my grip on her shoulder. I'm ready to hold her here until she's forty, until feminist consciousness rises in her like bread in a hot oven, through no will of the oven's. One of the cops starts the car. Tina tears away from me and I launch myself after her but stop halfway to the curb. The car's pulling off too fast for her to catch it, and the cop who's stayed behind isn't interested in her. He walks past her to ask if I'm the resident, and I point toward Katy, standing on the porch. Meanwhile, Tina plants herself at the curb, howling Darren's name at the taillights of the retreating police car.

The commentary in my mind kicks in again. We should have talked to Tina about boys when she was little, it says—when she still thought we knew about the world. It doesn't mean that we should have told her about sex; she knew about sex. It means we should have told her how few people really are saved by love, and how many people go under trying to save the rest. It means we should have warned her about all the things that go wrong between women and men so she'd be immune to every one of them. It means that if we'd said the right words, none of this would be happening.

I look away from Tina toward the porch. I can't tell which of the cops this is that Katy's talking to, and for a second this seems to matter. I take a step toward them, stop, take a step back toward Tina, and stop again.

In a decent world things like this wouldn't happen. Or they wouldn't happen this way. The car carrying Darren turns the corner and is gone. *That's it,* I think, *it's over,* but it doesn't end. Tina's rooted herself at the curb and won't stop sobbing Darren's name. He's everything she's ever lost and the premonition of everything life will take from her. She's oblivious to the rain, the cold, and the neighbors, who've been drawn outside by the flashing lights and are standing in clusters in front of their houses. I walk the rest of the way to the curb and touch her arm.

"Sweets, it doesn't have to be like this," I say.

She twitches away with the eloquent fury of a six-year-old. She's moving further away from us with each block the police car travels. Already she's beyond the reach of pleas, commands, and touch. The rain seeps down. I wrap my arms around myself and press the wet wool of my sweater against my skin.

Across the street, a clutch of people drift in from the corner to ask what happened, and the neighbors who've been there longer tell them what they know, or what they think they know, as if none of this had anything to do with them, although their children—for better or for worse, for richer or for poorer—are watching everything, and fitting it together with what they've been told, and with what they haven't been told, and are making sense of the world in ways even the closest of us can still only guess at.

# Cleo's Back

**GWENDOLYN BIKIS**

*I*

I was standing in the kitchen right next to my telephone, so it didn't have to ring but once for me to pick it up.

"Babysis."

"Hey, Marla," I answered, a little meekly. Not weakly now, but mildly. The last we'd spoken, we'd argued over Daddy's budget, over the price of margarine and grits, but really it had been about the heat, and the thrumming little headache I had, and the way my sweaty elbows was sticking to the kitchen table while Marla told me *she* would teach me how to keep a budget, because— And I'd hung up. She had not called straight back, so I knew *that* conversation was a for-sure done deal. Sometimes someone has to cut Marla off. Like a talk show on the television.

But "How you doin', babysis?" Marla's asked me now, asked me laughingly—and before I had a chance to utter "fine," she'd went on: "I talked to Cleo yesterday."

She's called to torture me, I thought. "Did she ask after me?" I asked.

"Tammy. She knows better."

Marla knew that she could say this to me because she knew I wouldn't hang up in her face—not this time I wouldn't. I closed my eyes and sucked the insides of my cheeks and found it in my voice to ask her calmly, "How is she?"

Unlike Marla, I have never, ever been "inside." ("Went inside today," she'll say, so casual-like.) But that fact only made it worse, my trying to imagine Cleo there. I imagined Cleo's hands, ashy, clutching sweaty at her dull-steel bars.

"Tammy baby." Marla laughed. "She is getting out. Next week."

I sat down, hard. "Marla. Are you fooling me?" Because if she was, I was gonna kill her. Cleo coming back was almost more good news than my Cleo-burdened mind could handle.

"Next week," Marla said again, "Cleo's coming home." She said it, so happy she was willing to share this happiness with me. Cleo. Marla's play sister—Cleo, my . . . girl—is coming back—back for good if *we* got anything to do with it.

So I've written my last prison letter to her, sent my last prison package to her. No more letters, no mo' packages, 'cause she's really coming home. . . . All the loneliness of missing her, all the grieving, worrying, and wondering over her locked up inside there, all of that is over, like a load slid off my shoulders: Cleo's back.


2


A few days back, me and Marla drove to Belk's together to buy Cleo a brand-new set of dress-out clothes. Marla's got a silver sports car, and it's always air-conditioned and smelling like mint freshener, and she's got a tape deck always playing new soul sounds, the smoothest Floaters, Moments, O'Jays. I likes me a ride in Marla's car, so much nicer newer sweeter-rolling than the bucket of old bolts *I* own. Smooth as a silver minnow we turned into the Cross Creek Mall's parking lot, we slid into a parking space, we nosed up in it and slowed into a stop. All smooth.

"What ought we buy for her?" I wondered out loud, really *cu*rious as to what Marla would think was right in clothes for Cleo. I watched her purse her lips, drop her car keys in her bag. Does she really know what Cleo is, I wondered; has she faced that yet? Does she know that if we want what *fits* for Cleo, we wouldn't be going nowhere near the women's section?

"She's saying she wants sports clothes," Marla answered, "So that is what we gonna get her. This is dress-out." Marla spread her hands like Cleo did, hunched her shoulders just like Cleo would, then shook her splayed-out fingers like how Cleo will: "This a *big* deal, sis," she said in Cleo's voice. Then she grinned, to herself; and I saw that Marla had been missing Cleo too—as much as me, but in another way. Missing her with tenderness and grief, covered over with anger. Whereas *I've* missed Cleo with an ache like something'd done been cut from me— cut right off my body.

All these months, I've been turning my radio dial away from any too sweet songs—"love jams," Cleo called them. Songs like "Stay in My Corner," or "Have You Seen Her," the Chi-Lites wailing sweetly, have done broke me up for months:

*Why oh why did she have to leave and go away . . . ?*

For months, I've had to stroke myself toward peace and comfort, on more restless feverish nights than I want to remember or admit to. My thighs, my arms, they've been aching to wrap up 'round her velvet-covered muscles. My flesh, it longs and tightens for her touch of liquid onyx. My center quivers, still, at the thought of slender fingers—of long, strong, stroking fingers, Cleo's firm calm hands. My fingertips itches to be pulling at her soft-napped hair, digging deep into it. But of course Marla, she won't see none of my longing—not as long as Cleo's gone. Long as Cleo's gone, I still can hide it.

We climbed out of Marla's car and flip-flopped 'cross the hot soft asphalt in our lime-green skirts and summer sandals. We'd matched our clothes that day, and it hadn't been on purpose. Marla's blouse was royal blue; my skirt was lime and blue. Striped, unlike her solid. But them skirts, they matched exactly.

"What's her size?" I asked as we pushed through the door into softer light and coolness. Even though I knew, I asked. I had to let Marla think she knew something more about Cleo than I myself did.

My sister steered me, by the elbow, toward the left side of the store—the boys' section; and all I said was: "Huh huh huh." So it's cool that Cleo's who she is, I thought—long as Cleo's not with me? Was that it now?

Marla ignored me, pushing on ahead. "She'll take a medium in shirts," she said. "For pants, she's size 29 in waist, 34 in length." By now, she's buzzing here and there, touching one display, then buzzing toward the next. I just stood there in the middle till she decided to buzz on back to me.

"What do you think, Tammy?" she asked me, looking 'round at nylon sweat suits, bright team T-shirts, basketball tank tops.

I walked us toward the T-shirts, and I picked a medium-sized red one; then walked us toward the tanks and picked a morning-glorious purple one with red trim; and right beside it hung purple pedal-pushed jeans that made it all a match. Cleo's color, her blackness, made the red, the purple come alive. It's Marla taught me that.

"All in the right size," I said, and handed the pile of clothes to her; Marla took them with that snort-laugh that she has. She knows why I know clothes. We walked toward the counter without a breath of argument.

She laid the clothes down on the counter and began to pick and snatch at them. "You know they gots to search the seams and hems for lock picks and handcuff keys and all. Let's us hope they won't be tearing up these jeans shorts."

"But they are letting her *go*," I said, and heard my voice edge up.

"*They* got ta be the ones to let her go, though," Marla answered. "And they ain't letting her go until the minute they get ready to. You ain't gone until you gone from there." She reached into her bag for her wallet. "I'ma put this on my Gold card, Tammy."

I nodded, too tight with sudden worry to want to figure out the clothing's price. Just like Marla, to drop a load like that on me, in the middle of the Belk's and all those nice clothes Cleo would love. If she ever really saw them, I could not help but think. I saw Cleo shuffling over cement, I saw her skin—the liquid onyx—faded, dusty-gray.

But no, I told myself, and began to neatly fold the clothes while the salesclerk, a young brother in a tie and a dress shirt a bit too big around his neck, punched in a sale price for the lady right in front of us. No, I said—just to myself, so Marla couldn't mess my mind up more: Cleo's coming back, and it won't be but a few more days.


3


Later that afternoon, Marla sent me out to Cleo's auntie's for her things. "She hasn't got a phone," Marla said, "but I talked to her the other day. She won't be leaving for work till early in the evening—so if you go right now, you'll be over there in time to catch her." Marla had to meet with Cleo's lawyer, set up Cleo's vocational assessment appointment, and call up to the prison—which was the one thing that she really hated to do. So *I* couldn't hardly say to her that I wasn't much inclined to meeting Cleo's auntie Miss Arlene again. I cannot mention, not to Marla, that I'm *embarrassed* to be seeing her again.

Marla has the right kind of insurance, so she let me take her car; and I know just where the auntie's place is, which corner by which little store that only just sells lottery tickets, cigarettes, pigs' feets, cold beer, and the worst sweet wine I'd ever smelled or touched my tongue to. Cleo did, but I *couldn't* drink it, that Ripple Night Train, Thunderbird that smelled like rotting fruit to me.

Miss Arlene's building looked the same, with a new gray coat of paint, and the same old beat-down patch of yard in front. The lobby stunk like a more sour brand of that sweet wine—and I tried to hold my breath while I rang the auntie's buzzer.

"Who's 'at?" her voice came over the intercom.

"Tammy Moore—I'm Marla's baby sister," I said, praying that she'd let me up: that she didn't remember me with my hair all frazzled, my neck all flushed and sweaty, my wrinkled clothes that I had thrown myself back into.

I guess she *didn't* remember, because she right-quick buzzed me up. I stepped through the lobby door and sipped a little breath in: the stairwell smelt like fresh disinfectant. Up three flights, and down a hall to the third door on the left: my last time here, I'd stumbled, with Cleo's hand holding mine behind me. Last time, we'd slipped in through the door that now I knocked on. I stood straight up in front of the peephole and listened to a door chain rattle, and one-two-three locks snap open.

"How you doing, baby?" she asked me as she pulled her door wide open to me. Cleo's auntie Miss Arlene is thin and long-boned like Cleo, but her worn dry face has no family resemblance that I have ever seen.

"Doing fine," I answered, stepping into her front room—remembering how I'd sneaked through, that last time.

"I boxed Cleotha's things up," she said, and turned and pressed my hand between hers, just for a second. "I appreciate all that y'all have done for her," she said.

I nearly choked. "Yes, ma'am," I gulped. Maybe Marla was the only one who knew—it wasn't homework I was helping Cleo with, back

there in her room behind that closed door. This sweet church-girl
face of mine can fool a lot of people, but it can't fool my own sister.

Miss Arlene had three boxes in all, one completely full with Cleo's
tennis shoes. "I'll he'p you tote them down," she said, throwing on a
sweater.

Uh-oh, I thought—this is where she'll let *me* know what *she* knows.
Would she give me Bible pamphlets—would she ask me if I pray? I
wondered this the whole way down the stairs with Cleo's boxes; but we
made two trips, carrying the biggest, heaviest box down between us,
and we said not much of anything to one another.

"Tell Cleotha," she said, when I got in the car and rolled the window
down to wave goodbye, "I got a frying chicken and some yams with her
name written on 'em."

And that was the all-in-all of it: I promised I would send Cleo over,
and Miss Arlene waved goodbye and had nothing more to say to me. I
sighed in sweet relief: this country-fresh face ain't failed me yet.

That was a couple days ago, forty-eight long hours ago. I've taught
three classes, washed dozens of dishes and two loads of clothes, eaten
four meals, and missed a couple, waiting that whole time. Hanging on
a thread, waiting for the phone. Yesterday morning Marla called.
"Tammy." Her voice was tight, and my heart clutched in my chest:
Cleo isn't coming home, I thought.

"We are scheduled to meet Miss Timmons at twelve thirty-eight
tomorrow," she said, still tense.

"Twelve thirty-*eight?*" I asked.

"Hm-hm-hm. You don't know how ridiculous them people is *yet*,
Tammy?"

Uh-oh: she was in *that* mood again. What had one of them done
said to her?

"I just spent a half an hour on the gotdamn phone with some buz-
zard who kept trying to tell me he wasn't 'authorized to give out
inmate location information.' I asked him who *was* authorized, and
he ac-tu-ally tell me, 'You people have to learn to let go of your children.'"

I closed my eyes. How long have we done had to learn just that?
"Marla," I asked, rubbing both my eyes, "you didn't say much else to
him?"

"Tamara. That musky scaly snake ain't gonna get his satisfaction out of me. I simply told him, 'Transfer me,' and I gave him an extension number that might take me to somebody human. Which I got. I got an older black woman who told me we needed to be ready for Miss Timmons by exactly twelve thirty-eight."

"Praise God," I said, and I hung up the phone so happy that I came in here and spent the rest of my day fixing up my room for her. I set my old record player up, stacked the "love jams" close beside it—the Bloodstone, Blue Notes, Bobby Womack songs that I've avoided the whole time she's been gone. Now she's coming back, I can enjoy them once again.

I hung the painting that I did of her, Cleo, as she leaps up toward a fire-orange ball of sun. Beside the painting, I hung her old poster of the long-armed player stuffing the ball down in a basket.

I lined her tennis shoes up under the bed again, almost all of them, nearly each and every pair; every pair except the lucky black high-tops she wore when she played ball. I got fourteen shoes, seven pairs, all lined upside the wall side of the bed—this queen-sized bed that neither squeaks nor sags, that is going to be the softest warmest comfort she's done laid in since forever.

This is the first room I ever had that I could call my own. Marla and I both love each other, so we know that we don't always need to be breathing in each other's air. We have known this since our childhood, when we all three—me, Ruthanna, and Marla—had to sleep all stacked together. That is why both me and Marla have always called this "my" room, even though it's inside her apartment; even though I rent my own house now. When I first came to the "big city" for to visit Marla, for the very first time I had a room for only me, a door that I can close, a bed that's all my own. I'm giving up my room to Cleo, but that just means that when she comes to stay in here, she's gonna do what *I* want to.

4

The telephone rings, just once, before Marla picks it up out in the kitchen. And then she calls to me: "Tammy?"

I sit up from the bed, my throat tight. Cleo isn't coming after all, she's—

"That was her lawyer up in Raleigh," Marla says. "They are starting on her out-process right now. Are you ready?"

"Yes," I call out, as calmly as if she's asked if I am ready to go down to the post office. I take a steady breath, and pick up my bag of Cleo's clothes and coming-home presents. I softly close the door, so that walking up into my room will be a surprise to her, and it will make her smile the way she smiled when she slung that winning wild-throw basket, in the last two seconds of the game, from almost all the way across the court—and the ball dropped straight down like it had been *pulled* through that basket. Neatly. Sweetly.

I dash through the kitchen, lock the door behind me, and climb in Marla's car while she revs it up impatiently. Before I've even reached over for to fasten up my seat belt, I feel the tension in between us, the little car space tightening. Marla's chewing gum, I notice; and by my noticing, I know that she is agitated. Marla is one person who can chew so smoothly, you'd usually never know she even has a piece of gum inside her mouth. Usually she will take a few slow chews, from way back in her jaw, three chews in maybe ten or fifteen minutes— when she is calm, that is. It looks to me like *now* she's chewing with her two front teeth.

I lean forward and I push a tape into the "play" slot:

> *Fight it, fight the power*
> *Fight it, fight the power . . .*

by the Isleys roars out over car speakers. Marla punches "play" to "off," slaps her gears into reverse, and speed-backs out the driveway.

"Dag, Marla," I complain; she will get us killed before we get *near* Raleigh, all because anger, for her, is such an easy attitude. She says not one word to me until we get onto the highway that will take us there, straight up from Charlotte to the exit for the prison.

"Against all my better instincts," Marla finally says, "I am making you a part of her parole plan."

"You are making me a part of Cleo's plan," I say, "because your *in*stincts knows she does whatever I ask her to, and you can't—"

"You're right," she quickly says, supposedly to agree with me, but *ac*tually to cut me off. She knows that I was getting ready to say, "You can't admit to *why* Cleo listens to me." Marla won't admit that Cleo does what *I* say to because . . . because I've got her nose open. Marla might not want to know that I can use that phrase; and she surely won't admit into her mind the thought that I know that phrase's meaning 'cause I also know its method.

Traffic's thin this morning, and the day is bright and sunny. It ought to be the perfect kind of day to bring somebody home—and it would be, except for Marla's mood: that gum is *cracking* in her mouth. I know that it is hard for her to go up in there, even though she'll brag about her trips "inside." Even though I've never gone inside, I've heard about each step: about each dark corridor, each endless wait on a hard plastic chair in a crowded room where orders were orders and people were owned by crackers once again.

Even though she hates it, it is going to be Marla going up inside this prison after Cleo. "You're too soft to go inside," she told me yesterday, and it was not to my good advantage to be arguing about how soft I really wasn't—I do not *want* to have to go in there. I am going to sit inside this car and drive it 'round next to the gate when they are ready for me.

About halfway there, near Asheboro, Marla turns on *Black Talk*, on the Raleigh soul station. Usually she loves it, the call-in show where everybody has five minutes, and she could take up twenty, on whatever given subject; but today, she turns it down so low it's hard to hear the words—so that I know that she just needs to fill the silence in between us.

When finally we arrive at the outside prison parking lot, it is exactly twelve twenty-three; and we pull up to a booth and offer proof of who we are to a man whose elbows and arms—it's all I can catch a look at, before I look away—have the pink cooked look of an old dry piece of smoked ham meat.

"Drive in through the gate," he twangs, "and to the left, to the back of Module C."

I feel the air around me thin out as we drive through, and I gulp for breath: I am inside a prison. Marla hadn't said that I would have to come this far inside.

Marla sees me wipe my sweaty palms on my skirt, and says, "We are not inside, Tammy. We just on the grounds around the outbuildings. They can't be kidnapping you out here."

"Ha-ha-ha," I say. She's making fun of my so-called softness once again.

We've driven 'round the back of Module C, an L-shaped building made of something looking like cement, painted in the moldy gray of old worn-out packed-down street dirt. We park beside an opening in the wire fence that surrounds the back of Module C.

Marla turns the car off. "Wait here," she orders, and opens up her door. As though I'm gonna move an inch out of this car. I know she's only giving orders 'cause real soon she's gonna have to take some—and that taking orders don't agree with her digestion.

I give her Cleo's clothes, in a red and purple pile, and she gets out. I watch her as she walks in through the gate, and stops to talk to a white guard, who opens up the metal door into the building. Marla walks in, and the door slaps closed behind her.

I climb around the front seat to the back, where me and Cleo could sit together in some privacy—and, if she wanted to, Cleo could stretch out them long legs of hers.

I wait. And wait. And wait, not wanting to look at the dashboard clock to see if I've been waiting long as it is feeling like—because it feels like half an hour. What if Cleo isn't—

But then the door opens, and Marla steps out; but then it's Cleo, coming out now with a shopping bag and duffel in her hands. And she's wearing her new clothes the way I wished for her to wear them: the red tank over top of the purple T-shirt, all tucked into her purple pedal pushers. Against the building's wall, the colors seem to pulse. And she's got her high-top Converse on, the pair of shoes I missed. It is the sight of her old "lucky" shoes that breaks me up—I've missed those shoes so much, the happy sorrow fills my throat.

I step out the car, leaving the back seat open so she'll come back here. I offer to take her bag, to hide my face. "I got it, babysis," she says.

Marla smiles at me, tightly, and walks back to the trunk; and Cleo sneaks a pat on the back of my neck. I bite my lips.

"Looking good, Cleo," I manage. How can she be looking this good, coming out of there? She's got the same sweet barbershop smell, the same strong body, her same old swagger.

It seems she's heard my thoughts, 'cause she looks at me, then stops to pose and pull an arm muscle. "Good black is hard to crack," she says, and grins.

We get into the car—me and Cleo in the back together, where we roll our windows down.

"I like your hairstyle," I offer, admiring the tight sparkly curls that makes her hair look sudsy-soft.

She runs her hand across the top of her head as though it is her halo I've done complimented. "Thanks, babysis." She smiles at me. "It's callt an S-curl. My girl Rita done it for me. It's the newest style in perms."

I feel my shoulders rise: who is "my girl Rita"? I am getting ready to ask just this, when Marla interrupts:

"Well, I've got news for you, Cool Cleo," she says. "Out here, that's one style that has *been* done come and long since gone."

"Why *are* you lying?" I scold Marla. "Lots of people have S-curls," I say. "And they look good with them."

"Oh yeah, maybe out there in the country where *you* are," Marla says to me, glancing craftily at Cleo through the back mirror, "but not in the cool slick city now."

Marla frowned down toward the road in front of her as we came up to the gate. "Anyway, Cleo needs to start thinking more about what is *in* her head than what is *on* it." At the gate we stop again, and Cleo rolls her window up and hums while the guard asks us to open up our trunk.

"Ssshhiit," Marla hisses, and climbs out to open it.

Cleo hums and looks out the window.

"Y'all have a pleasant evening," he says as Marla climbs back in the car.

"I wonder do they think they're serious when they say that," Marla says as we drive through, to freedom. Cleo rolls her window down again. Marla flips her right turn signal, turns off of the prison road, out onto the road that leads to open country. "Have you been working on your math?" she asks Cleo.

"I'm up to trignomics in the book, but who's go' check it for me?"

"I'll get a tutor at the Girls' Club to do it, and I want Tammy to be helping you with your classwork, your reading and your writing."

Well, Lord knows I would love to do it, but who could guarantee that's all that it would be, just homework? Certainly I can't. I press my thighs together to control the sudden pulse between them.

"Now," Marla instructs, turning around to look at Cleo for a second, "I want you to stop for a minute and breathe deep and feel how good this feels—feel it when you get to thinking how it might be easier to be inside."

Cleo sucks her teeth. "Inside ain't easy." She looks out the window at the tree line past the prison. "Inside done made me hard," she adds.

"Let's get up off the truth now, Cleo. Inside done made you soft. You got a lot of proving of yourself to do to me."

Cleo tsks her teeth again and jerks her legs back and forth.

I suddenly remember the giant box of Good and Plenty I bought her as a present. I bring it out to sweeten up the moment, shaking it in rhythm like the Choo-Choo Charlie TV commercial, and I smile at her:

'Member those first kisses that you gave me? I am asking with my smile. 'Member their spicy taste of sweet black licorice? What I mean to be my meaning, without Marla getting in the middle, is that I want those Cleo kisses back. "Got some candy for you, Cleo," I say, and open up the box to pour some in her hand.

Cleo grins down at her palmful of pink and white sweet pellets, and puts them in her mouth—all of them at once—and chews. "Mmm," she says, and grins; but she is looking at my thighs. "I likes Good 'n Juicy candy too," she whispers in my ear, while Marla's too intent on checking her rear blind spot and changing lanes to notice us too closely. "You got you some of that?" Cleo asks me softly in my ear. "Got you Good 'n Juicy?"

I love-slap her and shake my earrings, but my nose is stinging with my held-in tears—I have missed her nastiness so much.

But now Marla, you know she has a sense when something that she disapproves of is taking place, even when she can't see it. So she has to say, "You and Tammy can have your little visits on the weekends." As though *she* is Cleo's rightful righteous mother. "I am laying down the conditions right now," she continues.

"Who are you, our mama?" I ask. My mama's passed away, and Marla hasn't filled her place, even if Marla was the one who raised me.

"Who you anyway, my PO?" Cleo flares.

"That's the other condition," Marla answers. "I've set you up with an officer that I personally know, and between us we are going to know what you are up to every woke or sleeping minute. You can't afford to blow this one now, Cleo."

I know I'm supposedly a part of this big plan . . . but me, all I want is just to slather warmed-up cocoa butter all over her back, her arms, the ropy scars across her neck and shoulders; I want to kiss her throat. I want Marla to forget, just for a minute, about the worrisome little details of this parole plan. What Cleo needs, more than a vocation, a parole officer, a raise in reading scores, is love.

I want my sister to plug her Isley Brothers tape back in so we can cruise back down to Charlotte inside some kind of happy groove; so I can smile at Cleo and dream of loving her all the whole way down. I want Marla to forget, just for a single second, that her loved one could be snatched from her at any minute. I want to forget that fear just for long enough to *enjoy* her loved one's presence. Cleo's really back.

## 5

Marla's driveway's soft and squishy in the afternoon heat, and my sandals sinks into it as I step out the car with Cleo's shopping bag in my hand. It is really *heavy,* and I look to see what is in it—math books and a big thick dictionary.

"That bag too heavy for you, baby?" She's leaning over me; she's so close I feel her body heat; I feel my arm hairs rise as though a warm and furry breeze has blown across them; I feel my gaze go soft: I want her heat, her weight, on me; I want her thigh between mine. Thank goodness Marla's run up ahead of us to open up her door; because my breath has suddenly become very hard for me to catch, and an uncaught breath is very hard to hide.

Cleo takes the bag from me, and for a precious minute, her hand is holding mine. My first time touching her again, like touching thirst to water—for just a second.

Marla's finally noticed us. "Cleo!" she calls, from just inside the house; and Cleo steps away. I breathe, deep from my stomach, and straighten up my skirt, and follow her.

In the living room, Marla points Cleo toward my room; and I see that Marla's opened up the door already—so much for surprises.

"You like it, Cleo?" I ask. "I fixed it up for you." As if she couldn't see that.

"Yes, I do," she says, and she turns and pops me a noisy play-kiss, right on my cheek.

She heaves her duffel bag up on the bed, and I see her biceps bunch and glide; and I long to lay my palms along her gathered strength. When she notices my noticing, she grins.

"You've got mo' muscles, Cleo," is all that I can say; it's all that I can do to keep my hands still at my sides.

"I hit the pile a lot," she says.

"Huh?"

"That's jail talk. That means she lifted weights out in the yard." I jump, a little, and then I turn around; of course Marla has done followed us all the way up into my bedroom. What made me think she wouldn't?

"Cleo," Marla says, and points at her. "Didn't Tammy tell you? Your auntie dear is waiting for a visit from you."

Not right *now,* Marla, I almost say, and bite my tongue before I do; because if I do, Marla's going to insist—yes, right now. Right this red-hot minute.

". . . But you can relax a little if you want to first," Marla says. "I've got a ball game on the TV, so come on in and have a sit-down. There's a can of Coke in the refrigerator too."

Cleo sighs, and rolls her eyes toward me, and plods heavily out to the living room.

Damn! The tears I feel fill up my eyes are due to pure frustration. I feel like beating on a wall. There goes my kiss, there goes my hug, there goes the love I want to tell her I will give to her. I'ma have to drive back home tonight, and go back to my teaching tomorrow, and Marla knows that she can hold me off until it's time for me to leave.

6

The game is boring, with UNC-C losing to State, to a score so high it's getting to be a little bit embarrassing. I hate to see teams lose by lots and lots of points; it makes me feel *sorry* for them, they look so tired, galomping and galomping up and down the ball court even though they know they've lost.

Cleo's on the couch, scrunched so low her chest is only 'bout six inches higher than her sliding, swinging knees. That is one thing I'd forgotten about Cleo, how she never, ever will sit still, how she'll always be tapping, rocking, shifting, swaying, as though it is her body that helps keep her mind in gear, helps her keep her focus. She reaches for her can of Coke, and slurps on it. Cleo's known for no home training, so I only squinch a little bit, trying to pretend that I don't care.

A commercial for a sports drink comes on, and Marla stands up from her easy chair. "I'm on my way up to the Eckerd's for a new pair hose. Y'all want anything?"

Cleo lifts her can and shakes it. "'Nother can of Coke," she says.

Marla frowns. "Who you talkin to? Get your own damn Coke." And she walks out the room.

One second later, when she comes back in, we have already turned toward each other; our hands are almost touching. "I'ma only be a *min*ute," Marla warns. "That is all. Just one minute."

We wait until the front door slams before we move into a hug, and then into a kiss, with Cleo's hands both on my neck, pulling me closer, deeper; and her tongue, yes, spicy with that Good and Plenty, is moving in and out inside my mouth. I moan, and come up for some breath. "Cleo. Let me fix you lunch." Because I feel we really shouldn't be getting nothing started—it is just too *frus*trating—and fixing lunch for her is almost as satisfying. For right now.

Cleo groans, and rolls her eyes again; this time up toward the ceiling. "Country," it sounds as though she mumbles, but I ignore it. Call me country, I don't care—I know it is more easy to pry myself away from Cleo than it is from Marla's sight.

So I walk out to the kitchen, and after a few minutes, Cleo follows me. I reach in the breadbox for the whole-wheat loaf, and reach two slices toward the toaster. I poke my head into the refrigerator, and pull out mayonnaise, and bacon. Tomatoes on the windowsill, cheese inside the dairy bin. I close the refrigerator door, open up the bacon package and lay three long strips along the skillet already shiny with fresh grease. By now, the scent of toast is filling up the room, and Cleo's sitting in the chair behind me—I can smell her hair dress.

"What you want on it, Cleo?"

I turn a little, and I thought I knew just where she was; but I didn't know she was right directly up behind me. Pressing her . . . you know . . . up against my behind. I feel a wetness spread inside my drawers; I reach behind me and—

The back door opens.

Cleo moves away. "I wants lots of mayonnaise, and a slice of that there cheese," she says, in a somehow normal voice as Marla walks into the kitchen with a plastic bag. She reaches in the bag and hands Cleo a can of Coke.

"Thank you," Cleo grunts.

"You are welcome," Marla answers.

"No lettuce?" I ask, amazed at how *even* my voice sounds. "No tomatoes?"

Cleo makes a face. "Nu-uh. No."

"You still don't like you any vegetables?" Marla asks.

Cleo screws a tighter face. "They didn't give us none in there."

"That's how you know you need them. When did *they* ever give you what is good for you?" Marla turns to go out to the living room.

The bacon snaps and sizzles; I turn it over, and the toast pops up. I pull a plate out of the cupboard, throw the hot toast down with just my fingertips, and reach to open up the mayonnaise. I smooth it over the toast, slice a tomato anyways, slice some cheese, drop the bacon on two paper towels, pat the grease away, lay the three strips on the toast, and close it all up like a sandwich. Cooking calms my nerves like nothing else.

"Here, Cleo." I turn to hand the plate to her—and she's grinning at me, has been grinning this whole time, laying back and slowly flapping both her knees and grinning 'round a toothpick she has stuck into the corner of her mouth. She rolls it to the gap between her two front teeth; and I feel my throat catch.

I put the plate in front of her, and she reaches for the sandwich and begins to eat. I have never heard Cleo turn down food, or say that she's not hungry.

At my elbow, Marla's telephone rings. "Get that for me, babysis?" Marla calls in from the bathroom.

I pick it up, and know, by all the background noise, that I'm talking to a pay phone. "Marla Moore?" Behind the voice, a siren wails.

"May I ask who wants to speak to her?"

"Johnetta Harper. I'm calling from the emergency."

One of Marla's clients. "Here she is, right now," I say as Marla walks into the kitchen drying her hands on a towel.

She takes the call into the living room, and stays on as long as it takes for Cleo to finish up her sandwich and ask me if we got some snack cakes.

I ought to tell her we got Moon Pies, like the country peoples that she knows we is. I am getting ready to say this, but Marla's back here in the kitchen, with the phone hung up and her bag and car keys already in her hand. "I need to see about Miz Harper's daughter." She puts the phone back on the counter, and is already halfway out the door.

"Cleo"—she points, on her way out—"go and see your auntie." And she is gone, so quickly that I can't help but think—forgive me, Lord—that this emergency is nothing but a blessing to me.

Cleo's more than grinning now; she is smiling so wide I have no trouble seeing her front-tooth gap. "Zippity doo dah, zippity day," she sings, dancing her fingers happily across the tabletop.

I giggle.

"How long you think she'll be gone?"

"I'm trying to remember who Miz Harper is. If I'm remembering right, she is the one with the daughter who was almost ready to deliver."

Cleo smiles, rolls the toothpick in her mouth again. "That means we got *hours.*" She spreads her legs; she opens up her arms. "Come to mama, baby." She slaps her crotch, and I feel my blush creep over my body. I feel how hot this kitchen is.

"Let's go into *my* room, Cleo," I say, and grab her hand.

*"Yo'* room? I thought that you was giving it to *me.*"

"I am, but for right now, it's mines again."

"Meaning we playing house like Tamara want it played." She drops her arms. "Okay . . . I can stand to go that way." I pull her up behind me, pull her to my room.

I take her hand and lead her to the bed.

"Nuh-uh," I hear her grunt.

I reach over and kiss her, right on the corner of her lips. "Come on . . . baby." I whisper that last, that "baby," 'cause I know that she ain't really ready for it. Not *yet.*

I squeeze her hand; and this time it's me, pushing her down on *my* bed. I gives a tiny push, so that now she's sitting, with her hands on my arms wrapped 'round her, like she's almost getting ready to maybe pull me off. I kiss her jaw, and she sets back to look at me, with confused amusement drawing up her forehead.

She pulls my arms away, moves her hands down to my hips, and down some more, and gives a squeeze. "You ain't go' try and flip it on my ass now, is you?"

I give a little "tsk," and say what Marla says: "That is jail talk, Cleo."

"You ain't answering my question," she replies.

"You gonna have to let me touch you." I reach my lips toward her cheek, and taste the velvety skin there, just where her two lips begin to plump to fullness.

She pulls back again to look at me. "Okay, baby," she says, and she's laughing, like am I really up to this?

So I put my arms all around her, hold her like her mama oughta. Hold her like I ought to have myself, long ago. I'm so glad to have her back; I'm so grateful to my older sister for getting Cleo back for me. My face is warming up with held-back tears, so I just let them go.

My warm rain is falling on her shoulder, and she reaches up to stroke my hair. "Nobody never cried for me," she says, in a small and distant voice; and she sounds so surprised.

And anyways, it isn't true—it's just that all the tears I'd cried for her, she'd never known about. They'd all been shed in my lonely midnight bed, into my bitter pillow, far away from her in prison.

I turn my head to kiss her cheek; and it is completely dry. "She lacks the capacity to cry," Marla's always said, but I never could believe it.

I feel her squirm, but I make her to lie back, and I cover her up with my love. Everyone at home has always, in *all* ways, loved me. I'ma show her what that feels like.

. . . And if Marla were to ask me, "What'd you do with Cleo last night?" I'ma tell her:

We danced to Smokey's "Cruisin"—we swayed and slow-danced down to the bed, where we undressed each other. I rubbed her over, slow, with warm cocoa butter till she shone like polished dark wood. She moaned, and my tongue went everywhere—yes, *there*—while her hands tightened, twisted through my hair. She moaned, and shook, and heaved with what I recognized was dry crying.

# La Maison
# de Madame
# Durard

**NONA CASPERS**

Marie undid the buttons on her coat so the fabric fell open around her hips and the hem draped her ankles. She hoped this made her look dramatic, like someone from out of town. Peter Schneiweiss and a few townies were bowling. Chrissy stood at the end of the bar in her jacket with squirrel fur around the collar, leaning her bony hip on a stool, like some sort of time traveler from the Wild West. Marie walked over and leaned her back up against the bar.

"Hey," she said, poking a finger into Chrissy's side.

"Hey," Chrissy said without moving her unlit cigarette. Her foot on the bottom rung of the stool was tapping—she was already buzzed on something.

"You ready to have some fun?" she asked.

Behind the bar, Peter's father stopped wiping glasses and leaned over to stick his face between their heads. Deep lines ran from his mouth to his eyes, which made him look sewn together like Franken-stein. Marie pictured his wife in their apartment upstairs, sitting on a sofa night after night watching TV and waiting for him to come home after closing the bowling alley.

"You little girls want anything?" he asked. "Potato chips, Good 'n Fruity, Life Savers?"

Chrissy rolled her eyes and pushed off for the restroom. Marie fol-lowed.

The restroom was dim and smelled like an overdose of air fresh-ener and stale urine. Marie followed Chrissy into the first stall and bolted the door. On the back of the toilet Chrissy set her pocket mirror, an X-acto knife she'd stolen from seventh-hour industrial arts, and a tiny plastic bag half full of THC. She poured the powder on the mirror and divided it into crooked lines. By the way Chrissy's hands were shaking, Marie knew she'd already been doing some. Why did Chrissy always have to start without her? Marie's stomach felt sick from nervousness. Once she had snorted nutmeg in Chrissy's basement, but nothing had happened, just a slight headache. Now she remembered what the school counselor had said in his speech to the freshman class about drugs. Once you begin you can't stop. Marie hoped she wouldn't stop; she hoped this was the beginning of a new life for her.

Chrissy sucked the powder up her nose with a section of cafeteria straw, looked up, and smiled with watery eyes at Marie.

The restroom door squeaked open, then footsteps. Pressing her finger against her mouth, Chrissy handed the mirror to Marie, and climbed on the toilet tank. Marie sat in front of her on the edge of the seat—holding the mirror and straw—and peered through the crack between the door and the frame. Mrs. Hellerman, crazy Marilyn Hellerman's mother, ambled into the stall next to theirs and peed like there was no tomorrow. She came out of the stall and stood on her tiptoes in front of the mirror above the sink, tugging at her girdle through her beige slacks and checking out her flat, wide behind. Through the opening Marie looked into Mrs. Hellerman's dissatisfied eyes in the mirror. Mrs. Hellerman glanced across the room at the closed stall door.

"Who's in there?"

"It's just Marie Ann Schroeder," she answered. "One of Lawrence Schroeder's daughters."

Mrs. Hellerman looked back in the mirror and stuck her finger under her glasses to wipe her eye. "How's your sister doing?"

Marie's older sister had been head cheerleader, majorette, valedictorian. Now her sister was on scholarship studying to become a physical therapist at the University of Wisconsin.

"She dropped out of college," Marie lied. "We think she joined a commune in California."

Chrissy dug her boot into Marie's behind.

"Really?" Mrs. Hellerman said. She shook her head and walked out the door. Chrissy let out a hiss, climbed down from the tank, and left the stall.

Marie felt a little guilty, not because she'd lied, but because she loved her sister and because once Mrs. Hellerman had given her a ride home from school even though it was miles out of her way. She didn't know why she had to lie about these things. She wished her sister had joined a commune and that she and Chrissy could go live with her. But one weekend during Christmas break they had gone to visit her sister at the University of Wisconsin in Madison and all they had done was pop popcorn and watch TV in the dorm room. Chrissy fell asleep at 8 p.m. "Isn't there some sort of demonstration or love-in we could go to?" Marie asked. Her sister had just laughed and poured more butter on Marie's popcorn.

Marie didn't know if she would have had the guts to go to a demonstration or a love-in. Sometimes at night she sat up in bed and counted the hours she'd already lost watching TV or driving her uncle's tractor around the field or babysitting her brothers and sisters. Two thousand at least. One night she'd climbed on top of their shed in the backyard. Balancing on the flats of her feet, she walked back and forth across the apex of the roof and recited phrases she'd learned from her foreign-language dictionaries. She gazed out over the rolling hills and pastureland pretending she was in the northern hills of France, where one of her great-great-grandmothers had been born. *"Voilà la maison de Madame Durard,"* she said.

In the bowling alley restroom, Marie sat in the stall and looked at her face divided by the crooked line of powder on the pocket mirror. When she sucked the powder deep into her nose, a sharp pain shot up her nasal passages and behind her eyes; the back of her throat tasted bitter.

"Chrissy, do you realize we're fifteen and everything important on the planet is taking place without us?"

Chrissy drank some water and blew her nose. "Life is small," she said. It was a quote from the only poem she had read for second-hour English.

Marie tried to pee. She imagined the powder absorbing into the vessels of her nose, her cells opening up. She closed her eyes and swallowed.

In the booth for lane five, everything glowed and expanded: the long shiny wooden lanes, the white walls, the bowling pins. Chrissy sat in

the scoring chair rearranging the pencils in the cup, then the cigarettes in her pack. She switched one unlit cigarette for another.

The three men sitting in the booth next to theirs wore green-and-
white hats advertising Black Cat snowmobiles and carried vinyl bowling bags. One, the bus driver who had taken them to and from junior
high last year, had a blond mustache that hid his whole top lip. He
nudged the guy next to him and they glanced at Marie and Chrissy
then rolled their eyes. Rednecks.

She flipped them a hidden double bird below the bench. She
wanted to lean over the booth toward them and hiss, "I am a drug
addict." She had tied her white button-down shirt above her hiphug-
gers so a strip of skin showed. Now she bent over to take off her shoes
and showed Mr. Mustache the crack of her butt.

"Your ass is showing," Chrissy said.

"I know my ass is showing," Marie said. "It's called body language."

Chrissy shook her head; she didn't get it.

Marie swung her hips as she walked over to the jukebox and pushed
the buttons in for "Gypsies, Tramps and Thieves." She wished she
were part Lebanese, like Cher, or a real drug addict traveling around
the world, like Janis Joplin: Marie with long black hair like Chrissy's
instead of blond. Marie swinging her hips across the five lanes of the
bowling alley, singing "Gypsies" in a throaty low voice. Applause,
applause. Peter Schneiweiss sat about two feet away from the jukebox
with his face buried in a big hardcover book.

"What you reading?" Marie asked him.

Without looking at her, he held the book up in front of her face. On
the cover a comet shot out of the night—it looked as if it were going
to shoot right off the cover. "How ethereal," she said. *"La vie est petite."*

When Marie got back to their booth Chrissy was still bent over
undoing her boots to put on her bowling shoes.

"Chrissy, we'll be old or dead before you get those off."

Chrissy slowly looked up. The whites of her eyes were ultra-white
and her pupils had spread out over her whole iris. She held out her
foot. Marie took the heel, tugged, dropped the boot on the floor.

While waiting for the pins to reset, Marie picked through the balls on
their rack. It was the last bowl in the game. She weighed each one
carefully and wiggled her fingers inside the holes. She settled on her
usual, the black ball with blue swirls.

"That ball's too heavy for you." A loud voice came from behind her. Mr. Mustache leaned back in his chair and grinned at her. He took a swig of beer and Marie saw the lump move down his red neck and under his plaid shirt collar. She felt like saying, "Get a lip."

"What do you mean?" she said.

"Well, you go in the gutter with it every time."

"I just used it last turn and got five down," she said.

"You did?" He bolted up and bugged his eyes down her lane and then back at Chrissy and her. "Why, looked like just another gutter ball to me."

Marie stepped up to the blue line. The ten pin stands for all the rednecks in this town. The next for everyone who thinks they're smarter than me, the next for Mr. Hegle for calling me a goddamn pig for eating my sandwich in world geography. She closed her eyes and tried to think bigger than just herself. Tuesday in world geography they'd read about the smog in Los Angeles, where one of her uncles worked as an Air Force mechanic.

She tried to decide what the eye pin would be. Chrissy's drunk father. She held her wrist stiff and pointed straight for him. The ball hopped out of her hand and picked up speed. She could see where it had been at the same time that she could see where it was going. The ball blasted head-on and pins popped up. The red neon sign above her lane flashed the word STRIKE. She pictured the sign flashing MARIE MARIE. The sign went blank.

Wiping her hands on the back of her jeans, she wagged her butt at Mr. Mustache, then turned and looked at Chrissy, who was smiling straight ahead of her as if someone had wound a knob on the back of her head that pulled her skin back.

Marie stooped close to her ear. "Chrissy," she said. Now her voice was booming, really echoing. Her hands were sweating and her teeth tingled. "We gotta get out of here."

The sign flashed GAME OVER: Marie 165; Chrissy 97.

Outside the snow floated down light and even. Chrissy stuck her hands in her coat pockets, smiled up at the sky, and opened her mouth.

"Let's hitch a ride to the ballroom," she said.

Marie watched the snow fall and collect on the concrete. It was dark except for the two lamps above the green metal door of the bowling alley. The junk lot in the field across the road was black, the wrecked cars denser clumps of black. Beyond that was Chrissy's house, and farther, the gray spire of St. Mary's church, then the water tower that said "Hello, You're in Church Grove," then Marie's house. Marie's hands had stopped sweating and now her head felt full of air, like one of the balloons that floated over her house after parades in Minneapolis or Chicago. Marie would stand on the back lawn waving: Hello, Balloon!

A blue Nova pulled up in front of the bowling alley and Tommy and Mark Geiske stepped out. They were on leave from their Army station in the Philippines. They hunched their shoulders and pulled their heads into the hoods of their parkas. They looked like two giant turtles pulling their heads into their shells.

"What's the matter?" Marie said. "They don't have snow in the Philippines?"

They hunched deeper into their shells. "It's an island," Mark said. "They have jungles."

One afternoon a few months earlier Marie had been fooling around with the radio in their living room and heard an interview of a man who had traveled all over Europe and Asia. He'd gotten malaria hiking around in a jungle in Burma near Mandalay. Now instead of feeling cold, Marie felt feverish and about to die, pictured herself and Chrissy weakly swinging machetes through thick green ropy brush.

Chrissy was catching snowflakes on her face. Tommy and Mark huddled close to the car looking at their boots, every once in a while checking out Chrissy's backside. Marie walked over and stood next to Tommy. He was about two heads taller than she was, so she had to crane her neck just to see his chin sticking out of his parka.

"You wanna blah blah blah?" he asked.

Marie tugged at Chrissy's belt loop. "Chrissy, what did he say?"

"I don't know." She turned around and wiped the snowflakes out of her bangs.

"Well, look into his hood and tell him to repeat it."

Chrissy stepped up to him and squinted inside his hood. "Bloodbath," she said.

Marie stood on tiptoes next to her. Tommy's head was deep inside his hood, which was lined with yellowed fake fur. He had the thinnest lips she'd ever seen; under them a pointy chin stuck out like a ledge. Chrissy was right, his eyes were totally shot, his eyeballs getting a bloodbath.

"Gone to Guam," Marie said.

"Say it again, Tommy," Chrissy instructed. Then: "Car," he said. "Ride."

The back seat of Tommy and Mark's Nova smelled like pot and dirty laundry. The heater was blasting. Marie looked around the car for signs of the Philippines. In the middle of the seat, the stuffing bulged out of the vinyl; up front the radio and tape deck were broken. Chrissy pressed her open mouth against her window.

"What do you see?" Marie asked.

Chrissy shrugged. "Nothing. My mouth is hot."

Tommy drove down back roads, farm after farm swooping past the windows. The wheels hummed. Where the snow had been packed down on the road the sound was muffled, but when they hit a bare spot the gravel crunched and rocks spun up against the fender.

*I can feel it,* she thought. *I am moving.*

Mark lit up a joint in the front passenger seat. He held his breath and turned to them in the back seat, waving the glowing tip in front of them.

"Have you two beauties ever had Thai stick?" He smiled and looked at Chrissy, who was still looking out her window. His hood had fallen back from his square face. His buzzed-off hair was growing back in tight, bright curls that looked like meringue. His little-boy ears were pinned flat against his head. Chrissy toked slowly and handed the joint to Marie, who took a light hit and handed it back to Mark.

"Maybe you and me should switch seats," Mark said.

He stuck the joint into his mouth, reached back between the bucket seats, and ran his hand up Chrissy's knee. She slid closer to her door and his hand fell onto the seat between them, as if his arm were dislocated from his shoulder. How long could he stay in that weird position? Marie had read about a Chinese acrobat who could twist her head behind her knees, lie on her neck, and arch her back around like a table. She sighed, picturing herself and Chrissy curled around like that on tall red platforms, South Chinese tigers parading in circles around them, bleachers of Chinese clapping and roaring for them.

"I want to go to China," Marie whispered.

Chrissy pulled her mouth off the window. "Too far," she said.

How would the sky look from China? Marie thought about other galaxies full of spinning planets. She felt as if she could stick one arm out the window and poke a finger into Jupiter.

Mark was looking out the back window and sucking on the joint. Tommy stared at the road through the flecks of white, bobbing his head with the windshield wipers.

Marie put her hand inside her coat against her chest and felt her heart thumping under her fingers. Her life wasn't small, like the poem said, but dizzyingly huge. She picked up Chrissy's wrist and tried to find her pulse but Chrissy pulled her arm away. Tommy and Mark's hearts must be beating rapidly, like drums, the hot island jungles flowing through their veins. She leaned forward so her face was directly in front of Mark's face. She could smell the stale pot on his breath.

"Tell me what it's like," she whispered. "Tell me about the Philippines."

Mark stared back at her with bloodshot eyes. "Lots of pot," he said.

"No. I mean, what does it look like? What does it feel like?"

He shrugged and took another hit off the joint. "I don't know," he said. "It's hot. We jog a lot."

Marie slumped back in her seat and shut her eyes. She kicked the back of Tommy's seat. She leaned forward and clapped her hand next to Mark's ear three times. The roach flew out of his mouth onto Tommy's lap. Tommy hit the brakes, and as the rear end of the Nova swung across the road into the ditch, Marie grabbed the seat with both hands, sat bolt upright, and screamed, "Wheeeee!" Mark put his head in his hands, Chrissy's forehead hit the window with a thud.

While Tommy and Mark tried to push the Nova out of the ditch, Marie followed Chrissy down the gravel road, Chrissy walking as if she knew her exact destination. A car drove by and Marie turned and stopped to watch the shadows and fluorescence trail after it. Chrissy kept walking.

The snow was failing hard now, not in flakes but in small clumps pounding down on Marie's shoulders and head. The clumps filled the ditches and covered the road. The lowest branches of the trees were white and bent. Chrissy cut through the ditch into a field. Marie watched her feet imprint fresh snow. They could be hiking across northern China. "Tell us what is happening in the rest of the world," the villagers would say.

Marie stuck her hands in her pockets. Shutting her eyes, she held her face into the wind and took a deep breath—the Arctic breeze numbed her lungs. When she looked up she saw miles of white powdery plains spread out before them.

Suddenly there was a sound like thousands of people mumbling. Marie stopped and tried to focus her eyes. About ten feet to her right Chrissy was walking slowly, her hands in her pockets and head hunched into her squirrel fur collar. Marie felt something on her foot. She looked down and saw a big, dingy gray turkey, and then two turkeys. She stopped and stared at them and they stared back.

"Chrissy, do you see turkeys?"

"Of course I see turkeys. We're walking through Kemper's turkey farm."

About forty feet ahead was a long white turkey barn and they were surrounded by turkeys, thousands of shit-covered, gangly turkeys with red eyes. They walked forward, the turkeys walked forward. They stopped, the turkeys stopped. Marie broke into a run, the turkeys gobbled and trotted beside her, as if they were escorting her, their rubbery necks stretched out, their wiry legs struggling to keep up, their dirty white tails dragging in the snow.

Marie ran over to a wheelbarrow that had been left in the field. She dumped the snow out, turned it upside down, and stood on the top, balancing one leg on the handle and the other on the barrow's bottom. The turkeys swarmed around her.

"The world is ours!" she yelled.

The turkeys broke out in a chorus of gobbling that rose to a clamor and then died down.

"No more school," Chrissy yelled beside her.

"Life is big!" Marie yelled, but she felt the fear in her voice.

She scooped up snow and threw it at the turkeys, a field of blank red eyes watching her. Marie's heart beat hard. This is my life! she thought. A pain shot up her ribs and a gust of wind hit her face.

On the ground next to her, Chrissy slouched deep in her coat, her neck sunk into her shoulders, her long arms limp. Her face was the palest frozen blue. Who was she? Who would she be? Marie watched her friend cough and melt to her knees, then to her stomach. She stuffed a clump of snow into her mouth. Marie had a quick fear that Chrissy had gotten truly dumb. She slid off the barrow and lay on her stomach next to Chrissy, her neck weak as a turkey neck.

The wind was blowing snow into her face. Snowdrifts puffed out of the ditches. The turkeys had stopped gobbling and were milling around them.

Chrissy's head popped up. Vomit erupted out of her mouth onto the elbow of Marie's coat. She sat up and wiped the vomit from Chrissy's face with her fur collar. She touched her cheek. Even though her own cheek was numb, she expected Chrissy's skin to be warm, but it was cold. Chrissy's eyeliner had spread over her eyelids, so she looked like one of those lost lonely girls on old movie posters who never go anywhere.

"Chrissy, remember that movie where Katharine Hepburn has a tiger?"

She folded her arms under her face, lay back in the snow, and went to sleep.

Marie pushed to her knees and shook Chrissy's shoulder. She stood and grabbed her under the arms and dragged her a few feet toward the road. But it was useless. She could never drag her all the way to the road, and even if she could, what then? She would have to drag her to the highway. The road was empty as far as she could see. She pulled Chrissy's squirrel collar over her head. She lay down beside her and put her arm over her.

She wished she had the power to reverse the order of things. The turkeys would stumble backward into the barn. Chrissy would wake up, swagger to her feet, stick a cigarette in her mouth. Marie would follow her to the highway. They'd hitch a ride to Marie's house, lie on the braided living-room rug, watch *Bonanza* reruns, eat saltines.

They'd go back to sixth grade, when Chrissy used to hang from the bus window as it rode up to school and shout, "My Marie! My Marie!"

During lunch hour they sat on the wide windowsill in the grade school bathroom, gossiping about the girls they hated, and the international concert tours they would see when they were in tenth grade and hitchhiked around the world.

A loud high voice was screaming in Marie's ear.

"God, are you two drunk or what?"

She opened her eyes and saw a blue down coat open over a denim shirt embroidered with daisies and leaves. It was Sheila Kemper.

"What the hell have you two been doing?" Sheila yelled. "You must be freezing." She looked like she'd lost weight since the last time

Marie had seen her, which was just this afternoon in the school cafeteria. Sheila's round apple face was hollowed out and her eyes were sunk like shadows. Even in her bony state her breasts bulged against the denim shirt and reminded Marie of a picture she'd seen of an Austrian milkmaid.

"*La maison de Madame Durard,*" she said.

"What are you saying?" Sheila brushed the snow off Marie's back and then Chrissy's back. She held out her hands for each of them to grab. "God, we thought you were dead or something."

Mr. and Mrs. Kemper smiled at Marie. Marie smiled back. The car was hot, a steady stifling blow of overheated air. She and Chrissy huddled in the back seat with Sheila and her two brothers, who were holding their noses and staring at them.

"Where were you girls going?" Mr. Kemper asked.

"Dad, leave them alone," Sheila said. "Their ride got stuck over by the main road near the tracks, and they got lost walking across the fields."

Mr. and Mrs. Kemper looked at each other. He wore a red Russian felt hat that stood up square above his forehead. Mrs. Kemper wore a hand-knit scarf with bright teal blue figures woven into a yellow background. Mr. Kemper turned on the radio to country and western and the car sped down the road.

"You guys are gonna have to wash your clothes, you know." Sheila spoke to them slowly and clearly, as if they were children. "I mean, they really stink, you know, like turkeys." She screwed up her nose. "I don't know how you could stand laying out there with all them. They poop in their own feed bins. When I'm filling their bins, they trample each other."

Marie felt the blood painfully returning to her fingers and toes. Her head ached. She was going to be sick as a dog tomorrow. She would wake up late and have to shovel the drive, then pull her brother in his sled to the neighbor's hill and push him down the hill and drag him back up. She looked over at Chrissy, who was leaning against the window with one hand over her face, crying. Marie had no idea what to say to her. She realized that this was only the beginning of not knowing what to say to her.

The two boys stared at them and made faces and pushed each other. The heat was crowding her; her skin felt pricked with thousands of pins. She sat back in her seat, folded her arms over her chest, and shut her eyes. Chrissy's elbow poked into her side and her raspy, broken breathing made Marie feel tired. She pulled Chrissy's arm closer.

Marie would have to go into the world all on her own—it was so unfair. She looked out the window at the lights of the town, the gray spire of the church, the water tower. She squinted and tried to see the hills behind her house, the hills of France. Then she tried to see the powdery plains of China. Chrissy was right; it was too far. She was only a Church Grove girl. Even as she thought this, her life felt small with loneliness and fear. But there was also a tinge of something else, anticipation, the miles of dark, dense space.

"So where'll it be?" Mr. Kemper asked.

"Yeah," Sheila said, "where do you guys want to go?"

The Kempers looked at her, their faces round and inquisitive and smooth as hills. Marie and Chrissy looked at each other.

# Teratophobia

**PEGGY MUNSON**

Ever since Sarah left me, I've been dreaming that Dave is pregnant. He walks through my apartment naked, midriff jutting out and penis hanging down, burping like a guy with a giant beer belly. He seems oblivious to his condition, patting his stomach in satisfaction every once in a while, haunting my dreams. In this way, he parades through my REM sleep like a film extra for months. When he finally reaches term, Dave gives birth to monsters. A hairy cyclopean beast with a spiked devil's tail. Then a hideous creature with bile-colored skin and breasts. Some have faces of people we both know. Some have smooth skin where a face should be. One does not have arms but fins, not lungs but gills, and can't breathe once it leaves the amniotic sac, has to be plunged into bathtub water. Over the weeks, Dave's babies grow extra arms, third eyes, chest hair, claws, tentacles, sinewy tails. One has a hole all the way through its chest where a heart should be, and Dave moves his hand in and out pretending to be David Copperfield. They grapple for me. They think I am their mother. But when I look down at my own body in my dreams, I am hermaphroditic too, not mother or father but both. Dave is so proud of his monster babies. He holds them up to suckle at our breasts.

I slept with Dave once six years ago, but we'd known each other since childhood. He appears in my dreams a lot, even though I haven't seen him for a long time. I don't know why I'm dreaming about him and not Sarah. Maybe because for six weeks or so after he and I had sex, my period was late, and Sarah and I never had to think about that. I hadn't been with a man for a year before that, though I

had enjoyed a few sexual escapades with women. The summer before
I slept with Dave, a guy raped me with his hands. He didn't use his
dick, just shoved his hand up inside of me after I said, "No," repeatedly and told me he wouldn't stop until I came. He'd driven me on his
motorcycle to watch *No Exit* at an open-air theater, then took me back
to his apartment, which was mostly mattress, and raped me. It was our
second date. Later, a friend of his told me he had date-raped a whole
string of women, and they were trying to press charges. I didn't tell
her about me, because I didn't know if I'd been raped, since he
fucked me like a woman could. I had nothing to call it but manual
labor, since manual is like the French word for hand, *le main*. And he
did men's work, he raped me, he raped me with his hand.

Not too long after I slept with Dave, I met Sarah. Sarah was in my
Theorizing Personality class. She had John Lennon glasses and a
retro-hippie dyke chic which made her seem articulate and reason-
able. We went out for coffee after class to talk about Jung. From then
on, we decided to analyze the personalities of people in the class,
instead of paying attention, and passed notes back and forth which
said things like "Rabid womanizer who takes feminist theory classes to
improve his chances of getting laid." We both dated around for a
while before we fumbled together on her ratty old futon, running our
tongues around each other's nipples, kissing furiously, and tentatively
moving our fingers inside of each other.

Our relationship ended over minutiae. We had graduated and
moved to San Francisco by then, and I often would get sad when we
were out walking because in some neighborhoods people just abandoned junk on the streets. I didn't care about most things, only the
mattresses. Some days we'd run upon a mattress propped up against a
fence, like a vagrant, full of history. They seemed to have such distinct
personalities and started intriguing me. I began sneaking out at night.
I had a big Volvo station wagon then, and Sarah was a heavy sleeper.
I'd quietly put on my pants and shoes and coat, grab my work gloves,
lighter fluid, and a lighter, and slip out. I'd drive to the location of the
latest mattress spotting and heave the thing into the back of my car.
People were always happy to help. A psychologist friend of mine who
worked in prisons said you can always see danger in people's eyes. I
never had any problems; people were glad about what I was doing.
When Sarah was out of town, I'd wait until early morning and drive

south to the dump: then I'd pay the five-dollar fee and leave the mattress there. But more often than not I'd drive past the high-numbered streets in the Sunset district, find a dying bonfire on the beach, and throw the mattress in. I usually tried to say something priestly then. I would douse it with lighter fluid and toss in a piece of rolled-up, lighted newspaper if necessary and watch it burn. I felt such relief every time I did it.

I only got caught one time. Sarah was standing in the doorway with her pajamas on. "What the hell is going on?" she demanded.

"I couldn't sleep." I shrugged. "I was checking out the bonfires on the beach."

"Don't lie to me."

"I can't tell you what I was doing," I said. "You'll send me back to therapy." Sarah had been working as a crisis counselor for gay teenagers.

"I don't fucking believe this, you're sneaking around on me."

"It's not what you think." But she was already yanking on her jeans and grabbing her keys. Later, she listened quietly to the whole story and said, "Well, I met somebody I like at work, anyway." Before long, she left me for a nineteen-year-old activist.

I burned the mattress we shared and bought a new one. The day after I burned it, I went back to the beach with a garbage bag, collecting the skeletal remains. I cried against the sound of the waves. The fog moved in, turning the beach into an ethereal landscape.

I thought I had burned all of my ghosts, but then the nightmares started.

In one dream, like Leda and the Swan, I've been raped by a monstrous animal. Not only does the baby kick; its tail lashes against my womb. I tell Dave I want an abortion, but he won't let me. I drink strange teas, try to abort it myself. But then my body becomes so large I look like a human Volkswagen. When I finally break water, all my friends gather around the midwife to watch. I see the hairy head pushing out, the webbed fingers, its sinister tail. I yell, "Cut the cord," but no one does; it keeps pulsing with life as the thing feeds off of me. The midwife puts it on my chest. I wake up in a snuffled scream.

That's when I finally start taking the sleeping pills my doctor gave me when Sarah left. Every time I take them it feels like a suicide; the sleep is so heavy and deathlike.

———————

I met Dave in sixth grade. Because he had a crush on me, he told the whole class he crouched outside my window and watched me undress at night. He lived down the street in a dark house on a hill. Nobody believed me when I told them I left my shades down, even though he had the color of my underwear wrong, told people I wore polka dots. I stopped trying to protest. Doubted it myself, wondering what I'd let him see, searched my drawer for polka dots. Started undressing under the covers with the light out. Before I could fall asleep, I'd clutch my chest and cry into my pillow. And finally, I just stopped caring, dressed and undressed with the shades half cracked. People looked at me differently in school. I became class president that year but I never could stand up and speak. I'd get this panic inside of me, an urge to lie on the ground and cover myself with leaves.

Dave had bad teeth, big ears, and gangly arms. But he was popular because he was funny and told good stories.

By eighth grade, with his braces off, he'd become pretty cute, and everybody liked him. I'd quietly disappeared under a mound of permed hair and poorly applied eye shadow. I decided the best way to reinstate my social status was to develop an infatuation. It wasn't hard, as he was charismatic and he knew more about me than most people, since he'd been observing me like an anthropologist for years. One time he asked me to dance at some girl's basement party. The basement had track lighting with dimmer switches on everything, and they were all turned to the very edge of darkness. Dave put his hand on my lower back and rested it on the top of my jeans pocket. He moved us around in tiny rivulets for two songs. Someone's Coke dribbled on my shoe; he breathed softly on my neck; I watched moving silhouettes of boys and girls in beanbag chairs. The whole room reeked of popcorn and perfume. My body wanted to push closer to him, push into him. I felt so betrayed by my physical impulses. But I was too afraid to dance with someone who hadn't seen everything about me already. He was the only one who really knew the truth about me, since he'd created the rumor. And it was easier to be close to him than other boys, since I hated him enough to care at all.

He didn't call me after the party, and I was angry and disappointed. The phone did ring at the exact moment I was trying to put a tampon in for the first time, a week later, and I wondered if it was him. I desperately wanted the ease of movement the Tampax commercials promised. But the tampon didn't slide right in like the package said. I felt bad when I couldn't relax, as the instructions instructed. The blood was all over my hands, all over the tip of the tampon, dripping down my legs and onto the bathroom tile. My mother was calling my name, yelling, "Phone call." But I just stood there, poised with the tampon pointed at my crotch like a gun, my finger on the trigger, one leg up on the porcelain like the diagram said, thighs smeared with blood. I finally got it in, and cleaned up the blood. When I walked downstairs, I felt like something was prying my legs apart, like there was a spit wad inside. I tried to act suave.

"Who called?" I asked my mom.

"Oh, some boy. He hung up."

After that, I began sneaking down to Dave's window, watching him undress at night. Pulling his shirt over his ribs, unbuckling his pants, lowering them so that I could see his underwear, walking to the window, and drawing the shades. I even took pictures one time. I wanted evidence, evidence of what I had done. After I got the prints back, and was sorting them in my room, I realized there is no female word for Peeping Tom.

Sarah left town in June. She always hated Halloween but had no other symbolic connection to monsters, except for a while after she came out, when her born-again parents thought she was one. Suddenly, I realize it's time for me to get out there, to forget her. My friend Diane always has parties geared toward single lesbians, because she likes to play around. It seems risky and appropriate, then, when I go to her Halloween party as a final act of separation. There are several sexy vampires. I dress as Glinda the Good Witch, a long white gown and fairy wand, white wings and a giant blond wig. The three people I know—two vampires, one Medusa—stand in a line and do a synchronized sway to the music while eating and talking with people in masks. For a while I just watch, wishing I had a mattress to burn.

Finally, a woman dressed as Dorothy comes in, carrying a rather stiff, stuffed Toto, and I ask her to dance to Monster Mash. She has a strong presence. I can tell that beneath her Dorothy braids and gingham clothes she's one of those tough little tomboys who starred in my fantasies for years.

"I'm more afraid of good witches than bad witches," she whispers.

"I'm afraid of anything that's supposed to be good for me," I answer truthfully.

When Dorothy dances, she slides her legs from side to side and clicks her ruby heels together, and every time she does it, I think to myself, *There's no place like home.* When the song ends, Dorothy leads me to a back room, and on the way I point out my three friends who are lined up against one wall, and intone to Dorothy, "Lions and tigers and bears." Dorothy raises her eyebrows. Once we arrive in somebody's bedroom, we sit on the bed and talk for a while. Then we remove each other's wigs, laughing as we pull out the bobby pins. I stroke her short hair, which feels soft and smells like lavender. I've always liked stroking hair that is finite; I hate getting tangled up. She kisses my ear very slowly, which always turns me on. Then she moves her tongue around my earlobe and wraps her wig braids around my back like a braided whip to pull me into her. We kiss and touch each other gently until she has to leave with her ride, who bursts in on us when we're lying next to each other. She writes down her phone number on a paper cup, picks up stiff Toto, and walks out. I forget to tell her I'm leaving tomorrow for a week, don't worry if I don't call. I feel like a bit of an asshole for not telling her. I know I won't call tonight.

I leave around two in the morning and drive from the Mission to Potrero Hill, through the warehouse district south of Market. Drunk, ghoulish people are still hovering around street corners. It was drizzling a little earlier, but now the skies seem clear. I circle around for a while, then head up Divisadero, toward the water. Eventually, I see a couple of masked call boys leaning against a fence where a dirty old futon is resting. I have a knack for finding mattresses now. I pull up and shout from my car window, "You guys want to help me heave that thing into my car? I'm trying to clean up the neighborhood."

"Gladly," one of them says. "My boyfriend threw me out. And now my bed's been rained on." He kicks the futon. "This thing has nothing but bad memories for me."

"You might want to come along then."

"Where are you going?" The other one says, his eyes wide and inquisitive.

"You'll see." We heave the mattress in the back and they sit on top of each other in the passenger seat. One of them is dressed like a court jester, holding a feathered eye mask. The other is wearing a Batman costume. I drive them through the Richmond District, thinking I must be crazy to pick up strangers on Halloween, but they seem harmless and very young. And quite pretty; one of them has striking blue eyes and black hair, with wispy baby eyelashes that could stop traffic. The roads get flatter as we near the ocean, the sky becomes broader. I pull up into the beach parking lot. They exchange a look with each other. I hand one of them the lighter fluid, the other a matchbook from a club downtown, and today's paper. They both stare at me wide-eyed, and one turns to the other and says, "Shit, Dorothy, the Good Witch is a pyromaniac." His friend lets out a boisterous laugh.

We drag it through the sand like a beached seal, and I realize we're going to have to rip it open to get a flame, since it was damp earlier. I take out my pocketknife and cut it down the center, so the cotton innards are pouring out. One of them douses it with fluid, and the other tosses in a match. We warm our hands and laugh nervously, then jubilantly as the flame picks up. The jester turns a cartwheel. "This is much more therapeutic than that New Age fire-walking crap," he says, and we grin. The mattress smokes a lot, and we wave Batman's costume cape over it, pretending we're sending out signals to someone. It's a perfect night for this: the cops are tied up with parties in the city.

I get home late after dropping them off and fall asleep to the sound of people singing in the streets as they walk home from the Castro masquerade. The only nights I sleep deeply now, without pills, are the nights I watch a mattress burn.

I drift in and out of dreams on the plane. The monsters are in pieces this time, headless or limbless, searching all around themselves for their lost parts. I wonder if the parts are inside of me, in my belly, clamping on my stomach, feeding me thoughts.

I think about finding Dave when I get to Manhattan. I still have his old address in my book. The dreams seem to be drawing me to him. I want to tell him I fuck women now, drive "dyke" like a chisel between me and his ego. I know he got a woman pregnant when he moved to New York, and I imagine it could have been me. To his credit, I know he paid for her abortion in its entirety. I still talked with him periodically then. They were both getting into drugs at that point, though, nothing serious yet, but he did know all the trade names and sometimes called them by letters, like X and H. All these years I've tried to

give my own pleasures an alphabet, to name things; I can't do it. I
want to know the secret of creating hidden alphabets. When I used to
go out with men, I pursued wandering road boys who couldn't be tied
down. It was always semi-unrequited. I tried living in espionage, devel-
oping intrigue, but the strategy of being that kind of woman befuddled me. It seems I'm always writing in code, hoping someone will
know what I am talking about.

Just before Dave and I slept together, he said something odd.
Unprompted, while we were watching a movie, he said, "I really think
rapists should be castrated."

I was surprised, got quiet, then started kissing him, feeling around
his mouth with my tongue. That's how it started. And then the night
just went on and on. He had incredibly soft hands, which I didn't
expect. I left his house in the early morning, walking back to my childhood home, though I was an adult then. I arrived at the yard just
as the paper was being delivered. On the front page was a story
about a woman on a plane whose lung collapsed. A doctor on board
had to operate with forks and knives from the airplane meal, and he
sterilized them with little bottles of airplane vodka. When I later
reflected back on Dave and me having sex, I would imagine being that
woman, totally conscious, waiting for a man to bring back my breath. I
pictured the flight attendants coaching me like Lamaze instructors
when he finally got my lung to work, telling me to just *breathe,* to
*breathe.*

I could almost feel her first jagged, miraculous breath.

I take a taxi to Michael's apartment. He offered to let me house-sit for
a week, and I had enough frequent flyer miles to travel for free. As
soon as I get to his place, I'm already wanting to go outside, to walk
quickly through Manhattan and stalk the unknown. I dress up a little
for the walk. The air outside his apartment smells like tar. I think
about how grungy it is here and then a woman leans out an open window and takes a deep breath, as if she's in the country. As if the air
here is good.

As I'm walking toward the Village, I overhear three women talking
about dykes. They're visiting New York without their husbands for
some businesswomen's conference. One husband was afraid his wife
would run off to become a lesbian. Another chimes in. "Yeah, my
boyfriend was afraid I'd become a LESBIAN, too." They enunciate the

vowels like they are saying YETI. My body starts shaking and I wonder if I'm overreacting, if I overreact to everything. Like with the Rapist, who still invades my thoughts when I am making love, watching theater, walking down a dark street. The really strange thing, I guess, is that he fucked me like a woman. To any judge, this probably doesn't count at all.

I suddenly remember I have a Lesbian Avengers flyer in my pocket that someone gave me in San Francisco. I pull it out and shove it into one of the women's hands as I walk by her. She says, "Thank you," like an automaton, looks surprised and a little frightened.

I finger the piece of paper in my pocket with the phone numbers of people I know in New York. Sarah never knew about Dave or the Rapist. I kept that part of my history a secret, since it happened in my hometown during the summers I was back from college. Plus my lack of memory and details about the Rapist are hard to explain. I got on his motorcycle of my own volition, thought I'd like the feel of the breeze through my hair and didn't wear a helmet, and I knew he'd been drinking. But where I came from, that's just what girls did. And when I was visiting my hometown, I was simply a girl. I do remember he complimented me on my hair, and I felt beautiful for a second. And I remember when he laid me on the bed I said, "No," and he ripped off my pants. Or I said, "I don't want that" or something to that effect. I know I told him to stop. I know the mattress was flat and had no box springs, was just lying on the floor like an old dog. He led me right to the bedroom. Then he raped me and he drove me home.

I stop at a pay phone to call Dave. I just have to. I am sick of the monster dreams and know what I should do.

"Shit, what a surprise," he exclaims. "What have you been up to?"

"I'm a designer at a Scandinavian bedding company." What I mean to say is, I've been sleeping a lot these days, trying to make up for dream time. What I mean to say is, I'm working at a health-food store, trying to earn a living wage, spending my off-time at the women's hot-tub place and burning things.

"Is it a desk job? That doesn't sound like you."

"Well, I thought I'd work for a few years with benefits and then become a criminal like you."

He laughs. "Hey, I'm having a party tonight. Why don't you come. I heard you're into women now."

"How'd you know?" I slump against the wall by the pay phone. I'm irritated I can't tell him.

"It's gotten around. There will be some lesbian filmmakers here. Stop by."

I ring the bottom doorbell. I once had a fling with a girl who was a total submissive, liked it when I was rough with her, and I reminded her of my floor number by writing on a slip of paper: "Bottom = You = My doorbell." We'll just see, Dave, I say to myself as I feel my knees quivering. We'll just see who ends up on top. When he unlocks the door, he gives me a big hug. He's still attractive to me.

I notice one woman right away. She's beautiful, with painfully dark eyes and full lips. I mill around with a beer, not talking much to Dave, trying to make conversation with some of the others, and finally ease over to the woman. We make small talk. It turns out she's a filmmaker, and will be in San Francisco soon to preview a piece of her work. I ask her name, tell her I'll look for it, then forget most of what she says. I'm distracted. As it gets later, I wander into the back, into Dave's bedroom. There are bars on the windows, which could be a hindrance. I pry open one window as far as it will go. I shove out a pillow, a couple of blankets, and the top sheet. Then I peel back the bottom sheet and cut a gash in the side of his mattress with my knife. I pull out what I can, though the job's not easy. I manage to extract some springs, which, after burning, will remain like a rib cage. And I pull out some stuffing, rip off the remaining pillowcase, and fill it with the mattress innards. I heave those out the window too, then cover the bed with a remaining blanket and some coats.

After the party, I retrieve my goods from the alley, wrap them up in the sheet and hail a cab. That night I sleep curled up with Dave's pillow and blanket, and I dream about the woman on the airplane. I dream she is getting her breath back. Then I dream the awful part, what comes out when she breathes. First she starts coughing, then grabs for a handkerchief, then coughs up something that looks like a small bug. But it's not a bug. It keeps growing, tentacles looming larger and larger beside her, monster eyes poking out. Then it wraps itself around her neck, like an octopus, covering her eyes and choking out her breath.

———

The next night I go out with an old friend.

I lose both Annie and my beer while I'm dancing, but I don't care, just want to shake the years off of me. While I'm looking around for her, a woman strolls up to me. She has a ring in her eyebrow, and we start dancing, silently, because it's too loud to talk. It takes me a minute to realize she's the filmmaker from Dave's party, and I feel vaguely awkward, like she knows my secret crime. She looks different tonight, dressed up. Usually I can't feel sexy in public, but we dance through four songs with our bodies close together. I still don't want to tell her my name, because just saying it connotes history. When we finish, the floor is pulsing too loud to talk, so she shouts in my ear, "I've got to catch up with some people. Will you find me later?" I nod. There's a certain comfort in being here. New York swallows everything. It frees up the body to dance.

They're playing loud music, and I keep forgetting to breathe. I'm thinking of how, and where, I will do the burning. So when she sneaks up on me, I let out a gust of air. "Whoa," she says. "I didn't mean to scare you." She grabs my arm lightly and steers me off the dance floor so we can talk.

Then she says, "You look like you're thinking about somebody."

"I was," I say, although I was actually thinking about burning Dave's bedding. I feel sweat dripping down between my breasts.

"Old girlfriend?" she asks. I nod and she says, "Ah."

"Well, you know what they say about getting back on that horse." She touches my arm in a friendly way. "Lesbians are great at transference. That's why we're so good in therapy."

I laugh. "I'm a therapy dropout."

She thinks for a moment. "Well, some people are just better at field-work."

She leads me onto the back terrace, and we talk for a while, warming our hands in our pockets. She tells me she's here working on a project, but she'll be in San Francisco, like she said, later in the month. We eye each other then, trying to pick up signals. She doesn't waste any time, pulls me so close I can feel her chest thumping. When she kisses me, the metal stud on her tongue clicks against my teeth like a coin in a jukebox. I never thought I'd find metal sexy, but it feels solid and good, and I'm surprised at how assertive she is, and how much I want her there. She moves her hands in slow holding patterns

on my back. Sometimes I'm afraid of women who seem so sure of what
they want. I wonder what it would be like to wake up with her. Kissing
that metal tongue in the morning might be like kissing someone's
braces, and then I'll be back to square one again, just a kid groping
around in a dark closet.

I focus on right now, her tongue a spoon stirring the most liquid
part of me.

"Hey," I say when we've pulled apart. "Can I see you here tomorrow
night? I've got to leave now."

Hours later, I wake up in Michael's cramped apartment and for a second I don't know where I am. I hear two men yelling at each other in
Spanish in the next building. Then I see a woman with them; she's trying to push them apart. The red highlights in her hair look like flecks
of blood. They seem to be fighting over her, but I don't speak their
language, so I don't know. She finally gets them to calm down, and I
realize I'm clutching Michael's Superman sheets, and I want someone
to hold me. The threesome starts laughing, as if they had only been
playing out a scene from a play. One man gives the woman a long, tender hug.

I drift off to sleep and the awful creatures sweep through my
dreams again. Then I cut a hole in my own belly, and reach in to grab
the monster I know is there. I stick my hand in with my eyes clamped
shut. If I see the thing, I know I will turn into it. I know the monster
will have my eyes, my freckles, my ears on its hideous body. In the
dream I float outside my body, shaking it. A furry hand reaches out
from the belly. I shake the body and say, "Wake up." When my eyes do
snap open one of the men in the window is gone. I long for the
woman with her metal tongue. I want her to be my anchor.

The next morning, I stuff my backpack full of Dave's mattress innards,
the springs and stuffing. I figure I'll take care of this stuff here, and
transport the rest back to San Francisco to burn there. I leave the
apartment in thick-soled shoes, thinking about erasing my whole life
and starting over, today. When I've finally decided to put it all behind
me, I suddenly think I see Dave through the glass front of a café and
I'm straining my eyes, trying to find out if it's really him. My heart
pounds when I see him, and I suddenly remember how much he likes
breasts. When he tried to touch my breasts, I pushed his hands away

and moved my breasts where his mouth could reach them. I can't really remember if I liked it, but I know he did.

The problem was, I kept thinking of that other guy, the Rapist, simultaneously remembering and trying to forget. When I faked coming with the Rapist, I said his name, because I knew that would make him believe me. I hate saying his name, even now. But I also hesitate to call him the Rapist; that name is like producing a monster with your own body. I could for convenience's sake call him Dick, to distinguish him from Dave, but I never even saw his dick, and I touched Dave's, and the skin was so much softer than I expected. I didn't want it to be soft.

Usually, I think what I call him doesn't really matter, because no one will believe me. He's just an ordinary guy, respectable in every way but one.

I know in some cultures they don't name their children until they know what those children will become. Maybe then it would be okay to be called the Bearded Lady, as if your name was just an observation. Maybe then it wouldn't sting when other people yell "dyke" at me from passing cars. When I see Dave through the window of the café I think to myself: I touched his dick. The thought seems remote and strange, since I've called myself a lesbian for five years.

But then, sometimes, giving birth to the monster in my dreams feels good, sensual. Sometimes I look down and see his head peeking out of my body, glazed in my blood and still attached to me, breathing my breath. I feel my whole body relaxing. The monster is attached to me. The monster is my own child. For a moment I feel centered in love, before I scream, "No!" and snap awake. The "No!" echoes through my thoughts as I confirm that I am no longer sleeping. I think about the Rapist, how he looked startled when he finally realized I meant it when I said, "No," like he'd woken up from a bad dream. And when he rode me home on his motorcycle, I told him, "I'm sorry," as you do when you have rudely awakened someone from a dream state. I felt the motorcycle seat between my legs all night.

A woman in the café springs up to get a second cup of cappuccino and Dave slides her shopping bag to where he's sitting, then casually gets up and walks out with it. Our eyes lock for a second, and though he's almost a dead ringer, I see that he's not Dave. This guy has a tiny scar on his face that looks like a diamond on a card. I avert my eyes. You're never supposed to do that with predators. I mumble to the sidewalk and the guy keeps walking by me, fast, up the street. Then I follow him for a few blocks. He stops at a magazine stand and picks up *Sports Illustrated*. I grab *Seventeen* because it's close and bury my head in it.

I see him tuck the magazine into his bag, then he hails a cab and is gone. Just like that. I take a few steps toward the street until the vendor yells at me for walking off with his magazine, and I have to buy it, even though I don't want it. I used to read *Seventeen* all the time, because I thought I would lead a lonely, bespeckled life if I couldn't apply makeup well.

Dave once told me he wouldn't stop at night on a long road trip until he counted three dead animals. He called it the "roadkill trinity," a sign that he should rest for the night. I'm like that in New York, waiting to see any piece of violence that will let me know it's time to sleep. Now that I have witnessed a theft, I feel somehow relieved. I feel like I can walk around by myself for the day without being afraid.

I wander the city until the lights go down, eating one soft pretzel after another. When I know the club will be open, I hail a cab and get a driver who looks like a female version of the Elephant Man. Her features are gargantuan, one side of her head is flattened, there's hair on the back of her neck and moles behind her ears. I think how in some countries parents used to kill their female children. Some of them must have dreamed about giving birth to monsters. Some dreamed the daughters would grow up to be monsters. This is probably why girdles were invented, and push-up bras.

"You been robbed yet?" is the first thing she asks me.

"Um, no." I laugh. Instinctively, I reach for my backpack.

"Didn't think so," she says. "You don't walk like someone asking for trouble." She gives me a broad smile, and her teeth are perfect and lovely.

I have her drop me off a couple of blocks from the club. When she counts out my change, the rearview circles her unnaturally large forehead. I give her a big tip.

My old therapist said that naming your fears helps them seem more manageable. I suppose I should call a monster a monster, but it's hard when you know he's somebody's child. How do I explain the fact that I went willingly back to his apartment, or that I sometimes watch horror movies, just because they're an excuse to grab on to somebody's arm. How do I explain my childhood friend who has married three convicts? There is always the thought that if you call a bad situation something else, you can rewrite the alphabet, and it's like writing a story with a happy ending. It brings everything a little closer to the fairy tale you expected. You see, I still don't know if I can call that guy the Rapist, and I can't mention his real name. Where would I put it in my life story? A comma at the end like a draped sacrifice, a period at the end to show however small it becomes, it never completely disappears.

I walk in the direction of the club, then duck into a side alley. I swing my backpack down and unzip it. I take out a spring and put it around my wrist. It actually looks pretty good, like a piece of futuristic bondage gear. I leave it on. I take out a tuft of stuffing, pull out a match, light it on the ground, and watch it burn down. "You fucker," I curse at it. The fire lasts for about a minute and then it's gone. I keep on walking, feeling lighter.

When I show the bouncer my ID, she looks at it, then looks at me and says, "Good haircut." The photo was taken when I had long hair.

Music starts moving through my body immediately, and I feel energized and excited. Sarah and I stopped going dancing after our first year. There was too much temptation, being around other bodies. I wonder where she is now, but for a moment it doesn't matter. Here I am.

After an hour of milling around, I find the woman from last night. She's dancing in a group of people, doesn't seem to be with anyone in particular. I reach into my pocket, where Dave's number is, curl my fingers around it and squeeze them into a fist. I go over and dance close to her until she sees me, moves in my direction. They're playing something by PJ Harvey. The music is slow, sinister, hard. She herds me over to the wall with her body, and for a second I just want her to take me home and fuck me. It seems easier than talking.

"So, it's you again. *The Book of Laughter and Forgetting*," she says.

"What?"

"Milan Kundera. I never read the book, but I love the title. I often judge books by their covers."

For a second I smile. She's so witty and cute.

"Didn't you say last night that you're trying to get over someone?" she says.

"Oh yeah."

"I'd ask how you know Dave, but I'm not sure I want to know." She shakes her head back and forth.

I break into a mischievous grin. "Well, I used to be a Peeping Jane. He lived down the street from me. I watched him through his bedroom window."

"You're kidding." She laughs. "Is that what you do for kicks in San Francisco?"

"No, my life is pretty tame. I spend a lot of nights combing the beach."

She looks around, somewhat nervously. "Look," she says. "I'm sorry if I came on strong last night. I don't know what came over me. I'm not even from the city."

"It's quite okay," I answer. I can't tell her she could be even stronger if she wanted. I just don't have the guts right now. I've been out of this scene for too long.

"Are you sure?" she asks. I nod my head.

"So you don't want to ask where I'm from?" she queries. "I like background checks."

"Well, I had previously assumed you were from New York."

"Pennsylvania," she says like she's giving a sales pitch. "Land of steel, but I can't wear anything but sterling. I'm allergic." All of her piercings are silver.

"I used to believe it was Transylvania," I say. "Where all the monsters lived."

"It's a common misconception."

I reach up to touch her hair but she deflects my hand. I hate being pushed away. "Wait a second," she says. "Let's go somewhere else. This place is starting to creep me out." We leave fairly quickly and I forget about my backpack, then I have to drag her back to get it. We walk and walk. The pack starts to feel like another body, and a spring begins poking into my spine. At some point, we lean up against a wall, and she's pressing herself against me, holding me tight with her whole body. She starts kissing me deeply. Her lips are exquisite and she feels so gentle, so good.

Tonight, I want to tell her, I will give birth to a monster. It will be a hybrid of everyone I have ever known, a hideous combination of regrets. Tonight, I want to tell her, I don't want to sleep alone. I want to feel her hipbones pressing into me, find the stowaways in her body, forget about everything but tonight. She presses her body against me and kisses me hard. Her arms pin me to the wall. When I want more of her, she pulls back. She strokes the back of my neck. I grapple for her, pull her into me. For a second, she takes a breath, and I almost open my mouth to speak, to confess my crime. But then she kisses me again, and her tongue closes the top of my mouth like punctuation.

When we're walking the three flights up to Michael's place, she says to me, "Dave and I went out with each other for a while. Is that okay with you?"

"Sure." I turn my key in the lock and lead her inside.

"I went out with some enigmatic guys, but that was a long time ago. Some women don't like it when I tell them what a big history I had with men."

I excuse myself for a second, go into the bedroom, and spread out Dave's stolen covers over the bed, fluff the pillow, and pretend I'm retrieving something. After we've talked for a while over tea, she takes my hand and pulls me toward the bedroom. I like the way she takes charge, so I don't even have to think. She pushes me down onto Dave's blanket, which smells vaguely of unfamiliar things.

I kiss her hard, run my tongue around her teeth and nudge the edge of her metal stud so that she moans. I bite the hoop in her eyebrow, suck on her neck, run my tongue around the labyrinth of her ear. She lifts my shirt up, starts teasing my nipples with her fingertips and tongue. Before I know it, we are naked, exposed, my fingers pushing inside of her, her palm pressing against my warm cunt until I'm so heady I forget myself. Eventually, after we've fucked each other into exhaustion, we drift off. Her head is resting on his pillow, and I dream about the woman on the plane, the tentacled monster, her labored breathing. I dream about the monsters in my body, the ones who are waiting for me. Then I dream about the Rapist, but this time I hold him down, I hold him down and I peel off his face as if it is a mask. I peel off layers of skin and muscle and bone until there is nothing left but a blank slate.

In the morning, I wake up wanting to burn something. It must be like a nicotine fit, this daily compulsion for pyromania. I think of how bodies, even at a cellular level, are constantly discerning between the self and foreign invaders. Pedestrian decisions can be so treacherous or miraculous, but burning is definitive, complete.

She stretches beside me. "Did you hear someone took some stuff at Dave's party?" she says offhandedly.

I look away, rearrange the blankets and covers. I want to be close to her, but already I'm keeping secrets.

"You know what?" she says sharply. "He got my friend pregnant, before we went out."

"Dave?"

"Yeah. He was also a jerk to me. I chased after him, because I had this rebel boy fantasy. He represented something I thought I could never be. He has a history of mistreating women, but I shouldn't tell you that if you're his friend. I don't know why I went to his party."

She pulls me gently onto the bed and wraps her arms around me from behind. It feels so comforting I want to cry, but can't. "Hey," she says. "I'd like to see you in San Francisco. If my film does well, I might be moving out there to work on something new."

"A little continuity would be nice."

"You're sweet, and you seem stable."

"I'm not at all." I laugh. I get up and pour us both some orange juice. I notice how the light plays on her forehead and glints off her metal, how her lips look beautiful and slightly used. She picks up the spring-bracelet I laid by the bedside. "This is really funky," she says. "Where'd you get it?" She puts it on her own wrist and admires it. The scene looks almost domestic, and I wish I could capture it. It has created itself so perfectly.

"What'd you say your film is about?" I ask, evading her question.

"The main character is a woman who keeps growing hair in strange places on her body. She tries to pluck it and wax it and shave it, but it keeps growing back. So she starts cutting it off and saving it, like they used to do with hair of the dead, and makes things out of it but burns them, because she loves the smell of burning hair and wants to get rid of it. Still, she can't seem to destroy it. She can't make it go away." She laughs. "My work is very experimental. It probably sounds weird."

"No, that's fascinating," I say, handing her the orange juice. "My last girlfriend was much too literal."

"I like a little mystery in my partners too." She smiles broadly. "So, where'd you say you got that bracelet?"

I pick it up, finger the snaking coils. I think of Dave sleeping on his lopsided bed, the discomfort of springs pressing into him, and I laugh out loud. "Probably at some women's festival somewhere. I don't remember."

I notice she has left her boots by the bedside. They're tough-looking shitkickers.

"I just thought of something," I say to her, realizing I want to entice her into staying with me longer. "I have an image you might find visually interesting."

"Really?" Her face shines with excitement. "A collaborative effort?"

"Yeah, get dressed," I say, squeezing her hand and savoring the moment of innocence before creation or destruction. Then I give her a wry smile. "And grab that lighter over there."

# Bang Bang Bang

**NATASHA CHO**

Fuck, what a time you end up having:

*Car Chasey and Claire*

You ever played car chasey before? Claire loves it.

Just watch the pedestrians crossing the road: they're walking, and then they realize that Claire's car isn't slowing down, and their last steps across the road are sprinted. Car chasey's a sport, see.

Claire laughs loudly as she chases, her knuckles curved around the steering wheel. I laugh too.

Claire does hit things in her car—animals so far, not people. Last time, she got a very large dog—blasted into it as I sat beside her in the passenger seat. BANG: I felt the collision, and I felt myself moving forward until I heard the confident click of my seat belt. We got out of the car and watched the lines of blood which were traveling out from under the car like oil. *Tag—you're it!*

And that's how you play car chasey.

## Stories About Dying

Dying is not always sluggish.

Look at the jig of freshly netted seafood suffocating in the open air; a drowning victim's violent intake of ocean; the last sprint around the yard by a beheaded chicken.

And light does not die in the eyes when it comes to death. Bullshit, that is. Claire's dog—moments before he died—his eyes were shiny with panic. And my father—his eyes like round vowels, his mouth open as if in mid-sentence—

Dying is definitely not always sluggish.


## The Runt Boy

The night I met the Runt Boy, I had a girls' night out with Claire, Lisa, and Helen. We went from pub to pub. I drank and smoked until I saw sparks. The others had even more than I did.

Then we went running down the streets, glowing from our beers and yelling out our stories. We could have met a cat along the way and pelted it with something. Can't be sure. But I know that we ran up to this car that had stopped at the lights and we kicked at it and shook it until the lights turned green. The young girl who was the driver looked ready to shit herself.

We ran over to a park and tried out all the playground equipment there. *Watch this, watch this,* Lisa called to us. She was standing at the top of the slide. She pulled down her jeans, squatted, and pushed out a heavy dark shit onto the slide. *That's the surprise for the next kiddie who sits there,* she told us, pointing to where the shit rested. Fuck, it was funny.

After a while, Claire wanted to leave the park and walk toward the city. We all agreed. Before we left the park, I frothed up a mouthful of spit and left it on the seat of the swing I'd been using.

We walked into this particular area of town, and watched all the men coming out of the nightclubs. While the others were talking, I vomited into a corner.

This young guy—a Runt Boy—was walking out of a bar with another guy. The night was still sparkly, and we watched as they kissed each other good night.

BANG: We grabbed the Runt Boy as soon as he was alone, a few side streets away. He really was a runt; he was so young, and his forearms were so smooth and breakable.

*Shit, shit,* he cried out. *Don't hurt me.*

But the others held him down, and I razor-bladed RUNT BOY into his chest, him screaming the whole time. Then we all hovered over his chest, reading the inscription aloud like it was on a plaque. After that, we had him standing, and we were about to let him go.

*Hang on,* Claire told us, and she walked up to him while Lisa, Helen, and I held on to him. She unzipped his trousers and rammed his trousers and underwear down to his ankles. All the vapors of his fear were rising, you could see that.

She brought her face right up in front of his. She smiled, opened her mouth, and brought her teeth together with a hard click.

Wish you'd been there to see it: Claire kept her face right up to his and she kept snapping at the Runt Boy with her teeth and he was shrieking in fear and we were shrieking with laughter.

After a bit, Claire let him go and shoved him away and we watched him run down the street so fucking fast, his trousers jiggling round his ankles. Pants-down, the Runt Boy had this awkward kind of gallop that just made me laugh and laugh.

*H*A

Claire came back to my place so we could have a drink to celebrate our time with the Runt Boy.

*Congratulations,* Claire said to me.

*Congratulations to you too,* I told her. *You were great. Ha.*

Claire smiled. And then she kissed me on the lips.

So:

Only a few hours ago we'd chased after the Runt Boy, and a couple of weeks before that we'd gone chasing in her car, and now we were both huffing after each other, dragging the clothes off each other's bodies. In the past, we'd rarely even hugged, and now every gesture was a fantastic infringement upon that history.

Everything was anatomical from there on in: I saw the muscles on Claire's neck move in and out as she dipped her head down over my body. Her hips were like handles to her body, and I pulled her in. Spit trails were left all over each other's bodies; girl drool was to be found on both of us.

We were rubbing our skins together, warm and oily, our bodies tensing and untensing. Girl girl girl everywhere, and there's not much more to say.

We finished up lying together on my bed, she and me, still huffing.

*B*IG *B*ANG

BANG:

Claire and I woke up in an embrace and we stared at each other. I saw the black-blue look on her face—same as the one on my own face.

Fucking hell.

# Nicolette:
# A Memoir

**JUDITH BARRINGTON**

When I first went to work at Perelada Castle in Spain in 1963, Nicolette and I had been lovers for just three months and my parents had been dead for six. I was nineteen, ignoring the grief I wouldn't let myself feel, and eager to find adventure. Although it was torture to be separated from her, I never considered changing the course of my life because of our affair. Even while I was still in London, our times together had been furtive and infrequent, our contact mostly limited to long, expensive telephone calls, each of which I faithfully recorded in my small diary with a series of cryptic initials. Now, living in Figueras, just over the border from France, when I couldn't stand her absence any longer I would place a call at the *teléfonos* building, where I would wait for several hours before the connection was made. I wrote her passionate letters and received, in return, letters which I chose to read as equally passionate, but which, in retrospect, might have seemed to an outsider like the words of an effusive, affectionate relative.

Much of the time, Nicolette faded to a dull ache, but still she leaped into painful focus if ever I had nothing to do, or was alone and sober. Then, one day in August, I arrived back at the small hotel on the square where I lived, to find an airmail envelope with her slanting handwriting on the front. I took the stairs two at a time and tore open the letter as I sat on the side of my bed.

"Darling Judy," she wrote, "I must go to Italy in two weeks' time to deal with some financial business." It seemed that, in addition to the small inheritance that Nico's father had left her—long since spent—

he had also left a house, a large mansion in the northern Italian village of Luserna San Giovanni. "...a house I have loved my whole life," she wrote. "A house that I must now sell, even though it will break my heart in two." The problem was, she explained, that her father had left it jointly to her and her sister, Gully, with whom she did not get along. Desperate for money and miserable at having to live in a cheap, but isolated, house in Wales, Nico now planned to meet Gully in Italy to negotiate a deal. "My darling," the letter ended, "won't you drive over and meet me there. You will be such a help. I can't manage without you."

It wasn't exactly a quick drive across town (it was some five hundred miles from Figueras to Turin along winding two-lane roads and over mountain passes), but I didn't hesitate. My busiest weeks as the tour guide at Perelada Castle would be over by then, and I could take some time off. Even if my employers didn't agree, I would go. She couldn't manage without me, she said.

I drove for most of two whole days, crossing into France after a three-hour traffic jam at the border, skirting the Camargue and Marseilles, and cruising along the spectacular Grande Corniche past St. Tropez. I spent the night in an uncomfortable little inn in the foothills and the next morning crossed into Italy by way of the Col de Tenda tunnel and headed toward Turin, where I was to meet Nico at the bar of a luxury downtown hotel at six o'clock. It was ten to six when I ordered myself a vermouth at the hotel bar, after cleaning up and changing in the opulent rest room off the lobby. I sat on a high stool, as if in a movie, waiting for my lover to appear.

My family had always hated Nicolette, but my mother hated her most of all. In 1955, Nicolette had waltzed into the lives of my Uncle Guy and Aunt Joan—a woman my mother adored—and had rapidly disappeared to Italy with my uncle, breaking up a thirty-year marriage. (I was eleven, and nobody talked about it in my presence, but I heard plenty, just the same.) Underneath my mother's outrage at the divorce and at Nicolette's "shameless" behavior, lurked other, less legitimate complaints about the interloper: she was flashy and overdressed; she smoked untipped cigarettes in a long cigarette holder; she had married *three* different men before Uncle Guy—indeed, she commanded way too much attention from men; and, worst of all in the eyes of my middle-class British family, she was *foreign*.

Her history was somewhat murky. She was French—no, she was English—no, she was Italian. She was the daughter of a count—no, she came from humble origins in the Aosta Valley. Mostly she spoke with a not quite believable upper-class British accent, but sometimes she rolled her *r*'s or threw out phrases in French or Italian. Then for a while her English would become redolent with one of those languages until the persona of the retired brigadier's wife took over again. The mystery irritated my mother, who was apt to throw out remarks like "Well, she must have something to hide then!" For me, though, listening behind half-closed doors, the mystery was an essential ingredient. By the time my mother finally agreed to let Nicolette and Guy come for a very brief visit, I was fourteen and felt as if Grace Kelly had been invited to tea.

It started badly. The couple arrived early and my mother, flustered and angry, emerged from her bedroom after my father had taken their coats. Sweeping into the hall, Mother glanced at the oak chest on which our large black cat, Banjo, liked to sleep, and swiped at it. "Get off, you naughty cat," hissed my mother, sending Nicolette's mink stole flying away into the kitchen. Nicolette was delighted by this piece of farce, but my mother failed to match the newcomer's peal of laughter and remained embarrassed the whole afternoon. Nicolette had the upper hand, but wisely she didn't overplay it.

It took less than an hour for my uncle's new wife to make me fall in love with her. She decided correctly that I was the only member of my family who could be charmed (my father and brother were both vulnerable but on too tight a leash), and so devoted her exclusive attention to me. I sat at her feet while she listened to my favorite records and asked me grown-up questions that no one had ever asked before: "Have you seen any interesting plays lately?" and "Don't you just *adore* that new Ella Fitzgerald record?"

A few weeks later, a letter arrived from Italy inviting me to go and stay with them. "Absolutely not!" said my mother, and that was that— for a while.

It wasn't until I was nineteen and my parents were suddenly dead— drowned in a Christmas cruise-ship disaster—that the neophyte passion I nursed for Nicolette—a crush which had perfectly wedded my budding desire to play the hero to her film star sophistication— exploded. We had only met twice since that first time at my home in Brighton, and both times I had judiciously failed to mention the meeting to my mother. But now, plunged into a tragedy which I couldn't yet comprehend, I received an invitation from Nicolette to spend my two weeks' compassionate leave from work at the house in Wales where she and my uncle had recently moved. My uncle was too ill and too upset to come to the memorial service, but Nicolette would "represent him." She would take the train to London and stay the night at my flat before going with me to the service. Then we would go back to Wales together.

The day before the service, Nicolette's train pulled into Paddington Station right on time. People hurried from the train, but there was no sign of Nico until, finally, as the crowd dispersed, a first-class carriage door flew open and she appeared. The way I remember her is with a drink in one hand and a long cigarette holder in the other, slowly descending the steps in her fur coat and high-heeled shoes, but could she really have been the icon I recall, or have I cast her as the permanently old-fashioned star in a movie that my memory made of that oddly unreal time? I tell myself I was in shock; I should know better than to trust my memory.

"Ah, there you are, dearest Judy!" she said, kissing the air close to my cheeks, and exuding a strong aroma of champagne. "Oh, you *poor* child. I just don't know what to say."

"Don't you have any luggage?" I asked, anxious to change the subject. "I'll look for a taxi."

She gestured back to the carriage, where a small man in a camel-hair overcoat with a fur collar was handing down suitcases to a porter. "Mr. Sherman says he'll take us to your place, darling. Such a dear man! We had a nice chat on the train."

Mr. Sherman turned out to have a Rolls-Royce waiting in the forecourt of the station, which did, indeed, deliver us to my shabby Lexham Gardens flat, where my neighbors peered through their windows in disbelief as the chauffeur carried cases and bags up the three flights of stairs. Mr. Sherman whispered something to Nicolette and handed her a card, then winked at me before jumping back into the Rolls and cruising off toward Knightsbridge. "He's staying at the Dorchester," Nicolette said as we puffed up the stairs.

Later, after she had changed her clothes and tried, unsuccessfully, to engage me in conversation about the accident, she settled by the gas fire with a large scotch, while I cooked a meal which I'm sure was unappetizing, since my culinary skills were nonexistent. She pushed the food around her plate and drank a good deal of wine before, quite abruptly, she said she was sorry but she had to go out for a little while. It wasn't until I heard the downstairs front door slam that I thought to ask when she'd be back, so I ran to the window and slid it open but I was too late: she was climbing into a taxi and my shouts went unheard.

For a while I wandered around the flat aimlessly, switching on the old, flickering TV, then turning it off impatiently. Finally, picking up a book someone had left on the couch, I tried to read. All my flat mates were away for Christmas and it was strangely silent as I turned the pages, occasionally getting up to make some instant coffee. Around eleven, I started to feel both worried and tired. Where on earth could she be? We had to leave early in the morning to drive to Brighton for the service. I wanted to go to bed.

By midnight I was furious. She had no key, so I couldn't go to sleep. Anyway, I had no idea where she was or if she was all right. I told myself that she was almost forty years old and could damn well take care of herself, but I didn't believe it. Then I remembered Mr. Sherman and his wink. *The Dorchester*, she had said. I looked it up in the phone book and dialed the number. "Mr. Sherman, please," I said, hoping I sounded forceful. "I'm sorry, he's out," said the desk clerk. "I don't know when he'll return."

"Listen," I said with as much authority as I could muster, "it's extremely urgent that I contact Mr. Sherman. Do you have any idea where he went?"

"Well," said the clerk hesitantly, "I did hear him telling his driver to go to Crockfords Club when he left about ten."

I ran downstairs and knocked on the door of the flat below mine, where four young men lived. I knew Tom was staying in town for the holidays and prayed he might be home. He appeared in his pajamas, rubbing his eyes.

"Tom," I said, tugging at his arm, "you've got to put on a dinner jacket and take me to Crockfords. It's a gambling club in St. James's."

"Okay," he said sleepily. "Which day do you want to go?"

"Now!" I said, giving him a push. "Go and get dressed."

The uniformed parking attendant looked askance at Tom's battered blue van, but finally let us pull up in a corner. I took Tom's arm as we walked through the entrance and explained to the host that we were with Mr. Sherman. I had never been to such a grand or decadent-seeming place before, but the surroundings were not uppermost in my mind as we were escorted along a red-carpeted hallway into the gambling room. I looked around, barely noticing the designer clothes and the jewelry, and certainly having no time to worry about my own hastily donned evening dress. My hair was a mess; my shoes were scuffed. At any other time I would have been mortified, but Tom by my side was elegant in his bow tie and I was busy scanning the crowd. I spotted her at the far side of the room, perched on a stool halfway along a roulette table, with Mr. Sherman standing beside her, his hand, heavy with rings, lying on her bare shoulder. She hadn't been wearing that dress at dinner. How had she changed after she left the flat?

Mr. Sherman seemed not at all surprised to see me and shook Tom's hand in a friendly way. Nicolette hiccuped a little and told me she had won a lot of money. Indeed, there was an impressive pile of chips in front of her.

"Well, cash them in," I said shortly. "We're going home now."

Again, Mr. Sherman was not surprised. In fact, he seemed rather relieved. When she descended from her stool, I realized why he was so agreeable about handing her over: she was too drunk to stand up. Swinging her purse in a wide arc, she lost her balance and fell against the glass doors that led out onto the patio bar. There was a huge crash as Tom leaped forward and caught her round the waist. The room fell silent, heads turning in our direction, as Tom and I took her by the arms and walked her between us out to the van. Mr. Sherman never even said goodbye.

The next day, I stood stoically through the memorial service and then gathered with the family at my sister's house. I remember very little of that day, but one memory lingers with perfect clarity: I am in the kitchen with my sister. We are scraping bits of potato and fatty roast beef into the garbage. "I know you're going up to Wales with Nicolette, but if you like you can stay here instead," she says, without looking at me. What would have happened, I will wonder over the years, if I had gone back into the dining room and said to Nicolette, "I've changed my mind"? What would have happened, I will speculate, if I had simply put her back on the train and waved her out of my life?

But I didn't change my mind. I went to the silent, green valley of Llandyssul in the bitter cold of that January, driving straight through the night with Nicolette dozing in the passenger seat. For the next two weeks, I spent most of my time sleeping, drinking, and writing notes in response to hundreds of condolence letters. Several times we went out for lunch with people Guy and Nicolette knew, and once they made me put on an evening dress and go to the Tyvieside Hunt Ball. I remember nothing about these occasions beyond a vague image here and there, but I know they happened, because they are noted in the datebook for that year which I still possess. I walked through the days on automatic, numb with shock, but pretending that nothing at all was wrong. The only thing I do remember with the full richness of emotional memory is the day Nicolette and I walked along the river path at the bottom of the water meadow. Beside the swirling river, muddy with rain, we stopped and turned toward each other. When our eyes met, I felt a charge go through my whole body.

Then, at Easter, she invited me back again. I arrived after another grueling night drive in a rainstorm, winding along the narrow lanes that followed rivers and snaked over humpbacked bridges. When I finally pulled up beside the old lodge, I discovered she had sent my uncle away to visit his son. We had the house to ourselves.

Sex and death make a potent combination when they start to over-lap—merging into one enthralling entity. Death became a formidable presence there in that old house, where I refused to talk about my dead parents, refused to cry, refused to acknowledge that anything at all was wrong. In spite of my denial—or perhaps because of it—death was all around us as Nicolette and I fell into bed together. It beat against the old windowpanes as she placed my hand on her breast and whispered into my ear what her body wanted from mine. It crammed itself into the corners of the room and entered me. I didn't yet know that it wouldn't go away, no matter how deeply I lusted, no matter how hopelessly I loved.

The storm was beating on the roof as I felt her legs wrap around mine, but at that moment I panicked, throwing off the quilt and bolt-ing into my clothes and down the stairs. I started the car and drove furiously down the lane, but the storm had soaked the mossy banks until many new springs overflowed across the slick surface of the road and I skidded in a half circle, ending up with my back wheels in the ditch.

For a few minutes I just sat there, the car making those little creaks and groans it makes after you switch off the motor. Then I got out into the pouring rain and walked around to the back. I could barely see the wheels in the dim red glow of the lights masked by sheets of falling water, but they appeared to be buried in deep mud. The nearest farm was half a mile back up the lane, but I could hardly wake up the farmer to tow me out of the ditch at this hour. Anyway, I would have to walk past Nicolette's to get there—walk right past the lodge with its bedroom light still glowing through the darkness and Nicolette waiting there with her silk nightgown slipping off a shoulder and a bottle of brandy by the bed.

I stood very still in the night as the water seeped through my clothes and dripped off my eyelashes and nose. No dog barked. No owl hooted. There was only the steady rain, sloshing into the puddles on the one-lane road and drumming on the leaves of the beech trees that grew along the bank. My stomach had a strange, sinking feeling: a yearning and an anger; a terrible fear that threatened to spill over into a mysterious and overwhelming joy. I knew I wasn't going to do anything about the car: perhaps I had intended all along to go back to the house, even if I hadn't ended up in the ditch. Hadn't this dash for safety been a sham—something to relieve the guilt that already permeated every feeling I had for Nicolette? And, indeed, as I walked back to the house, I was, for a few minutes, free of that guilt. I had put on a good show of trying to leave; I could almost believe that I had no choice.

Even out there in the wilds of Wales, Nico, as I started to call her after that night, had found her way into the social life of the county set. We moved from cocktail party to cocktail party, interspersed by the occasional dinner at someone's home or a pub lunch with a group of rowdy fox hunters. In between, there were the nights, which stretched out long and warm, filled with words of love mouthed from lips to ears, while slow caresses and sudden passions built into a nightly rhythm that merged with the humming and the sudden rushes of the spring wind that rattled the casement windows. I felt important and protective when I drove Nico to a party, the slightest hint of sunshine giving me an excuse to put down the hood of the little green convertible I had so recently inherited from my mother. I wanted to squire her into the large, square rooms with their chintzy sofas and sporting prints on the walls—to hold her hand possessively as we threaded our way through crowds of men in dinner jackets and

women in little black dresses, and to hold the car door open for her
when we left in the small hours of the morning, but I very quickly
picked up her ability to be lovers by night, aunt and niece by day.

"This is my niece, Judy," she would say to our hostess, after kissing
her poutily on both cheeks. Then, dramatically lowering her voice to a
pseudo intimacy, she would add, "She lost both her dear parents in
the *Lakonia* disaster, poor child." And I would blush and turn away to
find a waiter or a young man, who would supply me with a large
whiskey or a champagne cocktail. As I wandered away, I would hear
Nico extolling the virtues of my "poor dear mother," and telling the
gathering crowd just how "absolutely ghastly" it was for me. In my
embarrassment, I tried to pretend it was someone else she was talking
about, despite the glances that came my way as she warmed to the
story.

There was always a gathering crowd. At parties it was a group of
men who clustered around her, and I noticed that their expressions
closely mimicked those of my father and brother that first afternoon
when she had come to our house: wide-eyed and slightly befuddled—
but eager. At other places, like the shops in Llandyssul, she attracted
a crowd of whoever was handy. Even before she went into the green-
grocer's or the bakery, the royal manner in which she strode along the
village street caused a little stir of attention from the locals—some of
them slightly hostile, but all of them eager to follow her inside. The
pseudo intimacy that she dispensed here too sometimes involved
retelling the story of my sudden orphanhood, but often, she simply
requested or supplied a piece of local gossip. "Gladys up at the farm
has"—here she looked around and lowered her voice—"her *nephew*
from South Africa visiting, you know." And, even though this same
nephew had visited many times before, Nico managed to provoke in
her listeners a very real doubt that he *was* Gladys's nephew and to
raise the specter of family secrets too awful to imagine.

Toward the end of that spring visit, I realized that Nico herself had
secrets. From time to time, she would ask me to drive her into the village and leave her there for an hour, with no explanation of what she
was up to. The first time this happened, the morning after a particularly passionate night of lovemaking, I got it into my head that she was
going to buy me a surprise present, but when I picked her up she
offered nothing and was oddly silent as we drove back along the lane
by the river. Every few days, a green van would pull up by the garage

and a man in a sheepskin coat would haul out a big box and go round to the back door. Whenever Nico heard this van, she would frown and say, "Wait here a minute," and hurry to the kitchen as the man knocked on the door. Once, I followed her a few minutes later and found her standing on a chair, apparently putting away a bottle of scotch on the top shelf of the china cupboard. "I said *wait,*" she snapped. So I turned away, hurt as I was so often hurt by her changing moods, and went out for a walk across the meadow. It wasn't until a year or more later that I grasped the full extent of her drinking and began to find the bottles she hid all over the house. By then, she was buying from a village further away, her line of credit having long dried up in Llandyssul.

As our affair unfolded over the next few months, my guilt escalated. This was my first sexual relationship. I tried to hide from everyone the fact that I was involved with a woman, but still, my flat mates and friends picked up that something was going on. The part of me that was enamored with Nico had no outlet for my intoxication, although I longed to shout it all over town or, at the very least, to confide in some-one. After a while, the mixture of exhilaration and reticence led my close friends to conclude I was having an affair with a married man and I let them believe this, even while I lived with the terror that the real truth might come out. I muttered under my breath when I talked to Nico on the phone, afraid that someone would overhear. I rushed to the mail in case anyone noticed how often I got letters with that same sloped handwriting and a Welsh postmark. Discovery, or even suspicion, I assumed, would bring about the end of everything I had left to count on in the way of normal life. In fact, I pretty soon began to consider ending that life before I could be found out. Fantasies of suicide followed my increasing bouts of solitary drinking.

When I talked to members of my family, I found myself seeing Nico through their eyes. I was supposed to despise her as they did, or at least laugh at her pretensions and at her disturbing sexual power, and, in a way, it wasn't difficult for me to join in with them, though now, looking back, I can see what psychic havoc that must have wreaked. Whenever I talked to my sister-in-law or my cousin, Nico's latest out-rage was quite likely to come up: "You'll never guess what *that woman* has done now . . ." was the inevitable opening, and I would slide into a gleeful solidarity with the family that was genuine enough to fill me with the guilt of betrayal, as we all joined together in despising the

woman only I knew was my lover. Then there was Guy's first wife, my
Aunt Joan, who was also my godmother. I had always loved visiting her,
but now my visits were strewn with potential pitfalls, as Joan detailed
Nico's bad influence on Guy and her outrageous drunken behavior in
public.

And it wasn't just the living who demanded my loyalty in this cam-
paign against Nico: How could I forget that my mother had been
reluctant even to allow this woman into her home? How could I reconcile that with my constant and painful longing to have Nico in my
bed—to have her as far inside my body as I could get her? Everywhere
I turned, I betrayed someone: when I was with Nico, it was the family I
deceived, and when I joined the fold of the family, I denied not only
Nico but also my own deepest feelings. I wanted her with an intensity
and desperation that had to keep pace with my unexpressed grief. As
long as I could stay in love, I felt no pain or, at least, only the exquis-
itely distracting pain of an impossible affair.

Waiting at the bar in Turin, I was not particularly surprised when six
o'clock passed and then seven o'clock and eight o'clock. Nico was
never on time. But still, as I ordered drink after drink, and ate all the
olives on the bar, I felt a panic rising. Then, a little after eight-thirty,
she strode in through the swinging doors.

"Judy, darling!" she said. "We got so held up, but I *knew* you'd be
here." I noticed the man and woman who had quietly followed her in.
"This is my old and *very* dear friend *carissima* Santina, and her
absolutely *adorable* husband, Sergio Lupo."

I shook hands with Sergio and Santina, immediately liking them
both, although part of me ached to be alone with Nico so I could tell
her how horrible the months had been without her. But Nico insisted
that we all sit at a table for a drink, after which Sergio suggested that
we head back to their home in Ivrea. Nico had arranged for us both to
stay with them.

Over the next few days, between stolen moments of lovemaking in
Sergio and Santina's spare room, or in my car parked in a gateway
somewhere outside Ivrea, I listened, understanding only a word here
and there, as Nico and Santina talked in Italian about people they had
known growing up together in Luserna San Giovanni. Santina, I
noticed, always called Nico "Paméla," which supported the theory that
her origins had been at least partly English. I played out my role as

Nico's helpful niece, while in the little room divided by one thin wall from Sergio and Santina's room, our lovemaking became more and more furtive. Dishonesty was becoming a way of life.

It was a relief to get out of the house when Nico and I drove to Luserna to begin the house business. La Fontana, the disputed property, was an ivy-covered villa with a quiet, overgrown garden and, of course, a fountain dripping from stone ledge to stone ledge, where the gravel paths intersected near the front door. After we had wandered around for half an hour or so, Nico dabbing her eyes with a handkerchief and muttering to herself in Italian, Gully showed up in a rented Ford. She was utterly unlike Nico: no hint of foreignness and no charm. The only thing I recognized in Gully that I had also encountered in Nico was a ruthless egotism which boded ill for the negotiations.

Nico was desperate to get some cash but Gully didn't want to sell. Although I had only just turned twenty and knew virtually nothing about property or the law, they both seemed happy to use me as a go-between as well as advisor. That first morning, the three of us talked in the garden to the hum of bees, Gully's impatience and Nico's sorrow only occasionally disturbing the tranquil beauty of the place. But as the days passed, things got worse. The meetings moved indoors; chairs were dusted off and papers strewn over marble-topped tables. When I suggested leaving them alone, Nico insisted that I stay, although frequently she would flare up at Gully: "I need a break from this. I'll be back in an hour." Then she would take my arm and guide me to the car so I could drive her down the street to the village bar, where she would knock back a few brandies. Sitting in the little tavern like a cave with whitewashed walls, she would relax, throwing her head back to laugh with the locals, and shouting out witticisms in Italian, which she sometimes translated for me. Sooner or later, in a moment of alcoholic sorrow, she would grip my arm tightly. "Oh, Judy, Judy!" she would moan. "It's my father's house, where I grew up. Oh, D'o, D'o! That woman should not end up with it!" And she would wipe her eyes with a piece of fine lace and put her lips close to my ear. "I love you so much," she would say. And I believed her.

Although this visit, like so much of my time with Nico, was fraught with melodrama, there were also moments that shone through with great clarity—moments that seemed to put the whole careening affair into a kind of stasis. I remember sitting on a little ottoman next to the dressing table in our room, while Nico cleaned her face and put on her makeup. This was something I had loved to do in Wales, where she sat at a mirror in the bay window of her bedroom, looking out over the greens and grays of the valley. As she wiped the cream off her skin, her face always seemed to emerge with a kind of naked vulnerability that, at first, scared me. I didn't know this pale, ordinary woman, who seemed unrelated to the magnificent figure that Nico had made of herself and that had assumed epic proportions in my fantasy world. I wasn't even sure if I wanted to know her. But here in Italy, as she caught my eyes in the mirror, I felt a surge of protectiveness as she sighed, reached for a cigarette, and began to paint on her face. Later, I would wonder about that so rarely exposed face, and realize that I had never really known what lay underneath the public Nico—what fears stirred under the sophistication; what history lay buried under the vodka and the whiskey. For her, our intimacy was just another kind of show, a role that she adopted and discarded with ease as it suited her. And for me, half a child, half an adult, stunned into a confusing numbness by my parents' sudden deaths, the show worked just fine, even while those moments at the mirror fixed themselves into my memory, hinting at what I would never understand.

Six days after the rendezvous in Turin, I took Nico to the airport. We had reached an agreement with Gully, renewed our passion, and, as usual, were about to go our separate ways. I wasn't looking forward to the eighteen-hour drive back to Figueras, or to the busloads of tourists I would continue to guide around the Perelada wine cellars for another two months before I could return to England and, perhaps, see Nico again. Longing to throw myself into her arms and kiss her passionately, I tolerated, instead, her public "aunt and niece" display, as she kissed me on both cheeks and held my hands in hers for a moment. "Thank you darling," she said, already turning toward the gate. And then, almost over her shoulder, she said, "You've been an angel. Where would I be without you?"

After that summer in Italy, we continued to write and call. For another year, or perhaps two, we met occasionally and made love whenever we could. I'm vague about the time involved because mostly I pretended it wasn't happening—even while being obsessively in love. When we were alone together, we never talked about our relationship, which led me to accept that it was an unspeakable—and consequently unthinkable—thing.

It ended when I transferred my desperate passion to another woman, even though I continued to meet Nico for a while longer, without telling her what else was going on. At first, this new development threatened to break through my denial about what I was doing: falling in love with one woman could be an aberration, but doing it twice surely created some kind of pattern. I was accustomed to lying to everyone and to seeing myself as some kind of pervert, but now I was presented with a terrifying vista of the future. This was not the life I had anticipated. I had always been a good girl—even a *nice* girl. I'd been a top student at my all-girls school. All I'd known of sex was a few kisses in the back seats of cars with boyfriends I hadn't much liked. But now my life was doomed. I would forever be skulking in unsavory places. I'd never have friends I could talk to. I was possessed of a horrible secret.

I didn't really *think* all this. I didn't have the words or the knowledge of how "people like me" lived so that I could process it in sentences. But it was, nevertheless, enveloping me in its wordless set of terrors when Nico came to London to see some old friends for a few days and demanded that on her last evening I join her for dinner at a restaurant. Afterward, driving her back to the station to catch the night train to Wales, I stopped under a tree along Birdcage Walk near Buckingham Palace and cut the engine.

Turning to face her in the dim illumination of a streetlight, I said bitterly, "I've fallen in love with another woman and it's your fault. You've turned me into a lesbian."

It was the first time I had ever uttered the word and I intended it as an epithet. Indeed, Nicolette recoiled from it as if I had struck her. There was silence except for the ubiquitous hum of big-city life, and I glared at her, burning with righteous indignation as she shrank away from me, apparently silenced by the power of that word we both so dreaded. "Now, Judy darling," she began finally, reaching a gloved hand out toward me, but I interrupted the speech I knew was coming. I didn't want to hear how she was sure I would meet a perfect young man and that this was just a difficult time for all of us—whoever "all of us" were. "I'm taking you to the station," I said. And did.

We continued to drift apart, although, of course, we were still connected by the family, and when I did, as she had predicted, get married to a young man, though not, as she had also predicted, a perfect one, she was there at the wedding, in the second pew, sobbing loudly. Eleven months later, having realized my mistake, I left the marriage and began to come to terms with being a lesbian. The word transformed itself into something altogether different, as I found other lesbians and left behind my suicidal shame and my *Well of Loneliness* kind of existence. Eventually, I started to regret that night in the car on Birdcage Walk.

By this time more than seven years had passed since the Wales days, and Guy and Nico were living in Wiltshire, renting another in a long line of country cottages attached to large estates. This time they were enjoying their proximity to several market towns, which meant for Guy some new horse-world acquaintances, and for Nico a selection of pubs and off-licenses where she could buy on credit. One spring Sunday, I drove down there through the rolling green of Berkshire and turned into a long, tree-lined driveway that stretched away from the stone pillars at the turnoff. After a while, the drive curved around to a sweep of gravel in front of the Georgian mansion, where a carriage and four would have seemed more appropriate than my little purple Austin mini with the bright red women's symbols stenciled onto the doors. Following Nico's directions, I skirted the great house and bumped along a grassy track to their cottage, where I ducked my head through the doorway and found the two of them preparing a haphazard meal. Nico was far from sober. I tried not to remember all those nights when she had passed out and I had undressed her and put her to bed; the time she had fallen down the stairs; the sickness and the maudlin tears. It had been a while since I'd seen her, but I quickly remembered how to adopt the cheerful pretense that all was well, as I toured the house and then settled down to chopping carrots.

As always, preparing lunch took way too long, and it wasn't until after three o'clock that the three of us sat down to roast leg of lamb, amply flavored with rosemary, and slightly blackened roast potatoes. When we finally cleared away the plates, Uncle Guy wandered off to take a nap, while Nico and I moved into the shabby living room.

"I've wanted to tell you," I began, but Nico, perhaps sensing that something she didn't want to hear was about to invade her house, interrupted me.

"Let me make some coffee," she said, and hurried into the kitchen. When we sat down again with the little Italian coffeepot between us, I said firmly, "Now, let me tell you what I want to say."

Nico looked nervous, but laughed and said, "Go ahead, go ahead! You young people are so intense with your speeches about things!"

"It's about that night in London—you remember, when we stopped in the car and I told you that you had turned me into a lesbian."

Nico shifted uncomfortably and muttered, "Long ago . . . old history," but I continued.

"Well," I said, "I know better than that now. I want you to know two things: First of all, I would've been a lesbian even if I'd never met you. You didn't make me one. And secondly, however I came to be a lesbian, I'm not sorry about it anymore. In fact, I'm glad. It's all right with me, it really is."

Nico sipped her black coffee, which, judging from the smell, had a large shot of whiskey in it, and looked at me speculatively.

"But you must get married," she said at last. "I know it didn't work out that first time, but you can always try again. You can't live with women all your life."

"Of course I can," I said sharply, annoyed at how out of touch she was with the new world I had so recently discovered.

"But, Judy," she pleaded. "At least find a man who'll turn a blind eye . . ."

But I wasn't about to look for a fake marriage. "You wait and see," I said. "It'll work out fine."

Nico went to the kitchen and poured herself another drink. I started to get out of my chair to follow her; I wanted to convince her—to make her see everything the way I now saw it. But the slightly sweet smell of alcohol lingered in the air and something told me that Nico wasn't going to be glad for me, no matter how hard I tried.

Years later, after a bout of shock therapy (which she claimed had erased all her memories of the years in Wales) and several periods of drying out in various institutions, Nico got into a recovery program and gave up drinking. After she became sober, I heard about her only from family members, most of whom had mellowed over the years, feeling sorry for her after Guy died and she grew old alone. I had moved to Oregon and made a life with my lover far enough away for only intermittent family news to come my way. I didn't hear about it

when she was finally hospitalized for the emphysema that all those cigarettes had left her with, but I did get news of her death in time to
consider flying from Oregon to England for the funeral.

I considered it carefully. For thirty years I had gone back and forth:
sometimes sorry for her, as fragments of tenderness fluttered alive in
my memory, more often furious at her for taking advantage of me at
that particularly vulnerable moment in my life. She had been twenty
years older than me, as well as my aunt, and the stories of incest sur-
vivors had resonated strongly with me during the angry years. By
allowing our bond to become sexual, she had isolated me from any
possible source of support, while proving quite incapable of helping
me into the grieving process herself. What's more, her homophobia
had strongly reinforced my own, putting me in serious danger of suicide. And yet at nineteen I was not entirely a child. Emotionally imma-
ture as I had been, still I had been complicit in the affair. I had wooed
her with long-stemmed red roses and love letters. I had driven five hundred miles for a chance to light her cigarettes. I had rolled around, crying with laughter, when she spun a wicked tale about Gully or imitated
the stuffed shirts at some dinner party. I couldn't deny the triumphant
joy I had felt at flexing my own seductive muscles for the first time.

These contradictions, and my inability to reconcile them, domi-
nated my life for many years. I wrote in my journal. I went through
therapy. Affairs came and went. I fought the old shame, learned not to
lie, and removed the erotic charge from secrecy, but the final step
eluded me: how to reconcile the starstruck, victimized child I had
been at nineteen with the young adult who strode bravely into her les-
bianism on the arm of an alcoholic and very damaged older woman.
That's a task that will surely continue for my whole life.

I decided not to go to the funeral. I had missed my chance: now it
was too late to convince her that my life was one I chose happily. She
hadn't been able to see it as a possibility but I could and did live my
life with women—one in particular. Nico carried on to the end believ-
ing that lesbians were an unspeakable subject and that she herself,
having had three husbands, was in no danger of being mistaken for
one.

I speak with confidence about this, even though I hadn't seen her
for more than two decades, because of something that happened just
a couple of years before her death. When I turned fifty, my friends,
who were organizing a big party for me, solicited written memories

from all kinds of people to put together in an album. For some reason, I put Nico on the list, and my friend Phyllis Oster, part of the "Friends of Judith Barrington Committee," sent her the request. Nico's letter, sent by return mail, might once have provoked me to anger, but now simply made me sad.

These were her final words to me:

Dear Miss Oster,

Thank you for your communication of the 4th May.

I don't know that I would call myself "Friend of Judith Barrington" but I am certainly her aunt; I am the widow of her paternal uncle, Guy Barrington.

Judith stayed with us for a time at our home in Wales, after the tragedy of her parents' death. After that we did not see much of her—she went to the United States not long after. I enclose a not very good photograph of her at that period.

Please give her my good wishes and congratulations on her achieving her half century on the 7th July.

Yours sincerely,

Nicolette Barrington

# How a Lady Dies

**EMMA DONOGHUE**

Breathing hardly seems worth the trouble today. Elizabeth lets out her shallow mouthful of air. Her shoulders subside; her head sinks back against the obelisk. She stares up at the tapering stone, but the sight dizzies her. Her eyelids fall. Fur is soft against her cheekbones.

There, between the breaths, is peace. A little more air seeps away between her withered lips. The forest inside her ribs is emptying. No sound, nothing stirring, no fear, nor inclination. How the end will come. This winter, surely. Perhaps this very month. Could it be today?

This is all she has to do, thinks Elizabeth with a sudden inspiration. No vulgar act of self-destruction is called for; nothing to trouble her conscience or her taste. It is necessary only to relinquish: the daily effort, the stale cold air.

Her whole self hisses away through the crack of her mouth. Her stomach gives a startling rumble. She feels it fold in on itself. Soon she will be quite hollowed out. The weight on her chest grows, but she tells herself not to tremble, not to resist, not to bother with another breath.

"Elizabeth?"

The voice of love is a noose. It keeps you dangling between two worlds.

Her lungs suck in a huge mouthful of air. Her stays crack mightily, like a ship turning into the wind. How this worthless body fights for life.

She turns to see her friend's anxious face, cooped up in a silk bonnet. Dark eyes, a high forehead traced like paper. By the world's standards, a plain woman, twenty years past her best. "I am only resting, my dear," Elizabeth murmurs.

"Do you feel a little better in yourself today?" suggests Frances.

"Indeed," faintly.

The only thing one can do in Bath that one did not do the day before is die. This is the undisputed bon mot of the season of 1759. Mrs. Montagu's words will be misquoted long after these swarms of visitors have dispersed to their respective altars and graves.

Every year more yellowstone houses seize their share of tawny light. Every day more carriages scurry across the valley. Each duke married off is replaced by another five; every beggar arrested leaves room for fifty more. What was once a gracious maiden of a town has become a bloated dowager.

Bath is known for social rules and hard drinking, exquisite refinement and filthy jokes. Money is the air it breathes. Half a guinea to the Bellringers to herald your arrival, another to the City Waits for the obligatory serenade, then two guineas' subscription to Harrison's Rooms, where the tea is only ever lukewarm. People come to Bath to take the waters, but also to take the air in the Orange Grove, to take heart at the sight of a handsome face. They take their turns at scandal and glory, pleasure and spleen; they take their time about living and dying. The town is full of sound lungs proclaiming their sickness, old men insisting on their youth, married women whispering their unhappiness.

"That's Miss Pennington," the gossips say; "she does not dance." Which, in Bath code, means: spare your breath. Her partner is bony and invisible. The lady's not for marrying.

Miss Elizabeth Pennington is a fortune, past twenty-five and still a spinster. Friends blame her health. Enemies blame her finickiness. She has come to Bath in the care of a humble companion, Mrs. Sheridan. ("Wife to the theater man, don't you know. With a houseful of children left at home.") Both ladies are vicar's daughters, but there the resemblance ends. The younger has all the money, it is said, and the elder all the wit.

What the gossips don't know is that a year ago Elizabeth turned up on her friend's doorstep in Covent Garden without a word of warning. "I am come to take up my abode with you," she stuttered, absurdly biblical. Words memorized in the hired carriage, sentences stiff with anticipated disappointment.

"I find it impossible to live without you."

She strained for a breath.

"You may shut your doors against me—"

The doors swung open.

She lived all that year with Frances and her Mr. Sherry and her children. Elizabeth taught the smaller ones Aesop's fables, poured tea for Sherry's visitors, and could always be relied upon to have read their latest works. When the new baby came, the Sheridans named her Betsy, in Elizabeth's honor.

She made sure to make herself indispensable. Sherry joked that his wife had no need of his company anymore; he stayed out late with poets and ballet masters. In letters from home, the Reverend Pennington asked his daughter with increasing querulousness how long her friend would require her. Elizabeth answered only with remarks on the weather.

She picked at her food, and fed the best bits to the baby. Whenever she was taken by a coughing fit, that long winter, she covered her mouth with one of her two dozen handkerchiefs, each of them trimmed with the best Bruges lace.

Frances refused to be alarmed by her friend's husky voice, the violet tinge about her eyes. All her darling Elizabeth needed was a trip to Bath: taking the waters and seeing the sights would restore anyone to perfect health. Especially one so young. Especially one so worthy of all life held in store.

And what could Sherry do but agree? What husband could object, except a brute? What could any man say who had the slightest sense of the exquisite force of female friendship?

They promised to write to him weekly. They left the baby with a good clean nurse. Before dawn Elizabeth is shaken awake by the rattle of carts, the bawling of muffin men.

"I declare," yawns Frances beside her in a perfect imitation of Lady Danebury, "this is such a fatiguing life, I scarce have strength to rise!"

This town was designed by the sick; every hour a different amusement keeps death at bay. At sunrise they go to the Bath in sedan chairs; the chair men's puffing breaths leave white trails on the air. The first time Elizabeth saw a bathing costume, she was so appalled she laughed out loud, but now she pulls on the yellow canvas jacket and petticoat and thinks nothing of it. What she shrinks from is the moment of ducking under the arch and wading out into the basin, under the gray sky. The water scalds, even on the coldest mornings. Elizabeth cannot help imagining that she is being boiled down to the bone, rendered into soup.

Oblivious to the heat that flushes their cheeks, ladies stand and gossip with their necessaries laid out on little floating trays: snuffboxes, pomanders, nosegays wilting fast. Clouds of yellow steam fill the air. In a far corner, Frances has her bad leg pumped on. She chats with the pump man as if he were family; she lacks any sense of the gulf between herself and the lower orders. Elizabeth can always make out her friend's voice in a crowd; still full of Dublin, after all these years.

Two boys dive in, raising wings of water. Elizabeth holds down her stiff skirts so no one can snatch at them. She tells herself that no one is looking at her, but lodgings crowd around the Bath, and footmen and beggars ring the walls, pointing out the fairest faces, the greatest dowries. One day someone threw a cat in, and there was a wonder: it could swim.

Elizabeth backs against a pillar, light-headed. She pulls her handkerchief from her straw hat to wipe her cheeks. She sinks deeper into the water, and fiery fingers lay hold of her stiff shoulders; for a moment she is relieved to the point of tears. She shuts her eyes and tells herself to trust in the waters. So many, of all ranks of life, have been cured, even some three times her age; there is a marble cross in the corner, hung with discarded crutches. Why can she not believe?

It seems to her now that these are the waters of death in which disease leaks from one frail body to another. The ghostly smell of bad eggs fills up her nostrils, and a stained plaster floats by. Flakes of snow drift down from the sky, then turn to rain; the whole world is made of vapor.

"My dearest?"

That smile that sustains her, like daily bread.

When Elizabeth climbs up the steps to join Frances, her costume weighs on her so she cannot breathe. But then again, she cannot remember when she last drew breath without a struggle. When she was a girl? A child? At home, there was an oak tree; surely she climbed it?

The Guides are stained brown from the waters. They tell her how well she looks today. Such a lie is worth half a crown each.

The leather of the sedan chair is still wet from the last customer. "Home now, and quick about it, before Miss Pennington takes cold!"

orders Mrs. Sheridan. Her voice is sharp with borrowed authority. But she has omitted to tip the chair man in advance; she finds it hard to persuade herself to make free with her young friend's fortune. Out of spite the man leaves the curtains open, so the rain drifts in on Elizabeth's eyelids. The streets are clogged with barrows.

Back in bed, the ladies keep the blankets over their heads to make themselves sweat out the poisons. Outside the muddy window, the pattens strapped to strangers' feet clink like blackbirds. To distract her friend from the cough that doubles her up, Frances recites some new phrases she overheard in the Bath. "My dear girl is vastly embellished, she is a perfect progeny of learning," she squeaks. "La, my dear, you put me in a terrible agility!" Lying there, chuckling and wheezing, Elizabeth should be perfectly happy. She is happier, at least, than she has ever been in her short and narrow life. Is she not here, in Bath, with Frances, the two of them curtained in their bed, forgetting fathers and husbands and children and all, shedding the ordinary world?

By eight in the morning the ladies are at the Pump Room, listening to the violins and forcing down the water.

"I declare," confides Mrs. Thorne, "I am laced so tight today my stomach is sore."

On the other side of the pillar, Lady Bennet sucks in her chalky cheeks. "I never put on red in all my life." Words fill the air like feathers, moving too fast to catch. "Your lordship's immensely good." "Nay, I grant you, he dresses prodigiously." "Oh, lud!" "Oh, monstrous!"

"Miss Pennington? La, she'll not last till Easter."

Elizabeth lowers her eyes and sips her glass of warm metallic water. For a moment she has the impression she is drinking blood. Frances must have overheard the Captain too; she gets two red spots high on her cheeks, and twice in a row she tells her young friend how becoming her lavender pelisse is.

Elizabeth knows better, knows what Frances cannot know, must never find out. She knows she wants to die.

The doctors think a young lady of fortune must have everything to live for. Each doctor who visits assures her that he knows where to fix the blame: frailty in the family, damp in the bones, tight lacing and spiced food, an excess of exercise or education, too many baths. One recommends enemas; another, marriage. Miss Pennington thanks them all and pays their fees without a murmur. She is coming to realize how very rich she is. If she was only a pauper, this dying would have been over with long ago.

At Mr. Leake's booksellers Elizabeth and Frances browse through the latest poems about the antiquities of Bath and the pleasures of melancholy. But they like the old books best. Sometimes they spend the morning on a sofa, reading aloud their favorite letters from their dear Mr. Richardson's *Clarissa*. Elizabeth often asks Frances for the scene in which Anna comes to see her dead Clary's body. "My sweet clay-cold friend," Anna cries, trying to kiss some heat back into the corpse; "my sweet clay-cold friend, awake."

Halfway through that letter, Frances glances up from the page to rest her eyes, and for a moment her gaze admits it. Acknowledges that Elizabeth is not simply ailing, not simply weak in her spirits. Truth flickers in the air between the two of them. And then Frances snaps the book shut and remarks, "How well that yellow lace becomes you!"

Elizabeth loves her most for the lies.

Frances hopes one day to write a novel. The heroine will meet unhappiness on every page, but she will never stop being good. She has never mentioned it to Sherry; she would prefer to surprise him. Elizabeth is the only one to know of her plan.

It occurs to Elizabeth that her friend is misled by the younger woman's pale, slim face, her gentle expression, her occasional verses. An unmarried, invalid lady is too easily assumed to be all soul, all sweetness. Frances seems to think that because the good suffer in this imperfect world, those who suffer must be good. Has she never peered into the back of Elizabeth's eyes and seen the greed, the rage, the morbid longings? How well does she know her friend, for all her devotion?

Elizabeth cannot face the public breakfast, held every morning at eleven. On good days, Frances may prevail upon her to visit a pastry cook's for a jelly or a tart. Elizabeth always tries a bite or two, then lays her spoon down unobtrusively and pushes the plate toward her friend, an inch at a time. Frances takes mouthfuls between her eager sentences.

They might try on hats at a milliner's, or visit the ladies' coffee-house, where Elizabeth sips the sweet black brew till the dizziness retreats to a distance. If the day is mild and the gutters stink, they buy violets to hold to their noses. They cross the path of the same people five times a day, with a curtsy for each, like nodding marionettes.

There's Mr. Allen, noted for benevolence; Mr. Quin, once the king of the stage; Mr. Gainsborough, whose rooms are stuffed with handsome ladies and their handsomer portraits.

Red-faced servants trundle wheelchairs up and down the streets. Elizabeth avoids the eyes of the desiccated women who let themselves be rolled along. But then she makes herself give one of them a civil nod. She need not stiffen at the creak of a wheelchair; she need have no fear, for herself, of such a drawn-out old age.

Down by the river, the ladies stand and look across at the sweet wooded curves in the distance. "Someday we'll drive to the hills," says Frances. "When you are feeling more like yourself."

If Elizabeth can catch a breath today, she and Frances will walk up to see the Circus. Mr. Wood is always there, overseeing the buildings his father dreamed of; this will be the first street in the world to form a perfect circle. He points out where the tiers of Doric columns will rise, where the Ionian, where the Corinthian. The ladies smile with their mouths shut, so as not to yawn. Elizabeth tries to imagine being needed by the world, having such projects, reasons to stay alive.

The wind pours down North Parade and soaks right through her. The air moves past her mouth too fast for her lips to catch. She stands still, waiting for a breath to come her way, utterly insubstantial. It occurs to her that she died some weeks ago and never noticed. Perhaps she is not the only one. Perhaps the whole city is populated with ghosts, and their faces are made of powder, and their hooped skirts are empty as bells.

"Race you to the bottom of the hill," says Frances with light irony. Elizabeth starts to laugh, soundlessly. She slides her arm into the elder's and offers her whole weight. Interlocked, they set off on the infinitely slow walk down.

Everyone goes to the Abbey at noon. Above the great door, stone angels on ladders climb to heaven and let themselves down to earth. Joyous and polite, they wait their turn, even the ones whose heads have been worn away by centuries of rain.

Elizabeth and Frances like to sit at the back. Bright colored light drips through the windows. Today the sermon is on Gethsemane. Then saith he unto them, My soul is exceeding sorrowful, even unto death; tarry ye here, and watch with me.

Her pale hand and her friend's brown-spotted one lie together on the pew. What, could ye not watch with me one hour? She steals a look at Frances, her serious profile, the drag of the skin around her eyes. The church is full of people, but for Elizabeth the world has narrowed to one face.

Watch and pray, that ye enter not into temptation: the spirit indeed is willing, but the flesh is weak.

If Elizabeth feels up to it, she argues with her Creator. Her illness, she tells Him, is none of her making. But this is only partly true, and she knows it. True, in Elizabeth's lungs, there is a sickness like a dreadful guest who sits and sits and will not leave. But in her heart squats the sickness that will not let her eat, will not let her live. Not long, at any rate. No longer than this companionship will be permitted to last; no longer than she may wake every morning to the soft nape of Frances' neck.

Her favorite part of the day is when they linger after the service and read the memorial tablets. Thro' painful suff'rings, tranquil to the last, Thy lips no murmurs, no repinings passed. . . . Some are in the shape of urns, bulging like stomachs from the wall; others are fallen columns. In testimony of regard to the memory of a pearl beyond price, this monument is erected by her much afflicted husband. One tablet is meant to be a curtain; the marble ripples beneath the letters. A woman truly amiable . . . translated into another world . . .

"This one lived to the age of ninety-two," marvels Frances.

Elizabeth leans over her friend's shoulder. Their cheeks are not an inch apart. What she has never explained to Frances is that she is choosing phrases for her own inscription. . . . *though sudden to her friends yet not to her,* as appears by these verses found in her closet after her decease . . . No, Elizabeth has written nothing worth marble. Her verses are thin leaden things. Nothing to leave behind her, then. Only a share in a much divided heart. . . . *but to none could her merits be so well known as to her affectionate friend, who considered her as her support, her comfort and advisor . . .*

"Here comes Mr. Lampton," hisses Frances in her ear, "and we've still not called on his mother." . . . *whose grief must be as lasting as breath . . .*

But how lasting is that? Elizabeth leans on a pew, wheezing. Darkness comes and goes about her eyes.

"My dear? Are you ill?" asks Frances. . . . *who henceforth can look to no happiness but in the hope of reunion with the dear departed in a happier world.*

That is the thought Elizabeth clings to. The other world, the only real world, when she and Frances will have outrun time. When need and guilt and incomprehension will have fallen away like hairs from a brush. Where the two friends may stroll forever between soft green trees.

They dine at three. How sweet, the press of a worried hand on one's wrist. But eating seems inconceivable. Elizabeth's mouth will only open the width of a finger, and the beef smells of blood. She has the impression that wine drains through her as the rain through peat; that food is too slippery to glue itself to her bones. If her friend bullies her to eat, tears begin to collect in her plate.

"Oh, my dear, my dear!"

The ladies sip port to celebrate the anniversary of their meeting. They forget to write to Sherry and the children. Elizabeth feels a terrible delight.

At five they go to the Theater, or to Harrison's Rooms. Lady Cholmondeley complains about the servants. "The very teeth in one's head aren't safe, if one sleeps with one's mouth open!" Every table has a literary lady or two. There sits Mrs. Scott, a little pockmarked authoress who lives at Batheaston with a female friend. It is said her husband tried to poison her before she ran away from him. "She is much to be compassionated, poor soul . . ."

For a moment, sipping her thin tea, Elizabeth lets herself imagine Sherry as a murderer. As a man who deserves to have his wife stolen away from him, before he wears her out with bearing a dozen children. But having lived in his house all year, observed his kindness and his chatter, Elizabeth knows the worst that can be said is that he is a bit of a bore. He has never seen his wife for the wonder she is; he has no idea of his luck.

Every other lady's friend is content with her share, she reminds herself, biting down on the frail edge of her cup. What would the world come to if they asked for more?

There is a Dress Ball each evening at six. Elizabeth refuses every gentlemen who asks her: "I regret my health does not permit . . ." Two hours of minuets, then an hour of old-style country dances; the young ladies go off to remove their hoops so as not to bruise themselves. Frances taps her foot and says it is not proper for a married lady to dance. Elizabeth always overcomes her friend's objections by the end of the evening. She smiles as she watches the older woman whirl across the floor with one widower after another.

But every night feels like the last night. Elizabeth sucks the marrow of pleasure out of each hour like a starving dog. This cannot go on.

"Quadrille!" cries Lord Humphry. "Ombre," contradicts his sister.

Now the ladies look on, and fan themselves; the rooms are airless. Elizabeth watches Frances out of the corner of her eye. She knows there are limits to what a friend may ask, even the dearest of friends. She knows their stay was never meant to last so long. Any day now, Elizabeth must let Frances go home to her family, to the baby she will barely recognize. This is where the story ends.

When the gaming is over, there is an auction at which an Ethiopian girl sells for five guineas. "Vastly amusing," shrieks her new owner. Elizabeth meets the small milky eyes of the child and feels all at once that she may faint. Blackness covers her like a cloth thrown over a birdcage.

Frances rushes her home at once, with a linkboy stumbling ahead with his torch. They pass two women in bleached aprons. "Harlots," whispers Frances in her friend's ear. Elizabeth clings to her arm. Her breath echoes in the narrow street. In, out, so regular, so unstoppable. Elizabeth tries to match her own breathing to her friend's. She turns painfully on her side and watches Frances' face in the moonlight that leaks through the window, across the pillow. Soft lines score the lofty forehead: a face worn out with feeling. Who does Frances love? Her spendthrift Sherry, her big Tom, her Charlie boy, her Dick the Dunce, her pretty Lissy, her baby Betsy. . . . How can she have any love left? Yet it seems to come as easy as sweat. She even manages to love Elizabeth, this dry husk of womanhood lying beside her, bitter, unsleeping. Sister of my heart, she calls her, sometimes.

But the latest letter from Sherry is under the pillow. Elizabeth read it by candlelight while Frances was downstairs shouting at the chambermaid to fetch a compress for Miss Pennington's chest. Her hand shook as she opened the letter; she almost set the edge on fire. One word told her all she needed: "Dublin."

The friends have had their season.

I find it impossible to live without you. If Frances were to wake now, this minute, and ask her, look her in the eye and ask, "What is the matter with you?"—that is all Elizabeth could say, like a child repeating her one lesson.

I find it impossible to live.

She cannot remember how she got through the days before Bath, before London, how she bore the weight of her short life without Frances to share it. And still less can she conceive of how she is to live, in a week or a month or two at most, when Frances and her family will go back to Dublin. Impossible.

A rough sea, a universe away.

She coughs, stifling it in the pillow. Then she lets herself cough louder. If she sounds bad enough, the older woman will wake from her shallow sleep and tend to her. She will stroke her friend's forehead, cluck over her tenderly. If Elizabeth coughs hard enough to wet the pillow, Frances will surely kiss her face. If she stays awake all night, she will look even paler in the morning, and Frances will scold her and coddle her and bring her hot wine. If she cannot breathe, in the bad time before dawn, Frances will lift her in her own arms and count her breaths for her.

As long as she keeps getting worse, Frances will stay.

Such thoughts, such weakness. Is it her body that's diseased or her mind? In the dark, Elizabeth cannot remember how to be good. How do they endure, those heroines of novels? A tear burns its way through her lashes. Today she is weaker than yesterday, when she was weaker than the day before. She's eaten nothing to speak of for a fortnight. Sitting in the Abbey at noon, Elizabeth's eyes drift up the walls, across the floor. Every inch is inscribed; the place is crowded with names, packed tight like a gala ball for the dead.

She glides out of her stiff body, slips through the stained-glass windows, soars up into the aromatic streets. She hovers round the Abbey, grips with one white smoky hand the stone ladder that the blunt-toed angels are climbing. She watches, she waits. How will it be?

She sees Frances roaming the streets, the ribbons of her bonnet hanging loose. Forgetful of her family, red-eyed for a year, heartsore for the rest of her life. Frances, transformed into a greedy girl on the doorstep of Heaven, knocking furiously, ready to make her demands.

Even within the dream, Elizabeth feels the implausibility of this. Suddenly she can see another Frances, a gray-haired Frances, revisiting Bath, only a little melancholy when she glances down South Parade to the stone bench where she used to sit with "poor Miss Pennington." And all around the visitor, the barrows and stalls and colliding sedan chairs, the nitty-gritty of Bath life going on just as ever, oblivious to the words etched on marble in the Abbey.

Elizabeth comes back to the present, to a warm hand wrapping itself around hers. This is what it comes down to: a firm grip that banishes past and future.

Feeling a tickle in her lungs, she withdraws her fingers apologetically, searching for her handkerchief. No one turns a head; racking coughs are no novelty in Bath. But Elizabeth stares into her snowy handkerchief at the bold red flag death has planted there.

She folds it over and over till only white shows.

Not yet. Please. I did not mean, I did not know, I thought—

Impossible.

Down the aisle, her heels resounding. Scandalized whispers on every side. "What ill-breeding, to run off from Service!"

I am only twenty-five.

She bursts through the great double doors of the Abbey as if they were veils. Out in the watery sunshine, she takes a great breath. And another.

Frances is at her elbow.

Elizabeth presses her fingers against her friend's hot mouth before she can say a word. "We have so little time," she whispers.

Tonight, Miss Pennington will dance.

# kays and exes

**CAROLYN A. CLARK**

Club grrrl sits on a corner lot at a T intersection, the outer walls the orange of rusty metal. A lavender neon sign hangs above the entrance. It spells g-r-r-r-l in cursive writing. Whenever I drive by in rush-hour traffic, I get lost in that third *r* as if it were a twisted chromosome, or the missing link. The club is as good as the missing link for my ex-girlfriend, Casey. I lost it in the breakup as we meted out territory like tribal warriors. Tonight, six months later, I break the pact as my lover, Kelly, and I enter through a maze of women standing out front, through the two musclemen guarding the door, the only men we'll see all night, through a dimly lit alcove where a young dark-haired woman greets us with a conspiratorial smile and asks for the cover, a relatively cheap five bucks. She stamps our hands with a Celtic design the size of a quarter.

It's Pride Weekend, so we've been walking all day, screaming on the streets, we're here, we're queer, get used to it. I'm dressed for marching in baggy overalls and a white tank top. At first I worry that we're underdressed. This is the club I describe to my San Francisco friends as the chi-chi girls' club, good for people watching. They nod doubtfully. To them chi-chi equals shallow. But as it turns out everyone else came straight from the Dyke March too. Because it's Pride Weekend, the place is packed. We automatically search the flushed faces for the ones we know.

We're standing in the doorway of the main room, taking off our jackets, adjusting our vision to the dark air, misty with smoke, when Kelly asks, "Is that Casey?"

"Where?" My eyes scan the scene, several women walking in different directions, others in conversation behind cocktails and ashtrays on short round tables.

"There, walking across the room." Kelly almost points. My breath hits my heels as I notice the long wavy hair the color of sand, the wide shoulders swinging side to side in Casey's trademark walk.

"Yeah, it's her."

"Shall we head in, Claire? I have to pee."

"Uh, I need a beer." I do an about-face and march to the kidney-shaped bar behind us in the first room. A red room. The shelves above the bar are filled with rows of exotic bottles, bottles I can empty thoughts into, empty memories into, reminding me of our last fight over a small shapely bottle acquired on a trip to Manhattan to visit her mother, who didn't know Casey fucked girls, namely me. We wandered into a hot sauce shop called Kapow and bought some Scorned Woman, on special. With a name like that we couldn't resist. One day after we broke up, I went to spice my taco and it was gone. Later, on the phone Casey reminded me that it was the perfect hangover remedy. She would need it more than I would.

"I'll have a Heineken. Kelly, look at that blue tequila bottle." I bounce my thigh against the bar in time to the music.

"I still have to pee. You are going to introduce me to her, aren't you?" Kelly knows all about Casey but has only seen her in photos.

"Yeah. Just give me a minute." To breathe, I want to say.

We wind through the crowd to meet our friends up front by the stage. We've come to see the Murmurs. They're a New York band, all girls. The singer's name is Heather and she looks like she's been marching all day with us. The other lead singer, Leisha, has us ogling within minutes, large lips, dark eyes on a broad pale face under cropped black hair, yellow baby doll dress with logger boots.

"So we're here. We finally made it out of the bedroom and into Club grrrl. Is this okay? Are we too close to the stage for you?" I have to ask because Kelly's been dying to go dancing, and I'm not sure if a live show will suffice. In the short time we've been together, we've learned to avoid assumptions. Kelly's more modest about getting naked even though she's got a labia piercing that makes me wince. And I'm the health nut with a drug history that is so foreign to Kelly she teases me about it.

"It's fine, Claire." She tugs the straps of my overalls for emphasis.

"Okay. It might get kinda crazy up here but I don't mind if you don't mind."

"No, not at all." Kelly looks up at the band. I don't know if she understands what I mean by crazy but I decide not to worry about it.

As the band warms up, two groupies in front of us begin to jump up and down slowly, like kangaroos, suspended in the air for a moment before they land on terra firma. The energy is contagious. They twirl around to stare behind them with bright liquid x eyes. One of them is a smaller slimmer version of the other, but they look the same, same pierced navels, same striped T-shirts, colored rings of Saturn around their breasts. The bassist hangs back in the corner. I focus on the drummer through Leisha's knees. Leisha has shaved. There is a small nick on her shin.

Soon the pack of women begins to sway, we grow pelagic, flipping, frothing. We're jostled left and right. I get nostalgic and lean into Kelly, craving contact. Then kd lang comes out of nowhere. Earlier I thought there was someone who looked like her standing next to Kelly. She had the floppy brown hair, the thin lips and big shoulders of kd, but she wasn't tall enough to fit the Big-Boned Girl from Southern Alberta image. Yet here she is, slamming, lifting, tossing girl bodies into the air—large hands on thick torso flesh. I cringe for belly piercings. The Murmurs roll from hypersonic "Sucker Upper, Starfucker" into lazy stone-eyed "I'm a Mess" and the mosh subsides. Soon whispers rush through the crowd.

I came out the same year kd came out to the press. Her announcement both grounded and repelled me. I grilled my friends about it for a few days. "Why'd she have to?" "Because she wanted to be free." "Didn't everyone already know?" "Of course, but not officially." Who knew the closet had so many shelves? Casey loved kd and wore out the repeat button when we made love.

Heather talks too much between songs. I never would have known this, but she points it out to us. "They tell me I talk too much between songs. They. So I'm trying to cut down, but I do have to introduce someone special tonight. This is Grandma Phyllis," she shouts, gesturing toward an enlarged photo of an old woman plastered to the bass drum. She sports brown penciled eyebrows, baby blue eye shadow, orange permed hair, and a denture-straight smile, shoulders covered in flower print polyester. "We have to thank Grandma Phyllis"—there is a rush of whistles and catcalls at Grandma Phyllis' name—"because she is our number one fan. Not to mention our fashion guru. When I was seven, Grandma Phyllis"—more catcalls from the crowd— "bought me my first instrument, a kazoo, and that was the beginning of my musical career."

The cigarette smoke starts to irritate my throat. No one around me has a cigarette. This is serious mosh pit territory. Kelly watches me look around and pulls me closer. She is out of breath, a sign that she is warming up to the flesh pounding around us. The girl in front of me, the one with the liquid x eyes, suddenly grabs her headband, an elastic ring of fabric that keeps her short brown hair off her farm-girl forehead, and yanks it off. She continues twisting the band around her hand until she mummifies her fist. Something about watching her is painful. As soon as the music starts, she jumps up and down again, slowly, high off the ground, untwists the band and sticks it back in its original position, slightly askew. Quickly she is back in action as she starts to throw limbs, kick boots. I realize that I've seen her here before, back when Casey and I were still regulars at Club grrrl. Casey loved the scene, loved hearing the bartenders shout out her name or the regulars waving to her from their barstools like a chorus line kicking up their legs in an old movie. I was more the misfit, playing with matches, drinking too fast, folding napkins. Casey always thought I was waiting for the drugs. Sometimes I was. Mostly it was to get her alone, even if it was only in the bathroom stall.

Our last night there, in the bathroom, Casey pulled two tabs out of a tiny manila envelope, the kind the dentist puts your bloody molars into before giving them back to you. She never let me carry the drugs. It was a thing with her. She poured the tabs into her hand, head bent in concentration. Impatient, I pushed her shoulders gently until she was leaning against the stall.

"Come on, Casey. Give me a kiss."

"Watch it! You're going to make me spill."

"And . . . ?"

"Not now, Claire. Here."

"Gee, thanks." I popped the small round tab into my mouth and swallowed it dry. It lodged, a hard lump in my throat.

At the bar, I waited for the first tingle, the first rush. It always hit under my fingernails first and behind my ears. Twenty minutes later, I interrupted Casey in conversation with another woman, "Wanna dance?"

"No, baby, I'm not wearing the right shoes." She never said yes.

I looked down at her weathered cowboy boots and chuckled. "No, you're not." I kissed her on the cheek and wove to the dance floor. Like always, it was awkward for the first few moments, standing on the fringe, wondering where and how to enter. I vowed never to let my body leave the ground. I stood near the edge and sank in. At first I floated. For all the bodily contact, slamming is a numbing experience. Body parts disappear, no hands, no breasts, just impact. Songs crashed and faded, one into the next. I kept my eyes open until I reached the Zen state I was there for. Then they closed in a halo of light that stuck to my inner eyelids. The music stopped but we kept dancing. I vaguely wondered why. Shiny black leather spun around me. Black leather Docs. Black.

I woke up quickly, surrounded by women's faces. I squinted my eyes at them. They smiled gently or frowned with concern.

"Don't worry. It could happen to any one of us." It was groupie girl. She was talking as much to the others as to me.

"Are you okay now? Can you stand up?" Some stood, others crouched nearby. Several of them touched me, an arm around my back, hands on my legs and arms. Warmth tingled wherever they touched. I wobbled to my feet. A line split between them like a wedding aisle, and Casey marched up the middle like she was walking her boots through mud.

"Hi, honey." I smiled shyly, still half inside the sheen of leather and the dark echo of fainting.

"Are you okay, Claire?" Casey talked fast. "God, why do you do this? It's so stupid." She looked around accusingly as the women whirled away. The band started to play again, a slow song that got faster and faster. Casey and I stood in the middle of the dance floor. A few women bumped into Casey, anger tangled in their brows. I led her back to the bar.

"You're okay, aren't you? Sit down, honey. You'll feel better soon." Her eyes clouded over, her full beautiful lips sneered in contempt.

"No, I'm going home."

Casey never forgave me for fainting in front of her friends and we broke up two weeks later.

---

kd lang jumps up on the stage. (It is definitely her.) And sings along with Leisha, who is, as the whispers inform us, kd's girlfriend. Leisha's eyes open wide as if she didn't expect kd to leap up next to her. kd is drunk or high or something, because her eyelids lie low and her hair sits in strings across her face. She leans into her girlfriend's shoulder, oblivious to Leisha's discomfort or the fact that she needs her balance to play the guitar.

Again, the music fades and groupie girl pulls the headband off her head so it sits around her neck like a choker. She twists it around her hand, while choking herself. Her friend laughs, while groupie girl raises her hand above her head, pretending to hang herself. Then quickly it comes off altogether again and is banded tightly around her fingers. Until the next song starts and it is instantly back in place.

The band takes a break. Kelly and I both have to pee still and that requires passing the back bar. The inevitable has arrived. We finally say hi to Casey, and I'm stupidly surprised to see that she's on drugs. Rings of black around her blue-green eyes, more pronounced than they ever were when we lived together. She's skinny, looks awful, and it's no consolation, only sad. We stare for a minute.

"How are you, Casey?"

"Fine. How are you, Claire?"

"Fine." We revert to the vocabulary of a level-one language class. *Il fait beau. Il fait froid. Ça va?*

"How's Dogma?" I'm struggling for conversation even though I know the shape of her cervix by touch. She stares at me. The band's not playing. It's not like she can't hear me. That was her cat's name, right? I say it out loud again. "Dogma?"

"Oh, yeah, Dogma. He's fine." She stares again.

Kelly saves me by leaning forward into my hip. She holds out her hand. Casey takes it. "This is my girlfriend, Kelly."

Casey brightens, tosses her head a little and says, "There's someone you should meet too. I mean, well, not that you should meet, but, well . . . This is Dahlia."

Dahlia is a tall, thin blonde with a layer of foundation almost as thick as Grandma Phyllis'. She takes one look at me and says, "This is Claire? I've heard so much about you. I feel like I know you." She ignores the hand I hold out and grabs me in a limp squeeze. She smells like hair spray. Instantly, I recoil as the silver sequins on her top scratch across my denim overalls.

I look from Dahlia to Casey and back to Dahlia again. "Well, Dahlia, then you probably do." I turn back to Casey, who says, "So, Claire, any fainting spells lately?" She and Dahlia laugh too loud as my face flushes red.

I glance at Kelly, whose face remains blank. I'm grateful for that lack of recognition, want to glide in and out of it, knowing full well I will have to destroy it later. I glare at Casey without answering her question. "We're going to catch the rest of the show. See you later." My legs shake as I grab for Kelly's hand and walk away.

It's not supposed to be like this, to be traumatized by an ex sighting. What's the joke? What does a lesbian bring on the first date? Her ex. Just last month there was an article in *Out* magazine on exactly why, socially, politically, and economically, lesbians never really leave their exes. We need them was the simple answer. Because we need all the community we can get, not to mention sex, since it's sex that makes us who we are. Even if our exes cheat on us, lie to us, or borrow too much money and never pay us back. So here I am, a freak in my own community. Legs gone to noodles at the sight of my ex, whom I haven't even seen in six months, a lesbian record for living in the same city.

It's great to have kd lang in the mosh pit but she just landed squarely on my foot. I swear she cracked my instep and suddenly I'm thinking: "What the fuck are you doing here anyway? This place is crowded with dykes who would do you sideways. It's dangerous. You're too famous to be here. You gave up your right to these peon clubs when *Ingenue* hit the charts, when people like my mother started to buy your albums." The pain dissipates somewhat. At least she offers me a drink when the song is over.

"Sure, I'll have a drink. I'll take a beer and a shot of whiskey, if you don't mind. Thanks." She can afford it, right?

"Whiskey?" kd's annoyed. She has read my mind about affording it. She's looking at me like I'm a freak.

"Yeah, I'm Irish. It's for the pain." That shuts her up and off she sends a friend to go get the drinks. She's not about to leave her honey up there onstage all alone. Especially with all us hungry girls in the audience. I could be taking her up on the drink offer just to distract her long enough to glance up Leisha's skirt.

Groupie girl is unwrapping the headband off her wrist again. I lean into Kelly's body, suddenly dizzy, my head limp on her shoulder. She looks down at me and we kiss, loud, lots of tongue.

Kelly always wants to go dancing after sex. This morning we lay in pink skins, heads heavy against the wall above her loft bed. Naked, wet, spent hearts beating fast. "Come on," she whispered slowly in my ear. "Let's go out tonight. Let's dance." She gave me a ring, a token, she called it, of our three-month commitment. It was wrapped in brown corrugated paper with a silver ribbon, and it was the ring she caught me admiring in a store a couple weeks back.

"You're sneaky. I'm going to have to watch out for you."

"Not sneaky. Ingenius."

"Well . . . clever at least." I smiled into her shoulder as she put the ring on my finger.

I take my shot of whiskey and toast beers with kd. I decide to forgive her and we dance to the last song with enthusiasm. I'm stomping on faces, on graves, on flowers on graves. We whistle and clap but get no encore. Groupie girl takes her headband off for the last time when the music stops. I want to grab the headband and cut it into a million triangles. Paste them back together to make a handkerchief, pour chloroform onto the handkerchief and stuff it in Dahlia's face. Just to see the smile go lax, to see the lipstick smear across her cheeks as she falls to the floor.

Instead, groupie girl leaps off into the crowd and I never see her again. Kelly and I climb up to the roof deck. In the blue night air I finally relax. We stand in the corner by the edge of the roof and look down. A line of traffic jitters below. Larchmont leads south. I stare at a white stucco building across the street with arched windows on the second floor.

"Are those Romanesque windows or Gothic? I always get them mixed up."

"Romanesque. Think rounded for Romanesque. Think of Gothic. Dark . . ."

"Gargoyles, " I interrupt.

". . . harsh angles, pointed turrets, the flying buttresses of Notre Dame." Kelly has a degree in architecture and gives a sexy lecture.

"Gargoyles," I say again until Kelly laughs at me. "Do you mind me picking your brain like this?"

"Are you kidding? At least my degree is benefiting someone."

Dilapidated storefronts stare back at us from below the Romanesque windows, a palm reader, a dry cleaner, a butcher. All closed for business, the blinds drawn against the irreverent celebration happening above and below this roof.

I start to think I'm paranoid. That no one is on drugs. I just wanted them to be so I could feel clean. Maybe groupie girl just has bright eyes, and maybe kd is tired from all that touring. As if to prove my point, Casey stands across the deck, laughing and smoking with her friends as if she hadn't dosed in ages. Kelly starts to kiss me, pressing her hands on my shoulders, leaning me against the wall of the building next door. I start to imagine us at home, in bed. I unbutton her shirt and she reminds me where we are by squeezing my wrist.

"Let's go dance."

"Wait, Claire. What was Casey talking about you fainting? Do you have low blood pressure?"

"That's so like you, Kelly." I laugh. "Low blood pressure. Of course, makes perfect sense. You're sweet."

"What?" Kelly's face crinkles in confusion.

"The last time I was here with Casey, I fainted on the dance floor, too much x, I guess. It was embarrassing but sort of healing. Casey never forgave me for it."

"Is that all?"

"Yeah."

"I wish I would have been there that night."

"Me too."

We have to pass Casey to get back inside the club. I mumble quickly, "Bye, Casey," and touch her shoulder lightly. I touch cold bare skin. Gothic. She says, "See ya." And takes a puff off her cigarette, as if she's Danny in *Grease,* trying to act cool in front of the boys. I wonder if her friends know that she started smoking only after we broke up.

# The Moon
# in Cancer

**DONNA ALLEGRA**

The fountain in Washington Square Park is the perfect place to meet. A fat moon shimmers in the cloud-choked sky. It's the second full moon this month, the kind that the old folks say changes people's hearts.

It's about to rain any second, but I'm back with my girls: Juice, Uzi, Pepper, Bagel, and Scoop. I'm Gumbie. Scoop and Juice bring up the rear and the six of us are posse pals riding again.

The toothpick Pepper always has poking out the side of her mouth bounces with excitement. She takes it out to say, "Y'know? When we was kids, we'd be up in each other's face all the time. Now getting us rounded up all at the same time happens once in a blue moon." She's beefing, but I hear in her voice the gladness I feel.

We're grown and made it out alive. Pepper and Bagel are girl-friends now. Scoop's girl, Fabronique, had to work tonight. It's not like back in the days when we was in high school and had to watch each other's backs all the time. The world was a war zone then, 'cause everybody knew us as gay girls.

"Do we have to go to a bar, Uzi?" I say. "Juice is trying not to drink nowadays."

"Gumbie, don't you get it? Juice has conquered alcohol. She don't need to hide out from bars. She's got the problem all licked."

Uzi pronounces like a judge closing a case, but it bugs me that Juice doesn't say anything. She hates bars, even a place for gay women like Temptations.

"C'mon, it's a Wednesday night. It's not like there's some dyke diner we can go to. Be chill, Gumbie. You've got the alcohol solution, right, Juice?" Uzi's not even checking Juice's response. I want to shake Juice for masking her face in some kind of neutral zone.

"And besides," Uzi plows on, "that magazine *The Lesbian Sheik* is having a promotion party. It's some kind of literary event. You like that shit, Gumbie. It's not just a regular bar night."

"You must be aching for some Mad Dog, huh?" Scoop kids Uzi.

"Nah, man. I drink upscale these days. It's Ripple for me."

Uzi turns her appeal to Bagel, "There'll be some dope music to get a boogie going . . ." She makes like a suave pimp talking to a country gal.

"So?" Bagel fluffs her cheerleader ponytail like she's the last bored working girl. "I'm white. I don't move, you got that?" She pops her chewing gum and looks Uzi up and down. Uzi breaks to smile first.

"Aw ite," Pepper plucks out her toothpick with a finality that makes the decision. "It's on like that, and everybody's welcome."

We head out from Washington Square. The June humidity makes me yearn for rain to wash through the haze.

"How's your brother?" Juice asks Scoop.

"He's still negative," Scoop says, her chesty plumpness somehow an invitation to snuggle up, sigh, and tell all.

"Mine too. I feel like I don't want Kevin to have sex ever again."

I feel for them. I used to wish I had a gay brother, but now I know I couldn't hack the heartbreak.

Uzi catches up to me and picks up a conversation we was having earlier. "So what's the big deal about choosing fresh vegetables over canned vegs, Gumbie? Don't they put extra nutrients and shit in all the preservatives?" Uzi's voice holds an argument in her question.

"Well, it's the difference between real flowers and plastic," I try to persuade her.

"You always got all the answers, don chu?"

"Uzi, you asked me," I hear myself whine. "Why you wanna pick a fight?" I'm frustrated with her, and I don't have all the answers.

We're a couple blocks from Temptations when Juice puts an arm around my shoulder and steers me to the side of the street away from everybody. I feel Uzi and Scoop turn their heads to see what's gonna jump off as Juice says, "Can I ask you a question?"

"As long as it's not a hard one," I say loud enough for everyone to hear.

When we're out of range, "Would you kinda hang tight with me tonight, Gumbie? I'm afraid I'm a do something stupid, like just up and leave. I've done that before—left a bar trying to stay sober and ended up getting high on the street. You know I'm trying to keep my head up on the positive tip, but every now and then it feels like gloom and doom."

I don't think she's ever told the others that she'd completely quit alcohol three years ago. She'd play like she was just slowing down on her drinking so nobody'd try to shake her with, "Not even a beer?!!"

I massage her at the shoulders. "I'm with you Juice. Anybody mess with you, let me know. Do whatever you need to." I feel warmth rise off her trapezius muscles. I'm feeling pretty played out myself. I hope tomorrow is a better place.

After a bit, Pepper comes over and offers me a toothpick. "So, Gumbie, what's with you and this sneaker show? Urban Airplanes is sponsoring this dance troupe thing?"

"Don't get me started about my job," I say, and launch in. "The Urban Airplanes Athletic Shoe Company wants a few Black bodies to dance, but the touring company is mostly white. Their packaging is frontin' like the inner city is this melting pot where we all hang together and dance alike. My noble Urban Airplanes employers appear benevolent in the public eye because Black kids get summer playground activities."

"That's good for the little niggas. How come you sound so down on it?" Scoop asks, picking up on her titties to ease the bra strap bite.

"It's hard to criticize, but this rich corporation advertises itself using Black folks' culture as decoration for coolness. What's up with that?"

"You mean you do all the work and they get all the glory?" Scoop says with an attitude of knowing the answer.

"Not exactly. The corporation folks do their jobs . . ."

"And the kids have mad fun, Gumbie," Juice cuts in. "You do too. I seen you in the recreation centers. Why can't you leave it there?" Juice prods, and I don't want this to turn into one of our head-bangings.

I take another stab at convincing her. "Urban Airplanes' image is hip whites with a supporting cast of other races. The public relations people present a Black thing like it's multicultural—that has better selling appeal than Marilyn Monroe or Elvis . . ."

"Well, this is America," Juice says, like the knuckleheaded kid I met in JHS 210.

"Which to them means whites rule with a few colored faces as accessories," I snap, and immediately wish I could've said it nice.

"They paying you any money for it?" Uzi demands.

"I get some chump change, but the real ducats go to the corporate types," I tell Uzi. "White professionals get rich off the backs of Black people. Again." I give Juice a look of Sunday school 'buking and she mimics me right back.

"It's not like kids aren't glad." Juice puts up her dukes, ragging me. "They get some entertainment and hopes to dream on." She crowds against me and wraps her arms across my chest in a wrestling hold.

"Nigga, get offa me." I don't really push her away. "Yeah, on the tip of it; but nine-tenths of the advantages go to Urban Airplanes. They market Blackness and make it safe for white people to buy at the store."

"Gee, what a new idea," Bagel chimes in, and shakes her ponytail at Juice, as if her cinnamon-colored mane is a hand puppet.

"So? That's the deal at my job," Juice grumbles. "Why you think we call it a 'slave'?"

At least Juice sounds a little defensive. I wish so bad that she saw things the same as me. But I can't change her mind.

"But what really pisses you off is that Black and Latino kids see their dance moves come down from white playground group leaders and everybody thinks the white folks invented it," Scoop concludes. Scoop's been in therapy school forever.

"And it's my choreography to boot." I wave my hand to give Scoop her point.

Bagel scolds, "Juice, you should know the deal by now, Ms. America. People see the performance group at youth centers and the assumption is that Urban Airplanes is 'helping' the disadvantaged. Meanwhile, back at the ranch, the multimillion corporation gets big bucks from plucking Black culture. That's the real American way, Juicey." Bagel sucks her teeth and pulls at the band holding her hair back.

The expression on Juice's tilted head shows something has shifted. She nods to Bagel and jeers "Maybe" to me.

We finally arrive at Temptations.

Bagel and Pepper stop into the deli next door for chewing gum and toothpicks. The rest of us go in and the bored-looking woman slouching at the door stands at alert, "You have to show some ID."

Once we sit at our table, Scoop goes, "I suppose I should be flattered for looking so young. Here I am twenty-eight years old and still getting carded, but ya know . . ."

Uzi cuts Scoop's diplomacy. "Well, you still Black and probably a hoodlum, nigga, so 'Let me see your ID.'"

"Thank you," Juice says.

The bitters swallowed, I look out for Pepper and Bagel to join us. I wave to Bagel in the lead and watch the two of them enter like grown-ups, no one asking for their ID.

I don't like to hang in bars. Even though there's more places for gay women to go besides the after-hours clubs, the women in Greenwich Village aren't like people we grew up with around our way.

I scope the room and scowl over the high-fashion lesbians acting like they're fabulous for smoking cigars. The freebie copy of *The Lesbian Sheik* shines from the table with a cover photo of an actress who played a bisexual in a movie. I glance through the pages hoping to find out she's gay and see the quote highlighted from the sleek pages: "I'm not a lesbian, but I feel now I really understand them. My boyfriend . . ."

I put the magazine down in favor of real people, but the scene at Temptations has an emptiness despite music and people dressed in corporate drag and power suits. I notice some straight guys making sure everybody knows they're with straight dates. The het girls cling to the guys and evil-eye any woman within stabbing distance. Nah, I think, no, thanks. Where are the dykes who put women first and don't sleep with men?

At the bar a few tables away from us, two high-heeled cigar girls seem to be hanging on to every word a man in a pinstripe suit is saying. His eyes roam over women's bodies as he talks.

Juice looks over at what I'm watching and shakes her head. "I'm from the old school. Either you're a lesbian or you're a bisexual. None of this 'I'm a lesbian and this is my boyfriend' shit."

"So you like the old days when butches were butches and femmes were femmes but we was all bull daggers to the fellas?" Uzi sucks her drink through the swizzle stick.

"Nah, not all that, but I can't get with women who claim to be gay, sleep with men, get married to 'em, and wear wedding rings on their last names." Juice reaches for her glass and glowers as she tastes the soda. "Then they go around getting mad because I can't see them as lesbians. What's up with that?"

"Why you always have to put a label on everybody?" Uzi says.

"I don't. I'm just keeping it real, kid. People should tell the truth about where they're at." Juice frowns around the room searching for a waitress.

"How can you look at somebody and tell if they're a lesbian or what?"

Juice gives Uzi a look like Uzi is lippin' but not saying nothing.

"And so what if she's a bisexual who feels it more for men?" Uzi puts her hand on her right hip and pops her neck in and out, daring anybody to say something. "Then what, huh? Are you saying that woman can't hang with you, Ms. Butch-in-the-streets?" Uzi takes a pull from her drink.

"Well, what about the women who call themselves bisexuals because they don't want all the weight that comes with being up-front that they're lesbians? That shit's from hunger," Juice throws back.

"So? That's real-life survival sometimes. And if you want to go there, then what about the ones who swear all up and down, 'I'm a gay,' and then go having affairs with men and keep it on the down-low?"

Now I have to jump in and say, "For one thing, there's a lot more hoops for honest lesbians to go through than the bisexers have to. Give me the butch bull daggers any day. Fuck them women who put men first and be so understanding of them. And then, the bitches go backstabbing sisters." It shakes me that I speak with more heat than I intended. I try to tone down when I see a shade of anxiety in Juice, who turns from Uzi to gauge my upset.

"Y'all is too much." Pepper takes out her toothpick and fans the air around Juice and Uzi. "It is getting hot in here. I'm supposed to be the one with the temper." She squeezes my shoulder and shakes my body in a playful way.

"You know what I say about all of that . . ."

"Don't say it, Pepper. I'm sick of hearing 'bout 'It's on like that and everybody's welcome,'" Uzi warns.

"You stop crabbin' and I'll shut up. Is it a deal?" Pepper tosses back.

"Bet," Uzi pronounces.

"Uzi, Juice shoulda let you stay with the name you wanted to go with, 'Bazooka,'" I tell her.

"Nah. She was on about 'Uzi' having more class. Probably the smartest thing you ever told me, Juice," Uzi declares, and shadow-boxes the air around Juice.

"Dumb bitch," Juice calls her as they pat each other's backs, careful not to hug.

I'm relieved Uzi decides to drop it. I think: Maybe it's good to be in Temptations. I need some dykes to rub shoulders with. There just aren't that many of us in the world and I want at least some part of my life to be about peace, some place where I feel I belong and all is well.

Even after all these years, I still felt whacked around losing my high school girlfriend to a man. But the way I see it, I lost Double Dutch to the straight world's bullying. William was the means to an end for Dutch more than he was a person she loved better than me. If she even really loved me.

Scoop asks, "How's your love life holding up these days, Gumbie?"

I snort and shrug. "If I can get a buzz off an attraction to someone, God bless it. Not much going on beyond that."

"Aw man, Gumbie. As Fine. Black. And Intelligent as you are? The babes should be paying at the door for that FBI service," Juice says.

"Hey, yo. But on the real side, I think the rules I made up for myself after my thing with Double Dutch got fouled—'Don't let anybody get too close, don't depend on anyone, don't care too much'—were right. Most people are too trifling and flaky."

"Maybe you're not really all that available for someone to get next to you, Gumbie." Scoop talks like she was born being a headshrinker.

"Well, I'm not up to rocket science in relationships, but it still seems like they'll mostly lead to getting your feelings squashed."

"But you rebound and come back sharper for the next round, Gumbie. That's just the give-and-take of life, kid," Scoop argues.

"I know the piece about pain and struggle make me wiser, but you know what, Scoop? I don't care. The hassle and heartache isn't worth whatever I supposedly learn."

"Aw, c'mon, you know better than that, Gumbie. All relationships take you through the fire, but most people believe they're worth the heat. I think you should keep an open mind," Juice encourages.

"My mind isn't the problem, it's my heart that's stopped."

A woman passes by our table and looks back at Juice. After the woman is out of hearing range, Scoop says, "Juice, how come you always cut the mustard with girlies?"

I wonder: How can you cut something liquid like mustard? The air inside Temptations is thick with odors of alcohol and cigar. Not even fresh air would cut the dankness.

"Juice has that star quality. Everybody wants to get a little piece of her." Uzi sounds mean, like there's something wrong with Juice for being so good-looking. I look at Juice, her lips like cut glass. She's handsome and yet not out of the attainable world. I couldn't handle the whole package, but she has so many aspects I wish I could get in a lover.

"'A profile like the Statue of Liberty,'" I quote how Uzi once described Juice. I tickle my palm over the velvet lower part of Juice's scalp. She's got dreads on top of her head and the lawn is mown below her ears. But it's more than Juice's face, it's her vibe that draws people.

Juice defends herself with Pepper's line: "Hey. It's on like that and everybody's welcome. Besides, I was high a lot back then. It's easy to pick up women when you're drunk out your skull or they are—if that's what you want."

Uzi sucks her teeth and looks like she's about to throw down something mocking, but doesn't. She just gets up and says, "Anybody want anything from the bar?"

"I'll come with you to get me another beer." Scoop follows Uzi.

A slow song is playing and Bagel and Pepper move to the dance floor.

"Time sure flies around." Juice looks at her watch.

"It always does." I wish I had something deep and wise to tell her.

"Everybody I know is like, forget it as far as having enough hours in a day. Saturday is the only minute free to do anything and then maybe get some rest." She carefully sips her soda through the thin stirrer.

"I need to be three different people or have a talented octopus as a household slave just so I can get some sleep. I go to rehearsals and my tired ass is dragging through every one of the seven seas." My voice tells me just how weary I feel.

"You want to leave, babe?" Concern laces her voice, but I shouldn't think it means anything. Juice is always considerate about people doing whatever it is they need to.

"How're you doing drinking soda?" I watch her face for the complete answer.

"I'm doing okay."

I can see she means it. What throws me—and I could be reading her wrong—is that I feel attention from Juice when she looks at me. She keeps her eyes open to what I say and do. We can be talking about the weather but sometimes the tide of feeling between us could move an ocean off the planet. I'd be a fool to hope or trust. Feeling sexy for Juice would only bring me grief. I feel my heart shore up against the prospect of pain. I shouldn't let my liking for her make me forget what I've learned about life.

But I wonder: What is safe to hope for? What do you have a right to expect from another person? Can you assume anything? Most folks are into hype and looking good, but no follow-through.

I look out onto the dance floor and see Bagel and Pepper wrapped around each other. They don't move much more than a slow drag, but they might as well be humping. I feel like a little girl, left out and unable to join in. Bagel and Pepper are really the big kids on the block.

"I don't know, jim. How come the older I get, the stupider I feel?"

"'Cause you realize you don't know everything, Gumbie."

Times like this rattle me, when Juice is so on-the-money about how I feel. I stand and say, "To pee or not to pee," then head for the john. When I arrive, one of the straight guys pushes out of a stall.

What the hell is his stupid ass doing in here? He tries to straighten his rumpled navy power suit and tangled red print tie. When he sees me, his eyes glitter with an eager excitement and his smile makes him look like a crocodile. I think about the distance between an open hand and a fist.

"Goddamnit! I thought I was by myself in the women's bathroom." I want him to know I'm pissed.

He sorta stumbles. "Anything goes, right, gorgeous? What's your name, sweetheart?"

"None of your fucking business."

"Now that's not a nice thing for a young lady to say." He speaks in a singsong way like he's coochie-coochie-cooing a little kid. "You don't have to be like that," he says, and moves toward me.

I smell soured alcohol on him and tell myself he's drunk and I shouldn't be getting mad. I've had enough times tangling with Uzi when she was hammered to know better than to expect sense from anybody that's pickled.

Juice would get quiet and sad when she was drunk.

The guy trips and, cursing, reaches for me to help break his fall. I step away and let him hurt himself. I don't have to pee bad, so I turn and leave. I want to get back to Juice to make sure she is still okay not drinking.

Everyone is at the table when I get back. "There's a straight man in the bathroom," I say disgustedly.

"Aw, man . . ."

Pepper shakes her head, saying, "Um, um, um," like a church-woman. Bagel rolls her eyes and says, "Damn, they just have to get into everything, don't they?" She adjusts her ponytail for a looser fit.

The laughter helps jolly me out of being so mad. I take comfort from the way my friends chuckle. It holds an understanding that takes the fangs out of a moment spent gnashing teeth.

We all notice a particular steady thump in the music's bass line and a phat beat unfolds with some scratch. "Oooh, this is my joint!" Bagel says of the song that's kicking on.

"Let's boogie, y'all." The bunch of us get up.

There's a look to us that makes the people in the bar sneak peeks. I've been shaping the same flavor into the Urban Airplanes Crew. It's a way of moving that looks like we're people from animated cartoons. The style grew out of our days hanging out in Uzi's family's basement. I'd break down moves I'd seen on *Soul Train* for the others and spin my body's vibe to it. When we'd find women's after-hours clubs to party at, we looked like family.

Bagel can shake her moneymaker like a regular around-the-way girl. She gets a lot of notice when we dance. It's not like she's out-standing, but people expect the rest of us to have the bounce. Bagel is the surprise to them. She calls herself uppity white trash. I don't think of her that way, but if she says it, I guess it's okay.

The slow-time bridge of the song comes up and I unfurl a riff of body rolls and quick steps around Juice that make her say, "Yeah, all right, you still the flavor-maker."

But Uzi goes, "This is just partying. How can you call doing that with the Urban Airplanes Crew choreography, Gumbie? And went to college to learn it?" She sounds indignant.

It whacks me that Uzi can be so blind about my work. Too hurt to say anything back, I don't even put her in check by reminding her of all the times I unraveled dance moves just to teach her a step.

"Uzi, you need to turn on your brain before you open your mouth sometimes," Juice whips out. "And besides, you've never seen what Gumbie's doing with those kids. Gumbie frames the moves so that they stand out and look bigger than life. Your tired ass couldn't even walk back in the day."

"But I was just saying . . ." Uzi protests.

"Now, Uzi. Gumbie and Juice go to the bone with being friends. You should know better than to dis Gumbie." Pepper laughs and swipes her toothpick at Uzi like it's a rapier.

"You was just asking for trouble, weren't you?" Scoop wiggles a finger at Uzi.

"But all it is party boogie, no big deal." Now where does Uzi get the nerve to sound aggrieved all of a sudden? But I see the tide of alcohol is making her weak, where before she was feisty.

"You don't want to go there . . ." Bagel warns like she's somebody's mother.

After the knock from Uzi, it makes me feel like buttered porridge that Juice'd stick up for me and brag on top of it.

The phat beat picks up and we're dancing again when one of the straight men comes over doing a corny-ass step out of rhythm. He tries to break in with the offer of his teeth as a smile.

It's the red tie guy from the bathroom saying, "All these good-looking women and no man? Here I come to save the day." He delivers this slippery line with a sheepish look, as if to convey that he's hip enough to get over.

He insists way toward me like he means business and Juice steps between us. She frowns him to back off, puts a restraining hand on my thigh, and speaks in a strong voice, "Yo, man. This is mine. Aw ite?"

He steps away mumbling, "Sorry, dude, no offense, all right? Peace, okay, bro'?"

I'd forgotten how tough Juice can be. She looks like a jaguar poised on a hairspring. I know I'd hightail up a tree from such a defiant woman.

"Dude," Pepper drawls to Bagel, who echoes "Bro'." They both cut their eyes on the man in the power suit. Pepper flicks her toothpick at his cordovans.

One of the cigar smokers rushes over. Her hair color is a mix of beige and straw, her skin tanned to alligator. "Is there a problem?" she asks with a pastel smile, her tone anxious.

Juice puts her arm across my shoulders and says, "That fella is cutting in where nobody invited him. I was just letting him know . . ." She keeps her eyes aimed like a rifle on the man.

The guy in the suit protests, "I was just asking for a dance . . ." He turns to Uzi with a smile of appeal. "Right, honey? Tell her."

Uzi folds her arms across her chest and you can practically hear, "Child, please. Don't even try it," as she shoots him all the attitude her mama gave her. "My name ain't no 'honey.'" She eyes the guy up and down. "Honey comes in a jar and you keep it on a shelf." She flicks her wrist like the swipe of a cat's tail.

Bagel pops her chewing gum loud enough to be heard over the music. I lean into Juice, chuckling. I turn my head so no one can see me rolling my eyes over this cartoon. Juice keeps a strong hold on my body. I feel a position I once held to like a law of life, something that has been a long time eroding, simply wash out to sea.

The woman tosses her striped hair, thumbs the cigar, and says warningly, "Well, then there's no problem, right, ladies?" She eyes us like she's a school crossing guard. Then she speaks more solicitously. "Would you like a drink on the house courtesy of *The Lesbian Sheik,* sir? We're a magazine that includes everyone."

"Well, damn, excuse me," Uzi says, moving her head in an S-curve as the woman with the cigar ushers the man away.

Bagel and Pepper exchange looks of disbelief and Scoop says, "Let's blow this hot dog stand," pushing up her titties as the last word.

The music intros some old school schlock, but most of the women in the room get up happy to dance. As Sister Sledge's "We Are Family" follows us out the door, Temptations feels like a glorified cellar.

Outside the rain has stopped. The freshened air is like smelling the difference between a pasture and a parking lot. I hear a distant rumble and think how thunder is such a soothing sound. Rain always reminds me of comfort and a place called home.

We're out on the street with no place to go, but we have each other's company.

Juice is being quiet, but looks like something is biting her. I can feel she's moved away and hope she's not wanting to drink. I long to fill the space where we connected a short while ago. Her vibe doesn't push me away, but she seems strained.

"Ain't that some stanky shit?" Scoop says.

"I guess we must be the wrong color," Uzi responds.

"Nah, it wasn't that. We just didn't carry big enough cigars, girl. The expensive kind," Bagel says.

"Designer dykes, jim."

"I'm telling you, fashion is everything these days. If you're not hip with the trendy program, they don't want you around."

We're kinda laughing, kinda something else.

"Them chicken-headed bitches couldn't even dance. Lame-ass motherfuckers. I mean, give me a break. If this is what being a lesbian is, you can count me out," Uzi says.

"Break it down for me, Uzi. Does that mean you're with the straight crowd now, gonna get you a man, some babies, the whole nine, maybe a couple extra yards?" Scoop intones, the model of innocent inquiry.

"Child, please, none of that mess. Wha'm saying is, these girlies aren't like folks around our way. When the shit goes down, you know we're not gonna be on the same side as them," Uzi declares.

"Yeah, that shit is deep, jim."

We're walking the long way to the subway station. Pepper and Bagel will go to Queens, Uzi and Scoop are Brooklyn-bound, and Juice lives in Harlem. My place is down here, by the East River.

"Let's not trip on this and get all wrapped up dropping more shit than a pigeon," Juice says. "You know how we do."

But Uzi explodes, "No, thank you, everybody is NOT welcome. You saw how welcome we was with the sheik lesbians."

"Okay, keep it real, but keep it right. Let's drop it now, y'all," Juice says irritably.

"Well, with their little condescending attitudes, they should put all that money they're making to good use and get some psychologic help." Uzi puts in her last word.

Juice throws up her hands in aggravation. "Uzi, you need to be pounded for about a month, then you'll be all right."

"Aw, man," Scoop says. "Call them 'Moon children' my butt." She puts her arms around Juice and Uzi at their shoulders. "Bitches, please. You Cancers is just the crabbiest people on earth."

"She's just jealous 'cause I can drink and she can't," Uzi accuses. But Uzi's wrong and I'm just realizing why. I feel like a spectator again with Juice the grown-up in this ball game.

Juice leans across Scoop to say, "I must really love you, Uzi. 'Cause if I didn't after all these years, they'd've found you mangled and decaying under the floor a long time ago."

"Thank you, thank you, thank you. I thank you, my mother thanks you, my father thanks you, my thank you thanks you." They pat each other on the back like boxers, careful not to hug.

We amble along Sixth Avenue. Just like Juice had earlier railed me toward the edge of the sidewalk so she could say something private, I herd her from the others' hearing. She looks at me with question creasing on her face.

"When were you and Uzi lovers?" I ask.

Juice looks embarrassed. "I'm not even gonna try to lie. It was a one-nighter. Back when you were first going away on tour and not sure if you'd be coming back to New York. Me and Uzi were both high. It didn't mean anything, Gumbie." She pleads for me to understand something I don't want to.

Why should I care what they did together? Juice wasn't ever my girl-friend. We weren't even best friends really. It's just that there was always something between us that was more and different than with the rest of the gang.

"Uzi wasn't the one I wanted, Gumbie. But she was there and I was drunk." Juice looks miserable now.

It shouldn't matter to me who Juice sleeps with.

But it does.

I feel like a castle with a moat around me. But then a sensation reaches through the twilight, maybe that blue moon pushing at the murky clouds. And I think: I don't want to stay stuck in a place that I'm bigger than now.

We walk and don't talk. A little later, I clear my throat a couple of times to say something. But all my questions tonight have the same misty answer: I don't know.

Uzi says, "You got allergies these days? How come you're coughing like that, Gumbie?"

"I dunno, maybe 'cause it's so muggy or from breathing in all that smoke."

Scoop and Pepper start feinting boxing moves.

"I'm a fuck you up good, mothafucka. Pop!"

"The fuck you will. Whap! You fuckin with the wrong fuckin bitch. Bam!"

Bagel referees. "Fuck you. Fuck that. Fuck it. Fuck."

"Why y'all niggas gotta act all ignorant and shit like you ain't got no edumacation?" Uzi asks reasonably.

I sidle up to Juice and say, "You wanna come by for dinner this week?"

She doesn't look at me, but I know she wants to. I can see the little smile she tries to tame. The gratitude I see alter her silhouette means everything to me. That look is worth going through the stench of a thousand cigars.

"Yeah, sure, cool, Gumbie."

"Why's everybody so quiet?" Uzi complains.

We're dawdling at the entrance to the West Fourth Street subway station, lollygagging like no one wants to go home.

"Bing-bong," Scoop sings the sound of the subway doors about to open.

"You going back to Brooklyn, old lady?" she asks Uzi.

"Yeah, and it better be quick before I die. I drank too much tonight."

"You always say that." I watch Scoop waiting for Uzi to draw a conclusion.

A halo of summer scents surrounds Juice. Something more than the haunting moon has caught up with me. I tilt Juice's head to show her the silver sheen push through the smoking clouds. The others turn up their faces too as Uzi says, "Oooh, look, y'all, the moon's on fire." She sounds like a little girl who's never seen the moon beam before.

"Yeah," I tell Uzi. "It's on like that."

I cozy my body into Juice, push her with my hips, and she moves closer, responding. So I wasn't making this all up. A belief I once held as solid ground washes out to sea.

With my arm draped around Juice in a shoulder hold I inhale the sweetened summer air. I look up to a blue moon and it doesn't make sense to be so careful anymore. A wave of feeling pulls me to turn toward her. We hug.

# Fire

**PAT ALDERETE**

Two things you found out about Fire right away: he was weird and he loved his radio.

I was sprawled with some of the girls on the sharp brown stubble we called grass. We were in the netherworld between Maravilla Projects and Belvedere Park in East Los Angeles. It was one of our favorite places to hang out since the Housing Authority considered it the park and the Park Patrol considered it the Projects. From a distance we saw a guy walking toward us but since I was with my homegirls I wasn't too concerned. He was dressed in a T-shirt and khakis, like any other guy, except he was carrying a radio on his shoulder and as he got closer to us we could hear the song "I'll Take You There" by the Staple Singers. We could see he was moving to a rhythm different than the music that was playing on his radio.

"Hey, Pata," Tina nudged me, "here comes Fire."

Fire's head was shaped like an anvil that'd been pounded on too long. He had bristly black hair that was full of cowlicks and greasy kid stuff. His eyes were small and dull with just a few eyelashes thrown in for protection. His nose hooked over uneven lips that stuck out from his always drooping mouth. And his voice, he always sounded like he was being strangled. He was around our age, sixteen, more or less.

"Ey, Fire," Tina said, "where you been?"

"Been out moving around," he gargled.

Tina rolled her eyes at Margo. "Yeah, you see anything?"

"Lots of things to look at. I been looking around."

"Yeah, you get around all right. Hey, let me see your radio."

Fire jerked back. "No! My radio! You can't have it."

"I didn't say I wanted it, stupid, I just wanted to see it."

"No! You can't touch my radio."

"So who the fuck wants to touch your stupid radio? Get outta here before I break it."

After he was out of earshot, Margo poked Tina in the shoulder. "Why'd you do that?"

"He pissed me off."

"So? He can't help it."

"Ay, Margo," Fuzzy teased, "you act like he's your boyfriend or something."

"Naw, man, it ain't that . . ."

"Then what? You'd stick up for that weirdo before backing up your homegirl?"

"Of course not, esa! I guess I feel sorry for him."

"You think he feels sorry for you? You think he'd ever do shit for you? Don't you know who your friends are?"

"Oh, it's just, you know, Fire just wants to be one of the vatos."

But I could see that Fire thought he *was* one of the guys. He never seemed to realize that he was the reason for their laughter, standing there with them, a goofy smile on his long face.

Fire went to McDonnell School, which was where they bused all the strange kids. It was down the street from our barrio and sometimes the younger kids in the neighborhood went to the fence at the schoolyard to stare. Trini, one of Margo's younger brothers, told me, "Yeah, it's weird all right! They got these kids wearing helmets and they're not even playing football or anything. And I seen this girl that was strapped into a wheelchair." Nobody ever saw Fire there but Trini told me they could hear his radio playing.

Fire was highly motivated to learn how to spell his nickname so that he could spray-paint it on the walls like the rest of us did. He was proud of his childish sprawl and he only used gold paint. You could always tell his placa, even if you couldn't read, because it was jagged, the letters crooked and uneven, like him.

Later that night as we walked through the park by Belvedere Plunge, we saw a couple of the guys from our barrio.

"Ey, Mousie," I called out, "que pasa?"

Mousie was leaning against the fence surrounding the swimming pool. Standing next to him, drowning in the dark of the broken overhead light, was Lio. Lio was only respected by the little kid wannabes. If he hadn't of grown up with everyone he would have been killed years ago.

"Ey, Pata," Mousie said, "what you girls up to?"

"Not too much, just checking it out."

Tina pulled a joint out of her cigarette pack and lit it, took a few puffs and passed it. In a few minutes, several joints and a couple of short dogs of T-bird were being handed back and forth.

After a while I started feeling good. When my head got heavy, I let it flop back on the grass, looking up. "Man," I said, "lookit how pretty the stars are."

"Ay, tu, nature girl," Lio teased, everyone laughing at me.

"Yeah, well it is."

"Aw, whatta you know about the stars?" Lio said.

"You're the one who doesn't know anything."

Before Lio could say anything, the sounds of a radio reached over to us.

Fire spotted us and smiled. Swaggering as usual, radio on his shoulder, he came over.

"Ey, man, what's happening?"

"You, Fire," Lio said.

"Whatya mean, Lio?"

"I mean you're what's happening." Lio picked up a can of spray paint and started shaking it, the rattle of the metal ball inside the can pinging in time. With short bursts of paint, Lio started writing his own and Mousie's name on the wall.

"Where's my name?" Fire asked, studying the wall carefully.

"It ain't here, can't you read?"

"Well, how come why not? I'm here too."

"Fire's a stupid name, I ain't going to have it next to mine," Lio said.

"Fire's a good name! I thought of it."

"Aw, whatta you know?"

"I know a lot!" Fire looked like he was going to start crying.

"You don't know shit, man, you're stupid."

A scream from down deep got torn from Fire's throat as he threw himself against Lio, his skinny arms flailing against the much bigger boy. His radio dropped to the grass.

"I'm not stupid! You're the stupid one!" he cried.

Lio pinned Fire's arms down by his side, laughing. "Mousie," he said, "grab the radio."

"Noooooooo!" Fire screamed.

Mousie bent over and picked up the radio, dangling it at Fire. "Is this what you want?"

"Yeah! Give me my radio." Fire struggled against Lio's grip.

"How bad do you want it?"

"It's my radio! Mine! Mine!"

"Yeah, well go get it." Mousie flung the radio over the fence where it plopped into the swimming pool with a large splash, the water gurgling out the music.

"Nooo, my radio." Fire had tears streaming down his face.

Mousie looked at Lio. "Let the fucking baby go."

Lio shoved Fire, "Yeah, you pinche baby, look at you crying."

"You fuckers!" Fire screamed as he started swinging at Mousie. Mousie swung once and knocked Fire to the ground, then put his foot on his throat.

"Listen," he said, dead serious, "don't you ever swing at me, you understand? I'll kill you."

Fire rolled up into a ball, crying hard. Margo went to him and placed her hand on his shoulder. "Leave me alone!" he said, knocking her hand off.

Everyone was laughing at Fire except me and Margo. We pretended we had to go pee behind the bushes but we didn't. We stood there shaking like we'd been tossed into the plunge too.

We stared at each other, not knowing what to say, when Margo opened her arms and we held each other. "Ay, poor thing," Margo said, "he never hurt nobody."

"I know, I know."

Walking out and rejoining the group, Fuzzy held out the bottle of T-bird for me.

Waving it aside, I said, "No, thanks, I'm going home."

A mean smile on his face, Lio asked, "What's the matter, Pata?"

"I'm going home too," Margo said.

Looking at Lio but talking to Tina, I said, "I'm tired and I'm going home. You coming, Tina?"

"Uh . . ."

"Come home, esa."

"Awright," Tina answered, grabbing the hand I offered and pulled herself up off the grass.

"C'mon, Fire." I offered my hand. "Let's go."

# French Press

**K. E. MUNRO**

"I know you're in there," she says. "I can see you. Pick up."

This is one of the disadvantages of living next door to an ex-girlfriend. We have matching houses out on the edge of the industrial zone, where the rent is cheap. I moved in first, three years ago. Marie moved in next door last year; we started to date, and after a while it seemed like a good idea for her to sublet her place and move in with me. We lasted six months before she moved back out again. So far, neither of us has been willing to trade cheap rent for a better location.

My study is directly across from Marie's bedroom window, and because I refuse to hang curtains or shades, she can look in and see me anytime she wants. She has venetian blinds, which she's been keeping closed since we broke up. Sometimes I look up and see them and want to laugh. As if I'd want to stare into her bedroom. As if I don't have better things to do.

She's opened them a bit now, just enough to be able to squint through them and see me at my desk. I can see her outline faintly, through the openings.

I reach over and pick up the phone. The answering machine clicks off and starts to blink.

"I'm working," I say. "What do you want?"

For a moment she says nothing, and while I'm waiting I put my finger into my ear and scratch. Marie hates vulgarity.

"I want my coffeemaker," she says finally. I take my finger out and wipe it on my jeans.

"You have your coffeemaker," I say. "You took it already."

"The other one," she says. "The French press. That's mine too."

"The French press is mine," I say. It is—I bought it last summer with money I made translating a brochure for a German aeronautics company. I bought the French press and a new duvet, and paid for my brother's Shiatsu classes. But I'm not going to bother reminding Marie of any of that.

"It's mine," she says. "I got it as an exchange when my mother gave me that juicer for Christmas."

"Marie," I say, "I'm working. I don't have time for this."

"Just leave it on the front porch," she says, as if I haven't spoken. "I'll come by and pick it up."

"Goodbye, Marie," I say. I hang up the phone. I can still see her outline behind her blinds; for a moment she stands there without moving. Then she shifts to the left, and the little dark openings close to thin seams. I sit looking at them for a while, and then I pick up my pen and my dictionary and go back to work.

When I get home that evening there's an envelope taped to the screen door. I take it down and open it with one hand while I'm putting the key in the lock. I've forgotten all about the French press, and when I see Marie's handwriting I'm momentarily confused. Then I'm annoyed, and I crumple the paper and the envelope together and toss them off the porch.

The phone rings as soon as I get inside.

"Pick up," Marie says to the answering machine. "I know you're home. I saw you come in."

I drop my briefcase and keys on the kitchen table and pick up the phone.

"It's not your coffeemaker," I say immediately. "If it was yours I'd give it back. I already gave you everything that was yours."

She's silent for a minute, and I look out the kitchen window and think I can see her outline faint behind her living-room curtains. She has the lights on and I don't, so she can't see me.

"You got my note," she says finally.

"I got your note," I say. "And it's still my coffeemaker. So please stop calling."

I can hear her breathing quietly on the other end of the line. Through the door to the study, I can see the red eye of the answering machine flickering.

"It's mine," she says. "It's mine and I want it back."

"You can't have it," I say, and hang up. I stand there for a minute, my hand on the receiver, breathing hard. I half expect it to ring again under my palm, but it doesn't, and I step away and rub the back of my neck. I'm sweating slightly.

I go to the sink and rinse out a glass, then fill it with cold water. I drink it standing with my back to the counter, looking around the room as my eyes adjust to the dark. I've reorganized most of the other rooms, but there are still gaps in the kitchen. The empty space next to the toaster where Marie's Cuisinart used to sit. The bare spot on the wall where her Chilies of the World poster was hung. The absence in the cupboards and drawers of a cream jug, an eggbeater, a garlic press. She took a lot of things with her when she went.

Of course, she didn't go far. I look out the window and she isn't standing behind her living-room curtains anymore, but I know she's there all the same. Neither one of us is going anywhere.

It's still dark when the phone rings, and I roll out of bed and fumble with the receiver, thinking of my father's heart, my brother's motorcycle, the family home in flames. I can't find my glasses to read the clock.

"Hello?" My voice is thick and foreign.

The line is silent, and I start to repeat myself. She cuts me off.

"I can understand wanting to keep it for yourself," she says. "But it seems like such a petty thing to do. It's mine. Why won't you just give it to me?"

I sink back onto my bed and stare into the darkness.

"Marie?" I say.

"I mean, it's not such a big deal," she says. "It's just a coffeemaker. But it's mine. I want it. You have no right to keep it."

I grope around on the night table and find my glasses. It's 2:30 a.m.

"It's two-thirty in the morning," I say. "Jesus Christ, Marie."

"Well," she says, and falls silent.

"It's two-thirty in the morning," I say again. "And you're calling me about a coffeemaker. I thought . . . Jesus, Marie. I thought it was an emergency."

There's a pause.

"Well," she says again, and then nothing.

I hold the receiver away from my ear and look at it. Then I reach over and carefully, quietly, hang it up.

I sit on the edge of my bed for a minute, my glasses cool on the bridge of my nose, my heart just beginning to slow. Through my bedroom window I can see Marie's front porch, and the square of light dropped onto it from her own bedroom. The house is silent except for the sound of my breath.

I take my glasses off and rub my temples and run my hands through my hair. Then I get up, find my slippers at the foot of my bed, and walk downstairs to the kitchen in darkness. I go to the cupboard over the sink and take the French press off the shelf. I wrap it in a dish towel. For a minute or two I stand looking at it, considering. The dish towel begins to unwind and I tuck it firmly back into place. Then I pick it up and carry it carefully into the bathroom. I put it on top of the toilet tank while I take my sweatpants and T-shirts and underwear out of the laundry hamper. I put the French press on the bottom of the hamper, and pile everything else on top of it.

Then I go back upstairs and get into bed, and stare out the window at the square of light on Marie's porch. It takes me almost an hour to fall asleep, but her light stays on the whole time.

I get home late again the next day, with a searing headache and a sore back from ten hours of copyediting on the office computer. The mail in my box is all the usual: a flyer from a pizza place, a phone bill, a bank statement. I look automatically for a note from Marie, but there isn't one.

I let myself in, drop my briefcase and keys on the kitchen table, and go to the fridge to get a beer. I've already drunk half of it before I notice the first change.

The blender is on the counter beside the toaster, in the space where the Cuisinart used to be. I look at it for a moment before I look around at the rest of the room. Then I see that the dish rack is on the wrong side of the sink. The terra-cotta pot of basil has been taken from the windowsill and left on the counter. I sip my beer and look around. Then I go to the door of my study and turn on the light. My books are in the wrong places on the shelves. I turn and look through the door to the living room, and I can see by the dents in the carpet that the furniture has been moved.

The phone rings suddenly, and I jump. I step into the study and realize that the phone too has been moved, and I can't find it. I go back into the kitchen and pick up. I don't say anything for a moment; I wait to hear what's coming.

She's silent too, so after a minute I say, "I can't believe you."

There's a pause, and then she says, "You didn't get rid of it, did you?"

I don't say anything. I don't want to give her the satisfaction of knowing that it's still in the house. And I can't think of what to say about what I did last night—the dish towel, the laundry hamper. It's a vague memory, like something I dreamed of, or just considered doing. I was half asleep. I wasn't thinking.

"I want the key," I say, twisting the phone cord around my finger. The dustpan is leaning against the baseboard instead of hanging on its hook. "You're not supposed to have a key anymore."

"You hid it," she says. "You hid it so I wouldn't find it. My God. That's such a petty thing to do."

"You broke into my house!" My voice is high and strangled, and I'm twisting the phone cord hard enough to make my finger turn red. "You came in here and moved everything around and went through my stuff—" I break off and reach for my beer, then put it down again without drinking. "Put the key in an envelope and leave it in my mailbox. Tonight. I want it when I leave the house tomorrow."

"Just give it back," she says. "It's not like I'm asking for much. Just leave it on my porch and that'll be it."

"Marie," I say, struggling to keep my voice even. "Listen to me. It's my coffeemaker. It's mine. I'm not giving it to you. And if you come into my house again I'll call the police."

I wait to see if she'll say anything else, and when she doesn't, I hang up. Then I turn out the kitchen light so she won't be able to watch me, and I finish my beer in the dark.

When I leave the house the next morning the key is in an envelope in my mailbox.

I've spent the night before going through the house, meticulously finding the changes and correcting them. I couldn't remember where all of the books went on the shelves, but I got most of them pretty close. I got to bed late, and I'm tired.

I stand on my porch with the key in my hand, looking over my lawn at Marie's house. Her curtains are drawn and her windows are innocent. I take out my key chain and slowly work the key onto it. I already have two copies—mine, and the one Marie gave back to me when she moved out.

At the time, it had seemed such a final gesture. We'd spent two days separating our possessions, carrying boxes and furniture from my house to hers, making sure everything was where it belonged. On the evening of the second day we shared a beer on my front porch and watched the trucks pull up to the glass factory on the other side of the empty lot. When we finished the beer Marie stood up and took the key out of her pocket.

"Here," she said, holding it out to me on her palm. I looked at it, then took it without looking at her. We watched the trucks for a minute or two in silence.

"Okay," she said, pushing her hands into the small of her back. "I'll see you."

"Okay," I said, staring down at the key in my hand.

She stood there for a moment, and then when I looked up she leaned down as if to kiss me. I turned away, just enough.

She stood up, brushed a piece of hair back from the corner of her mouth, and stuck her thumbs into her belt loops. Then she walked away across my lawn and hers, and up onto her porch, and into her house. She closed the door behind her, and I sat on my step and watched the trucks until it got too dark to see anything but headlights and taillights winking on and off.

Now I stand twisting the new key onto my ring, looking at the blind eyes of her windows and thinking. She had a copy made, of course. And if she had one, she could have more. What if she decides the couch is hers too? Or the television or the stereo or the washing machine?

I turn the key over in my hand, staring across the lawn at Marie's curtains. Then I turn and put the key into the lock and open the door and go to the phone. I call the office and tell them I won't be coming in this morning. Then I take out the phone directory, look up a number, and call it. I tell the man who answers that it's an emergency, and he says he'll send someone as soon as possible. I go into the bedroom, lie on my bed, and watch television until there's a knock on the door. Then I get up and let the man in, and he smiles and squats down in the hallway so that the handles of the tools in his belt knock against the floor, and says, "No problem."

I go back into the bedroom and watch television until he's done. When he leaves I take the dustpan off its hook and sweep up the splinters and paint chips he's left behind. I take three keys off of my key chain—two of them Marie's, one of them mine—and line them up on the kitchen counter. I put the two new keys the man gave me in the place of the three I took off. I stand there looking at the three keys on the counter for a long time.

The phone rings halfway through Oprah, and I reach over and pick it up without looking away from the television. I don't bother to say hello.

She waits a moment, then says, "You're unbelievable."

I pick up the remote and raise the volume of the television a notch. I say, "You started it."

"Do the landlords know you changed the locks?"

I don't answer. In Oprah's studio, a woman is crying.

"All I want is my coffeemaker. That's all I want."

"That's all you want right now," I say as an audience member stands up to speak. "Next week you might decide you want something else. You might decide you want the kitchen table."

"The kitchen table isn't mine."

"Neither is the coffeemaker." I didn't hear what the man in the audience said, but suddenly everyone is applauding. Oprah lets her microphone swing in her hand and looks around, waiting for them to stop.

"You're really unbelievable," Marie says again, and I shrug.

There's a pause, and then she says, "What if I said I'd give it to you? I'll just give it to you and you can have it."

"You can't give it to me," I say. "It's mine anyway." I turn the television up another notch, even though it's already too loud. I can hear Marie listening on the other end of the line.

"My mother gave it to me," she says. "I mean, she gave me the juicer and I took it in and exchanged it. You were there."

"I bought it last summer," I say. "When I bought the duvet. With the money from that German contract. You slept under the duvet for six months. You don't remember that?"

Oprah goes to a commercial break, and I hit the mute button. There is silence on Marie's end of the line.

Finally she says, "Yes. I remember that."

I turn my head and look out my bedroom window at Marie's front porch. Her mail is still in her mailbox and her newspaper is still on the mat. I can't see her in any of her windows.

"What's this really about, Marie?" I say.

She doesn't say anything. I watch two commercials while I wait.

"I want my coffeemaker," she says at last. Her voice is thin and choked.

"I'm sorry," I say. "It's mine."

The next day I go to work and stare at a computer screen and think about Marie's voice. Two assistant editors tell me I look tired. I leave early with a pile of manuscripts under my arm, and on my way home I stop at the Kmart and buy three sets of blinds.

When I get to my front door it takes me a minute to find the right key on my chain. Then the lock sticks and I have to jiggle the key and the handle until finally something inside makes a popping sound and the door opens. I step in and put the blinds on the floor, work the key carefully out of the lock, and close the door. The house is silent.

I go to the kitchen, drop the manuscripts on the table, and take a glass from the cabinet. Everything is back where it belongs. I fill the glass with cold water from the tap and slip out of my shoes. I'll put the blinds in the study and the bedroom, and tomorrow I'll buy curtains for the kitchen.

The locksmith's bill is still folded on the counter, and I pick it up and read it while I drink the water. Then I put it back down and stare out the window at Marie's front lawn. There's more mail in her mailbox, and a second newspaper on her porch mat.

I drink the rest of the water and put the glass down on the counter, next to the bill. The top of my right foot itches, and I rub it against my left calf. Then I turn and walk down the hall to the bathroom. I go in and open the laundry hamper and take out the stale tangle of

T-shirts and sweatpants and underwear. The French press is still there at the bottom, still wrapped in the dish towel. I take it out and put it carefully on the toilet tank while I pile everything else back into the hamper.

I carry it into the kitchen, unwrap it, and hang the dish towel through the refrigerator handle. I pick up the telephone, then put it back down. I want to tell her to open her blinds, so at least we can see each other when I tell her it's hers. I go into my study.

The first thing I see is that my desk has been shoved away from the wall, and the loose papers I've left on top of it have been scattered over the floor. I don't notice the broken window behind it until I step forward into the room and cut my foot on the glass in the carpet.

I go back into the kitchen and pull paper towels from the roll under the sink, run cold water over them, and touch them to the sole of my foot. They come away stained with red marks like flowers. I sit down heavily in a chair and lift my foot so I can see the bottom of it. There's a piece of glass the size of a quarter protruding from the skin. Without thinking, I take hold of it and pull. It comes out easily, and blood begins to well out of the hole it leaves behind.

The phone rings.

I half stand, balancing my weight on the heel of my foot, and snatch the receiver from the cradle.

"I'm calling the police," I say, before she can say anything. "I'm calling the cops right now." I slam the receiver down and then take it off the pins so she can't call back. Then I have to brace my hands on the counter and lower my head, because I'm dizzy and I feel like I can't breathe.

I stand there with my head down for a minute, and then I sink to a squat, and then I sit cross-legged with my forehead on my knees. I'm cold and my hands are shaking. Blood is pooling on the linoleum under my foot, soaking into my trousers. I grab the clot of wet paper towels and press it to the hole in my foot. I try to breathe. After a minute or two I lift my head and grab another wad of paper towels from the roll. I press them on top of the ones I already have, and watch them start to bloom from white to red.

In another minute I grab the side of the counter and pull myself upright. The phone is emitting a flat, plaintive note. The linoleum is spattered with blood, and the counter is smeared with red where my fingers have touched it.

I see a movement through the corner of my eye and when I turn my head I see Marie coming up my walk. She's wearing socks and no shoes, and her shirt is untucked. She's running.

The French press is beside me on the counter. I pick it up and tuck it under one arm like a football, then hobble to the front door to meet her. I get there just before she does, and fling it open before she can knock.

"You bitch," I say, taking the French press from under my arm and brandishing it. She stumbles back off the step, her eyes wide, her mouth open. "You want it so fucking badly, you can have it." I'm going to aim it at her head, but at the last moment I pull back and it hits the concrete step between us. The glass explodes and Marie shrieks and covers her eyes.

"And you can get the hell off my porch," I say, reaching without looking for the door handle behind me. "Because I'm calling the cops." I step back over the threshold and start to swing the door shut, but Marie leans forward and jams it with her arm. Her face is white and her hair has come out of its ponytail.

"I already did," she says.

I pause.

"You called the police?" I don't believe her, but as soon as I've spoken I can hear the sirens in the distance.

"He got in through your study window," she says, and for a moment I can't understand what she could possibly mean. She licks her lips and stares at me. "He got in through your study window," she says again. "Just before you came home. I called the police."

I stand staring at her for a long moment, and then I turn and look over my shoulder into my house. Nothing is out of place. I look back at Marie, then turn and hobble down the hall to my study. The sirens are getting louder.

"Don't—" Marie says, then stops. I reach the door of my study and look in. My answering machine is gone. There's an empty space on the desk where my laptop computer should be.

I stand there looking for a long moment, then turn around and walk back up the hall to the front door. Marie is still standing on the step, looking over her shoulder to watch the police cars pull up across the street. I reach the door and lean against it. I've left bloody foot-prints all the way down the hall.

Two men get out of the police car and start to walk across the street toward us. Marie turns and looks at me, and I look back at her, and all around there are too many jagged fragments, too much simple bro-ken glass and metal, for either of us to risk moving anywhere at all.

# Archeology

**BARBARA WILSON**

> *You may forget*
> *But let me tell you this*
> *Someone in some future time*
> *Will remember us.*
> —Sappho

The clearing in the woods was overgrown now, Clare said, but to me it seemed like an open meadow. Perhaps that was because it was early spring, and there were no leaves out yet on the vine maple and Oregon grape that had taken over. Only the sketchy lines of twisted twigs and branches were between us and the dark green hemlock and fir that shaped the clearing into a circle. The March day Clare took me to that place in the country—well over ten years ago now—a weak sun shone, and the wind moved restlessly, as if trying to settle itself, in the evergreens. Black crows flew overhead with the swiftly changing clouds. It smelled like rain.

"It looks very different," Clare said, in a wondering, somewhat dissatisfied tone. She walked inconclusively into the center of the clearing and back again, wearing a heavy old anorak and rubber boots. I stayed behind at first, for I was in twill slacks and a blazer over an ironed shirt. My polished low boots had already attracted clumps of mud from the road where we'd parked the car. Clare had picked me up for lunch at the office where we both used to work and where I still did. An hour later I called my boss to say I wasn't feeling well and would be going home.

"There's a lot of it around," said Frances sympathetically. She would not have suspected me of lying. Clare she would have suspected. But that was partly why Clare had to leave.

I had overstayed my lunch hour because I could never say no to Clare. It had been the same when she worked with me at Boeing (we were in the design division and spent our days making graphs and charts for the engineers); I had always fallen in with her plans. Today had been no different. When she had suggested over lunch—"Take the afternoon off. I'm restless with spring. Let's go to the country. There's someplace I want to show you"—I had immediately agreed.

"The main house was here," Clare said, pointing to the charred foundations in the clearing. "It burned after I left. Right next to it was the vegetable garden. We grew everything ourselves. The raised beds have flattened, but you can still see them."

She was standing close to me, the way she often did. There was something in her—southern Italian, grandparents from Naples, she said—that did not like physical distance. Always a touch on the shoulder and a stroking of the arm. She came closer to me than anyone except my husband ever had.

"The tree house. The sweat lodge." Clare pointed the structures out among the firs. I hadn't seen them at first. They looked tacked together with salvaged lumber and tar paper: children's constructions, not built for permanence.

"This was my—our—place," she said, leading me around the side of the clearing to a one-room shack next to a tall Douglas fir. There was a glass window and the door opened and closed. Even so, the weather had entered. The place smelled of the forest, not of people.

"It's . . . cozy," I ventured.

"We didn't have good boundaries in those days." She smiled. It was a face I loved to see smile, a thin face, olive-skinned with straight black glossy eyebrows, black eyes, white teeth, a faint mustache. When she wasn't smiling, she often looked anxious.

She wasn't much older than me—she was thirty-four, I was thirty-two—but she had been a lesbian for an inconceivable amount of time—since college. She'd been in gay lib, had started a lesbian rap group, had volunteered in a bookstore, had organized concerts, had lived on lesbian land in a separatist collective.

All during the seventies, while I'd been married.

There was a table still, but no chair. Under the glass window that was no longer weather-tight, was a shelf that looked as if it might have been a washing area. There were a few hooks on the walls and a rod that still held a washcloth.

It had been a red washcloth once. Perhaps it still was (when was the exact moment that something, having lost its purpose, could be said to have also lost its name?). Certainly, however, no one would ever use it again on her face or under her arms, or pull its wet soft dark redness between her legs. The texture peculiar to terry cloth—thread bunched in loops—had given way to something more like stiff, greenish-brown cardboard. It was greenish because of the lichen creeping over it. If I had found this squarish, flat object in the forest outside I might have imagined it to be a chunk of cedar bark covered with moss. Only the fact that it was hanging vertically from a tarnished towel bar alerted me to its former status—though "hanging" doesn't really convey the absolute immovable rigidity of the thing; it looked so stiff that if the bar was removed, the washcloth would keep hanging there in space, an upended flying carpet.

On closer inspection (the touching a fingertip to its surface), it seemed, however, that the washcloth, far from being indestructible, was held together by mere threads, or perhaps by memories of the soft young skin it had once stroked, and that those threads were weakened to the point of explosion. It had probably never been an extremely fluffy, *thick* washcloth, the kind that are more like soft caresses than cotton; undoubtedly it had come from a more utilitarian department store like Sears or Penney's, or even a more cut-rate source like Woolworth's or Chubby and Tubby's.

It wouldn't take much to start a hole going. It was clear that the edges of the washcloth, especially the bottom edge, were neither even nor intact, but frayed, so that tiny filigrees of thread feathered out minutely, like cilia in the bronchial tubes, barely visible filaments that fluttered with each breath of cold wind. A slight pull to one of the filaments and it would all unravel.

How many winters that washcloth had lived through, including its early useful years when it had scrubbed and soaped, been balled up and fiercely wrung out. How many years it had survived, helplessly absorbing moisture (for that was its dumb nature) through the window that never hung very well and whose frame was now warped and askew.

While I'd been looking at the washcloth, Clare had been wandering the room. "God, it's depressing, isn't it? I can't believe I lived here for four whole years of my life. That so many of us did."

"What happened to everyone?"

"Came, went, had meetings, fought, left. There were about a dozen of us, maybe six living here at any one time. The ones who were 'in town' were supposed to work and support those who were 'on the land.' The idea was that we'd trade off."

She ran her finger along the dusty windowsill, found a stone and handed it to me. "We were idealists." The word had a flat, cold sound in the room. "Or just stupid."

The stone she'd given me was small, rectangular with sloped edges, very smooth, pale gray. I rubbed its surface with my thumb and found it had an odd texture. It was absent any hint of the granular, which even the most well-washed of river stones have. I brought it up close to look at it better, and caught, very faint, something meadowy. It could hardly even be called a smell: only a few molecules bumped up into my nose. Not an entire meadow of wildflowers, only one or two. A stalk of lupine, a crushed sprig of love-in-a-mist, a poppy petal.

It was a bar of soap, hardened to stonelike consistency, but still keeping within it a trapped sense of spring.

I wondered who had brought it here and who had used it. Was it a special hand-milled French soap, a tiny feminine luxury in a brave new world, or was it something ordinary, like Dove or Zest? Had one of the women used it with the red washcloth, back when the washcloth had been full of rough vigor and the soap was capable of creating a rich bubbly froth?

Had it been Clare?

Clare sat down on the mildewed single mattress rotting on a slapped-together wooden platform, with a ragged Indian spread pulled half across it.

"A single mattress for the two of you?" I asked, standing awkwardly beside her.

"Her name was Sara," said Clare. "She called herself Sara Nightingale for a few years. A nice ring, don't you think? She was a musician— wanted to be one anyway. I think she's working in real estate now. She was completely neurotic." Clare smiled. "Though around here, it was hard to tell what was really crazy or not."

She patted the mattress to indicate I should sit next to her.

I perched gingerly, half expecting rats to crawl out from the stuffing, or the platform to collapse. I noticed that the cuffs of my twill pants were wet and streaked with mud. I still held the bar of soap, the fragrant stone, in my hand. I thought of the two of them, Clare and Sara Nightingale, young women living here on lesbian land, in this small house together, making love on the narrow bed. In my imagination they had a woodstove and a pot of tea brewing, and in the distance there were the voices of other women.

I had lived with my parents until I got married and now I lived alone.

"It's good to spend some time again with you," Clare said, picking up my hand and studying the palm intently, the way she sometimes had at work, in a way that had both thrilled and disconcerted me. "How's the divorce going?"

"It's final soon, thank god." I sagged a little. Roger had veered between making things extremely unpleasant and looking at me with soulful, even doglike eyes. "Tell me just one thing I did wrong," he had often said at first. Now he was calling to make sure I didn't steal or destroy any of our precious possessions before we could settle on who owned, or deserved, what.

"When I first met you last fall, I couldn't *believe* you'd been married for twelve years," said Clare. She put an arm around me and snuggled gently. This too she had sometimes done at work, bending over me as I sat drawing graphs of lines converging and separating again. Frances had warned me about it.

"I've seen this before, Katherine," Frances had said. "Clare behaving . . . like this. She does it just to irritate me, I think. Just tell her to stop bothering you and she will. I'll speak to her as well."

I had not told Clare to stop.

"Yes, well," I said to Clare. "You know it was a high school thing, me and Roger. I never thought one way or the other about it. First I put him through school, then he put me. We were kids from Everett who wanted to work at Boeing like our parents, but to have better jobs than they had. That's all we ever wanted."

Clare stroked my hair, as if full of sympathy, and then laughed. "Oh no, I *liked* that you were married. I really felt I could talk to you. You weren't like *them*." She got up abruptly, as if the room had filled with ghosts, and walked a few steps to the windows. With mock drama, she

said, "Now you're getting divorced, what am I going to do? What kind
of a role model can you be now?"

I lay back on the bed, used to these sudden changes, these quips and
ironies of hers. Once, a few months ago, the day Frances finally fired
her. Clare had come home with me to the house I then shared with
Roger. She'd drunk up almost all of a six-pack we had in the refrigerator
and told me her life story: unhappy home with Catholic parents, four
other siblings, mother manic-depressive, father patriarchal and pun-
ishing. Majored in English, active in the antiwar movement, came out
at twenty, didn't finish college, and gave all her energy to political
work. The Boeing job was her first real job and she'd hated it.

"I took it to save money to go back to school. The only other things
I'd done were waitressing and office temping. I can't handle authority. I'm not used to it. I can't stand someone having power over me,
especially not an idiot like Frances. I liked drawing diagrams, but
everything else . . . It's just as well she fired me."

"What do you want to do.

"I want to be a therapist. Does that sound strange? I think I *could*
help other people. I understand a lot . . . from my family, and from living in a collective, about the things that . . . tear you apart."

Later she had reclined on the sofa and had let me give her a massage. I had bent over her a long time, smelling the strong citrus fragrance of her shiny black hair. I had felt her shoulders and her back. I
had stroked her legs from the thighs to the toes. Then I had turned
her over and had gradually found my way to her full breasts. She'd
had her eyes closed and was breathing heavily as I slowly approached
her nipples. Then she abruptly sat up, laughed, and said, "But,
Katherine, you're a married woman!"

I'd started divorce proceedings soon after, but when I'd called
Clare to tell her, she'd seemed surprised.

"Roger sounded like such a nice guy."

"He's boring. We don't have anything in common."

"But isn't that the good thing about heterosexuals?" she joked.
"They don't merge."

"Merge?"

"Lesbo-speak, Katherine. Anyway, I hope you'll think about it,
before you make a quick decision."

"I *have* thought about it. I just didn't know I could have anything
different from what I had."

"I know," she said, almost sadly, before hanging up.

After she left Boeing I didn't see Clare as much. She took out a loan and started back to school. From time to time she'd call me at work and make me laugh. But she'd never suggested getting together again until today.

I rolled on my stomach on the bed and caught a glimpse of something cardboard wedged between the mattress and the wall.

I fished it up: a dusty record album. The cover was torn at top and bottom around the caramel-brown border, and the photographic image on the front was water-stained, though still visible. It showed a woman with long hair standing on a rock in a desert setting with cactus behind, Joshua trees I thought, and in the very back, a mountain range. It was printed in a duotone of purple and green which gave the landscape and the woman an eerie look, though she seemed happy enough. She had her mouth slightly open and a row of front top teeth gleamed white. She was wearing a pair of overalls that looked too long; they lapped over her bare feet. It appeared that she was naked under the overalls; at least, she had no shirt.

Her hands were jauntily placed in her pockets, and I could tell she was meant, or meant herself, to look, not posed, but relaxed and at ease. And yet the green and purple tints, water-stained as they were, gave everything a sad look.

The words at the bottom were faded too; I could hardly make them out.

*"The Changer and . . . the . . ."*

"The *Changed*." Clare laughed. "Don't tell me you've never heard of Cris Williamson?"

I shook my head. Before I met Clare I'd never met a lesbian, or if I had, I hadn't known it, a fact that Clare seemed to find both delightful and very strange. She adored telling me stories, stories that she named "bizarre" and "demented," of screaming matches at collective meetings, of trips across country to something called "Michigan," of the strange antics of a group of women living in the woods somewhere near Granite Falls.

It took some weeks before I realized that all of these stories were in the past.

"Don't you . . . ever . . . I mean now . . . I mean, do you have a . . . girlfriend?" I asked her once at lunch, interrupting a complicated story of rivalries and squabbling.

And Clare had taken my hand over the lunch table and laughed and said in that cryptic way of hers, "Oh god, no! Isn't it obvious? I'm taking a break from the whole crazy bunch of them."

I never knew when Clare was joking, that was part of the problem.

I took the record out; it was in two pieces, almost as if someone had deliberately broken it in a rage. It was still shiny black but worn with much playing. I stroked the surface of one of the pieces. Like the soap petrified to stone, the record held within it some secret fragrance, some melody that called to me and that I wanted to hear.

"Was she at . . . Michigan?"

"Of course. And everywhere else. You couldn't go anywhere for a few years without hearing that stupid song." She warbled a few bars, something about a waterfall, and then came back over to the bed.

"This is like archeology, isn't it? These old artifacts from the glorious days of a lesbian separatist commune?" Clare had in her hand a candleholder in the shape of a woman. She was seated. Her wide lap formed a base for the candle and her arms came together at the hands to make a bowl. It was ceramic, of brown clay with a blue-green glaze. In the bowl were the remnants of a candle. It was still possible to see that it had been rainbow-colored.

Clare held it out to me, and I took it. It fit the palm of my hand in a pleasing way. "For you," she said. "I made it, way back in 1978 or '79, I guess."

She sat back down beside me. I could smell her black hair, which was so much stronger and more alive than the smell of the meadow stone. She had been letting it grow and it came down to her chin, framing her thin face. She had taken off her anorak and was wearing a heavy sweater underneath. I wanted to touch her, to snuggle her as she did me, but didn't dare.

"We wanted to be self-sufficient," she said, all in a rush. "I would be the potter and Laura would be the carpenter. Sara was the cook and Tressa was the gardener. We were the main four, and others came and went, an electrician, a welder, and lots and lots of women who couldn't do much of anything. We had a vision—it seems so stupid now—of a thriving community of women networked with other communities across the country and the world. We dreamed of being independent and self-sufficient. . . ."

"But why is that stupid?"

"We wanted to change the world. We thought we could. But we couldn't even decide what to do with someone who wouldn't wash her dishes!"

It was one of Clare's jokes, but it was not a joke.

She lay back on the bed, suddenly exhausted, and I lay back with her. The mildewed mattress creaked. I could see the pattern of the Indian bedspread close up: gray elephants linked trunk to tail, in a never-ending procession.

The light was fading, and the wind had come up even more. Overhead and around us the firs moved in agitation.

"You always talk about those days as if they were terrible. But surely—you must have had fun, you must have laughed and danced and listened to . . . Cris Williamson."

"We laughed and danced and listened to Cris Williamson," Clare repeated, almost mockingly, but also with a kind of longing I had sometimes caught in her voice. "Sometimes I think—I'd had such a strong Catholic upbringing. And I hated my father. And I was rebellious, *loved* the big marches of the sixties. And being a lesbian was the most rebellious thing I could think of."

"If I were a lesbian," I said tentatively, "I wouldn't do it because I was rebelling against anything. I would do it . . . because I loved . . . someone."

"We didn't know anything about love in those days," Clare said.

Without breathing, I placed my hand on her stomach, and she let me. But when I moved it slightly upward, Clare sat bolt upright.

"Don't you understand?" she said desperately. "I'm through with all that!"

"Then why did you bring me here?"

"I brought you here as my friend, someone safe I could talk to. I don't have anyone else I can trust."

She began to cry.

Sorry now and flattered, I sat up too and put an arm around her, murmuring comforting words: "There, there," I said, and "Don't be afraid. You can talk to me. I *am* safe."

Her black eyes looked at me gratefully. Her hair smelled like oranges.

How much I loved her! I understood now that I hadn't asked Roger to leave because he bored me or because of some vague sense that something wasn't right between us, but because of Clare herself. I was in love with Clare and I wanted to be her lover, however long it took.

"No one else I know would understand," she began again. "It's why I don't have any lesbian friends anymore. Why I'm afraid to go to the places I used to."

I put the candleholder to the side and held her close. I couldn't have imagined jaunty Clare sobbing like this. "There, there," I said.

"I'm seeing a man," she burst out. "It's been a year and now he wants to get married, have kids. It goes against everything I worked for and thought I wanted. Married to a man. Becoming a breeder. Turning into a heterosexual. Flipping. Going straight!" She turned her tear-streaked face to me, and cracked, "Officer, I never meant to go wrong!"

Clare could not resist the funny side of things, even in her misery. But I couldn't laugh. "Who is he?"

"You know him. That cute engineer who was around when you first came. Frances had him transferred to another department, the bitch."

"She's not a bitch," I said, drawing the line.

"She *is*," said Clare. "I'm not a good lesbian-feminist anymore. I can say stuff like that!"

We stared at each other a second, then moved apart.

"There, I've confessed," said Clare in relief. "I've actually told someone."

"That's really why you brought me here?" I said, dully, getting up and going to the window, staring out. The rain had begun, a fierce spring rain.

"No," said Clare, laughing again, trying to cheer me up. "I was rescuing you from Frances! Aren't you bored with all those diagrams of trajectories?"

I laughed too, in a forced way, and said, "It's freezing here. We'd better go."

We closed the door carefully behind us, though there was no reason, and made our way back across the clearing. It had seemed a shorter path than going around through the trees, but once we were inside it, I felt tangled up and persecuted. My good twill pants tore on a blackberry vine and my blazer was soaked from the rain. Clare strode ahead in her anorak and rubber boots.

During the drive back we were mostly silent. I watched the road, the signs that said Granite Falls, Monroe, Snohomish, Everett. She exited there and dropped me in front of my house, the house that was empty and mine alone now, without suggesting that she come in.

Just before we said, "See you soon," I remembered that I'd forgotten the little candleholder in the shape of a woman that Clare had given me.

But as with so much else, I didn't mention it.

It's a long time since I went to the site of the lesbian commune with Clare. I run into her sometimes in Seattle, where I now live; occasionally she's with her husband or little boy. He's not so little now, of course; I suppose he must be eleven, for Clare got pregnant three months after our excursion and she married soon after that.

Her husband and I sometimes see each other at work too. I like him well enough. I have wondered if he knows about Clare's history, not that it matters. She probably wouldn't talk with him about it, and if she did, how could he truly understand it?

"I never know what to say to her," complained my partner Louisa, once after we saw Clare on University Avenue with her son.

It had been a cold fall day and Clare had on a heavy red coat that made her olive skin glow. With her dark hair and eyes she could always carry off dramatic colors. After getting her B.A. she had gone on to graduate school to earn an M.S.W. and was working as a therapist. I had stayed on at Boeing, in the design department, and had ended up replacing Frances when she retired.

All our graphs and diagrams were done, easily, on computers now.

Clare and I had a laugh, as always, about the old days at the office, when Clare used to drive Frances crazy, and then Clare said, in that way of hers, touching my arm as if no one but us existed, her face close, her smile so white, that if *I'd* been her boss in the old days, then maybe she wouldn't have quit.

I breathed her citrus hair smell, noticed that she bleached her mustache now. Her face was still a little anxious when she wasn't smiling, but not *as* anxious, I thought.

"She always flirts with you," said Louisa afterward as we continued down the street to do our shopping.

I didn't try to deny it.

"I never understand these women who suddenly go straight!" brooded Louisa.

We've had this conversation before. "It must have been a hard choice for Clare to make," I'll say, and Louisa will reply, "Heterosexual privilege is not a hard choice to make."

Louisa is my age and works at Boeing too. Before that she was a carpenter in an all-women carpentry collective, but she speaks about it with affection, not disdain. Her longtime lover Paula is still one of Louisa's best friends and they get together sometimes and tell stories. Louisa has the record *The Changer and the Changed,* and once they played it for me and Paula got tears in her eyes and said, "We had so *little* then. You can't imagine. A few books, a few records, and the things we made ourselves, pottery and jewelry."

"It was so lonely," said Louisa. "To have to create your own reflection in order to see yourself for the first time."

"Singers like Cris Williamson were part of that creation," said Paula. "She made us feel strong and alive and very, very brave."

I listened to the record and heard only a pleasant voice and slightly sappy lyrics. I would never have their early history, much as I wanted to. I had only my own, with Roger, alone and unknowing. He has remarried now and looks puzzled when he sees me, as if I remind him of something he'd almost succeeded in forgetting.

"She probably was never really a lesbian, you know," said Louisa, still rehashing.

"Who knows? Who's to say?"

"Because you can't just wake up one morning and say: Everything I thought I believed is no longer important to me."

"But that's what happened to me with Roger." I laughed and hugged Louisa close. I find it strange, and rather touching, that after all these years together, Louisa is still jealous of Clare.

Louisa laughed too, only partly at herself. "Well, obviously. You went in the *right* direction."

I spend my days with diagrams so perhaps it's not unusual that I see Clare and my separate trajectories in terms of geometry. Our paths crossed just at the moment I was leaving my husband and she was finding hers.

There was a point in space, an instant in time, when it seemed we were alike, two women in our early thirties, both in transition, both briefly bisexual, both aware of some possibility between us.

A possibility that was over as soon as the lines of our separate trajectories met and passed.

That point in time exists only in our memories, or perhaps only in my memory. That point in space exists now only in my memory as well. For recently, one Sunday in early spring, I had occasion to drive to Spokane for a weeklong conference. I took the highway that led across the mountains, but before I went too far, I recalled that Clare's commune had been nearby, somewhere in the vicinity of Granite Falls.

The name of the exit was the same, but almost everything else was different. New housing developments keep springing up where there were only orchards and farm or ranch lands before. In search of privacy and the rural life, people keep moving further and further out of the cities, bringing suburbia with them.

Where there had once been a clearing and a few structures, there were only bulldozed piles of earth. Another few months and it would have been completely unrecognizable. Happy Valley Glen Estates.

I got out of my car and walked to what might have been a meadow tangled with Oregon grape, vine maple, and blackberry vines, and surrounded with firs and hemlocks that rustled in the March wind. Once there had been a tree house and sweat lodge and a burned-down main house and a little shack where Clare had lived with Sara Nightingale. Once there had been a mattress with a torn elephant-patterned bedspread, and a broken vinyl record in a torn cover and a red washcloth that looked like bark and a sliver of soap that looked like stone. Would these artifacts have been bulldozed into a heap of splintered wood and carted off to the dump?

Or would a few of the small remains have just been plowed under, to be covered up by a grid of asphalt streets and overlarge houses with big picture windows?

Somewhere, perhaps, several feet under *The Randalls* or *The Wallaces,* the bar of soap and the washcloth would lie, until they completely disintegrated and were no more. The broken vinyl record would exist for decades, perhaps centuries, but it would never be played again, and perhaps no one would know, in times to come, how much those lyrics, so bravely sung by the long-haired woman in the overalls, had once meant to women who wanted and needed to be brave too.

Only the ceramic candleholder in the shape of a woman would keep its name and something of its purpose. In a hundred years or more, when these unbuilt houses too were gone, someone might find it in a vacant lot and hold it up and admire it as ancient.

Would they know that it had been made by a woman who loved another woman? Or would they care?

The spring sky was huge that day I stood in the open field, with piles of earth around me, while below me the remnants of a once-fresh world and its meaning crumbled into nothingness. Except for the figure of a seated woman whose arms made a circle, to hold what remained in memory.

# The Lake
# at the End
# of the Wash

**KARLEEN PENDLETON JIMÉNEZ**

I remember how quick he had always been to take a dare. He smiled back at me for just a second and then dove from the ledge into the brown water. It would have looked real graceful except he had a bony-thin, twelve-year-old body that was nothing like the TV divers from the Olympics. A few years later I learned you weren't supposed to dive into the wash lake that had a lot of rocks in it. Some kid that was the son of a friend of my mom had died by diving on a rock. My mom told me about it and I agreed with her about how stupid kids can be, 'cause that day when I jumped off the ledge, I felt my foot hit a rock two feet under. I didn't tell my mom that part, though. She always worried a lot about me. She said it had nothing to do with trusting me, she just didn't trust anybody else. I guess it could have been Sal's fault for daring me to jump after him, but I followed him. I followed him anywhere. I was in love with his skinny brown body. I touched it as much as I could get away with and he touched me back the same. Don't get me wrong, there was nothin' goin' on between us.

I might've liked him, but he already had a girlfriend. Besides he didn't think of me that way anyways. One time his mom said people might think we were boyfriend-girlfriend, hanging around together so much. I felt all happy for a second until Sal started laughing and I did too so that he wouldn't know that I liked him that way. And it made more sense to laugh anyways because it wouldn't be right for me to like him as more than a friend. So we both laughed at his mom and told her how stupid that would be and I felt even more stupid when I looked down at myself in a maroon and gold V-neck jersey and blue jean shorts. Boy clothes. Brother hand-me-downs. What could I have been thinking in these clothes liking Sal?

The girls Sal liked wore makeup and bras already—even if nothing had started growing yet. They wore their hair stiff with junk in it, tight back and curly in the front like the Cholas at the high school. They made out like the Cholas too. That's why he liked them. That year Paula was the one he would take behind the classrooms. Afterward he'd tell me how they kissed with all the details. I'd listen. I wanted to know all the parts, everything he did to her. How her lips tasted, if she kept her eyes open or not, it there was anything under the bra, if they laid next to each other or if he climbed on top like the movies, if she was soft, and if he actually liked touching her frozen sticky hair. I shouldn't have asked everything, I know. 'Cause of how much it hurt my stomach when I thought of him touching her and not me. It's just I had to know. Not about her and him, but about it.

He liked telling me. Talked about her all day. Sometimes I'd even have to go with him to buy her things. I'd get mad finding little candies or sometimes even little rings for her, but Sal wasn't very good at picking things out, so I thought I'd be a bad friend to him if I didn't help. Besides, she was very pretty with big dark eyes, shiny black hair, and cute little lips. We were in the sixth grade and she already wore colored Guess jeans and frilly tops, so I couldn't let Sal buy anything dumb for her. Not while he was my friend. It still made me mad, but I figured as long as he was spending most of his time with me, it'd be okay.

We stole candy from the Chinese liquor store, looked for bums in the Christmas tree fields, searched for dead bodies in the wash, planned an escape to Seattle if our parents ever got too mean, and played a lot of basketball, but what we loved most were summers at the lake at the end of the wash.

The boxers that he always shows the top inch of are open to the sun, the smog, and me. I wish I could get some to show off too because they're more important than just underwear. If you're Mexican, you wear boxers, no doubt about it. Only white boys wear butt-huggers. But see, all I got are a bunch of panties. The word "panties" alone makes me squeeze my eyes and look down when my mom says it. I hate that word. My mom says they don't make anything like boxers for girls, so I better just forget it. My only stand against her is that I only let her buy me white ones. If I have to do it, at least they're all just plain white. I try not to let anyone see them, though. I hide them under my jeans, but when I swim, they're under soccer shorts. Blue soccer shorts with a gold L.A. Aztecs seal on the corner and a white T-shirt. That's my swimsuit. I wear it every time we come to the lake. My mom tries to buy me a swimsuit from the store, but they're all worse than the panties. Every one I've seen has flowers or bright colors. My mom knows she has no chance, so she bought me a couple more T-shirts, so I wouldn't be wearing the same thing all the time. She says this will be the last summer, though. She says my body will change after that. I don't know what she has planned, but she's never going to get one of those flowery things on me, no matter what my body does. Besides they're already showing on my chest now. Doesn't bother me if Sal sees them.

At first I thought I was going to die because they were so sore. I figured anything that hurt so much next to my heart meant the end of my life. I was afraid to tell my mom because I didn't want her to get sad. I never know what to do when she starts crying especially when it's my fault. So I went on with my secret until my mom asked me one day if they were sore. I told her "No" real quick and acted insulted. Nothing on my body could hurt me and if it did, she'd be the last person to know. I'm glad that I found out it was okay for them to be hurtin', though. Otherwise I'd still be worried about dying.

It's important to find out body things. They showed us a film only girls could see last year and said I'd start bleeding, but that hasn't happened yet and I don't know anyone that has it. They showed how you could still go swimming with it and that was all I was worried about. Sal asked me a bunch of questions about it later and I explained as good as I could, but it was all pretty confusing. Sal and I talk about that stuff a lot, but we don't tell anybody. It's our secret like the place we go swimming. It's also a secret that we take off my bathing suit and his boxers in the water. See, we figure if nobody's going to tell us right what's happening to our bodies, we need to inspect each other. At first, we'd just look at my sore spots through the T-shirt. You could see them pretty well 'cause the shirt stuck to the middles. One was much bigger than the other and we used to check them out. But we thought it'd be better to see them in the open. I took my shirt off because it was for helping us both, and we looked at them all day. Later he asked me about under the Aztec shorts. I admitted that some hairs had grown, so he wanted to see. I'm not stupid. If he was going to learn all about mine, he was going to have to show me his, so we both took them off. Of course, I took my panties off as quick as I could under the shorts so he wouldn't see them. He threw his boxers over them on top of a rock. That's how it all started. Now we always take our suits off. I got an old swim mask of my brothers and we take turns looking at each other. Sometimes I open down there as wide as I can for him to see. Whenever I do, a lot of bubbles come up fast 'cause he starts laughing and then I do too. When I go down and look, I bump into his thing on purpose 'cause I want to feel it. Sometimes he gets mad, but I say the water is so brown I have to get close and that's why I bump it. He shows me how it gets big and small in his hands in the water and I can't believe it.

Sal's always thinking of things to do. He found a hole in the concrete with a knob that made water come out when you turn it. It was clear water and I don't know where it came from. We'd pretend to take showers in it and all the white water would splash into the brown.

The next day I stole my mom's hose and we left early. We shot the water through the hose at each other and then shot it above the ledge so we could dive over the white water into the brown and the rocks. Sal dove up high all morning and never hit a single rock. I just held the hose and watched because I knew I would hit a rock. By noon, he was real tired and laid down on the cement ledge in the sun. I laid down across from him until we were all dry and hot. I like to feel my skin get dry in the sun. The skin gets smaller and tighter when the water goes away and it stays warm all over. It makes me go to sleep too, so when the cold water hit me, I got so scared I almost fell off the ledge.

Sal held the hose water over me laughing.

"Here," he says, "it'll feel good. I'll do it slow over your body."

I let him and he goes up and down my back and legs. It makes me want to sleep again 'cause it feels so good like he said. As soon as I close my eyes, I feel the hose jerk hard between my legs and the cold water rush up inside me. I jump up mad and start yelling at him, but he's laughing and doesn't care.

"I'm sorry," he says, "I'm sorry. Come on. You could put the water on me now."

But I'm still too mad.

"Oh, come on. Here take it. Take the hose, it's your turn."

He puts it down and lies on his stomach and closes his eyes. The hose starts to slide off the ledge, so I grab it. Cold water is still slipping out between my legs and all I feel are my muscles moving fast down there.

I put the hose over his back and legs and go up and down for as long as I can till he looks almost asleep. Then with one fast move I open his butt and stick it in as hard as I can and he jumps and squirms out of it like I tried to, but I got him good and I pushed harder in for as long as I can until he flips over and then we both laugh.

We got a new game. What's important is to make the other person as tired as you can with the water light all over the body. That's what makes the surprise so much fun. I like how fast it happens and how my body gets when he puts it in. It's like when I fight my brothers and my body's so strong against them, but then there's that second when all of my muscles stop trying and everything goes tired.

But I like it better when I make my hand as hard and strong as I can and push it in him. I think he likes that better too because he wanted me to keep doing it to him. I can hold it there for a while 'cause I'm pretty strong. My brothers tell me I have to be strong, and now I'm glad 'cause I like doing this on Sal's body for as long as I can. We did it to each other all afternoon.

When we were about to leave, I heard my name and saw my brother on one of the cement walls near where the dirt patch is. He yelled that my mom needed me home. The new game had made me forget about the time. We got out quick and luckily my brother didn't notice the hose. I'd be in big trouble if my mom knew I stole it.

He did see us naked, though, and my brother has a big mouth. He told my mom about us taking off our suits. He's jealous 'cause I got more friends than him and he's already in high school. That's why he gets me in trouble. I didn't see what the big deal was. She says we're too old to be playing like that together, and now I'm not allowed to go to the lake with him anymore. The whole thing is pretty stupid to me, 'cause she thinks we like each other that way or something, just like Sal's mom. Why can't adults understand anything? I'd never be a girl that Sal would have as a girlfriend. We're best friends. We share candy bars, knives, and secrets. That's the kind of stuff best friends do together.

# They've Got My (Wrong) Number

**K. L. ROBYN**

Anita and I almost became friends. But there was something about pushing her buttons. She was friendly, but edgy with me. Distant. Like maybe I shouldn't know anything about her life. Hey, she was the one who called me. So it was an accident, a numerological phenomenon: she was reaching for some Katherine—apparently it just wasn't me. But I think she must've had trouble seeing me as a person. Still, she called again and revealed just a bit more. Like about her friend—*Katherine*—who was exhausted from law school. And her cousin *Cathy*, the sociopath: her free spirit; her problems with money. I listen. Ask questions. She never asks about me and I don't offer. I don't tell her how much I understand all this. How I'm the black sheep of the family; how sometimes I'm exhausted just getting up in the morning. I don't tell her I'm a lesbian. Or that I recently lost all my friends. And my work. But I'm good at listening.

Anita started as a wrong number.

I answered on the first ring.

*Is Katherine there?*

*This is she.*

*Yo, how ya' doin'?*

*Who's this?*

*Anita!*

*Anita who?*

*Is this Katherine?*

*Yes.*

*Oh man. I think I have the wrong Katherine.*

*How do you spell it?*
*K-a-t-h-e-r-i-n-e*
*Yeah, that's not me.*
*Sorry.*
*'S okay, bye.*
We hung up.
Then it happened again:
*Cath? Girl, it's Anita. / Oh yeah? / Oh God, I did it again. / That's okay. . . .*

For a few weeks it was going on every couple of days. Both of their phone numbers—the K(C)athy's—were similar to mine. A sequence of numbers out of place or transposed—something like one had the first three numbers and the other the last four—and when Anita forgot which one she was dialing mid-call, she talked to me. And I responded. It's hard to hear the nuances of spelling on the telephone. You have to really know someone. After a while, she told me all about her friend and her cousin and their numbers. She was embarrassed, I guess. But I didn't want her to be. I liked her voice. It had the round velvety tones that are common to young black women. So I assumed that's what she was. Nothing she said ever led me to believe otherwise. And I found myself trying to warm up and smooth out my sharp white Midwestern twang, so she wouldn't be sure what my race was. I wanted her to think I could be black. Maybe. I don't know if it worked. My girlfriend thought I should block the number, but I liked the chance to talk on the phone. I certainly wasn't getting that many other calls in those early days after leaving my partner of seven and a half years for another woman.

My ex got custody of everything. The dog. The cat. And all our friends. She got the house, the yard, the herbs in the garden. She got the story of how we broke up. Of how I betrayed her for someone with money. A successful woman. Not someone like us. We didn't believe in success. We were artists and lesbians, success was out of our realm. So apparently was art, since neither of us was doing anything but working for low wages. But this "other" woman, well. She worked as a writer and had blown into my life like a Santa Ana windstorm and shaken us to our bones. We kept joint custody of only one thing: the vet bills.

Our dog was trying to keep us together. All three of us. She kept getting hurt. Wrenched back, ear infection, broken toe. We converged every few weeks on the veterinary hospital for her treatments. It was the only time you would ever see a dog wagging its tail excitedly against an examination table. The bills kept coming. My ex and I couldn't afford it. The only one making any money was my new girlfriend. She started issuing checks for the care of my first marriage's four-legged child. My ex had no choice. She took it. The money from the hot hand of success and betrayal. She's still mad about it. Of course that's my story. She won't speak about it. But I can guess. And our friends still don't call. I can say I don't even know them anymore. I didn't know anyone else then. Anita was it.

One day Anita inadvertently gave me her number. She left it on my answering machine in an irritated voice full of hurry and history after a long involved message to Cathy about the DMV and insurance and some outstanding warrants. I called her back and left a message on her machine to let her know it was me she'd called and not her cousin Cathy or her friend Katherine, but I teased her that since I now had her number I might call her periodically too. But I never did. I left it that she could call back if she wanted.

She did. And she explained about the warrants. They were her cousin's from a wide variety of parking violations. Actually every kind of parking violation. And Anita was really mad because the car was in her name and now she couldn't renew her registration until the tickets were paid off. She couldn't afford it and she was afraid a "boot" was in her future. I asked her what her cousin was doing about it. *Nodda goddam thing,* she said.

*How about payments?* I asked her.

*Well, that might work, but*—Well, lots of things but the main one was that the DMV wanted her there in person and she couldn't go because her cousin had the car.

*You lent her the car again?!*

*She's my cousin!*

Now that's family values.

Then came the icing on the cake. Another wrong number. A man named Sam—with a warm voice made gruff from untold stories—looking for his daughter. Again, a Katherine! He thought the coincidence of my name was so strange, he stayed on a minute. I told him there were so many Kathys in my fourth-grade class I had to be Kathy R. He told me he called his daughter every Sunday. This was the first time he dialed wrong, actually the first time he dialed at all in quite a while. His speed dial was on the blink. Better look the number up again. He told me he always liked to call her after Sunday dinner, didn't want to disturb her meal. I told him I was making pancakes. He laughed. We were having ourselves a nice chat, so I filled him in about the other Katherines and about Anita.

There was silence on the line. Then suspicion.

*Anita? Is this Anita?*

*No, sir, it's, well, you know, it's Kathryn, but not your Katherine.*

*You wouldn't be making a fool out of an old man, would ya?*

*Don't tell me you know Anita.*

*Anita's my daughter's best friend!*

This was too much. His Katherine was the same as Anita's. He even knew Anita. Met her at his baby's thirtieth-birthday party. What's going on here? I know we live in Hollywood, but . . . I could hear the "doo doo doo doo, doo doo doo doo" theme from *The Twilight Zone* in the wire between us. My life was taking on the character of a pitch meeting—"It's a fractured comedy: *Candid Camera* meets *The X-Files* . . . No, no, it's a docu-mind-drama: *Psi Factor* meets *The Celestine Prophecies*." In New York City this might happen on the street. People running into each other who know someone who knows someone. . . . Everybody says New York is just a small town really. "Six degrees of separation" and all that. But that doesn't happen in Los Angeles. The separations here run deep. You never run into anybody in L.A. Not on the phone.

Next week he called again. Still no speed dial. And three or four times after that. Always on Sundays. My new girlfriend and I were usually just sitting down to brunch when Sam would call, voice all honeyed and ready for a good chin wag. Taken up short when I answered. It got so he recognized my voice, just like Anita did. And I his. It would just be "Oh no, it's Sam, I did it again. How you doin' there?" And I'd keep him on the line a few minutes before letting him go. I got to looking forward to Sam's interim call to me on the way to his own Katherine.

He told me his daughter was the first in their family to go to college. Had married and divorced. "No kids, thank God." And now she'd gone back to law school! He was worried about her fatigue. She never stopped working, no matter what. He was worried about lupus. Her mother had died of it when Katherine was a little girl. He'd never remarried.

When I think of Sam, I can smell bacon frying on my end and strong coffee on his; I see Danny Glover in *Grand Canyon* connecting on a weekly basis with his grown kid; and I wonder about not disturbing that meal. You could tell how much that girl was loved. And also that some part of the story was missing. I wondered if they'd argued over it. Still, I regretted being the wrong Kathryn.

Then the calls just stopped. Anita and Sam must have fixed their speed dials. Or trained up their levels of eye-hand coordination. Or maybe they found out somehow that my own father and I didn't speak. That there'd been *indiscretions* (with a dead uncle) and *allegations* (of ongoing damage), and that we'd quarreled over these things, and that I'd lost. Or maybe what they'd realized is that I'd jumped ship on my own responsibilities—followed a whim and a wish for more than posture, for demonstration—and abandoned my former life, partner, pets, and all. And then went mad with the huge and hot winds of desire and ambition and the devastation of judgment until my work went too. But how would they have found that out? Maybe Katherine just moved.

Or maybe it was one of those *Hotel California* circumstances that are better understood as a dream. Something outside of time, jammed with meaning and deliverance. Maybe the calls stopped when we woke up. Maybe Sam and Anita were gods. Or angels. Disembodied voices who loved and stood by a low-down Cathy and an up-and-coming Katherine no matter what. Women different from me in only one clearly investigated way: the way we spelled our names. Maybe they came to tell me that, like the San Gabriel Valley's Santa Anita Park, life is anxiety and desire, and desire is the horse race. And you can bet on the sure thing that pays only slightly more than even, or you can put your two dollars down on the long shot and at least thrill in the rush of the match. Maybe even win the big purse.

But that's not even all of it. There was purity in those wrong numbers. Something to be cherished. Grace. They gave love big enough to hold liberty, to encompass the light and dark of law and license, constancy and excess. It had room for success as well as failure. And then they went ahead and fought it out among themselves.

So it's sad to me that I no longer hear from Anita or Sam and I don't get the news on Katherine or Cathy. I don't know if the wild cousin's tickets got paid and the car got its registration renewed, or if it got the boot. I don't know if the determined daughter got lupus or passed the bar. For the longest time all I got was my own answering machine, staring at me dumbly with its one unblinking red eye. Eventually, though, my phone did ring again.

# Life Is
# a Highway

**PAULA LANGGUTH RYAN**

Nobody wanted to ride shotgun with Pops. He'd be sitting there in the driver's seat of his rusted brown '75 El Dorado with its once-cream soft top now gone oatmeal gray, eating pistachios and pitching the shells out the window. Pops's black "Old Grand-Dad" T-shirt was faded to a mellow charcoal color that resembled the vats used to distill those fine spirits, and his stringy muscles bulged out from under his sleeves like a balled-up cigarette pack; his right arm draped across the entire front seat. With the radio blaring, he'd clench and unclench his fist in time with the country beat. And then he'd bap you upside the back of your head for no reason, just to show he could.

It was easy to know when Pops wanted to hit the road. His gangly legs would cover the hard-packed red clay from the front porch to the car in three strides. The long car door screeched as Pops opened it and then flung the passenger seat toward the dashboard.

"Okay, rugrats, into the car!" Pops's shout would bounce off the porch and down the hallway. "Denys, you're riding shotgun—shake a leg!"

I always tried to stay glued to the window when I rode shotgun, but Pops's arm span grew octopuslike and found you no matter how far away you leaned or how much you slouched down in the seat.

There we were: me riding shotgun, the twins and Cheryl bouncing around in the back seat, and Pops taking the back-road curves going fifty, not hitting the brakes but once and shelling pistachios all the while. "Sweet Home, Alabama" blared from the radio and my neck muscles were as frayed as my nerves from the slight breeze that ruffled my hair every time Pops's fingers curled and uncurled around his palm.

Bap!

My head snapped forward toward the dashboard and tears welled up in my eyes. I clenched my teeth and mentally screamed "Asshole!" as loud as I could without making a sound. I'd learned how to do this over the years, just like I'd learned to silently scream "I hate you!" with my face full of rage whenever Pops's back was turned.

The first time Pops ever bapped me upside the head I started to cry. I knew right away it was a mistake, but there was no stopping the sniffle that escaped from my lips or the wet splotches that spattered onto my coat sleeve.

"Are you crying, boy? You got nothing to cry about, you hear? Stop it right now, or else . . ."

My shoulders shook even harder.

"Stop it right now, or I'll give you something to cry about!" When he bapped me again, a sob erupted.

Bap. Sob. Bap. Sob.

I covered my head with my arms and Pops grabbed my left arm and twisted it down and toward him.

"No son of mine is gonna act like a pussy every time somebody starts to roughhouse with him. I ever catch you crying again, I'm gonna put you in a dress and start calling you Denise!"

I heard the twins snicker.

I never let him see me cry again.

I've decided that I want my tombstone to say, "He had a great passion for living."

I think a lot about tombstones and death these days. The doctor says that's natural when you've had a "near death" experience. Near death. What a crock of shit. I'm still halfway dead; at least the half that counts, completely dead from the waist down. And they call this living! I know living and, buddy, this ain't it.

Living is sitting high up on a hydraulic air seat, hugging the steering wheel of a big rig with both your meaty forearms and watching the highway speed by you at ninety and never hitting the brakes because cars are clearing out of your lane just as soon as they spot you bellowing up on them. Yeah, that's living.

I run my bandaged hands over the top of the bedsheets, all the way down my thighs to my knees. If I was a blind man, I'd be in worse trouble, I suppose. At least I can see that there's something beneath my linen-covered mitts.

Lying here in this crisp hospital bed, lots of these thoughts creep into my head. I've never had time to think on life before now. Too busy doing the living, you know. But it's moments like this, in the early morning after they've taken my temperature and before they come back to feed me, wash me, and clean out the bag of shit that is attached to me by a thick, piss-yellow rubber tube, that I start thinking about life. And these thoughts are always triggered by the oddest things.

Fucking thoughts.

I watch my hands run up and down my thighs and I think about Pops and how he saw himself doing his duty. Husband, father. He saw it, but he never felt like a husband or father. He felt like a trapped animal with no way out. He must have peered over the ravine of his soul and seen all his ugly and pitiful characteristics groping for him. And then he must have fell in, 'cause he spent his whole life thrashing in thin air, raging against his demons with all his might; trying to shake loose the demons himself.

I know what would drive me over the edge. Seeing my hands close round that piece of meat between my thighs, and not feeling a goddamned thing.

Every morning, when the nurse comes in to give me my sponge bath, she drapes a tented cloth across my waist, the way they do in the movies when a lady's giving birth. It's like she's trying to protect my modesty. Like there's anything left to protect. At first it pissed me off, her being so tender toward me. So foreign and so familiar at the same time. Made me long for my momma.

I flip channels with the TV remote while the nurse does her business on me. Usually she shows up while the talk shows are on. Geraldo, Sally Jessy, Oprah, and Donahue. Mostly they got freaks on, you know—guys who fuck their sisters and want to marry 'em. But that Donahue, he's not as bad. Some of the guys he has on are normal people who crossed the line. Why they'd ever want everybody to know their business, though, is beyond me. There ain't enough money in the world to get me on one of them shows. I could see what they'd call my show: Southern gentlemen and the pricks that won't rise no more.

Like I said, I don't like to talk about it. And I sure as hell don't want every bonbon-eatin' housewife getting their jollies off on my troubles. That's why I watch Donahue. So I won't see the nurse as she cleans between my toes, washes behind my knees, scrubs my thighs, and picks up my dick and soaps under my balls. Now and then, the nurse glances up at the TV too.

"Man, some of these people sure do have problems, don't they?" she says as she rinses off my left testicle.

I say nothing. I just keep my mind focused on their problems and crowd out any thoughts that creep in about my problems, or how I'd like to be like them, be able to walk on or off stage or sit up in a chair without restraints. The rage is within me, but I squelch it with my thoughts.

Good thoughts.

I'm grateful for the drape the nurse has put across my lap. As long as I can't see the nurse touching my still limp peter, I don't feel like I'm half dead. Keep my mind off the past. Time was, once, I'd get a hard-on anytime a chick got within five feet of me. I couldn't help myself. An image would pop into my mind of this chick straddling my thighs on my hydraulic chair, or some bitch's head bobbing in my lap as I drove into the night. It's easy to block these images now. Getting a piece of snatch is what put me where I am. The pain I still feel in my hands and head from the flying glass and mangled steel; images of flesh and bone make up for what I don't feel as the nurse towels me dry.

I could have accomplished a hell of a lot more in my life, but like my momma always says, I got distracted.

By the women.


Although I cursed Pops every day of my life, I only sassed my momma once. We was sitting at the kitchen table, finishing up dinner, and Momma asked me to get the iced tea pitcher out of the fridge. I remember it so well 'cause it was the day the school sent us home with a notice about a father-son picnic. I showed it to Pops as he sat on the front porch rail, picking the dirt out from under his nails with his buck knife.

"Picnics are for sissies!" He spat over the railing and flicked his knife so nail dirt flew in my direction.

"Well, maybe we could do something else that day, like maybe go hunting together . . ." Even though I didn't like Pops much I couldn't help this gnawing need I had to bond with him somehow.

"Haw! You think you're man enough to tote a gun through the woods and not go sniveling home to your momma the minute you hear a bear coming toward you." He said it like a matter of fact, not really like a question. "Go on, git inside and set the table for your maw."

So we was sitting at the kitchen table, Pops and Momma and me and the twins. Cheryl was already off and married by this time. Momma said something to me about getting up and getting her the iced tea. I didn't know the words were going to blurt out of my face like a stream of bile, but they did:

"Get it yourself, you lard-assed bitch!"

I heard Momma's breath whistle in sharply but she didn't move an inch. The next thing I knew, my face had bounced off the kitchen table and blood was spurting from my nose and lips.

Pops was standing next to my shoulder, his rough fingers buried in my hair and pulling my head backward. His bristly cheek was right next to mine and I could smell his yeasty sweat and my pasty fear at the same time.

His whisper hissed menacingly into my ear. "You ever swear at your mother again, I'll beat you within an inch of your life." He let go of my hair and my head flopped forward again. He sat back down. "Now, get your maw the iced tea and then get your ass into your room."

Lying here thinking about it, that was the first time I felt the hatred I was capable of. But it wasn't Pops I directed my anger at then. No—it was my momma. What she represented. What women represented. And it was the first time I truly sensed Pops's rage too. What was I trying to do, swearing at my momma like that? I guess I was trying to bond with Pops, on his turf. The namby-pamby Boy Scout route sure wasn't cutting me any headway. I thought we could find common ground in Pops's hatred for women. He musta felt threatened by me, though, this fourteen-year-old man-child poaching on his territory. When I spat those words at Ma I was only echoing words I'd heard

Pops say time and again. But when I did, I chiseled away at part of his power and he grabbed it back faster than a bear trap snaps shut.

That's my two-bit take on the event anyway. At the time, though, my only thoughts were that Momma had set me up. That she somehow knew I was on the edge of my own ravine and she asked me to get the iced tea to see which move I'd make. The sharp intake of her breath was a betrayal of her disappointment in me; I had dashed her hopes of me being something better than Pops. I think Pops may have sensed that too—sensed that she had thought me above him. He was pleased to have taken me down a notch in her eyes. His sense of victory stung even more than the slap of my face against the metal-and-Formica kitchen table.

But all that eventually backfired on Pops because he didn't back me up. Instead of sharing this bond of male dominance, he turned tail on me. I knew that women didn't have close friends, because they were always being catty, competing for each other's guys. But guys, man, guys were supposed to stick together, not turn wussy and possessive.

For about a week, I was able to stay mad at Momma. But then her disappointment started eating away at me and my rage at Pops festered like a pus-filled sore. I couldn't sleep at night, even if I jerked off first; that's how full of guilt I was. My rage shifted slightly day by day until I swore I wouldn't ever, ever treat my momma or any of my women the way Pops treated his. I ain't never raised my voice or my hand to any woman since—although I did come close with that redhead at the truck stop outside of Albuquerque when she left me with a bad case of the clap and a wallet full of nothing. Lucky for her she was gone when I woke up or my momma woulda rolled over in her grave, sure enough.

The nurses come in every few minutes to take my pulse, check my temperature, or smooth my sheets. They do that so I don't get bedsores. Inside-out ulcers, that's what bedsores are. Even a little pucker in the sheets can cause one if you're lying on it too long. I've puckered my fair share of sheets over the years and never got any bedsores. Now I'd never know it if I did. So I got to rely on the nurses to let me know if my ass is getting red and chappy. What are they gonna do, put some baby powder on it?

I'm thinking about writin' myself an autobiography. I'll call it The
Last of the Great Lays, 'cause that's what wound me up here, for sure.
I'd picked up this cute hitchhiker outside of Albuquerque and was
heading to Flagstaff and Dead Man's Mountain. That's where most
truckers buy it, late at night when they're all coked up and sportin' a
sleep tank that's been riding empty for three or four days. Shit, some
of those speedheads actually get a rush from turning off their headlights and emptying their air brakes at the mountain's peak. It's like
jumping out of an airplane, I've been told. You got your window
rolled down, staring into night air as black as pine tar pitch and it's
you and the road. No way to break your fall, even if you wanted to.

No turning back. Like skydiving with no parachute. One last thrill
before you die.

Fucking thoughts, good thoughts. All jumbled together.

I've got this babe in my truck, like I said. And it's getting late, the
temperature's down to about ten below—and we're about a hundred
miles from anywhere, so I ask her, "Aren't you afraid of some trucker
putting the moves on you? What would you do if someone said 'put
out or get out'?"

Now, most girls start freaking out you start talkin' like this, thinking
you're gonna pull over and rape 'em and leave 'em for dead. They
start playing "let's make a deal" with you, offering to jerk you off, but
swearing they're virgins and can't sleep with you. But this one, Tanya,
she was different all right. She looked me up and down real good and
said, "If they're ugly, I'd start walking. But if they're as cute as you, I'd
ride 'em all night long."

Sweet Jesus. I almost creamed in my jeans right there. Instead, I
asked her, "How about we find ourselves a bar when we hit Flagstaff
and I'll take you out on the town?"

"How far we gotta go?" She laughed this rich throaty laugh and
pulled her hair away from her face. "To get to Flagstaff, I mean."

I told her it was just the other side of Dead Man's Mountain and she
asked why it was called that and I told her and recounted a few stories
from those who had lived to tell the tale.

"You ever done it?"

I shook my head. "Nope. But that don't mean I'm no sissy. Those
guys are crazy, darling."

We were about five miles away from the peak when she started
undoing my belt buckle and said she wanted to give me a story of my

own to recount. She stripped down buck naked and I pulled over at the top of Dead Man's, so she could mount her pony.

She was so damned hot, I tell you. All the way down that mountain she rode my big stick. She was thrashing around so much I kept having to move her hair out of my face so I could see the road. Then it happened. Her arm flew backward and pushed the headlight knob in. Seventy miles an hour, sucked into the darkness on Dead Man's and catching some snatch. I used the looming rocks on my left as my guide and we went thundering down the mountain, setting history on its head. I let out a war whoop, coming as we rounded the curve.

A flash of light, headlights, screeching brakes, turn the wheel, Jesus, Jesus, we're flying through the air and she's a wildcat, clawing at my face, my back, trying to get off my lap, then glass breaking, Jesus, Jesus, her head sliced off clean and her body's bouncing around the truck cab, blood spurting everywhere, glass, blood, glass, my seat, ripped up and twisted, oh God I'm being crushed like a tin can, then the fuel's on fire and I'm trying to scramble out of the cab, pulling myself along on my hands and then everything went dark and still and it was . . .

Good.

I've been dreaming about my momma lately. But it's not really her, you know. In real life, Momma was always old, worn down. But in my dream she's young, and full of energy, and beautiful, like she was in the picture she kept by her bedside table. She was about seventeen in the picture, dark and lovely sitting on a swing with her head thrown back in laughter. You can almost hear her, she looks so alive. That's how she looks in my dream too. And in my dream I'm holding her in my arms, like she's my lover, and in my dream I'm making love to her and we're all hot and sweaty.

Yesterday, the nurse took the bandages off my hands for good. The scars are jagged pink crisscrosses, road maps of my life's experiences. Last night, I woke up in the hospital and I swear Momma was sitting on the edge of the bed, her hand resting on my thigh. When I looked down, I saw my hospital gown making a tent between my thighs and a sob escaped my lips as I reached out to grasp my erect penis. But my erection got distracted and went limp before I could feel my touch. If I could feel my touch. Maybe it was a fleeting figment—a nervous twitch from a dying man's limb.

There's some hot topic for Geraldo.

Of course, sometimes it's more nightmare than dream as Momma's face melts away and I find myself making love to Tanya, but her head's not quite attached and our sweat turns to rivers of blood and I wonder what Momma's trying to tell me, showing up in my dreams.

# Sand
# and Other Grit

**CHERRY SMYTH**

I try not to notice the bars on the window of my new home. But there are bars on the window. If this was a burning building, they'd find me, back flayed and charred, front untouched, flesh stuck to the bars, still breathing or dead from the fumes, in a pose of escape.

"Lie down," she said. "If there's a fire on the subway. Don't rush to the doors with the others."

I check the mottled floor of the D train. Could I lie on the foot grime and skin dust, the nose dirt people had rolled and flicked when no one was watching? Couldn't I squiggle free with the beautiful Latino or try to slide out between the old Jewish woman in the badly fitting wig and the Chinese girl with hair on her upper lip and a love bite on her neck, like a red petal from her flowered dress? I look for other ways out. "Just lie down," her voice chides me. There must be other ways out.

As if connected with me by an unseen force field, a young black boy hurtles out of his mother's arms and charges the electric doors. He must be about six. Using all the balancing skills he's acquired, he keeps upright in the shunting train and turns to charge the opposite door. He giggles extravagantly, a giddy sweat breaking on his brow, making his black hair glisten. His mother sits, dumpy and amused. He swivels and runs back to fling himself against the other door with more faith than any adult that it will not open. He laughs, full of the freedom of misbehavior. I want to stop him, stand between him and the door. Should the mechanism that rocks the lever that squeezes the doors closed suddenly fail, he will be gone, sucked into the deep, hideous tunnel. It's like watching someone else have a falling dream. Each time he springs clear from the door is like a jolt awake. I want the force of his small, inexhaustible body against mine, then to feel it go soft with sleep. I would pick him up, let him slumber on my shoulder.

I don't remember when my body began its fear of flinging into space.

I sniff for fire. I search for a tall, red bucket of sand.


One warm afternoon we're walking along West Third Street.

"Every city I go to, it's the same," she says. "It's always like I imagined it would be. There's always dark splats of chewing gum on every sidewalk."

She's right. Suddenly the pavement is no longer pavement, but a map of the work of mandibles and tongues and teeth and saliva. The blackened splotches of gum are flattened cities of dusty tar.

"Except Arica," she goes on to say. "Chile, near the border with Peru. It wasn't how I imagined. How could I? Nothing could've prepared me for the possibility of this town."

She leans forward as she walks, feet landing more heavily than they need to. No one would know that she has hips. She's worked on that.

I notice fresh chewing gum droppings, which still bear traces of Bazooka Joe pinkness, like newborn animal paws. I avoid them. She walks on, cutting through Washington Square Park, talking again.

"It's a green valley by the ocean. A narrow strip of verdant life. But the green doesn't go up into the hills like on the road to Hana, or rise in gentle slopes above somewhere like . . . that place you took me? Ballycastle. The green stops abruptly less than ten feet above sea level. Then sand begins. White, cratered sand. Nothing but. Can you imagine?"

"No."

Say "sand" and I see a long curve of strand with dunes bearded by marram grass. I see bundled walkers pushing into the cold North Atlantic wind, a wall of white, fine sand, blowing horizontally like salt, needling their faces, like tattoos.

"It's white, still sand. Sand banks. Sand hills. Sand mountains." Her hands climb in an expansive pyramid. She rises up on her tiptoes. This is one of the things I like about her, how her body digs all the way into a story, how she often has to stand during an argument so that she can stomp her point with her feet, lecture with her long, bony index finger. She may even blast her opponent with *"Au contraire."* French may silence them.

"You've never seen sand as white." A slightly accusatory note has snaked into her tone. "As untrodden."

I let it go. "You're right. I haven't."

My sand has little wizened mermaid purses, the filigreed backings from sanitary pads, bleached plastic bottles, scallop shells, smooth orange pebbles, glinters of silver and purple, broken mother-of-pearl. I don't know white, untouched. Except the Devil's Hill. The highest sand dune in the world. Our spot of the northern world. Early enough, you could catch it virgin. Climb through the back to the top. Then scramble over the lip and below would sweep its wide, deep skirt of tawny sand. And you would squeal a launch, fling your body, tumble, somersault, gallop, footprints turning up the whiter, softer sand below the crusty top layer, skidding to the bottom, coughing, laughing, all loose with dizziness, sand caking each strand of hair, sand under nails. A rough thirst.

But as we walk, I don't remember the importance of flying into space, I only remember the sand on Shirley Morgan's sandals.

Shirley and I had been meeting the O'Kane brothers at the Devil's Hill to swing off in pairs, roll in sand-choked kisses down the steep slope. Somehow Shirley's mother knew by the look on her face that playing in the sand hills was no longer a thing about building hospitals for wee sick dollies out of frayed towels and damaged parasols. When Shirley was forbidden to go to the beach anymore, we schemed an elaborate lie about visiting my girl cousins' dairy farm in Ballyrashane (the name on everyone's delivered bottles of milk) and Mrs. Morgan said yes.

Shirley went home from the country trailing sand from every step. She was barred from playing with me ever again.

Shame looks like a thin film of sand sticking to the heel of a Clarke's sandal. I had lied, I was sexual, and I had corrupted Shirley Morgan. I had committed the crime of a bad lot: I'D LED HER ON.

"Arica. Tell me more." She hasn't missed me.

"It's a funnel of green, no, a V of green, with vast inclines of white as far as the eye can see. They used to bury their dead in the sand, you know. The unmoving, unmovable sand accepted the skin, the hair and the bones and filled each pore, each eye socket like salt, like castor sugar, and stuck and preserved. Slowly, slowly"—her fingers trickle as she speaks—"grain by grain, the sand lets go, sieves away as the earth turns and the wind blows and forms a new bluff, another serrated crest. Then the bones tilt into the sunlight." She tells me how children grab them and run home. Archeologists fence them off and study them. Old people just look and nod and sidle on, their walking sticks testing the permanence of the dusty path.

"There are no tombstones?"

"No tombstones. These days they erect little white wooden crosses made of posts." She describes how some are surrounded by fences painted watery turquoise, which try to command new plots from the sly, shifting sand. How sometimes they build a thin structure with a flimsy straw roof to shade the grave or its visitors.

"Did you ever see the film *Woman in the Dunes*?" I begin, but we are too hungry to talk and curve into a pizzeria without taking time to clock the thickness of the crust or the lack of air conditioning. All of the staff are Dominican. I don't know if their hands know pizza.

It is a poor people's pizza place. Some of the eaters are enormous. Size does not indicate wealth in this country. In America I have come to learn the meaning of obese.

"Good pizza is good when cold too," I say like a serving suggestion into the silent space our ravenous eating provides. This is the kind that you have to stuff in while it's piping, almost too hot to bear and the cheese cooks on the roof of your mouth. Soon we will notice the crust getting rigor mortis, the cheese becoming plasticine, and that the mushrooms harbor that rubbery, vinegar taste of tin.

She doesn't remember to answer me about the film. I don't know if this means she has seen it but doesn't want to discuss it, she has not seen it but always wished she had, and so feels a remorse that shouldn't be dwelled upon, or has more interesting thoughts of her own which have ambushed my question, left it standing at the back of her tunnel.

So I stare out at a French bistro, at the rich eating with silverware on linen tablecloths, pinching lemon wedges, slurping oysters delicately. A polite kiss on an ironed napkin. White, silver, yellow, oyster gray.

Being a poet is nine-tenths staring.

I want to think about the film. About the Japanese entomologist who is trapped at the bottom of a sand gully by a woman with long, shiny hair and a svelte, supple body. Her bait is a ladder. Its absence is her net. The ladder is drawn up so that he is unable to leave her home at the pit of the gully. He tries to burrow out but has not the stamina of a crab or a six-year-old boy in a subway train. He learns how to be a tiny creature who must search for rewards differently, understand the meaning of dependency, and let go of ambition. He is tamed by the daily rescuing of the woman's house from the sand and by the woman's touch. He learns a new way of recognizing gifts.

I didn't know then but I wanted the woman. I wanted her to feed me pots of steaming noodle broth, wash the faintly snowing sand from my body and skim her gleaming torso over mine like warm golden oil. I itched in the napless velvet seat of the old Everyman Cinema with sand in my shoes, grateful for the dark in which my desire glistened and coiled. I am just on the verge of realizing something about who I have become in this story when she is already up and heading out. I have barely finished. This is a thing I like less about her.

We go down West Eighth and she directs me into a travel agency. She needs to book another ticket to ride, to leave me. I pretend that this is so normal it is boring. "C'mon," I mutter. I resent the fact that she is spending our time together to purchase the ticket which will remove her from me. I will not ask her to stay, but will find ways to build a fortress that she will not penetrate until well after she returns. I push back cuticle skin. I see half moons. I was taught to do this as an imperative part of the routine of my toilette. Shirley Morgan and I had pink plastic manicure sets. The tiny tools had imitation pearl handles. We clipped and sawed and buffed each other's nails and called each other missus.

Some of my girlfriends have had severe cuticle advancement. I have tortured them, grabbing their hands in limp-fingered moments and scraping back the skin till they screech and snap their hands away. I slowly learn that cuticle removal is simply cosmetic. Like sitting at the table to eat, rather than on your knees in front of the television, or perched on a settee with a book propped up. I learn that the etiquette my family bullied into me has no moral weight. This surprises me and I am surprised that it does.

I hear her give her dates to the travel agent. She is coming back a day later than she had told me. Her body shows no signs of betrayal. I have a tantrum, silently. I hate that love makes me this way. As if twenty-four hours makes any difference. Yet, I argue with the bitch

that has moved into my head, that was all it took to fall in love in the
first place. The time it took for the earth to turn once. It could be
vital. It could be the very time we resolve questions like: Can we ever
be nonmonogamous, or figure out a way to be on the same continent
for more than two months at a time? Or is there anything else to
know? Often it seems as though I understood all I would ever understand after eleven nights. The rest was greed.

I stare at the agent as she curls her neck to the phone. Her nails tap-
tap on the keyboard. Her face makeup doesn't hide her acne. I wonder if the damp, scented, chalky foundation makes it worse. Another
phone rings and she switches into rapid Spanish and her eyes gleam.
This is her lover, the man she'll marry. But why? This woman could be
a dyke—a chola controlla.

There is a fusty sample card by her computer terminal. "Sand from
the world's ten most beautiful beaches." It's supposed to make you
want to go there. Malaysia, Thailand, French Anguilla, Antilles, Poly-
nesia, the Seychelles. The sand is caught under little cellophane bubbles. Some is salt and pepper, some laced with nutmeg, and the rest is
pure coke. I wonder who bleached it. Where it was collected. Did
someone scavenge it from a building site? Did the travel agent scoop it
up in her long red nails? Did she drive with her lover out to Jones
Beach or ferry alone to Fire Island, a tiny plastic bucket swinging from
her wrist?

I have been to paradise. It was full of American trucks, Japanese
resort complexes, and poverty.

The air conditioning is too zealous. I pull a cardigan from my bag.

My lover is rocking her foot back and forth. She is wearing her Daffy
Duck socks. She is very particular about her socks, and although we
share the same foot size, I am not encouraged to borrow her socks.

The first time I left New York after we met, there was a minor sock
incident. We were staying at the friend of a friend's apartment on the
Upper West Side. She said goodbye to me in the bedroom. Perhaps I
didn't want to watch the front door close after her. She hugged me
and we didn't kiss because our lips trembled and there was no spittle
left to exchange. As she pulled away, it was like having a plunger
attached to my heart, a rubber sucker pulling it into a tight vacuum.
She was leaving to go to work. I was to leave by cab an hour later. She
touched me one last time with her whole palm against my cheek and
left. In less than a minute she came back.

"These socks," she said, without looking at me. "They are the wrong socks."

At the time, I really thought she had come back to take one more look, to smile one more time, touch the other cheek. My heart lurched forward and I almost laughed at her gallant and bold trick to forestall loss. Then she busied herself with the necessary job of changing socks, unfurling another pair and pulling her boots back on. The second goodbye was a flimsy, quotidian embrace and I did not listen for another return. Wobbling like a sea animal released back into its own habitat after months of captivity, I forgot how to function unobserved for an instant, then sat on the edge of the bed and cried, envying her being seen in the world where she wouldn't show her tears. I always meant to ask her if she put on the wrong socks because she was more upset than she seemed, or if the socks felt wrong because she was upset. And did she welcome or resent the chance to come back and change them and to see me one more time?

Now we have become professional about departure, participate in an unspoken dare in which neither of us will break down, neither will come back. We order a taxi, the doorbell rings, there is a ticking meter to obey, and one of us is swept up in traffic toward the airport before there is time for a backward glance. Clean and tidy, like the right socks.

Finally, she's ready to go, tickets in their folded pouch in her hand. We walk down St. Marks Place. I notice the white lips of a cowry shell lying in the untended earth surrounding a tree planted in the pavement. I don't point it out to her. I am still building the fortress. She doesn't mention the changed date and I cannot decipher her lip-chewing. Does she think I didn't notice? Is she relieved to spend an extra day apart? She is meek, hoping that I have the good grace not to bring it up. She smiles a wide fake smile that does not reach her eyes and I hate being a couple, walking through the Village, not holding hands. She dives into a corner store and emerges with a plastic-wrapped dish of pineapple, melon, and strawberries and two bright gerbera daisies. She makes them her gift. "You catch more flies with honey" is her motto. I have to smile.

We walk quietly downtown. We eat the fruit. The flowers are erect and jolly. A pink one and a red one. I linger near a shop with fashions for someone younger and skinnier and when I catch up she has lit a cigarette. The fortress doubles in size. I snort. She says she gave up smoking for me, so when she smokes it seems like she'll give up me for smoking. I try to make her see this with my eyes. She doesn't understand. It's easier to fight about smoke than changed dates. My pace quickens. I realize that she bought the cigarettes when she bought the flowers. They annul each other.

There seemed to be more ways to make her understand, to be understood before. Without words. Just a look, a sleeping position, a mouthful of water squirted down from pursed lips, the depth of the sound of breath being inhaled, a nod across a crowded room. In the eleven days. Now I need more words, more philosophy, more psychology, more psychoanalysis, more neurology, more sociology, more biology, more than the law of averages. More than flowers. I grit my teeth.

"Look baby . . ." she begins as remorse crosses her face. I slow down. "I'm sorry about the dates. I should've told you. I only found out this morning and I didn't want to spoil our day." I feel her touch on the untanned underside of my arm.

"It's cool here," she whispers as she kisses there.

The action is alive with memory. It traces a piece of white unfolded paper, a line of black type, a sentence from a letter she once wrote. The sentence was her fingers. She wrote that when she first met me, she dreamt of touching the cool white places on my body that were hidden, and although I had lived with them, they were not real till her desire named them. It felt like relief. Like finding a large rock with a shadow on a scorching hot day on the beach and stepping barefoot onto the cold dark sand.

I decide to postpone decisions about time and place. I pitch into space. I smile at her, move in her direction, and link her arm.

She lets the half-smoked cigarette fall and squashes it under her heel.

"It tastes bad," she says.

# The Butcher's Wife

**CARRELIN BROOKS**

I can taste the meat in her mouth when I kiss her. Meat and smoke and the tang, so faint I may be imagining it, of freshly culled blood.

"And how was work today, dear?" I say brightly. She's late tonight, a rush shipment must've come in. Overtime for everybody and a quicker slaughter than usual, extra messy with the animals bleating and floundering all over the place. I've learned to harden myself to it, the thought of what she does and how, just as she's learned not to tell me the worst bits. We're both learning. Together.

But the butcher doesn't say anything. I glance up at her from my armchair; she's standing by the doorway, looking down, and her face casts a pool of shadow that makes her look, for just an instant, like a blot of darkness in the brightly lit room. Her hands are by her sides and I think I see a smear, on one arm, that could be blood. She is normally so clean, so white, in the clothes she changes into after work, that for a moment my eye refuses to take in this new information.

"What on earth . . ." I start to say, getting up from the chair to go to her. The butcher doesn't say anything, but the expression on her face is forbidding.

"What's going on?" I say, my voice wavering. She looks so terrible that, for an instant, I am almost afraid of her.

"Davey," she says unexpectedly. It's the name of one of the other boys at work, one I dimly recall, drifting ghostlike through the parking lot in his white coat. "He got cut."

"Oh God," I say. "What happened?"

"It was his arm." Now that she's been jolted into speech, the words come quickly, without prompting. "I don't know how the fuck—it was something with the chute. The gate gave way. He cut himself really bad. It looks bad," she repeats.

I don't really want to ask, don't want to imagine moon-faced Davey—I realize now that I can't actually remember his face, that I'm transposing my various parking-lot glimpses of her co-workers into an approximation of him—floundering in the chute, suddenly an animal himself, bellowing and bleeding. "Is it—do they think he—?"

"Is he gonna lose it?" The butcher's face is grim. "They don't know yet."

I go to her at last, put my hand on her arm, try to touch her. But the butcher just stands there immobile, then she gives a shake like a dog and steps away from me. She turns without saying anything, goes down the hall to the bathroom, closes the door. I hear water running. I stand there for a moment, irresolute, then turn the opposite way, toward the bedroom. I will be asleep when she comes in, and I comfort myself with the thought that the butcher's big hands will reach for me, that her touch will somehow come to me through all the layers of darkness, that in the morning she will look at me, again, like she recognizes me.

The butcher and I go back a long way. Well, long by my standards anyway. In the beginning, the butcher's profession made me sick. She wasn't ashamed. I couldn't decide if that made it worse or better. She told me what she did, right there in the bar where she came up to talk to me.

"It's not just killing animals, you know," she said, draining her glass of amber-colored liquid. I looked at her meaty hands, there on the bar top, and shuddered.

"But that's what you do," I said. "Really, when you get down to it, that's what it's about."

"There's a lot of other stuff we do. It takes a lot of training."

"But how can you stand it?" I said, shifting on the sticky seat in my dress. My voice came out high and strident. "Isn't there anything else you could do?"

Since then she's explained, patiently enough, that the only other jobs she knows are driving trucks and working security. When things started to get serious between us, when it looked like I might stay, she told me about her father and how she swore she would never be like him. She explained that the abattoir, whatever I thought of it, at least offered opportunities for advancement. That they accepted her there. That her kind came as no surprise.

She described for me the stainless-steel rows, the shiny hooks, the chute. She went over the procedures, carefully explaining how the building was hosed down each night until it stood empty and gleaming. She assured me that they used the latest of the new technologies, that the animals died quickly, their pain negligible. Once she even mentioned that if I came to see the abattoir, to look at where she worked, I might change my mind. I looked at her then, and what she saw in my face made her stop talking. She hasn't mentioned it since.

I've been as far as the gates, and that's enough. Once in a long while I park down there and wait for her shift to get off. She comes out the door, spattered and weary in her whites, waving goodbye to the boys and slapping backs. Then she sees me and her face lights with such a child's joy that I can hardly look.

I've seen the boys that work with her. Just out of high school, most of them. Milk-skinned and crested with acne. Don't know how to do anything with their useless hands except slit.

Someone should string them up, milken their eyes, drain them. Then they'd know what it was about.

Someone should teach the animals to talk. That wouldn't stop the butchers, of course. Would they lie there at night, though, thinking of the things they've killed that day? Would the eloquent pleadings of the cows and lambs, the desperate verses of sheep, enter into their imaginations at all?

Would they kill me if they knew I was the butcher's lover? Kill me like they kill the others?

Would the butcher watch? Or would she join in?

I don't ask the butcher such things. She'd say I was letting my imagination run away with me, making things worse than they are. And besides, we've been together too long now, and she no longer wants to hear it.

"It's a normal workplace," she tells me when I wrinkle my nose at the uniform, at the sharpened set of knives she packs carefully for work each day. "Not like you seem to think."

She downs the last of her coffee, slams the cup. "You know? Coffee breaks? Lunch hour?"

"Do you wash off the blood first?" I can't help myself, it just slips out.

The butcher stiffens, glaring. "It's a clean, modern, fully sterilized workplace," she recites as if from an invisible brochure. "The blood, for your information, is minimal."

I don't believe her, of course. After she leaves, I imagine the fluids streaming into the drains, between their rubber-coated legs. Sweat and blood and the shit and steaming urine of terrified animals. The viscera of their dismemberment, the bile, the green gall. How could it not be messy?

You know what I really want to know, what I'd like the butcher to explain to my satisfaction? The line. That exact place, the moment that makes the things they kill flesh and not real anymore. That makes it okay to do what they do.

I'd like her to explain what it is she sees in their eyes if, indeed, she ever saw anything at all. Does she ask forgiveness of each one, I'd like to inquire politely, or does it all go by too fast? Is it a blur, like war?

But I know I won't ask. It's too late for that and besides, maybe I'm afraid of what she might say.

"How is he?" She hasn't mentioned Davey since the night of the accident but I don't need to say his name. We both know who I mean.

"He's still in the hospital." The butcher studies the paper, not looking up. Her arms are silvery with the old scars of her profession, accidental cuts from the sharp knives she wields. "They're waiting to see how it heals."

"What if it doesn't?"

The butcher shrugs, her face stony. She stands up and crinkles the paper into a semblance of order. "I'm going to be late," she says, perfunctorily, without looking at me.

"Okay," I say. "Have a good day."

"Yeah," she mutters, heading for the door. A second later I hear the slam as it closes behind her. She hasn't even said goodbye.

Not for the first time, I wonder what the butcher would be like if she were ever really angry. If I said the one wrong thing, if I kept on asking the questions she couldn't answer and didn't want to hear. At night sometimes I wake to feel her fingers moving over my body, the delicate lacing of sinew and bone. I can't repress the sudden idea that she's thinking of the cut, planning where it is the knife would go. I imagine her arm, reaching for me, holding me down. I imagine my eyes, open, unblinking, staring at her. Silent, my throat leaking blood.

"You and your imagination." The butcher's tone is warm, indulgent. She dips the sponge into the bath and lets it drip down my back. With her finger she outlines the places where the water's been, the ridge of my spine, the bulge and dip of the muscles.

"What imagination?" I repeat, lazy in the heat.

"The shop. I bet you imagine all kinds of horrible things." She shakes her head in exasperation, leans down to kiss me. I smile, wrap my arm around her, shift slightly.

"Hey!" The butcher's voice is a shout. There's a terrific splash.

"Oh, honey." I'm all concern as she splutters in my lap, splashing water. "Did you fall in?"

"Fall? I was—" But I cover her mouth with my own, forestalling her protest. "Get in here," I tell her, keeping my mouth close to hers. "But this time, try taking your clothes off."

The butcher is tired all the time. Lifting those heavy carcasses takes its toll. At night, in bed, I probe her massive shoulders. She is like a slab of flesh herself, red and undifferentiated. "Tell me where it hurts," I say, poking her, searching for a way in.

"Everywhere," she groans from her place in the pillow, the words coming out muffled.

I want to know. I'm searching for the difference, for the thing that makes her touch me with such tenderness before she heads off to another day of killing. I study the butcher, turned away from me. Does she want me ravaged on one of the hooks, would she like me drained? The butcher rolls in my wetness, but she has never expressed a desire for my blood, not yet.

I wish there was less of the butcher. If she was smaller I could manage her better, cover her limbs with my own, provide the kind of comfort that comes with size. If she was smaller she might kill only little things: chickens or maybe even fish, silent and stunned. Killing fish is not like killing cows, there's something deniable about the fact. I could love her then, I wouldn't have to be afraid.

Then the butcher turns over and takes me in her arms. She strokes me from the shoulders to the calves with one massive hand. I wonder, not for the first time, what my flesh feels like to her, if she knows the names of the muscles she touches and how they would separate one from the other. I wonder if it reminds her, touching me, of the work she does.

I try to stop her. "Shhh," I say, "you're tired." I put one small hand against her chest, holding her back. The butcher grins. In the darkness her mouth is a sea of red.

"Not for that," she says, guttural. "I'm never too tired for that."

The butcher takes over. She takes my hands in hers, leans over. I twist under her, knowing what's coming, dreading it. The butcher is going to split me open and make me cry. Like she always does. I hate it. I hate this. Everything is too much. The butcher doesn't stop when I pound on her shoulders, when I shove at her hands. The butcher knows what to do.

"Like this?" she whispers to me. "Like this?"

And then I am rising, in her hands, I am levitating somewhere above the twisted sheets, and the darkness breaks in me with the movement of her fingers, the light comes flooding in. The butcher raises her head. Her face gleams. "Yes," she says.

This is what the butcher does for me.

The butcher loves me.

The butcher is the only one.

I'm all there is, she tells me, holding me tightly, too tightly if the truth be told. The only one for you.

The butcher is a sadist. She will never let me go.

I like that.

None of these things are true.

There are two kinds of blood in the body, the oxygen-rich arterial, the thin veinous, traveling back toward the source. The heart is a muscle, pumping out its hours of loss, doomed to motion until it finally stills. The lungs are gray lace. Inside we are just like the other animals, just as naked and helpless. Inside our colors are like theirs: red, yellow, green, and blue.

"What have you got there?" asks the butcher, amused. "Why are you reading that stuff?"

She's come up behind me and I jump in my chair. "Jesus. You scared me."

"I got home early."

The butcher's manner is casual, too casual. She sits down, watching me. Her eyes glitter.

"How was work?" I'm trying to act normal, but my voice catches. It's the way she's staring. What is she looking for? What does she see in my throat, in the pulse that's caught and fluttering there? "Did you hear anything?"

"About Davey? I think he's going to be okay. He has to do these exercises, but he has almost all the muscle control back." She reaches in her jacket, extracts something. "I brought you something."

It's a box, long and flat. I take it, fumbling.

"What's the occasion?"

"Open it." The butcher's voice is a command, undeniable. Her eyes stay fixed on me.

I do. There's a covering of tissue and then, when I pull it open, the flash of silver. I lift the knife out, balance it on my palm. Even I can see it's beautiful.

"Do you like it?" The butcher's voice is anxious. She leans forward, ready to take it out of my hands.

"It's—it's lovely." I turn the knife so its weight fills my palm, the blade catching in the light. "I don't understand."

The butcher shrugs, embarrassed. "I know, it's not your kind of thing. But I don't know, I thought sometimes you get nervous when I'm not here. And besides"—she smiles at me tentatively—"I wanted you to have something from me."

I stare at the knife another moment, and suddenly, unexpectedly, my eyes fill with tears. "What were you doing out late so many nights?"

"Overtime." She takes my free hand in hers. "I wanted to surprise you."

It's ridiculous, but I feel suddenly like crying. I imagine the butcher, working overtime for me, but this time I'm not picturing the atrocities she commits. Instead I see her face, a study in concentration and love, and how she leans forward to steady the lamb as its eyes film, as it takes a final step in the chute and almost topples. I picture her hands, administering the killing blow, pregnant with a last dose of comfort. I see her loving the things she slays.

I make a noise, I don't know what, and the butcher is beside me suddenly, close enough to smell, blotting out the rest of the world. "Sweet," she murmurs, and I reach out for her, hands gathering her solid flesh. "Don't leave," I say into the butcher's chest. "Don't ever leave." She thinks I'm talking about us, and she clasps me tighter, but

I don't mean that at all. What I'm really saying is that I need her there, in the killing place, hosing the excreta of helpless bodies from her hands. I want to know that she's there and that, afterward, she is coming home to me. I want to know that whatever comes, and however inevitable our demise, she is there, holding my hand against hers and urging me on with those mild eyes that have seen all the mysteries the living can offer.

# The Art
# of Losing

**CATHERINE LORD**

*I*

One life, two women, ten years. A series, not a progression, copiously illustrated, concordance impossible. I LOVE YOU, written backward on a fogged car window. A look, your eyes widen, a kiss blown, the back of your neck, your dappled ass. My bare breasts, sand on my belly, a feather in my hair, striding. My head on your shoulder. Behind us, or you, or me, a fireplace, a church, a Christmas tree, a mountain, seas and lakes and breaking waves, a museum, flowers massed, tree trunks, granite, waterfalls. Feasts, front doors, backyards, rooms bare and rooms filled, a basket too big to wrap, candlesticks. Rocks shaped like hearts, flowers like cunts, the sympathies of nature. Our arms around family, friends, each other. Lying on the hood of a rose-colored Cadillac. Hotel rooms, café tables, art openings. Rabbits mowing grass at the edge of deep shade. Cactus spines embedded in a car seat. Fields of lavender. Rumpled sheets in a motel by a lake. Oak frames scuffed. A chocolate desert. Red newts, green moss. Bluebonnets. An armadillo at dusk. The insides of confessionals. Your first island. My cot by your hospital bed. Our shrink's gray sofa. The scar on your breast. A note folded. My face taut.

I pat a horse in the mist. You wave an armful of wild ginger. A child grins in Bali. A fish jumps in Spain. You walk on stilts. I mime a cactus. You hold a black puppy named Scarlet. I coax a pink cockatoo to whistle *Carmen*. Stuck at the end of the earth, waiting for a plane home, we weep over a picture of cats.

2

A black-and-white portrait, head and shoulders, natural light coming
from the right. My hair is uncombed, dirty, tucked behind ears that
stick out. I have my grandfather's ears. The part in my hair lands just
to the right of center. The focus is so sharp that every pore is visible,
but I still cannot bear the sight of myself: sleepy, eyes veiled, mouth
drooping slightly, lips cracked. It is a face unaccustomed to forming
itself for scrutiny, muscles midway between collapse into a slack gape
and the strain of a smile pulling crooked. I am twenty-five years old,
wild child in a rare interlude between girlfriends. In the privacy of a
room of my own, no audience but the blank white wall at which I stare
to trap myself with my own camera, I steal my own soul. Ten years later
I make you a gift of it. You put it in a frame. Ten more years and you
return it. You keep the frame.


3

It is not your birthday. We are being taken to dinner on your big
evening, the occasion of your first New York show. He is your dealer.
The two of you sit at one end of the table with the collectors and crit-
ics, insulated from the lesbian friends at the other end by a group of
clever fags. I am seated with the dykes. We plot and giggle and tip and
send your end of the table a parade of drag queens. Such is this restaurant's claim to fame. They bear a chocolate cake. Every dyke is a hero,
and tonight you're ours.

   You thank the dealer effusively.

   In the Polaroid, his arm lies across your shoulders. You have high
hopes for each other. You are both in uniform, black shirt under black
jacket, short hair, shaved napes, moderate piercings. He wears his
baseball cap backward so that a lock of hair falls guilelessly through
the half-moon. The red FAG embroidered on the front of the cap is
hidden. You wear a silky something under a leather jacket. He will go
bankrupt, then marry a woman who looks like a boy. In front of you a
pink candle skewers the cake. Behind you are fishnet and sequins. You
both know the formula: cheeks touching, heads vertical, look right at
the camera, and put the shit-eating grins center frame.

## 4

At first, you hated this snapshot. I had cajoled you out of the city, away from a comfortable bed, into a wilderness. It was hundreds of miles away. I did all the driving. I picked a trail that went uphill. I made you carry a heavy pack and eat dried meat among dirt and bugs and dowdy hikers. I seduced you to commit an art photograph, an academic exercise about representation and reality. I used you as a prop in order to escape the embarrassment of taking a tourist picture.

The massive cone of a volcano is barely visible below the clouds that occupy the right half of the frame, obscuring flanks of gray ash and millions of matchstick tree trunks whorled into fingerprints. You stand to the side, in the left foreground, your body slightly turned toward the mountain so that you can hold in each hand, directly over the volcano miles behind you, the two parts of a salt shaker. There is nothing but blue sky behind salt. Pepper, poised on the tips of the fingers of your right hand, is dwarfed by the smoldering cone. The salt shaker, which still sits on my dining-room table, reads on the bottom: MT ST. HELENS, 1980, MADE OF ACTUAL ASH FROM THE ERUPTION.

Elegant always, especially in the midst of devastation, you have chosen understatement: a man's white tank top, a long-sleeved white cotton shirt, cuffs rolled, and blue jeans. You manage to look ironed, urban, even in the hard wind that lifts your collar and blows your hair to one side. You wear on your left hand the rose-gold ring that I gave you on the first of your birthdays that we shared. Your other fingers are bare. Your eyes are hidden by sunglasses. I allow myself to think that what you feel about me in this moment is unreadable. In truth, you have both a slight frown and a slight smile, thus making it impossible, in this moment as in so many others, to distinguish forbearance from fondness. I remember the precise pitch of your protest when I made the photograph—Cather*innnnnnnne*!!!!—but I have never been able to decide whether you were a little girl speaking from the body of a woman or a woman in such pain she could speak only in the voice of a child. In either case, I imagine you enduring the inconvenience of my desire.

"Please pass the volcano," we would say, smiling to each other when we made dinner for friends, the perfect U-haul couple entertaining, icons of longevity in a world of quick turnover. And then, of course, we could explain the salt shaker's provenance, take the photograph from the refrigerator—with its tattered archive of vacations, friends, babies, their cats, our cats, cat cartoons, cat drawings—and by our words domesticate it, smooth it, cement it into the walls of our lives. As we learned by heart the story we were telling ourselves, we began to take turns speaking it, volleying lines back and forth, finishing each other's sentences like any married couple. In the end, you softened toward the photograph. Perhaps you came to love my delight in it. Perhaps you always had always liked it. Perhaps, polished by repetition, it had become a lullaby.


5


I hardly figure in our photographs, except of course as the one behind the camera, the one who took the photographs, offerings to your beauty, testaments of my fear, trophies of your misery. We want memories. We discard the present to gamble on a past. I operate the machinery of loss. You let me.


6


A walk-in closet stuffed floor to ceiling. White shirts are grouped together, then the black. Jackets with jackets, pants with pants. T-shirts are arranged by color and meticulously stacked on the shelves, a pile of whites and creams, then grays, then stripes, and finally a few reds, blues, and greens. It could be an ad for one of those organizing systems that aim straight at the abject fear of the slovenly, but these are insurance photos, a simple inventory of the loot in your undeclared war against the rich, or the middle class, or anyone who had money to burn, no matter how provisionally or imprudently. You scavenge thrift stores to reap the bounty of caprice and disease. You visit one on the day the new donations are sorted, another cluster on the day you drive across town to see your therapist, and the best one every other week when you see your drug shrink. First you scan for fabric, then you winnow by size, cut, and label. You move with practiced speed, plunging into seas of faded fabric to emerge with the unmarred object, the smell of money still upon it.

I watch you at work once, inspecting a jacket you have laid over a rack. You scrutinize it, inside and out: buttons, lining, pockets, collar, seams, everything. When these pass muster, your hands caress the entire jacket. You stroke the chest, move down the sleeves, turn it over, smooth the wrinkles out of the narrow back, and turn it again. You imagine how it might become you. You place your body inside it. You calculate the weight against your flesh. When you catch me looking, you abandon it. It's yours if you want it, you say. I'm not interested.

7

It's where you pop the question, long before gay marriage got to be an epidemic but well after you might have. It is a big beach, late enough to be getting cold. We have it to ourselves. The last of them are walk-ing splay-legged in the sand to sidewalks and trash cans and home. Marry me, you say, laughing. You go down on one knee. Darling, I say, I thought we were married.

It's not much of a picture, bad timing, too dark, hard to say what it was all about.

8

You stand in the backyard of our new house, the house for us I have just bought. This is capitalism. It is my money. I do not choose to share. I am a single woman, the title says. I soften this hard fact in a wash of pronouns. Our, I repeat as often as possible. We.

It's a gray spring day. The new backyard is red brick and ivy merci-lessly disciplined. I am celebrating, taking snaps for the parents, yours and mine. You stand hollow-cheeked, an immigrant to the land of prop-erty. I notice your misery only after the picture has come back from the drugstore, months and months after, catching it out of the corner of my eye one morning in the place it has come to live, pinned to the refrigerator with a magnet of St. Lucy holding her eyes before her on a plate. It is the face of my mother, in a black-and-white photograph with deckled edges, sitting in a homemade flowered bathing suit on her parents' veranda, the blue Caribbean behind her back. She is the same age I am, you are, at this moment of my passage into property, a beautiful redhead about to take her children to America to follow a husband too far gone to bring back, unable to do more than stare at the camera held by her father.

Every now and then you accuse me of switching one redhead for another, getting for myself a woman who will make heads turn, a woman who will stick it out through chill and rage and dead, dead silence, the perfect bloody stupid martyr. You gave me fair warning. Loyalty is one of your virtues. You gave me fair warning. You can't fucking touch a goddamn saint, I remind myself, wishing that you were neither neat nor clean nor organized nor driven nor beautiful. Saints don't have much more than virtue. Saints are designed to stay out of reach, holding their tongues, biding their time, counting their blessings, delicious with suffering.

9

Porn didn't do much for us. By the time we got around to it, perhaps, it was too late and too little. We checked out whatever there was on the shelves, which over the course of our involvement expanded from one or two tapes to maybe a dozen, pathetic next to the packed shelves of testosterone, gay and straight, monuments to a lust we weren't supposed to share. We used the various editions of lesbian desire until they wore thin, starting with big-breasted white women and moving on, as the eighties became the nineties, to shorter hair, darker skins, and flat tits, not mention a lot more leather and metal and lube. One way or another, no matter the advances in representation, it boiled down to wet pink bits with sound effects. The point began to elude us. We would forget. Our minds started to wander. Our fantasies would twitch and lie there, like pool balls after a bad break, or ricochet unpredictably, fluff banking dandy, soft butch kissing fag, femme top sinking the cue. You bought lacy bras. I missed your beautiful boy's chest. I wore tank tops. I looked like a truck driver. We wanted a legend who could walk in the front door and fix the mess with nothing but a tool kit and a lot of bravado. That tape was always checked out. The last straw was a baby butch going down on someone in a shower stall. When she came up for air, she was an ex-student.


*10*


It grew on us, adhered to us, became one of those customs couples invent to declare themselves a couple, one of the tricks by which two people enlarge themselves to fit a story they have already memorized, a story that holds them, compels them, tells itself to them because they are at once its center and its most eager audience. Instead of sleeping late on Sundays, and spending slow mornings in bed, in which case something entirely different might have been said, we would get up at dawn and go to a flea market, stumble sleepy through the chill with a bunch of yuppies trawling for a bargain.

Flea markets, trash cans, garage sales, thrift stores, these are your territory. Here, you learned to fend for yourself, get something for nothing, turn nothing into something. Here, you perfected the alchemy that would distill white trash into dandy. I apprentice myself to you. I am captivated. I watch you seized by another way of looking. Undaunted by quantity, you register every object, scanning for something you can use to invent yourself or else something to feed your work, a book, a postcard, one pun on gender or another. I feather the nest I am determined to inflict on you with plates and spoons, trivets and pillowcases.

While I wait for you—for in my memory it is always I who wait while you sift through one last table—I kill time flipping through bins of pictures: cabinet cards pried from their velvet mausoleums, snapshots that never rated the family album, wedding pictures, baby pictures, grandparents, mothers and fathers, uncles and aunts and friends and suitors, the occasional beaver shot, pictures of wreaths and corpses, magenta photos, sepia photos, torn scraps of photos, photos faded to the palest of browns, tintypes, photos with writing, photos held together with tape, photos bent to the shape of a wallet, round photos, oval photos, heart-shaped photos, painted photos, photos of cars, photos of fish, photos of deer, photos of movie stars, boats and sunsets and patches of dirt, oceans and rainbows and hats, cats and dogs, houses, monuments and straight roads to nowhere, vacation photos, insurance photos, police photos, publicity photos, news photos, art

photos, sports photos, fashion photos, photos of boyfriends, photos of
rivers and midgets, Christmas trees and bridges, banquets and flower
beds, gravestones and bicycles, rainbows and snow and girls feeding
bears, women of every sort and size and age, parades and conventions,
fountains and geysers and horses.

In these bins are our kind, tomboys and big-boned gals, mannish
women and men with a fondness for clothes. I look for the telling gesture, for the play that camouflages touch, for bodies that lean a little
too close. I buy in bulk, soft bodies packed with practiced zeal into
elongated rectangles—chiropractors, soldiers, postmen, camp coun-
selors, schoolchildren, nurses, and dowagers. One in ten, I repeat to
myself. Physiognomy is a fraud. I can spot them.

This is the carnage on the battlefield of magical thinking, the slag
heap of mimetic greed, a spirit world held together by nothing more
than an incantation. Quantity confounds reason, defeats taxonomy. If
there is an optical unconscious, these prints do the work of its dreams,
the labor of storage and revelation, the invention of the codes of
memory that free us to forget. Traces of whatever can be made visible
to desire, whatever can yield itself to the fantasy that the act of copying
might alter the thing that is copied, and so render it susceptible to
possession, these prints have lost the souls that craved them. Without
the charm of love or avarice or power, they have lost a palpable connection to the world they copy. There is no plot they thicken, no nar-
rative to which they have the slightest relevance.

Having forsaken the gift of memory for the bounty of representation, we are cursed by an inability to bury the remains. Does no photograph ever, really, disappear? Do they all, even if sold or discarded or
carelessly given away, one day or another wash back up to be pawed
and winnowed and patted into stacks, then dragged from market to
market waiting for someone mad enough to rescue them?

You bring me photographs of your life so as to map for me your
memory, show me what will give depth to my love. A baby Amazon on
a tractor. A teenager by a Christmas tree, towering over her brothers
and sisters. The willowy young wife, red hair to her waist.

You insist on cartography. We will want to have memories, of this
you are certain, and so we must take care to store them now. We photograph each other, and save the tickets, the postcards, the sweet
notes. We promise each other to organize it all one day when we have

time. Meanwhile, we nurture love in exactly the location where relations between people are transmuted into relations between objects.

*I I*

I bring you a dozen roses, long-stemmed, nested in white tissue in a gold box with a ribbon. We are just weeks in love, wildly, madly, for all eternity, a scandal and a delight, so mad for each other that I can catch your scent across a room of people, so lost in each other that you cannot quite conceal your trembling at the sight of me. How did I know the roses were your color—a color neither peach nor pink and certainly not rose? Did I guess because they were the color of the wine you preferred to drink, when we drank, sitting outside that first summer in the long California evenings? You say to me, tears brimming, that no one has ever given you roses. I fold you in my arms. You arrange the roses in my favorite vase, one of my grandmother's, take the vase with you as we move from room to room, making lunch, washing the dishes. You photograph the roses in the vase outside by the swimming pool. Some days later you take a few blowzy blooms and scatter the petals across the bed. I can see as I make slow and wondering love to you in the afternoon light that they are in truth exactly the astonishing, perfect color of your nipples, your lips, your labia, the undertone of your freckled skin. I vow to myself to lavish upon you roses of this color, to give you whatever you say you want, to give you what you don't yet know you want.

You will return the photograph to me, wadded into a thick envelope of souvenirs, an ordinary snapshot of a blue vase with roses sitting on the cement in the hard midday sun against a white stucco wall. A rosemary bush is just visible in the frame. For remembrance.

You will return the photograph after I have left you clumsily, brutally, in desperation and in sorrow. I inhabit a cliché, I tell you. I have been unable to control my feelings for her. I haven't been happy, for years. Neither have you. I know it is a cliché, I say, but I cannot help it. This picture comes from skin, mine and yours.

*12*

There is no way to photograph a woman so that she comes out looking like an executive. Studies prove this. If you look like a femme, you're stupid. If you don't, you take yourself too seriously to be one of the boys. Either way, you lose. Tailored suits and fabric about the neck and worst of all a smile demote you from executive to woman. I won't go near these costumes, so I come out looking like a lesbian. A photographer who makes ten times my salary shoots from below to make me all stubborn jaw and big hands. A woman in black jeans, no gray yet, in a fifties plaid jacket, clouds of cigarette smoke, trying to look like a big shot. No matter how often you kiss a lesbian, or how sweetly, or how long, she won't turn into a prince.

*13*

You are in the background, sitting on a bench, your back against a wooden house on stilts in the tropics. You wear a panama hat. Perfect banana republic. Damp pink tourists sit to your left. Between my camera and your body are mounds of green and red and white, glints of silver, blurs of brown. Strangers in a land where our kind is the main cash crop, we witness the butchering of water buffalo, waist-high piles of shit, muscle, and bone, rivulets of blood in the packed dust of a village square. Clouds of flies. It is a funeral feast. The corpse lies on a platform above our heads. The relatives ply us with sweet coffee and cookies. They use the instant cameras manufactured in their own backyards to sneak pictures of the monstrously tall white women who travel together.

*14*

We knew we had to have two so we could each have one. The one we had just put to sleep had persisted in treating you like the Other Woman until the bitter end. You had had it with triangles. We knew the new ones would be called Butch and Femme. We were so certain of our lesbian wit that we chose the names long before we went to the pound. He hooked you, somersaulting around his cage to say: Notice me! Look at me! I'm adorable! Get me the fuck out of here! Take me home! She chose me, pushing her brothers aside to stagger mewling for food to the front of the cage. A tiny, bony, matted, sickly little weakling, she was the runt, but she was a girl, and girl was enough. We couldn't have come home with two male cats. We were lesbians. Sexual difference rules.

He is classic alley, a muscled bundle of testosterone pumping alternately into charm and thuggery. She is long-haired, black with russet undertones, fur poking out between her toes, and improbable gray armpits. Perhaps Persian, perhaps Maine coon, perhaps just standard farm, she is in any event not more than a few drooping ounces of credulity. We cannot admit that biology is destiny, so if the cats must be butch and femme, he will be Femme and she Butch.

We try to make theory adhere to wiggling, slippery fur. It is just possible to say: No, *dammit*, Femme! to a kitten ricocheting off the walls of a small apartment. It is altogether impossible to say: Wake up, Butch! to a kitten who has eaten herself into a coma and looks like nothing so much as a hairy tennis ball with stick legs, or Stand up for yourself, Butch, to a cat who lies yowling, covered in spit and bites, rather than venturing to unsheathe her claws. We were the sort of lesbians who could not lower our standards for butch below soft. We surrendered within a week. She would be the queen, Cleo, as in Anthony and Cleopatra. He would be Tony, except that we soon learned you can't put tony into an alley cat. And she, we had to concede, silly in her growing bulk, was hardly majestic. Cleopatra, no. Queen Victoria, yes. Cleo became Chloe, as in Chloe liked Olivia, Olivia liked Chloe. Virginia and Vita. Vita and Violet. Leonard and Harold enlarge the closets.

Saccharine, glossy, yielding flesh pillowing that essential core, that hole in the doughnut of femininity, that emptiness waiting to be filled, Chloe was content. The marked term rolls over and purrs. High femme, old school. He, though, was no Olivia, no tomboy, no boyish androgyne, small tight body making sport of the sure gestures of masculinity, spilling the secrets of the war between the sexes. He was another story altogether, a daddy with an eye for the boys, a graying guy with silky skin, a guy who would never let himself run to fat, a fag through and through. Max he became, one morning over coffee, short for Maximilian, a name of emperors, and besides a classic fag name, all edge and dapper artifice, admitting nothing about class.

Max and Chloe. Catherine and Lizzie. Catherine and Chloe. Lizzie and Max. You're the fag hag, I'm the butch. You take him, I take her.

We rush to the cliché, wallow in the territory of pansies and poodles, girls who draw horses, women who look like them. We are two spinsters living together for companionship who treat their animals, as if they were children. We make a spectacle of ourselves. We tell stories about Max and Chloe to our kind, homos with pets, indeed anyone who will listen. We include the cats when asked how we are. We cuddle them, spoil them, train them to our ends, and speak to each other through them. Over the years we take hundreds and hundreds of photographs of them: kittenish, sleeping, eating, airborne, jealous, lounging, hiding, begging, fighting, adorable, fearless, pissed, wise beyond their years, frisky, serene, curious, fooled. Max sprawls on his stomach down the length of the dining-room table, a strictly forbidden place. Chloe sits sleek on a terraced garden bed, a black inkblot amid verdant green. Max, seized with the urge to kill creatures weaker than he, uses Chloe as a doorbell, biting her until her howls get him evicted from the house. Why not say through them what we cannot say to each other? Max is bullying Chloe. Make him stop. Chloe provoked him. Chloe can hold her own.

*15*

The camera loves you, which is to say you love it.

*16*

You kneel before her, *Peter: A Young English Girl*. A painting looks at a woman whose face is hidden. She's on a storage rack and you need to get down to where she's kept these days. Standing to your left, I aim down to make the photograph, one diagonal in the spokes of unrequited looks that converge on you: me, *Peter*, and the curator standing to your right, a regular guy grown accustomed to hosting the pilgrimage of queers. You have eyes only for her, *Peter*: same short hair, same man's jacket, same white shirt, same straight back.

17

One lesbian is driving downhill, along a winding country road. Another lesbian is driving uphill, along the same narrow, empty road. When they meet, they screech to a halt. The first lesbian rolls down her window and screams: BITCH! The second lesbian rolls down her window and yells: CUNT! The first lesbian floors it and careens off, narrowly missing her ex just around the next bend.

18

We travel well, we used to tell ourselves, meaning I suppose that we thought we could land on our feet unwrinkled, two serious ladies with wheelies who like books, antiques, and museums. Yet we exude the anxiety of women traveling alone. No one in foreign countries ever offers to sell us pot, though we are invariably asked whether we are sisters, and it becomes simpler to say yes. We fret about delays and detours and dangers. We bicker about why your suitcase is always so heavy and why the hikes I pick are always so long and steep.

It ends, one way or another. We couldn't find our way home. We'd finally lost it. It wasn't there anymore. I weep on the drive home, or you do. I can't believe we're doing this, you say when you drop me at the airport. The returns are impossible. I'm begging you to stay, I say the day you move out, leaving nails in the ghost frames of our archive. The break is not clean. You can't expect me to put up with this, you say at our last appointment with the shrink. I won't share you, you say. It's an emergency. We have interrupted her work. The pages of her forthcoming book on relationships are scattered across her desk. I can't let you back in, I say, after the drive over the mountains past the fruit stands. Take the peaches, I'll keep the melons.

I divide the pictures in two. Snap. Half for you, half for me.

19

The picture is taken from the hillside above us. We are tiny behind a foreground of spikes, daylilies and shastas, crocosmia and glads, rose mullein and red-hot pokers. The plum tree is covered with ripe fruit, so it must be June. The oleanders are still small, the wood of the rose arbor not yet weathered. We lie together in the hammock. You are wearing cowboy boots and sunglasses. Your head is on my shoulder. I am barefoot. My jeans are dirty. We are in our garden, being photographed for a series on lesbian domesticity, on couples who love each other and have made a place for themselves, in our case a garden, lush and green and wild, in which we can live happily ever after, like our parents didn't. It is a young garden, not even two years old, the gift of paradise I wanted to offer you, the closest I could come to paradise by planning and digging and planting, so that I can give you the life I want you to know: cut flowers, herbs, fresh lettuce.

It is, of course, not so simple. Beauty is not truth. The tangle of foliage obscures the dirt. I want you to give me a life of cut flowers, herbs, and fresh lettuce. I ache for an anarchy of green. You are living in someone else's paradise. We wage a battle, at ground level, for ownership. I invoke botany. You ignore the tedious details, harnessing passion to your side. If I yield, putting daylilies in the shade, cyclamen in the sun, hibiscus where it will grow to block the view, later I steal victory at any price, ripping out the lilies, letting the cyclamen wilt, chopping down the hibiscus before you can stop me. You hate to see me put plants out of their misery. I hate to watch them waste away because of your ignorance, or strangle their delicate neighbors out of your reluctance to apply discipline.

The photographer warns us that every domestic relationship she has documented ended soon after she made her portrait: lesbians eating hamburgers, lesbians comparing their tattoos, lesbians playing poker, lesbians eating brown rice, lesbians taking their dog for a walk. History. Water under the bridge. We are too proud to be superstitious.

Lesbians in a hammock is a technical failure, since the view camera has vignetted most of the bottom left corner into oblivion. The photographer substitutes another view, lesbians on back porch. We sit some feet apart in deck chairs. I talk to the cat. You look at the camera. Not a flower is visible.

20

You are sweeping for mines, a fury with bandaged arms. After the door slams, I wander the house looking for holes. On my bulletin board, a rectangle of cork shows through the postcards and the snapshots. You were twenty-five, on your first big trip, out of Arkansas to Yale, learning to invent yourself. Jeans, tank top, arms crossed over denim jacket, beautiful cheekbones. All you have is potential.

21

Two lesbians, they love each other, one gets breast cancer, she dies, the other goes on alone. A real tearjerker of a film. Two lesbians whose love withstands adversity, model victims, touching, sharing, *processing*. Sitting close on a cheap lavender sofa, under something framed and uplifting. Bad haircuts, short in front, long in back. Talking heads. I take you to see it, wanting to show you the way I really love you, wanting to put the movie before you like a proper picture, not a point-and-shoot, the sort of photo that comes out better than the real thing, the sort of photo one wants because it's true, the way you could show it if only you had the proper equipment.

You rage. It wasn't like that. You weren't like that. You didn't help. You let me down. You ignored me. You have no idea how lonely I felt. Why did it have to happen to me? Why does everything bad happen to me? You fucking ingrate, I think, floating weightless into my silence. You whining bitch. After all this time, haven't you learned how to be sick?

PHOTOGRAPHERS DO IT IN THE DARK, said the bumper sticker on the way home.

22

You're a redhead, transparent. Everything shows, all the surprises, all the imperfections. There are days I can see rage moving under your skin, seething along blue veins under that perfect surface, boiling under the freckles, down the lean arms, along the clear bone of your jaw, in the veins of your neck. At other times you go underground.

Your skin is empty, as if you have hidden the life that quickens deep inside, removed exactly what I am mad for to a place below any surface I can reach. You cool. Your body grows heavy. You close to me. To bring forth speech requires sweat in depths I can only imagine. You hesitate for minutes before you manage a word, or two, in reply to the questions with which I try to rouse you. Do you want to go to a movie? Shall I make dinner? When do you need to go to work? What did you do today? Do you love me? Will you always love me? Have I said something? Forgotten something? Done something? Thought something?

I don't name what we are living. If I abstain it may be temporary, not a misery that settles into your cells and that you will come to claim for your own protection, name as a molecular weakness, a chemical imbalance to be rectified through weeks and years of patient experimentation.

So little skin between you and me. I photograph around you, in spite of you, hoping that if the prints come back with a smile, it might make it true.


23


We visit another volcano, live this time, pouring lava down to the sea in a great black shiny delta that looks like oil or wax or anything but the sandpaper it is. At night, you can see the flames. People throng to see the flow that has cut roads in two, incinerated houses, exploded trees into charred bone. Dusk is the recommended time. The procession of curiosity seekers, dutifully carrying flashlights and water bottles, picks its way over hardened lava to the spot where a rivulet of molten lava pours into the sea. We walk to the edge and watch orange seep into waves, break into great globules that float out burning across the water, hissing and spitting and steaming until surf drowns flame and featherweight black boulders bloat with water and slip under. We are hypnotized. I know that I can describe the scene far better than my camera, but I photograph because you are afraid of the edge. To absolve myself from bringing you so close, I push the button to make something to see. It comes back dark sticks and orange blurs in a gray field.

24

A postcard, sent by our friend Felix, to thank us for being us, one installment in a correspondence that involves sending pictures of cats and clouds back and forth between New York and Los Angeles. STATELY ROYAL PALMS, FLORIDA, the caption runs, explaining nothing. It is a chromolithograph of progress, one of those forties photographs, usually of dams or bridges or hotels, retouched over the edge into drawing. This one is atypically monochromatic for a genre that mandates hope. There are only two points of color in its gray-brown field: far back on the right, at the end of a tunnel formed by the trunks of the palms, a blob of red, presumably bougainvillea; on the left, in the foreground, near a bush, the red skirts of two girls holding hands.

We have not spoken for months. I telephone the morning I learn that Felix has died. When he was poor, he lent us his apartment. We managed in his single bed with four cats. I want to remind you. A female voice intercepts, brightly sensible, a computer. The party you are calling will not accept calls from this number. I make inquiries. Your moat costs four dollars a month. For a while, I keep my end of your bargain, calling from time to time just to hear the computer say the drawbridge is still up.

Later, I frame the postcard, give it a new title. TWO LESBIANS WHO HAVE LOST THEIR CLITORIS.

25

You find her because you know she will be there. After all those years she cannot have vanished without a trace. We already know the outline. Robin and Mary came together to New Mexico. They lived there for years in an old adobe, still standing a few hundred yards away from where we now sit with our friends after dinner. Robin wore the pants. Robin did the farming, Mary worked in town. Mary was a nurse. Robin played the banjo. Robin kept notebooks of love songs. They quarreled. Mary left. Robin never spoke of her again. They are long dead. We have the albums, Robin's life arranged chronologically in many volumes. Black pages, white ink. Robin's childhood home, Robin as a girl, Robin in prep school, Robin's graduation from college, Robin riding with her girlfriends, Robin's roommate, their dogs, a thick red line and the notation: END OF ALBANY STREET. Another address, another roommate, more vacations, more road trips. The album thins to cars and scenery and dogs. Slowly we realize we are seeing evidence neither of weariness nor of growing humility, but detail erased with calculation, great blank spaces flaked from a worked surface. There are no human beings. Robin depopulated the years she could no longer endure, purged the memory of the woman who betrayed her, retracing her steps back to the place where everything still lay ahead, back to Illinois, then forward, west over the Rockies, and south to the final picture, a road to nowhere, a car beside, with the neat script: "New Mexico, 1941!"

You refuse to admit defeat. You retrace your steps, armed with a magnifying glass. There she is! There she fucking is!—you cry, Ahab in the uncharted seas of queer history. A speck on a cement guardrail somewhere in the Colorado mountains turns out under the glass to be a smiling young woman in a white blouse leaning back into Robin's encircling arms. It's your moment of glory. You sit under the bright circle of a desk lamp, waving your glasses in one hand and the magnifying lens in the other, triumphant in the knowledge that your eyes have been keen enough to catch the evanescent flash of love.

The photograph I did not make: the lines in your face show, the skin of your jaw sags, your carrot top has gone auburn, you wear a redder lipstick. Man's shirt buttoned to the top, you are the very picture of a schoolmarm, so beautiful my breath still stops.


## 26


We are camped at the headwaters of the Rio Grande. We make a house—laundry lines, kitchen, bedroom, reading nook. You reach into the icy water for stones, collecting the jewels, the smoothest, the roundest, the purest. Your patience is inexhaustible. I read *Moby Dick*, a book that bores you stiff.

A panorama. Mountains along the horizon, bands of forest, almost black, a foreground of curving green hills, a woman in a red baseball cap lying in the shade of a sapling that makes a tender vertical on the right side of the frame, the only relief in a hot field of cows. We have been resting, gazing at the mountains, your head on my shoulder. This is all I need, I say, all we need, a little pool of shade with room enough for us both. Then it doesn't matter how fast or hard or mean the world is. I ask you to photograph me on my island. To oblige me, you leave the shade and stand in the hot sun.

27

It is easier to remember your back thin against my cheek, or the sound of your car on the hill outside our house, than it is to endure these snapshots. I have carried them in a small black box to Lake Como, where a man invented photography because he envied his wife's ability to draw. I arrange them across my desk. After I write out each one, I shut it back up, Pandora refiguring the odds.

28

Flower alert, we used to say on walks around the neighborhood or in the country, a signal to look, to cradle, to inhale. A code, our code. We don't bother to learn their names, preferring to discuss each particular instance of sexual delirium in the language we already speak. A bee landing on the broad lower lip of a foxglove, fumbling inside, staggering back drunk, sticky, legs breaded with yellow. The entire thorned roundness of a barrel cactus swelling dark red among the rocks, prophecy of eruption. The cream throat of a burgundy daylily, the green veined shaft of an amaryllis, sweet wet cupped in the hollows of heliconia. Hummingbirds suspended, thrumming for the perfect pitch to lick nectar from deep violet mouths, moths groping in the dark for honeysuckle, white fingers laced in the beard of blue iris, the magnificent pornography of orchids.

　　Yes, and there are butterflies that smell with their toes. Plants confound sex. Plants make light of gender. Plants do it for themselves, plants do it with whatever moves. Skilled lovers, they are queer to the hairs on their roots, patient, inventive, perverse, unscrupulous in the pursuit of satisfaction and everywhere a shameless cornucopia of possibility, sweet nipples, wet holes, thrusting fingers, silky lips, tongues crafted to precision instruments.

We take shorthand in blurred photographs, revise the gynecology of homosexuality. We compile the guide to local wonders.

Remember that ladyslipper? Perfectly.

# Beauty of Blood

**JANE THURMOND**

For years my closest friends could fit inside a petri dish. Since I lived out in the country with Celia, who's like a mother to me, and a scarcity of other faces, and had a long commute to work in town, friends were hard to come by. As a substitute for people, I chose to focus on the microscopic world beneath my fingertips and just below my skin.

During one hectic weekend at the hospital, things began to change. I had just checked the wristband of a patient to draw his blood, a gunshot wound, a reckless hunting accident, and I cradled his tender forearm in my palm while I explored with my other forefinger. Before dialing me up in the lab, nurses had missed his veins over and over, leaving blotched bruises like irises whose purple petals fade to yellow edges. Beneath the pale skin a tired vein rolled and I held it down, inserting the needle. The patient relaxed, gratefully gazing through the test tube glass at the blood arcing from his arm, slowly filling each tube.

"That's it," I said, loosening the tourniquet, setting off its rubbery snap. I juggled tubes, the used needle, and my labeling pen. "You family?" I asked the patient's visitor, who had winced and rocked forward, doubling over as if the pain belonged to him.

He straightened and fingered the IV tubing. "I'm Dwayne. Michael's family isn't here."

"Listen, Dwayne, don't tell anyone I said this, but if you're around when they come in to draw blood again, don't let a nurse or doctor do it. They don't get enough practice. Insist they call me in the lab, my name's Judith Wiggins. It's rare I don't get a vein the first try."

Dwayne scowled at my name tag. "I've seen them try ten times before they hit it."

I taped a square of gauze over the new wound, which was surrounded by a field of tiny red punctures. The smell of disinfectant rose from the polished floor. Dwayne put pressure on the bandage as I placed a drop of blood on a glass slide and took another slide and swiped it up, transforming the drop into a thin film that ended in a perfect feathered edge. I labeled it and tiptoed from the room, waving to the pink wedge of Dwayne's face as the door creaked shut.

Back in the lab I gave Michael's red top to Chemistry for an SMA-6. I unstopped the purple top, let the blood flow into a capillary tube for a crit and lowered the smears into stain. This is a small rural hospital with no money for an automated Coulter counter. But I wouldn't trust one anyway. How can a machine detect the exquisite nuances of a cell? If it were my blood on the slide, I'd want a human, with nerves and reason and judgment, probing for abnormalities. When I put Michael's slide on the scope and gazed into the world of his smear I found white cells running rampant, red cells that looked as if they'd been bleached. Though typical of anyone who's suffered a shattering wound, his outpouring of reticulocytes was ominously high and he was throwing out blast cells in quantities I didn't like to see. Before moving on to the next patient, I phoned Dr. Osbourn to report the results.

During the following week Michael's condition became a gift to me, a rare opportunity for study. I'd drive home, my mind racing, and reflect on my findings with Celia, who's always game for a scientific puzzle. From her library we pulled references that shed light on the healing process. The body is remarkable, the way it rebuilds itself, and we watched Michael's struggle unfold across our coffee table.

Almost daily I bumped into Dwayne wandering the hallways of the hospital or grabbing coffee in the cafeteria. As much as possible, I avoided him. Then one day, by the salad bar, I asked him how Michael was doing and he latched on to me like he hadn't spoken to another human for months. So I invited him to my table and listened.

Dwayne was raised across the border in Beauregard Parish and Michael came from Canada. They'd met at UT, both working on their master's degrees in wildlife biology, and he had driven Michael to the piney woods with hopes of spotting velvet-horn deer, the subject of Dwayne's thesis. I clutched my iced tea and shivered, remembering the gray day when Daddy introduced me to hunting. Out the window nurses in sage-green surgical scrubs shuffled about. Smoke from their cigarettes hovered around them as if fog had settled in. My thoughts snagged on a tangle of twigs and I drifted back into Daddy's deer blind built into branches of a live oak. Back then I was barely big enough to handle a rifle.

"Judy Ann, that's a velvet-horn!" I heard my father murmur again, squinting through the scope of his .30-30. "Good for nothin' but stocking the freezer—they can't reproduce."

Beyond the blind, where we crouched in bright orange vests, grazed an odd-looking deer with irregular knots on his head where branching antlers should have been. Then out of the brush wobbled a fawn that reared and rammed the bigger velvet-horn in the ribs, forcing it closer to our blind.

"You'll never have an easier shot, Judy Ann. Line it up. Now, pull the trigger."

Against the shaking of my own hands, I lined up the crosshairs on its gray-brown chest and felt my finger pull back, and the gun's lunge against my shoulder. My ears rang as white tails shot up and deer disappeared instantly into the brush.

"You're about to bag your first kill," Daddy bellowed, leaping from the blind. "Now get yourself down here so we can find him—fast." Surrendering my rifle, I numbly descended the ladder. Without speaking, we followed the bright red spots, at first the size of dimes, stomped down trails shin-deep with gold and orange leaves, across the rocky bed of a trickling spring, past lichen-covered boulders. I dreaded finding the deer, but the dime-sized spots swelled and thickened into smears and, finally, a clump of skin and brown hair snagged on a low branch. I spotted the velvet-horn a few feet away, lying on its side. Crimson liquid pooled from its chest as its white throat wrenched back, head turning weakly against grass.

"Break his neck like I've showed you. Finish him off."

I took a step back, my arms stiff. "It's too close."

My father pushed me aside, sending a bullet through the base of the deer's neck and the smooth brown head relaxed. "Don't ever let an animal suffer like that again." He stooped for a dry reed and touched the tip of it to the deer's wide-open eye that sat in its socket like a polished stone.

I knelt and looked into the face of the deer. I ran my fingers along the thin white ring of fur around the eye, which had glazed over, but was watching me. Daddy heaved it over onto its back and spread its limp legs. "Velvet-horns never develop their, you know. We did this guy a favor. Even fawns will badger a velvet-horn to death." He released the legs and dug in his vest pocket. "Hey, big hunter, pull his head up on your lap. Big smile," he ordered, with the slow click of his camera.

"You're so soft," I whispered, running my fingers over the velvety antlers, small and misshapen like moss-covered stumps.

When Daddy brought the photos home, I felt sick at the sight of blood oozing out in shades of glossy gray, and I removed the one of me and the deer and buried it in the trash barrel.

Dwayne's fork clanked as he chased macaroni shells around his plate. "Michael doesn't seem to be getting any better," he said.

Gulping cold coffee, I snapped myself back. "What does the doctor say?"

"That he's progressing normally." He looked at me expectantly.

A week later Michael was dead. I noticed his empty bed taut with fresh sheets and questioned a nurse. "He seemed to have no fight," she said. When I pictured Dwayne steering back to UT alone, I felt a pang of sadness. Soon after, I received a card in care of the lab thanking me for being such a good friend to Michael.

I was no friend. Racing from room to room, I'd kept a safe distance from them both. Losing patients is part of the job, and if I let myself feel for anyone, I'd drive myself into a depression I couldn't crawl out of.

At least six months later, I was staring through the scope at a patient's marrow, awed by the picture of cellular development, from promyelocyte in actual mitosis all the way through to a segmented cell. I studied the paperwork that accompanied the smears in order to unearth the background of this patient in crisis, and found the description of a teenager named Jason who was succumbing to leukemia in the east wing. In such a small hospital it's uncommon to find the flesh-and-blood anomalies described in my textbooks, and my pulse quickened as I stared at Jason's threadlike chromosomes.

The lab phone rang and Dwayne stuttered, "Judith? Remember me? Dwayne?"

"Of course I do. I recognize your voice." The fact was, I rarely got calls from anyone but Celia.

"I finished my orals. Got a job in Houston." I heard him take a deep breath. "And I was wondering if you'd like to go out Saturday night."

I pushed my chair back from the desk and rolled across the polished floor, leaving the leukemia behind. "I get off at seven."

"I could pick you up at the hospital. We both know where that is."

What will I wear? I wondered, picturing my closet stuffed with yellowing lab uniforms wrinkled on wire hangers. "What's the attire?"

"Anything but a lab coat and those tacky nurse shoes. Dress for fun."

When was the last time I had gone out simply to have fun? The thrill of it caused my cheeks to flush. "Okay then," I stammered.

"A real honest-to-goodness date?" said Celia, crossing her arms. "To where?"

"To have fun. I don't know where." Not wanting her to feel left out, I stifled my delight. Celia scowled, picking through pecans piled into one of my mother's old serving bowls. We still had all of my mother's precious things—a complete silver service, china set for eight, lace doilies, photo albums and even her piano. She'd left hastily. Not me, thirteen years old at the time, not Daddy, not any of her possessions were as important to her as Ray Freed. My mother deserted us all for the lust of the church choir director. "I'd never do that," I blurted.

Celia loosened a pecan from between her teeth. "Do what?"

"Leave you."

"Slow down, Judith. It's only your first date."

After the scandal of Mother's leaving died down, Daddy had hired Celia to look after me. On her fiftieth birthday she climbed from his car, as bright and fresh as a perfectly poached egg. Her pear shape was stuffed into a starched white uniform and a yellow scarf swallowed her sturdy neck. I watched through my window as they unloaded her life—duffel bags, potted plants, a mountain of cardboard boxes, and a half-eaten birthday cake smeared with blue and yellow frosting.

Working all over the world inspecting rigs for Delta Oil kept Daddy too busy to worry about me, so he turned that task over to Celia. Before finally working himself to death, he came back for the big events—Thanksgivings, Christmas holidays, my high school graduation. But Celia, who quickly traded in her white uniforms for wild muumuus, was there for all the small stuff. My own sense of myself vanished along with my parents and she brought me back. Even now, when I see her hobbling up the path bearing a pile of cherry tomatoes in the curve of her shirt, or rearranging the fossils piled on our front stoop, I am overwhelmed by the treasures of our shared lives.

Through the years the two of us were content to hide ourselves away in the world. This date with Dwayne was a bump in our routine. But by Saturday morning Celia was excited enough to iron my outfit and hang it on the hook in the cab of the truck. Lenore, head tech in Radiology, trimmed my hair during our lunch break, and ordered me to neaten my nails. It was rare to feel a kinship with the memory of my mother, but old ties surfaced as I leaned in close to the lab's lavatory mirror to color my lips. Pinning myself into the privacy of a bathroom stall, I wrestled on a pair of stiff flats, new green slacks, and a houndstooth shirt I'd ordered from the Sears catalog. After I'd hit thirty my hips had spread, and I tugged the shirt over my new bulges.

When I emerged into the hospital lobby, Dwayne greeted me with a tiny bouquet of purple violets. "Street clothes become you," he said, embracing me. I stiffened up, startled by his bony arms clinching my back. As Lenore from the lab swished by and winked, I ducked my head. "You hungry?" He pressed the flowers into my palm.

"Thanks," I said. "Extremely." More than a decade had passed since my last date, and I fumbled as he guided my hands into the armholes of my winter coat.

Dwayne opened the passenger door of a sparkling new '84 Camaro and waited as I sank into the low bucket seat. He stopped at the hood and buffed a spot with the starched sleeve of his shirt. Nestled against the mudcat-brown velveteen cushion, his features appeared to turn down, shadowing his face with sadness. Before my nerves caused me to clam up, I complimented the upholstery and the new-car smell.

Shifting into fifth along the Interstate, he flipped on the radio and turned up the bass. "Do you like to sing?" The highway was crowded with speeding cars.

"Let's put it this way, I'm not gifted. We're not headed for Houston, are we?"

"That's the plan."

"Well, this *will* be fun. I never go down there. All that traffic. I can't find my way around."

Dwayne cranked the radio and tapped his left foot through a set of Top Ten tunes. "Ever heard of karaoke?" He turned down the volume.

"Kar-a-o-ke. It's Japanese. You go to karaoke bars to sing. Regular people, I mean, not pros."

"Didn't they just have a bit about that on the news?" I said, gazing out the window. Multicolored city lights flashed around us, strobing across the long polished hood of the car.

"You saw that? Then you saw me. I was working the KJ booth that night. Monday through Thursday I'm the karaoke jockey. That's where I'm taking you."

I wanted to spring from the car. "Oh, Dwayne," I moaned. "I'm not up for that."

"You don't *have* to sing. You can just watch." We rounded a corner where neon illuminated a packed parking lot. Sally's Seafood and Karaoke Bar was scrawled in lime-green light across the moonless January sky. "Welcome to the joint that's paying my bills," said Dwayne, opening his door. As he sauntered around the hood, his wheat-colored hair absorbed a tinge of neon green. When he stooped to open my door I was confronted by his long slender legs. "Don't worry about the crowd. I reserved a table." His flash of enormous white teeth startled me and I realized that, until then, I had never seen him smile.

Through the front door of jumbled pier pilings we faced an aquarium swarming with gaping tropical fish. Dwayne's palm warmed the small of my back. Beyond the entryway, collaged with shells, mounted marlin and swordfish leapt over stretched nets on sea-green walls. Cowboys crowded around tables cracking crab claws and swigging beer. Waitresses overturned buckets of bright red crawfish onto butcher paper as families covered their chests in wide white bibs that read "I sucked the heads at Sally's."

As we wedged ourselves into our stage-side booth, I could almost smell salt air. I tipped my head back against the aqua cushion to discover a high ceiling spotted with lights, like stars.

"I thought this was your night off," said a woman crowned with a wiry French braid. Stray strands of copper hair fell around her face.

"Sally, this is Judith Wiggins."

"So, you're the hero from the hospital." Her sturdy grip felt cool from carrying an icy pitcher of tea. "I've heard all about you. All good." A waiter's arm appeared with two slushy margaritas rimmed with sparkling crust. "I saw you come in, so I put in an order at the bar."

I lifted my glass and pinched the edge of it between my lips, sucked in the salt, then let a little liquid trickle onto my tongue. Heat shot from the center of my body right on out into my limbs.

"You didn't tell me she was cute too, Dwayne," Sally said, elbowing his arm. She bent down and whispered, "Dwayne thinks you walk on water."

I took another sip and buried my face in the menu. Along the bottom were detailed drawings of shells and sea life floating above dots of sand. The list of dishes appeared to drift under the surface of the sea.

"The Pirate's Platter is the best," said Dwayne.

I closed the menu. "Make it two."

In her tight black jeans, leather boots that zipped jauntily up the side, and black tank top, Sally didn't fit with this cowboyish crowd celebrating their Saturday night. "She seems awfully young to own a restaurant," I said.

"She's great to work for," said Dwayne. "I thought I'd hate this job, maybe stay a month or so, until I could find something else. But it's turned out to be a lot of fun and leaves my days open."

Sally resurfaced and placed both hands on his shoulders, his deltoids rounding her palms. "Dwayne, help me get the crowd warmed up tonight. Please?"

"If you insist," he said, cracking a smile.

"Great. I'll bring your Pirates in a minute." She topped off our water glasses and bustled to the next table.

"You guys are actually going to sing?" I was starting to feel edgy.

Sally appeared before us with two ocean-blue boat-shaped platters stuffed with fish fillets, oysters, shrimp, and hush puppies all fried to an even ocher. My foiled potato perched like sleeping quarters in the middle. I ate without a break, grateful for a task to keep my mouth busy.

Dwayne piled silverware on top of his empty plate and took a long gulp of water. "I've got to go warm up my voice." He gave a thumbs-up to the KJ sitting high in a side booth overlooking the stage, and disappeared down a dark hallway.

"I thought you could use another margarita." Sally brushed my shoulder. "Dwayne's been so nervous about asking you out. I didn't know what to expect."

"What has he told you about me?"

"What hasn't he told me?" Diners at the next table waved their arms her way. "Sorry, gotta go." She made another bouncy loop around the restaurant.

Lights dimmed and Sally stepped onto the tiny spotlit stage. Colored lights split the dark behind her, spinning magenta, gold, and lime over the cresting waves of her braid. A wide video screen floated above her, facing the audience. Another, smaller one perched at her waist level, facing her. When she took the mike from the stand her voice dropped an octave. "How's everybody doin' tonight?"

Scattered applause was the reply. "Sing one, Sally," slurred a tipsy silver-haired woman.

"Come on up here, Dwayne, and help me out."

Shrill whistles drifted up from the back as Dwayne hopped onstage. Orchestral accompaniment blared from the speakers, and before I had shifted back in my seat, Sally and Dwayne were shuffling their feet and clapping a perfectly timed dance routine from the score of *Grease*. "You're the one that I waa-nt," they yodeled, gazing into each other's eyes. Dwayne's bold voice leapt off the stage, his lithe limbs shifting in perfect rhythm, a genuine smile etching his face. Sally's voice bolted from her heart and held the audience captive through to the final note. Clapping and stomping erupted as Dwayne stepped down and Sally shouted, "You don't have to be a star, baby, to be in my show." As she raised the microphone, she introduced the next singer, a man with a potbelly and a beard, who sang a strained, but sincere, version of "Country Roads."

"Dwayne, you were great," I gushed as he scraped back his chair.

"Thanks," he said, grinning. As I followed the words to every song on the video screen above the stage, I hoped for the singers to hit their high notes, to remain on key and beat. When a man started in on "What's New Pussy Cat?" he fell so far behind, he had to start over.

I hadn't had a drink in years and, after downing my second margarita, streaming beams of stage light fuzzed the edges of sea life, the gurgling performers, and waitresses, graceful as mermaids. They glided over our table like shipwrecked treasure. Occasionally Sally drifted past. Dwayne was a diver, blurred by rivulets of water. Floating next to him on our aqua cushion, I let him take my hand in his.

On our way home I nodded off until Dwayne spoke. "This is my first time out on a date since before the accident, so I'm a little rusty."

Darkened stores loomed behind foreboding parking lots. "All I know is that I really like you, Judith. You've been so sweet. Kind."

"Dwayne," I snapped, "if this has to do with Michael—stop."

"Did I say sweet? I take it back."

"Let me tell you the truth. All along, I knew Michael was failing. I watched it happen through my microscope."

The wheels of the car hit the road's shoulder, sending off a spray of gravel until Dwayne jerked us back onto pavement.

"It was my job to know."

He gripped the gearshift knob. "Why didn't you tell me?"

"Because telling you wasn't my job. And, besides, I could have been wrong." Dwayne's knuckles looked like stone in the dark. "Real friends tell friends the truth, and I didn't have the nerve. You should know that."

He pulled into the hospital parking lot and coasted to a stop. "Judith, you're the only one in that building who even gave me the time of day. And you did comfort Michael." He glared at me, his big teeth pushing against his lips, his strong jaw jutting forward. "That's how I remember it."

"I wish you'd stop bringing it up," I whined. "I really don't like to think about it."

"What are you afraid of?"

Everything that I was afraid of glared at me from the dead space beyond the parking lot. Everything that I couldn't see or understand. "Do you know what I felt each time I saw Michael?" My voice was hoarse. "Nothing. Nothing but my own inability to help him."

"Oh, you helped, Judith." Dwayne shifted in his seat. "Look, Michael's family didn't even care enough to come down from Quebec, and I was all he had. Then there were these cops who kept grilling us about the accident—'Did you see this?' 'Do you remember that?'"

I stared at my truck, parked near the hospital entrance. Cool blue light from the emergency sign washed over the cab. My throat ached from the fear of exploding and I opened the door and bolted from my seat. "I'm so sorry he died," I blurted. My words fell onto the greasy lot.

Dwayne stepped out and stood by his car. "Life goes on."

I fidgeted with the wilted violets. "Thanks," I said, grappling with my manners. "I really did have a nice evening."

"Next time I'll be better company," he called after me as I rushed to my truck.

As I coasted through the parking lot, I looked into familiar patients' darkened windows and, though I could not see them, I pictured them in their beds. There was the pernicious anemia with dangerously low hemoglobin. There was the lead poisoning with polychromatophilia. There was the sickle cell and next to him the elevated platelets. And there was the chronic granulocytic leukemia, his bones breaking along with his parents' hearts. That I could change a patient's, a stranger's, life with only a few kind words was a responsibility that I was queasy to accept.

After I opened our front door, Celia swooped up from the couch in her bathrobe. "How was it?" She yawned, staying on my heels from the living room to the bedroom to the bathroom and back. "Where did you go? Was he nice? Did you have fun?" She fidgeted with a stained coffee cup.

"I drank two fish bowls of margaritas," I said, flopping onto my bed. "We'll talk tomorrow." I melted into my ocean of sheets, ears still buzzing from an evening spent too close to speakers. "You're the one that I wa-nt. Mmm mmm mmm, baby," I hummed, drifting in and out of sleep.

Dwayne and I agreed to put aside the tense conversations of our first date and pretend we'd just met. On our fourth date to Sally's Seafood and Karaoke Bar, I stood in the tiny practice room gazing into the full-length mirror. Through the insulated door I heard a muffled soprano emanate from the stage. I could sing circles around the last three performers, and Dwayne's prediction had come true—the performance bug had bitten. Powdering my nose, I reflected on articles about dating I'd borrowed from waiting-room magazines. They insisted that the passionate meeting of our lips was long overdue. "Are You on Schedule?" advocated more than our brief pecks good night. "Taking the Reins" advised that *I* become the suitor, and I considered this as I fluffed my hair, admiring my shrinking waistline. Flipping through the selection of tapes, I could almost hear my mother singing. After clamping headphones over my ears, I popped in a tape, propped the word sheet on the music stand, and searched through the selections. Should I sing "He's So Fine" or "Baby It's You," "Love Is Strange" or "Que Sera, Sera." Finally I settled on "Fever." I'd try to make it sexy, and I practiced it until I conquered every verse.

"Everything all right in there?" said Dwayne, tapping on the door.

"I'll be out in a sec." Filling my chest with air, I pulled the door open.

Dwayne looked sheepish. "I was starting to worry."

"I'm ready," I said, marching toward our table.

Further encouraged by a long-neck beer, I signed up to sing with a hesitant hand. "You'll be great," Dwayne assured me, massaging my shoulders as if I were a boxer about to enter the ring. But too soon the KJ announced my name and, despite the numbness in my legs, somehow Dwayne pushed me forward and onto the stage. Blinded by its yellow beam, I could feel the spotlight hot on my cheeks, but the song words on the little video monitor glowed green and reassuringly before me.

"Here's Judith Wiggins singing 'Feeevahhh,'" blared the KJ. Bass pumped through speakers. Familiar faces tipped up, encouraging me. Squinting at the lyrics, I opened my mouth to sing. A few words squeaked out, then my throat collapsed, as if it had melted from the heat of the spotlight.

The KJ's voice fell across the stage. "Sorry, you weren't ready. Let's restart that music."

I shook my head no, please no, but my accompaniment blared again and I sucked smoky air for a second take. My knees liquefied. Following the words that crawled across the big video screen facing them, the regulars in the audience snapped their fingers and sang each stanza for me. I couldn't look at Dwayne, but I was cheered briefly by the realization that Sally was still on an emergency run to a supermarket for cabbage, so she wasn't a witness to my failure. Catching up with the crowd, I wrenched out the chorus until the blessing of the last phrase arrived. On the final chord, everyone cheered as I stumbled straight to the bathroom. Inside the stall I froze, my eyes wide and alert, as if I were a hunted animal. The door creaked open, voices came and went. One voice cooed about how sorry she felt for that last girl until another voice shushed her in mid-sentence, probably pointing at my feet, rigid in the neighboring stall. When it was safe to emerge, I scrubbed my face at the sink. During a rendition of "Satisfaction," I slinked back through the restaurant.

Dwayne pulled my chair back for me to sit. "You okay?"

"I'm going to wait in the car until you're ready to leave." Dwayne waved, riveting his eyes back on the singer, a chunky young man with a buzz haircut imitating the drama of Mick Jagger's lips.

As I plowed across the neon-tinted lot, I bumped into Sally. "How's it going?" she said. I kept the Camaro in sight and disappeared inside without an answer. But that didn't stop her. After delivering the groceries, she returned and plopped down behind the steering wheel. "Tell me."

"I did it tonight. I got up there. It was awful. I couldn't find my place. I froze."

"My first time was in Japan. I felt like I had to do it to be polite. I fainted, right there onstage. I was sure I'd never sing again. Look, now I have my own bar." She pointed to her name in colored lights.

"Don't expect that story to change my mind. I'll never get up there again. Never."

At breakfast, Celia shoved aside a pile of seashells awaiting identification. Steam rose from her buttered oatmeal. "So, when are you going to bring the gentleman around?" she asked, tapping her spoon against the rim of her bowl.

Each fork I pulled from the silverware drawer was tainted by a spot of dried food. "Before he comes over, we've got to clean up," I said, throwing the forks into the sink. I pulled on my lab coat.

As my truck shimmied up the rutted gravel road that led out of our wooded acres, I squeezed one ear shut with my fingertips and sang. My voice was thin, but on key, and when I slipped across the quiet blacktop I began to exercise my range. Those days, on my way to the hospital, I was diligent with my practice and I began to believe that one night, when I was easier in my skin, I'd sing karaoke.

In the lab, as his condition grew more critical, I tracked the smears of the boy with leukemia. When I entered Jason's room his mother and father looked full into my face, their eyes brimming with the sadness that often accompanies love. The walls were painted a soothing green, the sky outside was blue, and the low winter light crept respectfully around the leaf-shaped shadows on the far wall.

"We'll get out of your way," his mother said.

"Coffee," his father grunted, and shuffled slowly toward the door.

Jason's body had puffed up, leaving his skin taut and free of wrinkles and he was covered with a rash. A picture of him posing in his purple band uniform draped with a French horn chided him from the nightstand. His eyes opened and I sat down and looked into his pupils. What is it like? I wanted to ask. "I have to do another test. A pinprick," I assured him. "Just one." He blinked as if to say yes and I held his middle finger lightly and quickly pricked it with a blade. As I milked the finger, working out a bead of blood, he didn't budge.

He opened his dry mouth and swallowed. "Didn't feel it," he whispered.

"Neither did I." I winked.

His mouth curled into a faint smile and I imagined the effort and ache that came with it. Pulling up a chair, I stared at his half-closed eyes and decided I could stay a few more minutes.

"I see you play the French horn. It's always seemed like a hard one to me, but I love the mellow tone. It sounds so, I don't know, noble." I straightened my tray, jumbled by my usual hurried tossing of tubes and needles and slides. "I don't play anything myself, but I come from a very musical family. My mother played the piano and the church organ. And she could belt out a tune." His eyes widened and he seemed to be taking this in. "And I'll let you in on a little secret. I'm trying to learn how to sing too. I practice on my way to work. It takes a lot of breath."

Jason's mother and father returned, sipping coffee from Styrofoam cups. "My beautiful boy. My beautiful, beautiful Jason," his mother intoned, smoothing his hair.

Before Jason died his eyes haunted me and, more than once, when his parents were absent, I visited him. The air was light and he was filling up the room. Nothing held us together but a few beads of his blood. I imagined his spongy marrow cranking out the stuff that could save him. But it was not enough, not nearly enough. And so I practiced, softly singing the words of the sweetest songs I knew, of hymns and childhood melodies, innocent things.

We became familiar, my voice and I, and I was learning that harmony came naturally to me, through my bloodline and fervent inner ear. My voice was clear, like that of a kid in a choir, and a few nights a week I found myself driving south through the traffic to Sally's Seafood and Karaoke Bar to watch. Dwayne climbed down from the KJ booth to say hello. On slow nights, Sally appeared with extra cake or cobbler, then she'd leap from her seat to approach the microphone, her back straight, her hair on fire. When she sang, I felt my body pull toward her, and was startled to find myself stretched forward, as if I might fly uncontrollably across the room. The light fell across the folds of Sally's blouse, around the delicate ridges of her ears, and bounced off the strands of her wine-colored hair, shiny as the polished cave of a shell.

"It's about time we had a man around here," said Celia, arranging a selection of homemade bread and smoked ham on my mother's antique silver platter. On hearing that I'd invited Dwayne over to meet her, Celia had polished the tray and it gleamed in the low dusky light flooding the windows. Around its perimeter she lined up fresh green onions, carrots, and crimson radishes from the last of her winter garden. Dressed in kelly green with pink accents, she fiddled with her stiff gray hair, which she had piled into a bun. It perched on the crown of her head like a pillbox hat.

"Don't go to so much trouble, Celia. He won't be staying long." I shut the bathroom door to soak away my nervousness. Worrying that Dwayne would see our house in all its disarray, I had spent the day straightening stacks of books and science magazines that crammed every corner, and dusting the cluttered shelves lined with earthly specimens that Celia collected from our land. I swept stray feathers and moth wings into a pile in the center of the living room and tossed them outside into the trash barrel to burn.

Celia came out to the barrel and stood next to me, warming her tough, arthritic hands at the fire. "It's been a long time since I've actually sent you out on a date," she said. I glared at her. "I'm not criticizing," she added.

"What's he going to think of me after he sees how we live?"

"Judith, do you think I won't know how to behave around him? Let me tell you, in my day I was quite a catch. When your daddy first hired me, I had a man. His name was Earl. But your daddy didn't want me flaunting Earl around you after what your mother had done, running off with that choir director like she did. So I kept him to myself until he realized I loved you more than him." She buttoned the top button of her sweater. "You had become like a daughter. Not blood, but mine."

I kicked the barrel, sending up a shower of sparks. "Look at me. Over thirty, and I've never been anyplace or done anything."

"Hum," she said, rubbing her hands together. Flames made the lines in her face appear deeper.

"Don't get me wrong. I love you and I love living here with you." I peered through gray smoke. "But I'm feeling this push to stretch, you know, discover other things."

"I wouldn't want to be anyplace else in the world," she answered.

As I relaxed into the bathwater, my new magnolia bubble bath rinsed over my shoulders. I scanned a test in *Redbook* magazine called "Is He the One?" By the time Dwayne arrived, I was dressing in my bedroom, dabbing gardenia cologne behind my ears.

"My God!" I heard him yelp as the screen door yawned behind him.

By the time I approached in my new batik skirt and blouse, he was picking through Celia's bone box that overflowed with the fragile skulls of small animals. Her assembled skeletons were displayed on a shelf that loomed over our heads above the dining-room table.

"Judith, why didn't you tell me about all this stuff?" said Dwayne, an armadillo spine dangling from his fist. I shoved a piece of ham into my mouth.

"Dwayne, I'd love to read your thesis," said Celia. "Judith says you're an expert on velvet-horns. Once I saw one right out there in the driveway."

"It looks like I could learn a thing or two from you, ma'am."

"Oh, I don't know," Celia answered coyly. "It's just a hobby."

Dwayne turned a full circle, taking in every detail of our private, our intimate, surroundings. He must think we're freaks, I thought, stamping my foot over a roving dust ball. I crunched into a carrot.

"Would you like to see the rest of the house?" said Celia, straightening the insect collection that hung on the wall. He followed her, nearly knocking a stack of mounted slides off the coffee table.

"Are those your parents?" he said, pointing through the doorway of my bedroom to a framed wedding photograph. I nodded. "You have her smile." He entered the room to get a closer look. When his trousers brushed the corners of my winter blankets, I felt the heat of a blush.

As Dwayne continued to wander about, hands deep in his pockets, Celia motioned me into the kitchen and whispered, "I just want you to feel comfortable, I mean, I just want you to know that it's fine with me for you to bring him back here to spend the night."

"Celia!"

"Well, Judith, it's natural. And what are you going to do? Make out in the car like a couple of teenagers?" Dwayne appeared in the kitchen doorway.

"Who does your taxidermy?" he said.

"I do it myself," said Celia, "in my workshop in the back."

"Don't laugh," I warned when we were alone inside his car.

"Who's laughing? I have to drive all the way to campus to find journals like that."

"Come on, Dwayne, I know you think we're crazy."

"Well, it's different, that's for sure."


Dwayne and Celia's friendship flourished. More often than not, I came home from work to find her exhilarated from a day of collecting specimens with him out on the ridge. A stack of his papers on velvethorns grew on the corner of her nightstand.

At the hospital I had taken up my own new studies. When Dr. Ruiz added prothrombin times to my responsibilities, I delved into the workings of the heart. Vena cava to right atrium to right ventricle to pulmonary artery to lungs. Left atrium to left ventricle to aorta and out, I recited, keeping time with my pulse. The lab phone rang, breaking my beat.

"Hope it's okay to call you at work. This is Sally."

"Sally, do you know the word 'arteries' means air pipes? People used to think that arteries carried air."

"I'll store that away to use on *Jeopardy!*"

I spun around in my chair. "What's up?"

"There's an ad in the paper. A disco's selling a whole set of lighting effects. Two hours down the coast. Tomorrow's your day off, isn't it?"

My pulse pumped wildly in my neck. "Should I meet you at the restaurant?"

When I cut my truck lights and plunged into the predawn purple of the parking lot, Sally appeared to be lit from underneath, crunching through white gravel flooded with moonlight. Thrusting steaming coffee and doughnuts toward me, she chattered as we dove into her Celica and rumbled out onto the highway. When a brightly lit oil rig backlit her silhouette, I followed the delicate ridges of her knuckles along the steering wheel, the whiter front tooth that pushed against her wide upper lip, eyebrows so thick they brushed the wire-rimmed driving glasses that sat high on her broad, freckled nose. She threw her head back in unabashed laughter. By the time we reached the Gulf I had pried from her the secrets of perfectly fried fillets, and heard her watery description of the island view from her parents' home in Ketchikan, Alaska, where she had been raised. With trips to Japan and even Russia under her belt, she was more worldly than anyone I had ever met, except for my own father.

I found myself answering all her questions about my mother's leaving. I had always imagined these answers safely silent inside a knotted balloon. If deflated I'd explode and collapse along with it, sputtering uncontrollably into dead space, from which there is no exit. Instead, after the loneliness and hurt and fear came spilling out, I was still there, slouched and startled next to Sally in her Celica.

Sally bit her lip. "Judith, I want to know more and more about you."

My hands shook. "I told you things I've never told anyone before, stuff I never knew I felt myself."

She pulled into the disco's parking lot, where we took in the bay, as smooth and metallic as a cookie sheet. Sandpipers skittered along the pilings and pelicans balanced at the end of the wharf.

I mopped my eyes with my shirtsleeve. "I could use a breather. Let's buy the lights."

Despite the disco owner's surly manner, Sally cut an admirable deal with him for a fog machine, black light, beacon light, torpedo light, a strobe, and two mirrored disco balls.

"You're pretty slick," I whispered as he disappeared back inside.

When she took my arm I held my breath, jamming my hands deeper into my pockets for fear that I would grab her perfect fleshy waist. A flock of pink roseate spoonbills lifted and caught a draft. Beyond the rippling bay, the thin barrier island held back the pounding ocean.

On the trip back the smell of fish we'd bought permeated the car and we opened all four windows. "Sally, how long have you known Dwayne?" I shouted.

"Just since he came to work for me, maybe nine months."

"I'm not sure what he wants from me."

She shrugged. "Why don't you ask him?" She flipped on the radio and fiddled with the dial.

"To tell you the truth, Sally, I think he and Celia are the ones falling in love. They have lots in common."

Sally shrugged and smiled. When the radio static sharpened to a golden oldies station, she puffed out her chest and jacked up the sound, belting out "Good Vibrations." I joined in and we swayed back and forth, singing in our highest, shrillest voices.

When I arrived home Celia was loosening a cactus from a plastic pot. "We need to talk," she said, digging a thorn from the soft flesh of her thumb. I draped my coat over the porch rail as she paced back and forth across the yard. "First of all, for months now I thought you and Dwayne, well, I was practically planning the wedding."

"Don't count on it," I said.

"This morning I happened to mention to him how deer tracks look like split hearts to me and he burst into tears. He could barely catch his breath. Everything just gushed out. Do you know his family lives less than an hour from here and they haven't spoken to him for over five years?"

"He mentioned that he didn't see them much."

"Judith, you don't suppose that Dwayne is, umm, I'm going to get right to the point. I'm just going to spit it out." She surveyed our deserted property as if someone else might hear.

I plopped down on a porch step and propped my feet on a split geode that revealed its crystalline center. Celia's hands balled up into fists. "Gay?" I whispered.

"Yes, a homosexual. I think he might be one." My feet slid off the geode. Celia clasped her hands. "I realized today that he and Michael may have been paired. Mates. Gentleman friends."

I sensed my pinched forehead. "I've never known a real homosexual before." I scratched my scalp, which had started to tingle. "How would you feel about him if he was?"

"I don't know," said Celia. "I've been analyzing that."

On Sunday I called Dwayne from the lab phone. "Let's talk."

"I can be there in an hour," he said.

We sat at the same table as we had nine months before when Michael was in the hospital, but this time spring brightened the sunny courtyard with bunches of pink flowers.

"Dwayne, what are we doing? I mean, when we go out, do you think of it as a date?"

His eyes pooled. "I've been trying to think of it that way, Judith."

I dropped my fork. "I'm not sure how to take that." Pushing back my full plate of spaghetti, I drew a deep breath. "Celia thinks you might be gay."

Dwayne's spoon clinked against his cup. He waited for two nurses to seat themselves across the cafeteria. "When I met you," he said, "I thought I'd give girls another shot. I've been waiting for the right time to bring it up. You're the first girl, well, woman, I've taken out since the tenth grade."

"Why me?" I heard myself whine. My mouth was dry, but I couldn't reach for water.

"I'm so glad you finally know." He rounded his shoulders and expelled all the air from his lungs. "Judith," he said, without looking up, "what if Michael's accident wasn't an accident at all." He shivered once and hugged himself. "I've never told anyone the whole story. Before he was shot, I crawled inside Michael's sleeping bag with him. Maybe someone saw." I organized the little packets of sugar into one neat row. "Judith, are you listening?"

"God, Dwayne."

"Afterward, Michael unzipped the bag and jumped up, naked. He was clowning around. Next thing I knew, he was flying toward me, blood everywhere. After the shot, no voices, no footsteps. No one came to help." Dwayne hissed through his teeth. "I tried to tell the cops that I didn't think it was an accident, but I never told them about Michael and me, you know, messing around."

"Do you actually think someone could have shot him on purpose and gotten away with it?"

Dwayne swiped a tear and held a hand up between us. "I plugged the hole in Michael's side with these fingers. I can barely remember how I got him to the hospital. I can't prove anything."

The sugar packets were perfect. Orderly. "What can we do?" I whispered.

He gazed blankly at the window. "Too much time has passed."

My lunch break was over, but I was unable to move.

"After Michael died, I let fear take me over until I wasn't me at all. But I don't want to live like that anymore, Judith. Friends tell friends the truth." He chewed a nail. "You said that on our first date."

"Now everything makes sense." I nodded. "And at least I can stop dousing myself with that gardenia cologne before we go out."

Dwayne grinned and his teeth were white as bleached bones. His breathing calmed.

"So, Dwayne," I fumbled, "what about Sally?"

"I knew it! You're all she talks about. She really, *really* likes you, you know."

My face grew hot and I sucked ice cubes inside my cheeks.

"I've been hoping you two might get together."

"Sally?" I repeated as if I'd never heard of her.

Dwayne shrugged. "Takes one to know one," he said with a weak smile. "Since everything is out in the open now, I met a great guy right here in town. Robert, the research librarian."

I swallowed hard. "Is he gay too?"

"God, Judith, can't you tell?"

The next day I checked a book out from Robert and read more about the doctor, William Harvey, who challenged other doctors who believed our arteries were filled with air. "I was almost tempted to think that the motion of the heart was only to be comprehended by god," he explained. Then in 1628 Harvey described this earthshaking idea, how the blood is driven around the body by the heart, "as it were, in a circle." As if I had just discovered it, I placed my right hand over my sternum and felt the squeeze of chambers. I detected something in there other than blood.

As I drove the truck up our graveled drive, Celia greeted me, waving torn pages from a magazine. She squawked over the engine, "Take a gander at this. Lesbian seagulls at the coast, paired for life." I stopped the truck, startled by the straight back of the printed *L*, the perfect circle of the dotted *i*. Letters curled across the page. In a photo two gulls perched at the top of a beach side boulder.

"You were right," I said. "Dwayne is gay."

"I've been researching it all day," said Celia. She shrugged and looked at the sky, which was turquoise and peach and filling up with billowing pink clouds. "And I finally decided: So what?"

I took both her bony shoulders in my palms and drew her to me, rested my chin in the crook of her neck. Her papery skin wafted my gardenia cologne. The orange sky washed over us. "That's nice," she murmured, stroking my spine.

I told Celia about Sally. "As soon as I asked Dwayne if he was gay, I knew that I was asking myself."

Celia folded her arms over her chest. "You want to know the truth? I've suspected it since the day I met you. I can't really put my finger on it, Judith. You were just, well, different."

"You don't suppose my mother knew."

Celia wagged her finger. "Even if she knew, it had nothing to do with her leaving."

"I used to wish that I had been born a boy so I could be with girls. I thought I was the only one in the world."

Celia scooped up a smooth stone and rolled it between her palms. "Remember when we found the tektite on that red dirt path we'd walked a thousand times?" she said. "I'll never forget how it caught the light. Such a rich black. Such a rare and beautiful thing."

Robert led me to a cardboard box hidden in the back room of the public library. "I order what I want," he whispered, fishing through and handing me a volume on gay American history. "The town council hasn't caught on yet. When you're ready to leave, make sure I'm the one who checks them out for you."

Each day during my lunch break, I nestled myself in the corner of the hospital courtyard and studied. The words shouted. They prickled my skin.

"Whatcha reading?" asked Lenore, passing me on her way to her lunchtime Bible study group.

A week passed before Sally had a day off. I phoned in sick to work. When I pulled up to her apartment she leapt from her front stoop clutching a wild red spider lily, ran to my truck, and flung the door open. Her polka-dot shorts brushed her pale thighs, which I had never seen, and I reached out and touched one ivory knee. She laid the lily across my lap and leaned to kiss my forehead.

"I've got a wild hankering for gingerbread pancakes," she said, pointing to a bullet-shaped diner on the corner.

That afternoon, lying in Sally's bed, I reflected on each part of her face. The vermilion border of her lip, the delicate ala of her nose, the frontal notch of forehead, her swooping zygomatic arch. Over her sternum I placed my palm and felt the chamber muscles pump. "After all this time," I whispered. Light from the streetlamps filtered through her window, which we cracked at first, then opened wide. The vast spring evening streamed in.

I examine Sally's fine hair under my microscope. I press petals from flowers she has given me between the pages of my notebooks. I lock her letters in my dresser drawer. Celia loves Dwayne, Robert, Sally, and, most important, me. We share meals together and our laughter lightens the darkened musty rooms of our home.

One night after dinner we all walked out along the ridge to admire the red-leafed maples and orange oaks bursting through the thicket of piney green. I could smell Sally's cucumber lotion. She looped her arm through the crook in my elbow and spread her palm to meet mine. The edges of our hands soaked up the angled light and looked transparent to the bone. I saw her pale skin through to her criss-crossed purple veins, felt the drum of her pulse, the beauty of her blood. Dwayne, Robert, and Celia lingered a few yards down, washed by breeze rising up over our field of trees.

Saturday night we drove Celia to the restaurant and, encouraged by us all, she sang karaoke. Dressed in her sky-blue blazer and canary pantsuit she slapped her hands on her thighs in syncopated time. When Celia's aging voice warbled out "Mockingbird," the audience quietly put down their silverware, stopped sipping their drinks, to catch it all.

At Sally's Seafood and Karaoke Bar dreams hover in the spotlight. The memory of my mother spins in the colored lights behind me, just out of sight, always at my shoulder. My lungs swell with her love of music. But under the houselights I behold my real family looking back across the table at me, their careful regard, their tender toothy smiles.

# Notes
# on the
# Contributors

**Pat Alderete**

"Fire" was a real struggle for me. Although it was relatively easy to write, I found it the most difficult piece I've ever read aloud. I was afraid people might think the cruelty in the story was stereotypical of Chicana/os, but the women in my writing group made me see that the meanness was the universal experience in the piece, though the setting was unique to my background.

Although the story is a work of fiction, Fire was a real person who endured much pain. I learned not long ago that he recently committed suicide, and I again questioned the ethics and morality of this tale. I worried that I might be exploiting him. Again, I was shown that by putting this story out, I was in fact giving him a voice he never had in life.

I wish he could have known how moving people find his story.

**Donna Allegra**

I'm in the lifelong process of clearing clutter from my life, so that I may put what I value most, first. Deep solitude is necessary to hear the soul's voice and trust its leading.

The audience I am writing for is lesbian, rather than the mythical "mainstream." It disturbs me to see so many lesbians water themselves down to be more palatable to a society that doesn't want us to be who we are or to critique that culture for its crimes against us.

My fiction, poetry, and essays have been published primarily in lesbian/feminist anthologies over the past twenty-five years. Most recently: *Does Your Mama Know?—An Anthology of Black Lesbian Coming Out Stories* edited by Lisa Moore; *Hot and Bothered*—short short fiction about lesbian desire edited by Karen X. Tulchinsky; *MOM* edited by Nisa Donnelly; and *Lesbian Travels: A Literary Companion* edited by Lucy Jane Bledsoe.

### Judith Barrington

I am the author of two collections of poetry and I edited *An Intimate Wilderness: Lesbian Writers on Sexuality.* This memoir, "Nicolette," a true story, was written as part of a book called *Lifesaving,* which I am just completing. Another memoir, "Poetry and Prejudice" (in *The Stories That Shape Us,* W. W. Norton, 1996), was the first piece I wrote that addressed my internalized homophobia—something I want to write more about. I was encouraged about the possibilities for dealing with this subject as literature when "Poetry and Prejudice" won the Andres Berger Award for Creative Nonfiction in 1996.

### Gwendolyn Bikis

Excerpts from *Cleo's Back* have appeared in *The Best Lesbian Erotica 1998, Close Calls, The Persistent Desire,* and *Does Your Mama Know?* "Cleo's Gone" is a recipient of the John Preston Erotic Writing Award.

I have written a vast amount of fiction (my work also appears in *Sister/Stranger, Conditions 15, Sleeping with Dionysus,* and *Catalyst*), but of all the fiction I have written, Cleo's stories have been the most enjoyable to write.

My work first appeared in lesbian publications in 1987; since then I have anticipated the day when identity politics is no longer lesbian fiction's main paradigm.

### Carellin Brooks

Carellin Brooks has been published in *Best Lesbian Erotica 1998* and the forthcoming *One Step Beyond* (Zero Hour Press). She also edited the anthology *Bad Jobs* (Arsenal, 1998). "I wrote 'The Butcher's Wife' at a period when I was pretty fixated on the darknesses in our lives," she says. "Maybe because of *Bad Jobs,* I was also thinking a lot about work. I was fascinated by slaughterhouse workers and by morticians. I didn't know very much about those occupations, and I didn't want to. Instead, I wanted to explore the tension between the symbolic value other people assign such occupations and the workaday atmosphere within those worlds." Brooks lives in Vancouver, where she is happy.

### Nona Caspers

Nona Caspers' novel *The Blessed* was published by Silverleaf Press. Her stories have appeared in *CALYX, Sinister Wisdom, Hurricane Alice, Women on Women 2, Word of Mouth.* A collection of short fiction received the Joseph Henry Jackson Literary Award. She teaches creative writing at San Francisco State University.

"'La Maison de Madame Durard' started with the voice of a fatally bored teenage girl and eventually turned into an attempt to relive my love-hate relationship with rural Minnesota. Marie must escape, but these farmers and bowlers are her people. The loss is incalculable."

### Natasha Cho

Natasha is twenty-four and lives in Melbourne, Australia. She has had successes in numerous literary competitions. Her work has appeared in publications in Australia and the United States including *Meanjin, New England Review, Sojourner, Tirra Lirra,* and *Verandah.* She is happy to see adventurous new queer writers being nurtured and on that note would like to say hi to her secondary school literature teacher Mrs. O'Shea. "Bang Bang Bang" is a bit like a James Bond film with Rosa Klebb and Pussy Galore as the main characters. It was written to show what can happen if women get nasty.

### Carolyn A. Clark

"kays and exes" started out as an assignment to write a piece including a celebrity . . . and grew out of my ongoing exploration of the collision between one's lesbian identity and the myths and legends of the lesbian community. The relationship myths, such as the ubiquitous ex-girlfriend, and the legendary role models, such as k.d. lang, can offer us a rich heritage or, by turns, a prepackaged culture, leaving us to navigate the murky waters of stereotypes rooted in a semblance of truth. I live and write in Los Angeles.

### Emma Donoghue

Born in Dublin in 1969, Emma Donoghue is an Irish novelist, playwright, and literary historian now based in Canada. Her books include *Stir-Fry, Hood, Kissing the Witch, Passions Between Women, Poems Between Women,* and *We Are Michael Field.*

"How a Lady Dies" was inspired by Elizabeth Pennington (1734–59), who turned up on the doorstep of Frances Sheridan (1724–66) to say she could not live without her. From Bath they returned to London, where Elizabeth died in Frances' arms. This story is one of a series of fact-based historical fictions, a form Donoghue sees as a treasure-chest for lesbian writers.

### Ellen Hawley

My first novel, *Trip Sheets,* was published in 1998 by Milkweed Editions. I edit a writers magazine, *A View from the Loft,* which is published by the Loft Literary Center in Minneapolis, Minnesota. For what it's worth, I have also worked as a cabdriver, a radio talk-show host, a waitress, a janitor, and an assembler.

I'm not sure how I'd define lesbian fiction, or where I'd draw the line between lesbian fiction and fiction in general. We're a community that's hungry for images of itself. The best-known lesbian writers, and maybe also the ones who are less well known, help shape our sense of ourselves and of our community. In how many parts of the world around us do writers have that impact? So it makes sense that lesbian writing focuses inward a good part of the time, looking at what we share, at what defines us. But what I want from lesbian writing, and what I want for myself as a writer, is the largest possible range. I'm not setting lesbian issues and women's issues aside; I don't want other writers to set them aside; what I want is for us to stake a claim on the world at large, and I want us not to set aside, or be asked to set aside, who we are when we do it.

### Karleen Pendleton Jiménez

I kept hearing story after story from lesbian and heterosexual women alike of their sexual experiences as little girls with other little girls. I felt so cheated. My brothers had convinced me early on that playing with girls was stupid and that girls refused to get dirty, so what was the point? Little did I know. It made me consider how much my childhood was more closely linked to a boyhood, and then I started remembering how we used to play as boys. In the age of defining queer, I decided this story of my baby butch lesbian self taking part in the kind of gay experimentation straight boys get away with before puberty would certainly give people something to think about. "The Lake at the End of the Wash" is a chapter from my novel *Not Everyone Turns Pink Under the Sun,* which I am hoping will be accepted for publication any day now.

### Catherine Lord

Catherine Lord lives in Los Angeles. She is professor of studio art at the University of California, Irvine, where she is also a core faculty member of the interdisciplinary program in Women's Studies. She satisfies her major habits, photography and things queer, as a writer, a curator, and an artist.

Her critical essays and her fiction have been published in *Afterimage, Art & Text, Artcoast, New Art Examiner, Whitewalls, Framework, Documents,* and *Art Paper,* as well as the collections *The Contest of Meaning, Illuminations: Women Writing on Photography from the 1850s to the Present, Reframings: New American Feminisms in Photography,* and *The Passionate Camera.* Her curated exhibitions include "Pervert," "Trash," "Gender, fucked," and "Memories of Overdevelopment: Philippine Diaspora in Contemporary Visual Art." Her work as a visual artist has been shown in the project "Something Borrowed" at the Museum of Fine Arts, Santa Fe. "The Art of Losing" could not have been written without the support of a residency at the Rockefeller Center for Arts and Humanities at Bellagio and its library's holdings on Elizabeth Bishop and horticulture.

### Amelia Maria de la Luz Montes

This story is dedicated to Juanita, who told me it helped her realize she was lesbian; to Dan, who told me he made love to his wife after reading it; to Jacqueline, who insists the narrator is a man; to Maria, who believes the narrator is a woman; to Barbara and Catriona, who believe that assumptions about the narrator's gender reveal more about the reader than about the story. I value complexity in gender, in sexuality. My writing expresses this complexity as does my queer identity. The fact that this story exists in an anthology which signals itself as lesbian helps, I hope, to elucidate the complexity of that term!

### K. E. Munro

I am a Canadian writer currently embroiled in the M.F.A. program at the Iowa Writers' Workshop. "French Press" was written in the space of about a day, in order to have something to turn in for class. Most of the discussion it generated revolved around the narrator's undisclosed sex/gender and the supposed implications of this little mystery. Enlightening, to say the least. My fiction has been published or is upcoming in *Global City Review, Prairie Fire, Bad Attitude, On Our Backs,* and the Masquerade anthology *Midsummer Night's Dreams.* I'm greatly in favor of neurosis and humor.

### Peggy Munson

I started writing "Teratophobia" (fear of giving birth to a monster) when I was staying alone in a wooded cottage, feeling edgy and scared about my solitude. Eventually, I realized it is not always the "woman in a dark cabin" urban legends that haunt women the most, but rather the stories of vague, indescribable sexual violations so many women I know have lived through and recounted to me. These are often the real "monsters"—shapeless experiences with tremendous visceral resonance. I believe telling these stories is one way of turning monsters into meanings, thus purging them by bringing them into light. Just about every single time I sit down to write, I'm afraid I will give birth to a monster.

### K. L. Robyn

K. L. Robyn's work has appeared in *Calyx, Earth's Daughters, Women Artists News, The Harvard Gay and Lesbian Review,* and *Sinister Wisdom.* She is the author of the forthcoming book for burned-out positive thinkers called *Clearing House: The Healing Power of Negative Thinking.* About "(Wrong) Number" she says, "This very short story may read like a memoir, but its truth has been stretched too far to be anything but fiction. That's the skeptic talking. On other days I might say it's a story about how the angels have never deserted me, even when they've had to trick me into hearing them."

### Paula Langguth Ryan

The main character in "Life Is a Highway," Denys, caught hold of Paula's brain one day and would not shake loose. She wrote the story to better understand male hostility toward women and to explore the odd bond that arises between a man, his mother, and his member. She also wanted to try successfully writing in a male voice. She invites you to tell her if she pulled it off or not. Paula Langguth Ryan resides on the Western Shore of Chesapeake Bay with her lovely wife, Lori. This is her first published story.

### Pat Schmatz

I spent three months in Japan in the autumn of 1995. I expected to come home with stories of the countryside north of Osaka or of the dramatic fall colors in the mountains surrounding Kyoto. Instead, I wrote "Tokyo Trains." My writing process is not so much about creation or invention; it's a matter of letting the story flow on its own terms. When I came out at the age of nineteen, all of my expectations of a linear life evaporated overnight. My life as an out dyke and a writer is a process of making plans, stepping back, and letting the inevitable metamorphoses occur.

### Cherry Smyth

In poetry and fiction I aim for emotional honesty and knowledge. I also lie. Writing teaches me how to persist through the irritations that arise between bed partners over time; how to navigate between cultures, around habits, and beyond the tiny retreats and returns that are part of being in love; how to call dislocation adventure and face the drop. More can be found in *Wee Girls: Women Writing from an Irish Perspective* (Spinifex Press, 1996). Nonfiction includes *Queer Notions* (Scarlet Press, 1992) and *Damn Fine Art by New Lesbian Artists* (Cassell, 1996). My novel and I shuttle between London and New York.

### Jane Thurmond

Often our blood families are replaced temporarily or permanently by families of our own making. I wanted to write a story that examines and honors alternative families, how we find each other and come to love what is unique about each of us. In small towns, where little support exists for those outside the norm, it's especially sweet to find alternative families that are flourishing. I make my home in Austin, Texas, where I write fiction and work as a graphic designer. Among journals and anthologies that have published my work are *Hers[1]*, *Indivisible*, *The Iowa Review*, and the *Austin Chronicle*.

### Barbara Wilson

"History and memory are my preoccupations; work that is funny, sad, dreamy, and very visual is more important to me than what genre it falls into. I have sought to evoke the feel of the times we move through, as well as to remember and investigate what has been lost and what remains. In 'Archeology' I wished to capture some of the utopian poetry and poignancy of the separatist movement of the seventies." Barbara Wilson's most recent books are the memoir *Blue Windows*, the mystery collection *The Death of a Much-Traveled Woman*, and the forthcoming *Salt Water and Other Stories*. She lives in Seattle.

# About
# the
# Editors

**Terry Wolverton** is the author of *Bailey's Beads*, a novel, and *Black Slip*, a collection of poetry. Her fiction, poetry, essays, and dramatic texts have appeared in numerous literary publications, including *Zyzzyva*, *Calyx*, and *Glimmer Train Stories*, and been widely anthologized. She has also edited several acclaimed literary compilations, including *Blood Whispers: L.A. Writers on AIDS*, and, with Robert Drake, *Indivisible: New Short Fiction by West Coast Gay and Lesbian Writers*, *Gay Fiction at the Millennium*, *Lesbian Fiction at the Millennium*, and the Lambda Literary Award-winning series *His: Brilliant New Fiction by Gay Writers* and *Hers: Brilliant New Fiction by Lesbian Writers*. Since 1976, Terry has lived in Los Angeles, where she's been active in the feminist, gay and lesbian, and art communities. In 1997 she founded Writers At Work, a center for writing workshops and individual creative consultations. She is currently at work on two books: *Embers*, a novel in poems, and *Insurgent Muse*, a memoir, to be published by City Lights Publishers.

**Robert Drake** is the author of *The Gay Canon: Great Books Every Gay Man Should Read* and the novel *The Man: A Hero for Our Time*. He is co-editor of the anthologies *Indivisible: New Short Fiction by West Coast Gay and Lesbian Writers*, *Gay Fiction at the Millennium*, *Lesbian Fiction at the Millennium*, and the Lambda Literary Award-winning series *His: Brilliant New Fiction by Gay Writers* and *Hers: Brilliant New Fiction by Lesbian Writers*. From 1986 to 1998 he earned his living as a literary agent, finding time to serve from 1993 to 1998 as book review editor for the

265

*Baltimore Alternative* and teach writing at community colleges in the city of Philadelphia and Anne Arundel County, Maryland, as well as the American University and St. John's College, where he received his master's degree in 1993. Born in Portland, Maine, and raised in Charleston, West Virginia, he presently makes his home in Ireland.

# Acknowledgments

The editors wish to thank Linda Rosenberg, Marcela Valdes, Valerie Cimino, and Betsy Uhrig for their considerable efforts on behalf of the *His* and *Hers* series. We also offer our considerable gratitude to Robin Podolsky, E. Scott Pretorius, and Gwin Wheatley for their editorial assistance.

Once again we extend thanks and kudos to Susan Silton for her striking cover designs and to Macduff Everton for his remarkable photography.

It is a privilege to work with the talented writers whose works appear between these covers. To them, most of all, we offer our gratitude.

All stories are printed by permission of the authors.

# Permissions
# Acknowledgments